MINE TO PROTECT

KENNEDY L. MITCHELL

Copyright © 2019 Kennedy L. Mitchell

All rights reserved. This book or any portion thereof may not be reproduced or used in any manner whatsoever without the express written permission of the publisher except for the use of brief quotations in a book review.

✽ Created with Vellum

To my husband, Gary, who loves me—quirks and all.

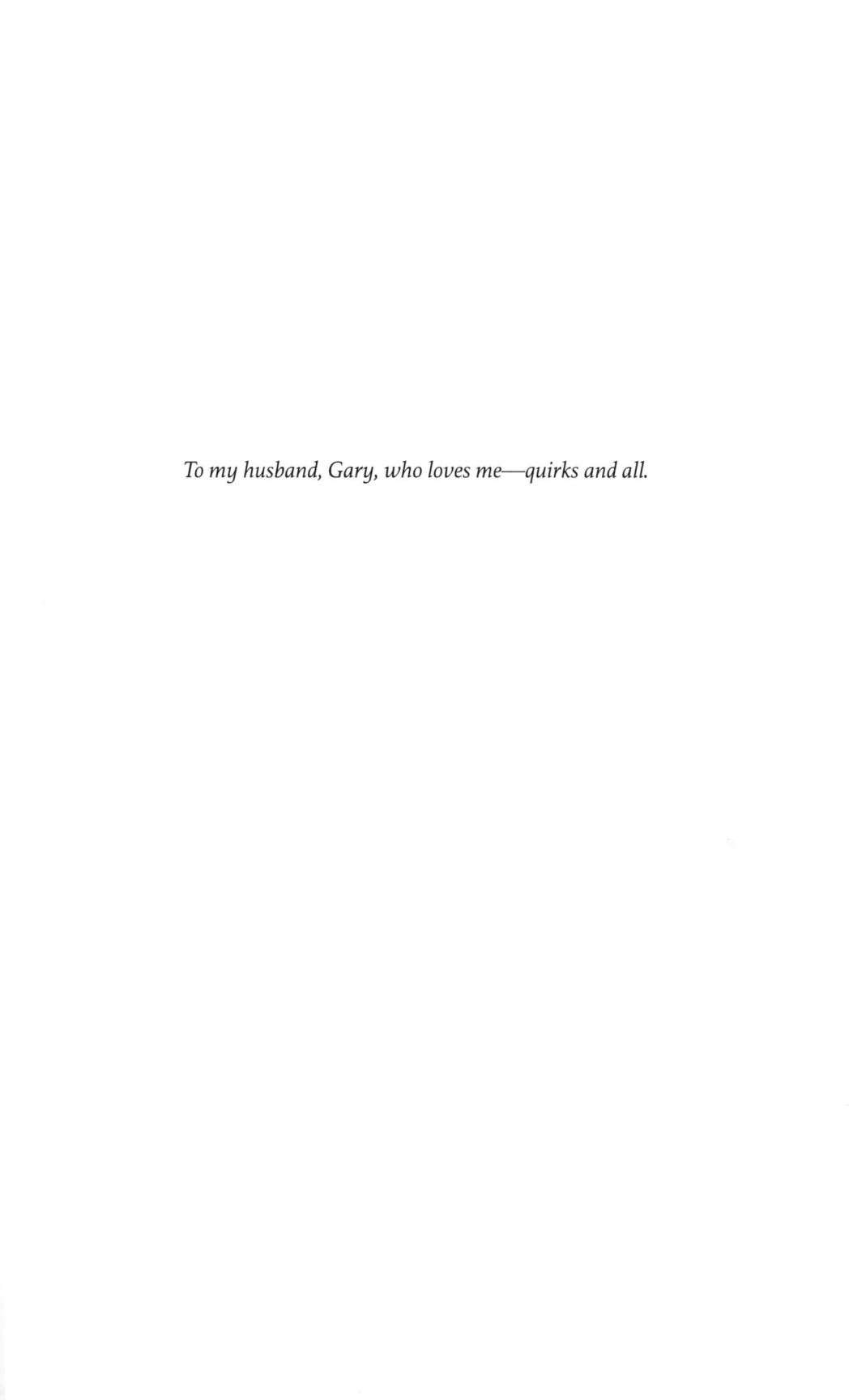

"A little stress and adventure is good for you, if nothing else
just to prove you are alive."
-Lady Bird Johnson

PROLOGUE

Christina Brown laid the worn paperback book on the stone picnic table with a contented sigh. With a smile, she scanned the picnic area from the spot she'd laid stake to hours ago to read in peace while her husband and sons hiked. She'd miss this place; the quiet it offered was vastly different than their home in Denver. Today was the last day of their seven-day vacation in the small town of Estes Park. For the past week, they'd hiked, explored town, and hiked some more in the gorgeous expanses of Rocky Mountain National Park.

"Um, pardon me," a man's voice said, interrupting her thoughts.

She bristled at the accompanying unwelcomed tap against her shoulder. With a scowl, she turned to tell the person to back off. But immediately her defenses softened at the unassuming man wringing his hands in front of his chest. A cautious glance around the area showed a few other families playing in the nearby stream and another packing up their truck, looking to head out. Unfortunately, her husband and boys were still nowhere to be seen. Having them nearby would be preferred, but even so, nothing immediately alarmed her about the man.

As a police officer's wife, she was coached and coached, and coached some more, on how to be alert at all times. Her husband even taught her a few key defensive moves just to be safe. But the man in front of her now, hell, she could knock him out with a simple shove and knee to the groin.

"Sorry to startle you. It's just that...." The meek man shifted his weight anxiously from one foot to the other and tucked his restless hands into the pockets of his worn jeans. "Right. Stupid me. I know better than to approach a woman like this. My late wife would kill me." He cringed and looked to the heavens. "Sorry to bother you."

Shoulders rounded in defeat, he swiveled around in a hasty retreat.

A pang of sympathy spread across Christina's heart. "Wait." He paused but kept his back to her. "What did you need?" she asked, engaging him even if all her husband's past instructions told her not to. Christina felt sorry for the man. He looked outright defeated in life. "Sorry, you just took me off guard."

His head dropped forward, his chin close to his chest as he said, "It's my young daughter."

Christina's brows shot up in surprise as she shoved off the concrete picnic table to stand. "What's wrong? Is she hurt, lost?"

He simply shrugged and pointed toward secluded restrooms on the other side of the picnic area. "That's the thing. I don't know. She's been in the bathroom for a while, and I can't get her to come out. It's a women's bathroom, and I feel awkward walking in." He paused and bit his lip like he was debating telling her more. "My wife passed three months ago, and this is my first time doing this alone. I'm not sure on the protocol."

A wave of relief washed over Christina at his explanation. She was a mother, after all; of course she'd step in to help this man and his daughter. Plus she knew the helpless feeling he currently had. How many times was she in the same predicament with her sons while she stood outside the men's restroom, nervously praying they would return unharmed or not need her assistance when they were inside.

"Of course I can help," Christina said with a reassuring smile to put the man at ease. "How old is your daughter?"

"Seven," he breathed in relief, returning her smile. "Seven going on sixteen."

Christina followed the man toward the bathrooms. A cool breeze rushed through, causing goose bumps along her arms beneath her long-sleeve T-shirt. It was early October, but it seemed winter would come early in the mountains this year. For a half a second, Christina paused her steps to glance to the van, wondering if she should retrieve the boys' jackets out of the car for when they returned.

"Gabby."

Christina's brows furrowed as her attention shifted back to the man at her side.

"My daughter's name is Gabby. Thank you again for helping out. You're a savior." At the bathroom's edge, he paused and pointed toward the ladies' restroom door. "I'll stay right here. And thank you again, really."

Staring at the closed metal door, a cautionary sensation zapped through Christina, settling in her gut. "Um, you know what?" she mumbled, turning back toward the picnic table that still held her book.

A low cry of a young girl's voice from behind the metal door halted her escape. Torn between being safe and helping, Christina flicked her eyes from the door to the man. In the end, the helpless child won. Could any mother hear that sad, desperate cry and do nothing about it?

Stealing her nerves and mentally preparing for any confrontation she squared her shoulders and shoved a palm against the door. Inside a single sink to the left dripped at a rapid, steady pace. The strong scent of urine and musk hung in the still air.

"Hello? Gabby?" Christina called before knocking on the first stall door, which echoed through the small cement-enclosed space.

No response.

The next, and last, stall door swung open when her knuckles rapped against the thin metal.

"Gabby?" she said, pushing the door to see all the way inside.

Empty.

A frown had tugged the corners of her lips down when something sharp pierced through the delicate skin of her neck.

She opened her mouth wide to scream for help, but a large leather-gloved hand slammed against her mouth, allowing nothing more than a muffled yell to escape. Warmth spread from her neck, blooming into more heat through her arms and legs, which grew heavier with each second.

Out. She had to escape. Had to get to her husband and boys. They needed her.

Rallying her fear into strength, Christina slammed an elbow against the person at her back. Darkness inched in from the edges of her vision.

"Save it." The man's tone was angry and harsh, unlike minutes before. "I want that fight later. It's my favorite part. Don't worry, we'll have so much fun."

1

Alta

Someone was watching me.

I felt it everywhere. From the hairs standing along the back of my sweaty neck to the unease growing in my gut, I felt it. Keeping my fast pace, I raced down the final stretch of the rocked path around Lily Lake. Heart pounding, my already rapid breaths came faster and faster, forming gray puffs of smoke in the cool late-morning mountain air.

Desperate to find the source, I cut my eyes right and then left, scanning the rocky terrain with as much scrutiny as possible while not tripping over my own two feet or running off the path directly into the lake.

But I found nothing.

Not even a single scurry of a chipmunk or slithering snake. But the person setting off all my internal alarms could be lurking anywhere. Because there was someone out there watching. This time I was right.

This time it wasn't in my head.

My frayed nerves urged a hand toward my hip belt, where I kept all the needed self-defense tools for a single woman on a solo run. After unzipping the small pouch, I tugged out one of the larger mace canisters. The cold metal bit into my already frozen hands but grew warmer in my firm grasp with each pounding step.

If I could only make it to the truck, get to Benny, I'd be safe. Damnit, I wish I didn't mind breaking the park rules and had brought him out here with me. But being a part of the Rocky Mountain Park police force meant I did care about the rules and knew them inside and out. Plus, I wouldn't want Benny to be tempted to chase after a moose or, even worse, his smaller frame draw the attention of a hungry bear in search of its next meal.

But right now I'd love to have his overly protective instincts and fierce bite by my side.

A steady crunch of gravel beneath pounding feet reached my ears.

Crap. Crap. Crap.

It was most definitely not in my head. Someone was behind me, and gaining ground quickly.

One hundred more yards until the parking lot.

All I had to do was make it one hundred more yards without being kidnapped or killed.

The sweat beading along my brow dripped down my temples and cheeks. A quick blast of wind, too cold for October, chilled my skin, making me shiver. An hour ago, when I dressed for the run, I didn't account for the sudden drop in temperatures last night. Which was why I looked a bit crazy out here running in only tights and a thin dry-fit T-shirt. If I paid attention to the weather, I would've also worn my running hat, gloves, and jacket, maybe even tossed in some of those hand warmer packets into my pouch. It could be eighty out here and I'd still be in a jacket and scarf.

Another crunch of gravel a few feet back drew my attention back to the situation at hand. This time I didn't stop from turning to get a quick look over my shoulder. What I found made my heart drop.

Whipping my head forward, I pumped both arms faster, attempting to put additional space between myself and the person chasing me.

At least seeing the man dressed in an all-black running suit confirmed it wasn't in my head like yesterday, and the day before that. Well, unless I'd dropped to a new level of crazy and had moved up to hallucinating.

Despite the cold and the man eager to kill me, I laughed at that thought. Maybe I *had* sunk to a new level of crazy. I mean, all-consuming anxiety and paranoia would do that to a woman, I'm sure.

Finally at the bend, I dashed full speed into the parking lot, my frozen fingers fumbling in my pack for the key fob. Once it was in my grasp, I pressed the unlock button repeatedly, making the headlights of the truck flash like a seventies disco. Out of breath, I faltered on tired legs as I lunged for the driver side door handle. The moment I had the door open, Benny leaped from the driver seat onto the pavement. I waited for him to run after the man, but instead he sniffed a few of the bushes, peed on one he deemed fit, and trotted back to sit at my feet.

"Seriously?" I said between pants. "I'm in mortal danger."

Benny's head whipped in the direction of the trailhead, a low growl rumbling in his chest, just as the man who'd chased me came into view. Every muscle tensed as I palmed the mace tighter, readying to spring into action if needed.

But I didn't.

Of course I didn't. Like always.

The stranger in black continued on his run, not even slowing his impressive pace to glance into the parking lot. Benny watched with little interest as he passed by. As the runner's form faded down the path, Benny turned back with a slight tilt of his head, giving me the eye he always gave when I got myself worked up about nothing.

Backside pressed against the hard metal of the truck, I leaned forward, gripping both knees. While I sucked down deep, gulping inhales in an attempt to calm myself down before a full-blown panic attack set in, Benny sat patiently, tail wagging along the blacktop.

It was getting worse. I was getting worse.

A short, high-pitched whine drew my attention back to the beautiful dog before me. Squatting, putting us nose-to-nose, I scratched down his thick, furry chest, giving him the love he deserved.

"I know, I know," I said as Benny's long tongue licked up my cold cheek. "I'm losing it. You don't have to give me that look." And like he always did, he gave the 'you need to get out more' look with his deep brown eyes. "I will, I promise. One day. Maybe we could find you a friend too." I swear his eyebrows narrowed. With a huffed laugh I shoved off the ground. "Come on, Benny Boy, let's get home."

Loading the 110-pound German shepherd into the truck's small cab was easy; making us both fit was where the challenge came in. After Benny was situated, I climbed in and locked the doors.

And locked them again.

And like always, I locked them again—you know, in case the first and second click didn't work.

With us secured from the outside world, I buckled Benny in and turned the key. The small engine rumbled to life with ease. Foot against the gas pedal, I pressed down slowly, revving the engine in hopes it would cause the heat to kick on sooner than later, and then pulled out of the parking lot, headed for home.

"OKAY, we have two hours before I start my next shift," I said to Benny once we were through the cabin door. Once, twice, and a third time, I flicked the multiple deadbolts before hooking the mace on the key ring, slid the knife from my calf into a similar holster tacked to the wall beside the mace, and placed my gun on the entry table. Throat burning from the run and cold air, I shuffled toward the kitchen while blowing hot puffs of breath into my still-chilled, somewhat blue hands. In front of the sink, I squatted and pulled open the cabinet door. Reaching into the dark depths blindly, I wiggled my fingers until the tips brushed against the chilled plastic bottle I searched for.

Hand along the counter's edge, I hoisted myself off the floor. Staring at the clear water bottle, I carefully inspected the seal under the cap, ensuring each plastic bit was still intact. As I screwed off the lid, the faint crack of the thin plastic snapping free provided enough reassurance that no one had tampered with it while I was out. Greedily I downed half the bottle as I walked toward the only bathroom in my tiny cabin. I chugged the final few ounces from the bottle of water, sat it on the vanity to toss in the recycling bin later, and reached past the shower curtain to flick the nozzle for the shower all the way to the right.

The running clothes had dried, but my skin felt clammy as I shrugged out of the T-shirt and yanked off my leggings. Steam billowed from above the floral shower curtain, filling the space with its humid warmth as I leaned closer to the mirror.

The dark circles beneath my eyes turned the greenish hazel iris a shade darker than normal. At least being outdoors most days gave my fair skin the opportunity to look sun-kissed, bringing out the natural tan freckles along my nose and cheekbones. My strawberry-blonde hair shimmered in the bright fluorescent light, making the varying natural hues pop.

From the outside, I looked like any other sleep-deprived, early thirties woman.

On the inside was a different story. That was where my scars hid. All left by one delusional man. One man who, even after his death, impacted every move I made, every thought I had.

Releasing a calming, shaky breath, I reached across to lock the bathroom door. Once. Twice. And of course a third time. Again I considered my reflection. What would I do if three wasn't enough to calm my intense paranoia? Would it stop at four? Five? Even the anti-anxiety medications weren't working anymore. Only my stubborn, overactive mind would scoff at the pharmaceutical company's attempt to alter its thought patterns. It was a blessing and a curse being so headstrong; I made it out alive because of it, yet sat here paralyzed by it too.

Stepping into the shower, I centered my thoughts on the nearly scalding water warming my chilled skin, letting it dissolve the memories eager to rise from the dark corners of my mind. Soothing scents of jasmine and lavender infiltrated my senses, regulating my breathing and lowering my pulse to a healthier level. In here, behind the locked front door, inside the cabin with film-protected windows, with a dog capable of ripping out a grown man's jugular—and enjoying it—with a hidden can of mace dangling from the shower head, I relaxed.

Even if I wasn't 100 percent safe, because no one ever was, the false sense of security all those measures provided allowed fifteen minutes of calmed breathing, regular pulse rates, and, on occasion, remembering happy memories. Sometimes I'd even let myself think about a future. Those thoughts typically involved me happy, safe, and not so alone.

But that was the tricky part. The fact that I had the urge to vomit anytime someone touched me was a significant roadblock to my happily ever after.

Outside the shower curtain, the screech of the cell phone ringing yanked me back to reality. Excess water flicked against the mirror as I shook off one hand to answer the call and turn it to speakerphone.

"Hey, John," I said as I ducked back under the hot spray.

"What the hell is that noise? Are you in the shower?"

My hands stilled where they were massaging my left calf. "Um, yeah." Answering the phone while in the shower wasn't the brightest idea, considering my boss was a guy. But we were so close after working together this long, sometimes his anatomy slipped my mind.

"Seriously, Birdie. That's really...."

"Unprofessional," I finished for him with a sigh.

"Distracting. Hey, I need you to stop by the ranger station as soon as you can. We have a missing woman on our hands, and I need you out there. Now."

"See you in fifteen," I responded, now working double time on rinsing the excess soap from my legs.

"And do me a favor."

"Yeah?" I smiled behind the curtain. No way would he let this offense go without some jab or innuendo.

"Think about me while you finish."

I barked a laugh. Yes, he was my boss, but he was a friend first. We were somewhat partners before his promotion last year to managing the entire park police team. All in all, we had 30 officers for the more than 265,000-acre park. We took care of the animals, maintained order on the trails and campsites, and managed the ever-growing crowds on a daily basis. It was a thankless job, but a gratifying one.

As I shut off the water, I thought back to what John said on the call. A missing hiker wasn't surprising, it happened often, but that wasn't the word he used. He'd said missing *woman*.

Odd indeed.

I wrapped the warmed towel around my torso and swung the door open, releasing a massive cloud of steam into the small cabin. From his oversized bed, Benny watched with a raised brow as I hurried through to the bedroom. In record time, I was dressed in a pressed uniform, still-wet hair tied back in a tight bun at the nape of my neck, and hat situated. After securing the tactical belt around my hips, I tossed a treat across the room to Benny.

"I'll be back later. Do you need to go potty before I go?"

In response, he stood, swiveled in his bed to put his lean backside to me, and lay down with an annoyed humph.

"Fine, then. No raiding the pantry while I'm gone either. Last time you got into the Frosted Flakes, your toots stunk me out for a week."

Yes, I was having a conversation with a dog.

And yes, I truly believed he understood.

All animal lovers did. Which I was to the extreme, if you believed what others said. Which was why I went to college for wildlife management. I wanted to follow in my father's footsteps and become a Texas game warden.

But that never happened. No, one man, one deranged man, snuffed out my dream and pushed me from the beautiful state I once called home. Made me move thousands of miles away from my family and friends just to find a sliver of peace.

One day I'd move on.
One day I'd feel safe again. Trust again. Live again.
One day.

I'D WORKED several crime scenes in this park and in the Smokies over the last few years, but this one felt different the minute I pulled up. Yellow tape marked off a small section of the picnic area, while across the way the Search and Rescue team hunkered around a map, all fierce-faced as they formed their plans. I stepped out of the park-issued truck and scanned the scene again, hoping to pick up any subtleties I missed initially. In a master's class I audited last fall, I learned to see what no one else saw, to pick up on the minute details that seemed ordinary until you zeroed in.

Three minutes I stayed by the truck, warmed by my heavy park police jacket, to observe the crowd. A few visitors gawked from their picnic tables, whispering to each other, probably trying to guess what was happening. To their right, five young kids chased a scurrying group of overactive chipmunks, squealing every so often when one got too close.

A booming, angry voice carried through the crowd, drawing my attention from the kids to the massive man surrounded by three teenage boys, towering over a volunteer ranger with a shaking fist.

That had to be the husband of... I looked down to my notepad to jog my memory.

Right, Christina Brown—the missing woman.

After mentally cataloging every detail of the scene, I lunged over the short wooden railing separating the picnic area from the parking lot to join the group. The quick flash of relief in the ranger's eyes when I approached wasn't difficult to miss.

I cleared my throat of the building knot and extended my hand between us. Dang, he was even bulkier up close. "Sir, I'm Officer Alta Johnson." His massive hand wrapped around mine and squeezed. Careful not to show a wince, I yanked my hand back and clasped both behind my back. "Our division manager read me up on what happened, but I'd like to hear your version."

"Where's my wife?" he growled. An angry snarl curled the right corner of his upper lip.

"Sir," I said calmly. "I promise you we're working on it, doing all we can at this point. I would like to hear from you what happened."

Strong tatted arms crossed over his broad chest. "The boys and I went on a hike over—"

"Which trail?" I cut in.

"That one." He pointed toward the Grand Ditch trailhead several yards away.

While still staring toward the trail, I nodded and motioned for him to keep going.

"We were gone for like four hours—"

"Why didn't your wife go with you?"

His frustration fell as a sad, wistful smile pulled at the corners of his lips. "Hiking is our thing," he said, motioning between him and the three boys. "Reading was hers. She loved coming out here and giving us time alone while she got some alone time of her own. They can be a pain in the ass— "

"Dad," the shortest one grumbled.

I bit back the smile that wanted to erupt at the kid's typical teenage sulking. We had a lot of those here. They weren't the first family to come to the Rockies to yank their kids away from their cell phones and iPads.

"Where are y'all from?"

"Denver. We came out last week. Been hiking every day since we arrived."

"Ever hiked this trail?"

"No, we've been to a new trail every day."

Hidden behind my back, I worked the cuticles of my thumbs as I processed his story, adding to the details John gave me in the briefing.

"Do you think she would've left on her own?"

A flash of annoyance and fury blazed across his features. Standing tall, he rolled his shoulders back and cracked his neck, clearly uncomfortable with what my question was referencing. Out of caution and self-preservation, I backed up a step and rested a hand on my sidearm.

His eyes narrowed at my hand. "Sorry, I didn't mean to scare you."

"I'm not scared." But I still wasn't planning on removing my hand from the proximity of the gun.

"She wouldn't have left us. And I'm a cop in Denver. She's heard the stories I've brought home. She knows not to talk to strange men, knows how to defend herself. Christina wouldn't have gone anywhere willingly." Strong hands gripped my shoulders. Revulsion at his touch, the closeness sent my heart racing. I held in a deep breath, counting in my head to remain calm. "Find her. Please. I know the statistics. We have to find her soon. You have to find her. She's our everything." The crack in his voice sounded sincere. One thing was for sure—whatever happened to his wife, this man had nothing to do with it.

"Birdie," John's strong voice called at my back. Sliding his hands from me, the man shifted his focus over my shoulder. "I need you for a moment."

Steeling my spine, I turned to face John. "I just finished getting his statement. We have what I need." Turning back to the man, I stuck out my hand once again. "I'll be back, Mr. Brown."

Within two steps, John was at my side, keeping pace with my long strides. "He wasn't hurting me," I whispered.

John sighed and looked to the sky. "I know, but...."

I stopped midstride and turned with raised brows. "But what?"

He paused to look back at the man and his kids. "Birdie, we've been side by side for years. Don't you think you flinching or nearly hyperventilating every time we happen to touch would be something a good officer like me would notice?"

"I thought I hid it well enough," I grumbled.

"Not so much. Listen, I respect it. I hate it, but I respect it all the same because I know the reason why."

"Hate it?" Playing the naïve card was bad form, but I didn't want to dive into John's feelings right now.

"Forget it. Come on, let's go talk to Search and Rescue to see where they're going to start the search."

Back in motion, we walked in silence for several feet before I spoke up.

"I have a weird feeling about this one, Johnny Boy. Something isn't adding up. Women don't disappear around here without due cause. My initial thought was she ditched the family, but after talking to the husband, seeing the kids, my gut is telling me she didn't leave them. She wouldn't. Something happened to her, I can feel it."

"Feel it?" John said in disbelief.

"Yeah. Call it a sixth sense or whatever, but I know when something isn't adding up or when something is out of place. This is it. But if she didn't leave on her own...."

"Then someone took her unwillingly."

His words fell around us like a heavy, somber cloud.

A burst of cold wind had me gripping the sides of the down coat and pulling them tighter together for more protection. Around us, the hustle of the Search and Rescue team gearing up overtook the calming nature sounds. The hairs on the back of my neck stood tall, and a shiver that had nothing to do with the cold racked my shoulders.

I closed my eyes and took a slow, deep breath in.

No one was watching me.

There was no one there.

While scanning from the dense forest to the wide stream, I offered up a quick prayer for Christina Brown that if she were, in fact, abducted, not lost or hadn't ran off on her own, that she was already dead.

That was my gift to her.

2

Cas

The thick wooden door trembled on its hinges beneath my pounding fist. In my periphery, several heads popped out from various offices along the short hallway in the U.S. Department of the Interior's headquarters, staring with suspicion and a bit of fear in their gazes. It was apparent to everyone that I didn't belong here. The admins and directors who milled about, still staring, were dressed in fancy-ass business suits or nice dresses, while I stood outside my boss's boss's boss's office in full tactical assault gear.

Apparently it was unnerving, even though I was standing in the middle of the United States Park Police headquarters. Our particular division of the Department of Interior was the oldest uniformed federal law enforcement agency in the US. We held both federal and state jurisdiction across the country. We were highly trained, deadly —some more so than others—and tasked with protecting the national monuments, the president, and his visiting dignitaries when needed.

We were hot shit, and we knew it.

At the curt command to enter, I resituated the snug Kevlar vest across my chest and turned the doorknob. Once inside, I cataloged every detail of the spacious downtown DC office. The oversized leather chairs, large dark mahogany carved desk, and the man sitting behind it were exactly what I expected to find. The director of park services continued to type on his laptop. He looked the part with his buzzed silver hair, deep wrinkles along his forehead and cheeks—from years of playing the political game, no doubt—and tired, cunning eyes.

Those eyes cut from the screen and ran a quick, assessing gaze. Having zero idea as to *why* I stood here, pulled this morning from the protection detail I'd been assigned, was unnerving.

What the hell did I do this time?

Fingers templed beneath his chin, he flicked a pointed look to the chairs, which I ignored.

"You wanted to see me, sir." A shadow shifted at my back. All senses zeroed in on the threat while I maintained eye contact with the director.

"Have a seat, Sergeant Mathews."

"I prefer to stay standing, sir." Every muscle twitched, eager to face the person still hiding at my back. Instead I focused past the director to the windows behind him. Using the reflection, I monitored the blurry form until it shifted closer to where I stood in the middle of the room.

The man's hand barely brushed my shoulder, snapping me into action. Jerking his wrist tightly against the middle of his back, I slammed his face against the closed door.

Heart racing, blood thundering in my ears, somehow his low chuckle flooded through.

I had him pinned, about to break his arm and dislocate his shoulder if I breathed too hard, and the man was fucking laughing.

"Damn, Mathews, still as quick as ever, you jackass. Good to see you haven't gotten any slower in your old age."

. The voice tickled a memory. Slowly I released his wrist, then forced him to turn and shoved his back against the door.

"Peters?" I said, very confused.

What the hell? I hadn't seen this jackass in years. We served two deployments together, but he was the type of person you wouldn't forget. Smart as hell, calculating and dangerous—similar to me. Well, all marines, I guess. There had been an edge to him that I recognized, making us both immediately respect the other and form an instant bond. Chandler Peters was someone you could call at any time, even if it'd been years, and he'd come running guns blazing to your aid. It seemed he felt the same way, which must've been why he was in the damn office.

"Have a seat, Sergeant Mathews. I won't ask again," the director ordered.

Peters smiled as his brows rose high on his forehead, taunting me. Bastard. With a growl, I released his shoulder and stalked to one of the leather chairs to do as I was instructed.

"I'm sure you're wondering why you're here," Peters said. At my subtle nod, his smile widened. "I almost don't want to tell you, just to drive you fucking insane."

The director cut in. "I do not have time for this, Agent Peters—"

"Agent?" My shock registered in my tone.

Peters nodded. "FBI. BSU—sorry, Behavioral Science Unit."

"Couldn't hack staying in action so you found a desk job. Nice," I said with a smirk. "Not surprised. You always were a lazy ass."

"Lazy ass, me? You're the one who's put on the pounds since the last time I saw you. Drinking too many carbs there, Mathews?"

"Fuck off," I grumbled. Because what else was there to say when he was fucking spot on. I had put on a few pounds since my demotion from team lead last month, and he was also correct to the cause. Damn beer.

"Gentlemen," the director cut in, once again trying to regain control of the conversation. "I have another meeting in ten minutes. You'll have plenty of time to catch up later. Now we must discuss Sergeant Mathews's new assignment."

That didn't sound positive.

Brows raised in curiosity, I leaned forward, pressing both elbows onto my thighs. A pointed cough swept my suspicious gaze from the director to Peters, sitting in the other leather chair across from me.

"I'll fill you in on the specifics on the plane tomorrow, but long story short, you're with me now."

What the hell? "Why me?" I demanded.

Peters shrugged and leaned back in his chair, but his tight shoulders and sharp movements radiated the tension he was trying to play off. "Why you? I know you, I trust you, and with you being USPP, your federal and state jurisdiction might come in handy at some point. You're mine until we're done."

"Done with what? What's this new assignment?" Damnit. A low throb pulsed behind my eyes as a headache began to set in. I hated vague, and the fucker knew it. Facts and strategy helped you make informed decisions. Both were needed for every assignment.

Sweat beaded down the column of my spine.

The last time I moved with too many unknowns, men died.

My men.

Peters's eyes held my gaze with cold intensity, making my pulse race with excitement. "We're headed to catch a potential serial killer."

VENTI BLACK STARBUCKS cup in hand, I marched up the short stairs of the FBI's private plane. Inside I had to duck not to whack my head against the low roof. Angling sideways, I shuffled to the open seat across the aisle from where Peters sat typing furiously on his laptop. The only acknowledgment to my on-time arrival was a quick nod.

Taking the 'I'm busy' hint, I twisted in the leather seat, getting as comfortable as possible in the tiny thing for the flight. Out the window, I saw the pilot and crew toss all my bags under the plane. The plane jolted as the final black duffel landed in the belly. Hopefully it didn't tip us over the weight limits for the jet. All Peters said yesterday after we left the director's office was to pack warm with enough firepower to make me feel comfortable, which meant a lot, then jotted down the address to the hangar.

The marines taught me how to use my hands and body as a deadly weapon, but still I preferred being heavily armed in hopes it never came to that. Hand to hand, I couldn't hold back, unlike the distance a gunfight provided.

The still-too-hot coffee scalded the roof of my mouth at the first sip, but I downed another swig anyway, hoping to clear the ever-present fog from my mind. Last night was another restless night. Hell, I couldn't remember the last time I slept through the night without waking up in a crazed panic with a loaded gun in hand.

Shortly after takeoff, Peters snapped his laptop closed and tossed it onto the seat across from him.

"Start talking," I demanded, my hot breath pushing against the window, fogging the thick plastic. "I understand I don't have a choice in taking this assignment, but I need to know what I'm walking into."

Peters's hard stare pricked at the nerves along my neck, making the hair stand on end. The soft leather groaned as I shifted in the seat and leaned back against the window.

He shook his head. "We need to get something else out of the way first. What happened to get you demoted?"

Wondered when this would be brought up. I sighed and scrubbed at my clean-shaven cheeks. Might as well get it out of the way now. If we were a two-person team on this assignment, he had a right to know what he was getting into.

"What? They let you in the FBI without knowing how to read?" I deadpanned. Yeah he needed to know. Didn't mean I'd make it easy for him. "You want to know what happened, read the damn report."

Peters smirked, knowing what I was doing. "I did read it, fuck face, but it was one-sided. I want to know your side."

"My side," I said with a huff.

"We served together, you fool. If you think you're the only one who deals with past shit on a daily basis, then you need to pull your head out of your ass. Who knows, I might understand why you did it. But all in all, I need to trust that you won't lose your shit again."

"I didn't lose my shit," I growled, my fingers tightening around the thin armrests.

"Tell me."

I scrubbed a calloused hand across my face and leaned back to stare at the ceiling. Maybe he was right. The person who documented my side of the incident wasn't someone who'd been in close-quarters combat, didn't understand the triggers that lay beneath the surface of every man who'd been cornered in the past and believed they were out of options.

"My team and I were on protection detail, stationed along the route the president would take that day to meet other dignitaries. We had a few protesters due to *who* he was meeting with, but it was orderly and nonviolent. There were even a few kids in the group, holding their parents' hands." I downed another swallow of coffee. Fuck this small plane. Sitting in the damn, tiny chair was too confining. "A group showed up minutes before the president was due to cross our path. The group was different than the others—we all knew it the second they walked up—so when the first guy drew his gun, we were prepared. Several of the guys yelled at everyone to get down, and we went into action—"

"You mean *you* went into action."

"We all did, but with my training, it came easier. Instantly. I took out the threats with the help of my team."

"You put seven men in the hospital."

I shrugged and turned to gaze at the clouds beneath us. "I took out the threat."

"The report mentioned all seven men had multiple fractured bones. No bullet wounds, no lacerations."

"I took out the threat," I repeated.

"Without endangering civilians around you."

Without looking to him, I nodded.

"And they demoted you because...."

"Excessive force," I said through gritted teeth.

"The men said you were amazing to watch. That you were efficient and calm through the entire attack, which lasted less than three minutes."

"I'm trained by the best to be the best. You know that."

"They also said they had to drag you off one of the men. That you were seconds from snapping his neck."

I turned, glaring at Peters. "He fucking stabbed me."

He raised both hands in the air. "I get it, man. Don't be pissed at me. Is close combat your only trigger?"

"You mean is getting stabbed my only trigger to want to snap a man's neck?"

"I guess," he said with an annoying smile. "Anything else I should be aware of on this assignment?"

"Nope."

"We're staying in the same cabin. What about sleeping?"

"Don't wake me up or move around at night and we should be fine."

"'Should be' doesn't give me much to go on."

At that, I smiled. The man could handle whatever I threw at him, and he knew it. "Damn, you'll probably do it now to see if you can survive. You're that much of a dumbass."

Peters's smile grew up his lean cheeks, making deep lines form along the edges of his eyes. "Challenge accepted, fucker."

"Hell, don't be pissed when I shoot your ass," I said on a chuckle. A sliver of tension eased from my shoulders. Everything was on the table now. A bit of the relief came from being with someone who understood. "Now that you know I won't go postal, give me the details of the case. Start with where in the hell we're headed."

The leather of his seat groaned as he leaned back and stretched his long, lean legs down the center aisle. "Estes Park, Colorado. We'll stay there while we work the cases in Rocky Mountain National Park."

Ah. So that was why he needed my state and federal jurisdiction. Interesting.

Clasping the warm paper cup between my hands, I leaned

forward and focused on the white lid now dotted with splashes of coffee.

"Tell me everything."

3

"Uniform or professional?" I mused to myself.

Dang, why was I making this so difficult? It was only a meeting with an FBI agent. An FBI agent who I still had no insight on as to *why* he was coming to the park. Yes, a second woman went missing three days ago, three weeks after Christina Brown went missing—who still hadn't been found—but why would the FBI take notice of two missing women?

Something else was obviously going on, hence the dilemma in front of me.

I held up both hangers. Ranger uniform to look official, but also possibly look less qualified since park police weren't high on anyone's radar for clout. Or a black pantsuit, which would give off the impression I wanted, but wasn't very official for a ranger.

"Ugh," I groaned and turned to Benny, hoping for guidance. "What do you think? Which one?"

I swear he actually rolled his black eyes, then trotted out of the room. Not surprising since Benny was a male dog.

"Fine. Leave me when I need you most," I grumbled under my breath. Which was a stupid thing to say since one, I was talking to a dog, and two, assisting in outfit choices wasn't the reason I adopted Benny six years ago. His intense obedience training from the military, harsh looks and deadly bite were. Okay, and all that fur was quite snuggly at night when he hopped onto the couch with me.

"Focus, Birdie." My gaze bounced between the two choices, once, twice, and a third time. Eyes narrowed at the dark green uniform, I sighed and tossed it on the unmade bed before shoving the other back into the closet.

Official it was.

Twenty minutes later, I shivered in the truck as I pulled into the parking lot; I lived so close to the central ranger station that the engine didn't have time to warm up before I arrived. After shifting into Park, I considered the long, sleek black Suburban two spaces down that stuck out like... well, a nice SUV in a parking lot full of white park trucks. Benny's nails scratched at the door impatiently as he turned his furry head to me.

The dog loved tagging along to the station because everyone spoiled him rotten with treats and long chest scratches. It didn't happen much, but today I couldn't push aside the urge to. Maybe it was meeting the FBI agent, or having an unknown man in my safe zone, or the two missing women. Whatever it was, having Benny within striking distance offered enough relief that I didn't have to pop a Xanax before leaving the house.

Yay me.

A cold blast of wintery mix pushed against the door just as I shouldered it open, buffeting me back into the cab where Benny was nudging my back with his head, eager to hop out.

"Benny!" I yelled as he shoved me forward with his heavy weight before I could gain footing on the somewhat slick pavement. Not paying me any attention, he leaped past, forcing me into the door and sending me tumbling out of the truck. My rear end slammed onto the cold blacktop as I held on to the side door handle with a death grip.

In the distance, Benny's long nails clicked along the pavement as he trotted toward the station's door. Damn dog.

Eager to not let my first impression with the FBI agent be one with a wet backside, I tugged on the handle to stand, only for the heavy door to swing shut, pinning me between it and the truck's running board.

"Jiminy Cricket," I grumbled.

"Need help?" a deep voice said above me.

My head whipped up toward the speaker. With a silent gasp, I shifted back for more distance from the unfamiliar man looming over me. A quick once-over showed him wearing hiking boots, dark jeans that fit snug around thick thighs, an untucked black cotton thermal shirt pushed up to his forearms despite the cold, exposing one fully inked forearm, and a short cigarette dangling between long, thick fingers.

When I found the courage to look up, I wished I hadn't.

Near black eyes bore into mine with an intensity that warmed my core. And scared the pee out of me.

The hand not holding the cigarette extended down, but his stone face never shifted, his gaze staying locked with mine.

"Thanks." My shaking hand gripped his steady one. Heat met my frigid fingers, sending tingles to erupt along my palm as it thawed. The ease with which he yanked me to my feet left an unsettling feeling at the display of his hidden strength.

After gaining my footing, I dusted off my backside while keeping my gaze locked on the stranger, which wasn't difficult. Something was alluring about him. Something that drew me into the darkness behind his eyes.

Something that called to me.

"I'm normally not that clumsy," I stated as I reached into the truck's door pocket to retrieve my gun. After securing it in the holster, I stepped closer to the still-silent man to make room to close the door behind me.

He didn't move, making me get so close that his fresh, masculine scent wafted up, causing my heart to race even faster.

"You here visiting someone or disputing a charge?" I asked, then took a steady step toward the ranger station front door. *Damnit, where is Benny?* Even as the thought passed, something about the man told me I wouldn't need Benny's deadly bite. This man, as intense as he was, wouldn't hurt me. A feeling deep in my core reassured me that he wasn't a threat, which was shocking. Every unknown man was a threat according to my fight-or-flight senses.

But not him.

Halfway across the parking lot, I turned, expecting an answer, but no one was there. A curious glance back to the truck showed him standing in the same spot, smoking the cigarette's remnants.

Hand on the station door, I paused for one more look at the strangely alluring man only to find him gone. *Huh.* I leaned forward for a different angle but still came up empty.

Dang. The quick twinge of disappointment was unexpected. How in the heck could I be disappointed about a guy who'd said all of two words?

With a shake of my head, I pulled open the glass door, allowing Benny to wiggle between me and the doorframe. The comforting sounds of volunteers and other rangers bantering, coupled with the scent of stale coffee, pulled a smile up my cheeks despite my lingering disappointment.

"Ah, there you are," Sarah called out from her perch on the corner of my desk.

As I walked toward her, a few volunteers called out to Benny, begging for his attention with treats and whistles. Sarah tossed her head back with an open-mouthed cackle when Benny tackled a ranger to the ground in an attempt to snag the treat he'd held out of the dog's reach.

"What are you doing here?" I asked as I sat beside Sarah on the desk.

Sarah was my one girlfriend in town, and that was due to her initiating it. When we first met, I was intimidated by her gorgeous exterior and outgoing personality. But after I got to know her, I found that Sarah was funny, charismatic, and wicked smart. There was something about her that drew you in and made you want to be around her, which was exactly what happened to me. Somehow in the few months we'd known each other, she'd coaxed me to open up about my past and broken down all my antisocial barriers.

She was fun too, opposite of me, horny as heck, and willing to jump on any willing male—or female, depending on her mood. I lived vicariously through her rambunctious dating stories and wild nights.

"I clocked out early at the coffee shop, so I decided to come up to say hi."

"And...?" I knocked her calf with the heel of my hiking boot.

"And I might have heard through the grapevine that an FBI agent was arriving today. I want to meet the newcomer, you know, welcome him to Estes Park," she said with a smirk.

Oh no. I knew that smirk. Whoever this guy was didn't stand a chance if Sarah locked her sights on him.

With a grin, I dropped my head forward and shook it back and forth. "What if he's not good-looking? Not all FBI agents look like the ones on TV."

"Duh, but have you ever heard that power is an aphrodisiac for some people?"

"No."

"Not surprising," she said with an eye roll and toss of her long, blonde hair over her shoulder. "You don't notice things like that, whereas I sure as hell do. Just like that friend of yours became ten times hotter the second his promotion came through."

Wait. What? "John?"

"Yeah."

No way. "My John?"

"Oh." Her smirk turned devious. "So he's *yours* now, is he?"

No, John wasn't mine in the way she was referencing. He was a sweet man, a fantastic friend, but that was it. An underlying tension had built between us recently as his feelings for me grew deeper than friends. But it stopped there. He knew I didn't feel the same way, and also knew that, with my past, I'm too broken for any sort of normal relationship. Plus the sympathy in his eyes when I sometimes caught him staring was a deal killer. I didn't want sympathy, didn't want anyone else telling me I was a victim.

Clearing my throat, I pressed both palms behind me to the desk and leaned back. "No. Not mine in that way. Never in that way. You know what I'm saying."

Sarah tossed an arm across my shoulders and pulled me close. I tensed beneath her touch, grinding my teeth to keep from shoving out of her hold.

"I know. I was just giving you a hard time. So, have you seen him? The FBI guy?"

I stood, very ready to sneak out from under her arm, and glanced toward John's closed office door. "Nope. I'm going in now. No idea why he's even here, you know. I mean the FBI. Something big must be going on."

Her eyes scanned over my face, and her lips pursed before she said, "Yeah, I guess. Tell me if he's hot. If he is, I get dibs, unless you want to join in, which you know I'm down for." She paused to scan my face, her lips pressing together in deep thought. "You want some lipstick or something before going in there? You're looking a little duller than normal today."

I rolled my eyes. Nope. My plain—dull, as she called it—exterior helped me blend into crowds, kept me from any unwanted attention. In college I learned the hard way the type of trouble a pretty face and outgoing personality could attract.

"Fine," she said with a dramatic sigh. "Good luck in there."

After the quick stay command to Benny, I smoothed down my top, tucked it tighter into my pants and then marched down the narrow hall toward John's office. As our division director, he was the only one who was allowed a legit office; everyone else had to share desks out in the communal room.

Murmuring male voices vibrating through the closed door caught my attention before I could knock. For a few seconds, I waited with my ear pressed to the door and listened, hoping to gain a hint of what this was all about.

Unable to make out a single word, I finally leaned back and rapped a knuckle against the cheap wooden door.

At John's curt command to enter, I twisted the metal doorknob and pushed the door open. Cold air brushed along my cheeks as I moved to the center of the small office. Immediately I scowled at the open window. Thirty-one degrees outside and this polar bear of a man had the stupid window open.

Behind his desk, John smiled with a straight-teeth grin as he gestured to the lone empty chair in front of his desk. My gaze shifted from John's extended hand to the man occupying the other chair in the office. Dressed in a black suit and black tie, he radiated federal agent. The man's ice-blue eyes met mine with an assessing glint. In the few seconds our eyes locked, my past, my thoughts—everything felt exposed.

Breaking from his observing stare, I nodded in greeting to the two men and carefully sat in the empty seat.

"Agent Peters, Alta Johnson. Alta, this is Agent Chandler Peters from the FBI."

A stiff silence followed the obligatory introductions.

"Nice to meet you," I said to ease the growing tension. "I'd say thanks for being here, but I'm still a little unsure as to *why* you're here."

Agent Peters smiled, one that was a bit mischievous and a tad sad. "I understand the confusion. But once I explain the details of the situation, you'll be glad we're here."

"We?" I shot a confused glance to John, who simply shrugged.

Agent Peters spoke up once again, swinging my attention back his way. "I have a partner here with me. He'll be working the case as well, though he's not FBI. Sergeant Mathews, a USPP officer, has both federal and state authority, which could come in handy depending on how this case develops."

"I see." But I didn't. Everything he said was clear as mud. "Where is he?"

Ignoring my question, Agent Peters leaned forward, resting both elbows on his knees. "Have either of you read any news regarding several missing women cases in other parks?" His calculating gaze shifted between John and me. At our simultaneous head shake, he nodded. "Twelve months ago, in Great Smoky Mountains National Park, a woman went missing. No trace. Then another. And another. Ten in total."

"That's terrible," I whispered in shock. I tucked both cold hands beneath my thighs to keep them from coming up to my mouth. That park was where I got my feet wet as a park officer years ago. Estes Park had only been home for two years. "What happened to them?"

His knowing blue eyes found mine and narrowed. "We don't know."

"What do you mean, you don't know," John said with more bite than I'd ever heard him use with a stranger.

"Meaning," Agent Peters said, angling his body toward John but keeping his gaze locked with mine, "we haven't found a single body. Not a trace. It's like these women vanished into thin air. There one second, then gone the next, leaving behind families, friends."

A million varying thoughts flicked through my mind. "You never caught the person responsible," I muttered as I looked out the opened window to the gloomy sky. "That's why you're here."

"You catch on quick. I like that. Yes, we believe the two missing women in this park are somehow related to the previous cases."

"You think he shifted hunting grounds."

Again his ice-blue eyes bored into mine. "Yes."

"Because you got too close?"

"We believe so."

I narrowed my eyes, forming a deep line between them. "You believe so?"

His shrug of indifference came off stiff, like the casual gesture was only for show.

"Who was the special agent assigned to those cases?" Surely one had been assigned by the park service instead of passing it off to the

FBI. "And why isn't he here now investigating this case instead of you?"

A creepy yet sad smile pulled at Agent Peters' lips, sending a bolt of caution down my spine. "You're perceptive. That will come in handy as we work the case."

"You didn't answer her question," John cut in as he leaned forward, pressing his forearms along the edge of the desk.

"Well, a special agent *was* assigned these cases but—" Agent Peters cleared his throat. "—she was the last woman in the Smokies to go missing."

4

Alta

"The hell?" John's voice lowered as he shifted a concerned glance to where I sat in shock at Agent Peters's words. "You're leaving out a lot of information. We need all the details you have connecting these cases before we agree to work with you."

Agent Peters broke his focus on me to acknowledge John, who was looking paler by the second.

"Nine women—"

The door hurled open, letting in a welcomed rush of heat from the hall. For a split second, I relished the warmth, until *he* walked in. My mouth fell open at the surly man from the parking lot, his scarred hand gripping the door handle. He stood eerily still, almost like he was just as surprised to see me, his near-black eyes burning into mine. The two others in the office faded into the background as a rampage of questions and unfamiliar feelings flooded through me.

"You," I said on a pushed breath, finally remembering oxygen intake was necessary for staying alive. Chest rising and falling in rapid succession, the cold from the office turned comforting against my too-hot skin. *What the heck is wrong with me?* This man was dangerous and a stranger—both of which I'd avoided at all costs the past several years. But here I was having a stupid hot flash like I was in high school all over again just from his soul-searching eyes.

The seat rocked to the side with a clatter as I shoved out of it to take a cautious step back. His eyes narrowed, but a small, knowing smirk pulled at the corner of his stone-cold features, as if my fear amused him. But it wasn't the type of anxiety I managed on a second-by-second basis. No, *this* fear was hot, sizzling in my veins, making beads of sweat build beneath my armpits and along my palms.

Our intense staring contest broke when a hard shoulder brushed against mine, making me tense all over at the contact.

The stranger's eyes narrowed on my shoulder, only to direct an angry glare at John, who now stood at my side. *Way too close* to my side.

"Can we help you?" John took an obvious step to angle himself between the man and me.

Thankful for the brief reprieve from the man's scrutiny, I glanced to Agent Peters, only to be more confused. He sat in the same position, leaning back in his chair, but now he smiled at the whole scene like it entertained him.

"He's with me," Agent Peters finally said with a deep sigh, cracking the growing tension. "He's the one I spoke about earlier. You always knew how to make an entrance, didn't you, Mathews?"

John didn't move.

Neither did the Mathews character.

Long, tense seconds ticked by on the old-school clock on the wall as the two continued their standoff.

"As I was saying," Agent Peters said, drawing out the last word in an obvious attempt to gain everyone's attention, "nine women plus the female special agent in charge of the case went missing in Great Smoky Mountains National Park in nine months."

Not ready to be in close proximity to Mathews again, I leaned against the far wall and kept my attention focused on Agent Peters.

Only after Mathews had stepped farther into the office in order to close the door behind him did John relax and turn back to the chair behind his desk.

"Ten women. How did that not make national news?" I questioned.

Mathews gaze burned into each inch of my body as he stared. Every instinct insisted I look, but instead of giving in, I willed my focus to stay on Agent Peters.

"It made the news in East Tennessee, but nothing on the larger networks. Mostly because we had nothing to go on. We had zero evidence from the crime scenes."

I chewed on the edge of my thumb. "And now you think he's here."

Against my will, my eyes darted to where Mathews leaned against the door, confirming what I already knew.

Not a single facial muscle flinched, indicating he couldn't care less that I'd caught him staring.

Fine.

Two could play that game.

Taking the opportunity, I observed every detail of his harsh, handsome face. High cheekbones for a man accentuated a strong jawline that was dusted with faint facial stubble. A thin nose had two distinct knots along the bone, indicating he'd broken it more than once. Dark brows and messy, light brown hair completed the ruggedly handsome look that he no doubt knew looked good on him. Because it did.

Then there were his eyes. They were captivating, holding me in place with some warlock power. Whatever it was, it called to me. Locked in his gaze, I felt safe, protected and, for the first time in a long time, alive. Instead of running from this stranger, I wanted to run *to* him. Wanted to feel his large hands running along my bare skin, my stomach, and inner thighs.

I startled at John's loud attention-getting cough.

"Sorry, I guess I forgot to make introductions," Agent Peters said. "This is Sergeant Cas Mathews of the USPP. Mathews, this is Ranger

Police Officer Alta Johnson and Division Manager John Cartwright. There, can we move on now?"

Right. Back to the case, the reason these two men were here. I cleared my throat and tried to swallow, even though my mouth had turned bone-dry. "What do you think he does to them? The women?"

"Birdie." John's tone was laced with concern.

I cut a hard glare at him with a slight shake of my head.

"We don't know. Without bodies to examine, there's no way of knowing. Hell, they all might still be alive, held captive somewhere against their will." My breath caught, that time not from the dangerously hot male, who was still staring, but from actual fear. "But my guess is they're dead since he's shifted to the Rockies."

I tucked my trembling hands into the pockets of my pants—which, of course, Sergeant Mathews noticed. Nervous energy had me pulling both hands back out and clasping them behind my back. "How will we catch him?"

Agent Peters shrugged. "We're hoping he's already made a mistake on the two abductions here, or will with the next one—"

"The next one?" I didn't even try to conceal the shock in my high-pitched tone.

"Yes," Peters said with a hint of disappointment. "There will be more, I'm sure, until we catch this bastard."

"What do you need from us?" John asked, clearly not pleased with the turn in conversation. Not surprising. He was over-the-top sensitive to my past and knew conversations like this would drum up bad memories for me. John was a good guy. Sweet, caring, and very attractive in a smothering type of way.

"We landed and drove straight here. We'll drop our bags off at the cabin, and then I would like to see the first and second scenes, preferably with the officers who were first on scene and spoke to the eyewitnesses."

Out of a grade-school habit I've never been able to break, I raised my hand with a tight smile. "That would be me."

"But I'll take you," John cut in, standing abruptly to his full five-nine height.

Unconsciously, my eyes drifted between the three men, comparing their features and builds. John was my height, but rounder compared to my lean frame. Agent Peters seemed tall with those long legs he had stretched out in front of him, but he was a bit lankier than John and Mathews. However, even without bulging muscles, anyone could tell Peters was capable of handling himself with ease against any threat.

Then there was Cas Mathews. A few inches taller than me but a mix between John's and Agent Peters's builds. Lean but muscular in all the places a man fit from doing actual work, not just lifting weights, would be. Strong arms stretched the sleeves of his shirt, and his exposed forearms had large, angry veins running down the thick muscle beneath. A bit of weight sat around his waist, but not enough to call him soft by any means. All that with his unnatural stillness and intense stare made him intimidating as all get-out.

"You weren't at both scenes." I said, staring at the floor to keep from gawking at Mathews more than I already had. "I'll take them. My shift doesn't start for another few hours."

"At night?"

Everyone's attention shifted to Sergeant Mathews. Those two words were all he'd spoken since he'd entered the office.

"Yes," I said, chewing on the cuticle of my thumb.

Well done, Alta. Solid response. Direct and to the point.

"We have park police available at all times to make sure our guests who decide to camp within the park are safe," John added.

"And the animals," I grumbled.

The same corner of Sergeant Mathews's lips twitched up, just as it had when he first walked in. Seemed I amused him in some way.

A loud clap echoed through the sparse office, making me jump. Agent Peters shoved out of the chair. "It's settled. Ranger Johnson will come with us to drop off our bags, then direct us to the two scenes."

Ready to get out of the suffocating office, I pushed off the wall, following the two men as they began to shuffle out.

"Johnson, hold up a second," John called.

Well snap. I held back an eye roll. "I'll meet you outside," I called out as they filed down the hall. I swiveled to face John and crossed both arms across my small chest. "What?"

He rapped a knuckle on the desk, his forehead furrowed. "I don't like it."

"Don't like what, exactly?"

"We don't know them. Let me go, tell me what the witnesses—"

"No, John. It's my job, and I trust… I trust them."

A spark of shock registered across his face before he schooled his features. "What was that between you and that Mathews guy?"

I shrugged a shoulder and turned to the open window, hoping to blame my cheeks' rosy tint on the cold wind. "Nothing. I wanted to get a read on him. Which I didn't. But him being with the USPP, he has to check out, right?"

"All those guys think they're gods. Fuckers," he grumbled, then shifted a few pieces of paper around on his desk. "I didn't like the way he kept staring at you."

I pursed my lips, not quite sure how to respond. Pretty sure saying 'I did' wasn't in my best interest if I wanted this conversation to wrap up sooner than later.

"You want me to ride around with you tonight on your shift? You know, like old times?" John's tone was wistful, nostalgic even.

Letting him down was the last thing I wanted to do, but I also didn't want to lead him on. "Nah," I said as I moved toward the open door. "I'll be fine. I like the mountains at night. You know that. I should go though. Don't want to keep them waiting."

"Check in when you're back. That's an order."

With my middle finger, I gave a fake salute and stepped out into the hall just as a wadded paper ball soared past my head.

"You missed," I called over my shoulder.

In the main room, I slowed my quick steps at the sight of Sarah smiling and laughing, surrounded by Agent Peters and Sergeant Mathews. Benny's soft head rested just under Sergeant Mathews's hand as the man scratched the thick fur.

Oh crap, what do I do with Benny? I rubbed at my eyes. Maybe I could run him home and meet them at the first scene.

Not wanting to interrupt the conversation, I tentatively approached the group. Benny glanced up with a 'please don't make me move' plea in his eyes.

"All set?" Agent Peters asked.

"Um, yeah I am, but I forgot about Benny."

"He can come too," Mathews directed over his shoulder as he marched to the front doors. I cringed at his ear-piercing whistle that sent Benny bounding after him.

Traitor.

"Okay...." I raised both brows in a silent question to Agent Peters, who merely offered a knowing smile before strolling toward the front doors.

Sarah's hand wrapped around my wrist, holding me back from following. "Wow. He's hot, right? Where are you going with them? Can I come?"

A pang of jealousy dipped my stomach. Flirting, talking, conversation came easy for Sarah. Plus, with her amazing looks, no doubt she could have both men in her bed by the end of the night if she put her mind to it. Which didn't bother me about Peters, but Mathews was a different story.

We'd only said a handful of words, but to me, he was mine.

Which had to be the most backward thing for *me* to think, considering that same mindset from someone else was what put me in my perpetual state of fear and unease. But the difference between me and the freak who stalked me was I wouldn't follow Mathews, leave him creepy notes, or drug him.

"I'm taking them to the two scenes where those women went missing." I'd keep the part about a possible serial killer to myself for the time being. Sarah wouldn't spread it around, but since it was an active case, protocol had to be followed. "I better go before they leave me."

With a fake pout, Sarah crossed her arms across her ample chest. "Whatever. I'm meeting that new ranger in a few anyway."

I tensed and frantically glanced around the room. "Oh no. Is she here? Please tell me she's not here."

Sarah shook her head and stretched her arms high over her head. "Nope, I'm meeting her at one of the trails. Your boy John thought I should include her since she's having a hard time making friends on her own. And since you don't like her...." Her mischievous smirk took a fraction of the hurt out of the accusation.

"Who doesn't like dogs?" I said, a bit exasperated. The woman was strange, so no, I didn't want to be friends with her. Either way, I was already at my max with Sarah and John. "I don't trust anyone who won't pet Benny."

"I don't blame her, Birdie. That dog stares her down like she's his next meal."

Okay, she was right. But I just assumed it was because he knew she didn't like him.

Which was absurd.

I mean really, who couldn't love Benny?

5

Cas

"What?" I inhaled deep, filling my lungs with smoke as I tucked the lighter back into my pocket. The dog continued to stare, unintimidated by my hateful glare. "I get it. It's going to kill me. Believe me, I'm counting on it. Fuck off, would ya?"

The asshole didn't.

Black eyes continued to judge with each deep inhale I took until the glass door of the ranger station swung open, ending the staring contest. Peters sauntered out, slipped his dark sunglasses on and tucked his hands into the pockets of his slacks.

"Interesting turn of events, wouldn't you say," he said and leaned beside me against the black Suburban. "Cute dog though."

"That dog could swallow your nuts whole as a light snack and enjoy it. Don't call him fucking cute if you want to keep all your body parts attached."

"His name's Benny, and she has a fall-themed bandana tied

around his neck. That screams 'flight attendant' more than 'killing machine.' Poor bastard."

With a grunt of agreement, I directed my attention back to his earlier comment. "You're going to make me ask, aren't you?"

The asshole's smirk grew into a full damn grin. "I don't know what you're talking about."

Liar. Eager to hear what he had to say, I gave in to his game. "You know exactly what. What the hell did you find so interesting?"

"You and her. What the hell was that? I mean, she's cute, I guess. A little plain, if you're into that type. And based on *your* reaction the second you stepped into that office—fucking late, I might add—she's most definitely your type."

Well hell. Thought I'd covered my reaction. Guess not. Officer Johnson wasn't just okay. She was... hell, I didn't even know how to describe it. There was something about her that wouldn't let me go. It wasn't her natural beauty—okay, some of it was the fair skin, freckle-dotted cheeks and lean curves that attracted me, but it was more than all that.

But no way could Peters learn that the moment Officer Johnson's hand gripped mine in the parking lot, my dick stood at attention and conjured other, less familiar feelings. If he knew I was interested, fuck, all this would turn into a game for him. He'd push every damn button to instigate, then sit back to watch the chaos that unfolded after. It was a game he'd enjoyed playing in the past as well, fucking conniving bastard.

"It's nothing," I responded, taking the last hit of the cigarette between my fingers. "You know me."

Yeah, he knew me. Heartless. Cold. Emotionless. A product of the shitty-ass life I'd lived the past forty years.

"Just don't fuck her over before we leave is all I'm asking."

I ground my back teeth to keep from shouting. "Shut the hell up. Nothing is going on. Nothing will happen. I'm here to do a job, that's it."

"Just saying, we have to work with these people while we're here. I don't want her all pissy because you did a fuck-and-ditch on her."

"I'm not into her," I grumbled. "Nothing. Will. Happen. Didn't you see her reaction? She's terrified of me."

"Who isn't?"

"You," I said with a laugh.

"And I'll just say this now," Peters added.

"Fuck, what else? When did you turn into fucking Oprah?"

Eyes alight with humor, he shot me an amused glance, reading straight through my protests. "Have your fun, but keep it quiet. It seems her boss has already called dibs on her pu—"

With a tight fist, I nailed him in the center of his chest with a hollow thud, cutting off his next words.

John didn't need to know anything at that point, and Peters sure as hell didn't need to be the one dishing out advice. He went through more women than I could count.

There was one thing I was certain of—Alta Johnson couldn't be mine.

With the heel of my worn boot, I stomped out the cigarette's cherry and ground the butt into the ground with more aggression than needed.

The glass door swung open, striking all my senses on high alert as the beautiful officer pushed through.

While she gnawed on the edge of her thumb—a nervous habit, I realized—her hazel gaze searched the parking lot before landing on us.

"Are you positive it's all right if Benny comes with us?" she asked as she approached the SUV.

With his damn knowing smirk still in place, Peters tipped his head toward me before rounding the hood to climb into the driver seat, leaving me alone with the only woman I'd ever felt off balance around.

"It's fine." I retreated two steps before she spoke again.

"That's considered trash, you know."

Taking a deep breath in to get my emotions in check, I turned to face her. Bad fucking idea. Hell. She was innocence and depravity wrapped into one confusing woman. Her tall, lean body was strong beneath the uniform that showed off the curves she did have. Like the fine, perky-as-hell runner's ass I'd like to sink my teeth into at some point in the near future. The soft, pink lips I wanted to suck between my own pressed into a thin line as those hazel eyes glared through my soul.

Hell, what is with me? She's just a woman.

The only woman whose similar ruined soul called to mine.

A woman who was too young to have as much pain and fear lurking behind those eyes as she did.

An enigma. That's what she was. A conundrum of young, beautiful, and understated, yet ripe with fear, hate, and anger. The feelings she evoked were nothing more than wanting to fuck her every which way before I headed back to DC, whenever that would be.

Remembering she said something, I glimpsed down to where she pointed to the discarded cigarette butt.

"Litter is litter," she said, still pointing with, if I weren't mistaking it, a slight tremble in her extended hand. Interesting. Either she was terrified of me, or I wasn't the only one who felt the heat when our hands clasped earlier.

One thing was certain—more information was needed on this woman. A full background, maybe some recon. No. Recon would be too creepy. I wasn't a damn stalker. I would start with the background and go from there. Surely Peters could get her file pulled quick with his FBI connections.

With a single nod in acknowledgment, I crouched to snag the crushed butt, then stuffed it into the pocket of my jeans. The effort earned me a tentative smile. But even with a smile, I could still see the sadness behind her eyes.

After dusting my fingers off against my thigh, I motioned toward the passenger door. As I held it open, like the gentleman I was not, she shimmied past and a waft of something sweet and purely feminine engulfed me. Releasing the death grip on the door, I slammed it shut after she was situated, then hopped into the back seat with the dog hot on my heels.

"Don't forget to buckle him up," Officer Johnson said, turning in her seat to smile at the dog.

"Who?" I stared out the window to avoid being distracted by her again.

"Benny," she huffed, as if my question exasperated her.

"The dog," I deadpanned, shifting to face her. She couldn't be serious. "You want me to buckle up a damn dog."

She nodded and twisted to face out the windshield once again. "I need him safe."

"Fine," I muttered, leaning over to figure out how in the hell to buckle up a fucking dog.

6

Alta

No way it was my imagination. The Mathews guy was strange.

Okay, strange wasn't the right word.

Intense. Focused. Authoritative. Dominant.

Who knew those traits wrapped in a hard, tattooed exterior would be a lure for someone like me. You'd think feeling the overwhelming intensity pulsing off him would make me run screaming, but it was just the opposite with this guy. I had to hold back from running *into* his arms and clinging onto him like a spider monkey.

In unison, our seat belts clicked into place. As Agent Peters backed out of the parking spot, I nonchalantly swiped both clammy hands down my thighs and said a silent prayer that a wet streak wouldn't be left in their wake. Who would've thought I'd be nervous due to the super-close, hot, brooding man and not from being trapped in the car, somewhat helpless, with two strange men.

It was odd, but what I'd told John was the truth, I trusted them. The Peters guy seemed harmless, and Mathews... well he looked scary as hell, but Benny seemed to like him, and something else settled in my gut the second he'd helped me up. Somehow, someway, I felt safe when he was around.

A feeling I'd never expected to have again. Such a welcomed relief that I was willing to stomach all the nervous energy that buzzed through me any time he was around.

The compulsion to flick the locks festered even with Mathews and Peters close.

Eyes on the lock button, I casually tossed out a question to distract them from my plan. "You mentioned dropping your gear off first. Where are you two staying?" Once, twice, and a third time—just in case—I clicked in rapid succession.

With my crazy ritual completed, I eased back against the seat, feeling more at ease.

"Directions say about five miles from here. I wanted to find something in the park, but it was too late notice, I guess. Nothing was available."

"Yeah, those cabins go quick, and those who donate to the park itself get top priority. A little 'I'll scratch your back and you scratch mine' action."

"Sounds nice." Peters glanced to the rearview mirror, a small smile forming at whatever he found. "I like my back scratched. How about you, Officer Johnson?"

I smiled at Peters's lame attempt to flirt, and he shot a welcoming smile back. A low growl of warning from the back seat made me turn to scowl at Benny. What was his deal?

"Anyway," Peters said, drawing my focus back to him, "it's a small cabin community just up ahead."

Keeping one hand on the wheel, he tossed his cell phone into my lap and nodded to the screen. I didn't need to look at it to know where we were going. I knew the community because it was mine.

"Looks like we'll be neighbors," I said. Catching myself peeling at the cuticles around my thumbs, I tucked both anxious hands beneath my thighs.

Neighbors. Great.

That meant *he'd* be close. Way too close, or not close enough?

My thoughts and emotions clashed as we continued to drive. *Of all the places in Estes Park, of course they end up by me. Fine, I'm okay, no biggie.* Except it was. There was no way I could stay away with them being within walking distance. I already wanted to see more of him and he was in the back seat. The way he made me tense, excited, scared, hot all at the same time was exciting—electric even.

I inhaled deeply to clear the wandering lusty thoughts that seemed to come out of nowhere.

Potential serial killer.

FBI.

Missing women.

That was my focus, not the brooding man whose eyes were burning a hole through the back of my head with his laser stare.

"Good," Peters said, still smiling. It irked me, like I was left out of an inside joke between the two men. "I'll want your help when reading through your notes and pictures from the two cases here. The close proximity will be beneficial for everyone."

Another low growl had me shooting daggers at Benny. Really, what was his problem?

"If you're open to it, I could use your help sorting through the Smoky Mountains case files too." Peters shifted in the driver seat, alternating hands on the wheel. "Without the special agent here, I'll have to decipher her notes, and I noticed in your file that you worked in that park for a while. You'd have a better point of reference when going through them than me."

"Of course. I'd love to—"

"No." The word was curt and commanding from the back seat.

I whipped around with narrowed eyes, finding Sergeant Mathews glaring right back. "No?"

"It's a great idea." Peters's light tap against my shoulder jolted me toward the window, my muscles' natural reaction to pull me away from the touch. "Mathews is the muscle of the operation, not the brains."

"Fuck you," Mathews grumbled.

"Why do you say no?" I asked, crossing both arms across my chest and leaning against the window to monitor both men at the same time.

Sergeant Mathews's dark eyes burned into mine, inching up the heat flowing through my veins from his closeness and the anger his comment raised. Reaching over, I flicked off the seat heater, which I never did unless it was over a hundred outside.

"Yeah, buddy," Peters chimed in. "Why not?" An undercurrent of humor laced his words.

"Am I missing something?" I asked, glancing between the two men.

"Do both of you fail to remember that the last woman who worked to catch this fucker went missing? Is still fucking missing?" Mathews hissed. "Since I'm the damn security around here, I won't take any unnecessary risks. This is a hard no for me."

His tone, completely void of emotion, and aversion to me working with them sank me lower in my seat. Disappointment swirled in my chest until it ached. I'd begun to think he felt the same undeniable pull between us.

Apparently not.

My cheeks burned as I shifted to stare out the windshield, hiding my embarrassment.

I was a stupid woman, inept at all things men.

Of course I read the signs wrong. He didn't want me.

Who would?

"If security is your concern, I can take care of myself," I said, attempting to hide my hurt and mirror his monotone.

"Really? She was an agent, had more training than you."

I huffed in annoyance and shook my head while tapping the passenger window with my short nail. "Turn at the next right. Anyway, you underestimate me, Sergeant Mathews. We go through the same training as any officer of the law. Plus I'm a black belt, and I have Benny here to watch out for me, since you seem to be concerned about the additional workload."

Only the tick of the SUV's blinker sounded as the two men sat silenced. The tension growing taut with each rhythmic click.

Crap. That was too pushy. Was that too pushy? Maybe, but he needs to know I'm an asset to this investigation, not additional work for him.

"You have my vote," Peters said as he navigated the SUV through the narrow streets. "And mine is the one that matters, so welcome to the team."

A grumble of discontent rumbled in the back seat.

The corners of my lips turned up.

Take that, asshat.

Birdie, one.

Sergeant Mathews, zero.

THE HOLLOW THUMP of my hiking boots against the aging, wooden porch steps followed theirs as Benny and I trailed the two men into their rental cabin. Somehow, inside was ten degrees colder than outside. Running my hands up and down my arms, I surveyed the front room. It was similar to mine, with a small kitchen equipped with the basics, which opened into an eating area and living room. The only difference was the two bedrooms where mine only had the one.

Both men disappeared into their respective rooms, followed shortly by the banging of bags being dropped.

The tips of my fingers tingled as they numbed in the frigid cabin.

Right. Might as well make myself useful. Surely they were cold too.

The precut logs I found on the porch were thankfully dry, protected from the light wintry mix by the overhang, and old, which was perfect for a fire. After grabbing a few, plus some tinder, I hauled everything into the living room and kneeled in front of the fireplace.

Too engrossed in the construction of a perfect teepee that would catch quickly, I failed to hear approaching footsteps.

"What are you doing?"

I sucked in a quick breath and shoved off the floor only to slam the crown of my head into the thick wooden mantle.

"Dang it!" I exclaimed, cupping both hands around my head to ward off the impending pain.

Wide, warm hands wrapped around mine, applying more pressure.

Even though the gesture was caring, bile rocketed up anyway, burning my throat. Flinging my hands down to detach the unwelcome touch, I retreated a few steps until my back hit the wall.

"Easy, boy. I didn't hurt her," Agent Peters said in a soothing yet frightened tone. "Hey there, Johnson, call off your dog, would you? I'd prefer my balls to stay attached to my body if you don't mind."

A few slow blinks cleared the moisture building in my eyes, blurring my vision, and I gasped. Benny stood between us, the dark hair along his back standing on end as he prowled closer to Agent Peters, teeth bared as he growled.

"Ruhe," I commanded to prevent Benny from attacking, pulling him to an abrupt halt. Adrenaline pumping, I slumped against the wall. With one more 'I'll eat you' glare at Agent Peters, Benny nudged his cold, wet nose against my leg, tucking his head beneath my waiting hand.

Thirty seconds maybe? That whole scene escalated quickly.

"The jugular," I stated as I held the aching lump forming on my head.

"What?" Agent Peters said, now several steps away.

"He's trained to go for the jugular, not your... guy stuff."

"I'd like to keep that part of my anatomy too. I hear it's kind of important for survival," he tried to joke.

I huffed a small laugh, more to ease the tense air between us than anything else. "Sorry. As you can see, I startle easy. Normally I don't let people get that close."

Agent Peters nodded as if he understood. "You feel comfortable around us, as you should. Even the mute in the other room is one of the good guys, though he doesn't act like it."

The way he seemed to read my thoughts and put me at ease set off alarms. Still rubbing my head to ease the throb, I watched him watching me. "What division of the FBI are you in again?"

He smirked like a cat playing with a mouse. "As I said earlier in your boss's office, you're very perceptive. I'm in the Special Sciences division."

"As in...."

"I help form profiles to assist teams around the US in finding and apprehending the mark, like our serial killer. If we learn his habits, how and why he targets these women, what his signature is, then we can stop him from taking another woman. Unlike in the old days when the police could only hope for a strong tip or the person to mess up."

I swallowed against a dry throat. "That's cool." But it wasn't. I didn't need or want a guy with his training around, one who would dig in my head.

Sergeant Mathews stepped into the living room, making me forget about my throbbing head. Donning a black North Face jacket and gray beanie, all he needed was a Harley outside to complete the hot-as-heck bad boy display of everything masculine. Without a word, he raised a dark brow as he glanced between Agent Peters and me.

Again I cleared my throat, hoping it would prevent my voice from shaking. "Agent Peters was— "

"Chandler." Sergeant Mathews jabbed his thumb in the direction of Agent Peters. "And Cas. If you're working with us, drop the titles, would ya?" He glanced to Chandler. "That damn agent title inflated his already big-ass head."

"You're good with words, you know that, Mathews?" Chandler joked as he slapped Cas on the back. "You should cross-stitch that on a pillow or something."

"Good idea. Then I could fucking smother you with it."

From my spot against wall, I lifted my hand and waited for them to notice. Both men smirked at my raised palm. "Are y'all partners or something?" I asked.

Chandler wrapped an arm around Cas's shoulders and tugged

him close for a tight side hug. "For this assignment, yeah, you can call us partners. But we've known each other for a while. We served a deployment or two together."

Cas shrugged out of Chandler's hold, keeping his eyes locked with mine. "Your command earlier, was that in German?"

My eyes widened. I didn't realize he'd heard all that. "How did you—"

"A guy in my unit had a bomb dog."

Chandler and I stayed silent, waiting for more of his story.

"And?" I finally urged, making the right corner of lip twitch upward.

"He commanded his dog in German too. Said a lot of military dogs were trained that way."

I shifted to gaze down at Benny, who was still nuzzled tight against my leg. We were perfect for each other. Two troubled souls looking for a way to get through the rest of our lives without additional pain or fear. I ran a hand over his head and scratched behind his hears. I loved him, and he loved me.

"Where'd ya get him?" Cas asked.

Benny's coarse coat tickled my palm. "A friend of a friend. Benny was in the military too, but—" With both hands, I covered Benny's pointed ears with my palms like makeshift earmuffs. "—his handler died, and they couldn't place him with anyone else. He was depressed, you know. He lost his best friend. They were about to put him down," I whispered. "Then someone who knew my situation suggested I meet him. We've been together ever since."

After releasing Benny's ears, I crouched to scratch his broad chest. A thick, wet tongue swiped up my cheek over and over.

"You're a good boy, aren't you?" I said to Benny's long snout.

Neither man said a word as I lavished Benny with the love I wished someone would give me and I could accept. Then without a word, Cas marched to the door and out of the cabin.

Chandler glared at the door and shook his head. "You ready?" he asked, extending a hand to help me up.

His hot hand wrapped around my freezing one. "Are all guys this hot natured? You and him both, your hands are hot even when it's freezing. It's not natural."

Chandler's brows rose up his tan forehead, deepening the fine lines etched across it. "Wouldn't know, don't hold hands with guys. It sounds like you don't either, Officer Johnson, if you're asking me that." His eyes narrowed. "How is that considering—"

"Birdie," I interrupted in an attempt to distract him from his train of thought. No way did I want the work friend of Cas to know I was completely oblivious to everything men. "If I'm calling you both by your first names, then you should call me, Birdie. All my friends do. Well, friend. I mean two friends. Two people call me Birdie. I have two friends."

Hand still warming mine, he shook it up and down with an amused smirk, which kind of pissed me off and made me smile at the same time. "Nice to meet you, Birdie. Now let's go catch this SOB before anyone else goes missing."

I trailed behind Chandler through the cabin and down the porch steps.

"What situation?" Cas asked, making me pause. He leaned against a porch post, cigarette pressed between two fingers.

"Will you at least put an ashtray out here or something?" I shoved both hands into the pockets of my coat and shifted my weight. "And you know they say that stuff will kill you."

"They said the same thing about the marines."

"But you took that risk to serve your country. What's this risk worth?" I asked, nodding toward his cancer stick.

"My sanity."

"You sure you haven't already lost it?"

A rusty chuckle rumbled through his chest. "Are you going to answer me or bust my balls on my life choices?"

My growing smile fell. "Let's just say we were mourning someone we lost." I inclined my head toward the now-running SUV, Chandler smiling behind the wheel. "We're ready when you are."

7

Alta

A SHARP BITE of pain registered as I rapped my freezing knuckles on the boy's front door. What was with this weather? This was when I missed Texas the most, the bitter cold and wind getting to me as the winter dragged on and on. Despite the awful cold temperatures, the winters here were somewhat magical. Snow-covered naked branches, frozen lakes, hot chocolate by the fire at night—everything about it was amazing, except when you had to step out in it and face the brutal elements head-on.

Huffing hot air into my hands, I waited impatiently outside the still-closed door, eager for it to open. Yesterday I told them I would come over late morning, which I guess technically meant around eleven, but to keep up my no-routine routine, I was early. Honestly, the coordinating of my no-routine schedule had become more daunting than ever for some reason. There were days I didn't care if I did the same as before. But that was a mistake. That's when someone would notice.

So there I was at a bit after ten in the morning, standing on their front porch instead of warm on the couch watching Netflix with Benny snuggled at my side.

I yawned wide into my cupped hands. Last night's shift went by without a single incident, which wasn't unusual but was welcomed. The peace of the night gave me time to think, process all the comments Chandler spouted as we surveyed the first and second crime scenes. The entire case was fascinating. All aspects of it, from the women who were taken in the Smokies to the special agent who was still missing to the two women here. Everything appeared well planned and executed with precision.

No witness. No evidence. No bodies.

'How' and 'why' were the first questions to find answers to.

I jumped back as the door swung open, revealing a mostly naked Chandler. Standing in nothing but a towel tied around his hips, he gestured inside the cabin. Wide-eyed, I scanned down his muscular chest and defined abs before averting my eyes and stumbling back even farther. A heel caught the first step, tipping my weight backward. The sense of falling flipped my stomach as I swung both arms in an attempt to right myself.

With a loud curse, Chandler lunged out the door and grabbed the waistband of my jeans, preventing my fall.

Heart pounding, both at the mostly naked man and the embarrassing almost-tumble, I pressed a hand to my heart, allowing my eyelids to flutter closed in an effort to regain some equilibrium over the situation.

"Birdie, if you don't stop overreacting, I'll start to think you don't trust me."

With a huff, I peeled my eyes open and focused past his bare shoulder into the cabin. "Sorry, just wasn't expecting this." I waved a shaky hand up and down his naked torso.

I wasn't a prude. Well okay, maybe I was technically, but not by choice. Well, maybe yes by choice, since I hadn't been on a date in years or been anywhere someone would have the opportunity to ask me out except for work. No one asked me out there though—not that

I wanted them to. Most of the rangers were twice my age, with more hair in their ears than on their head, and the officers... well, they all knew my quirks *too* well to find me remotely attractive.

Chandler's light brown eyes narrowed and flicked to where my index fingers fidgeted with my thumbs' cuticles.

"Right." His assessing expression morphed into a cocky smile. "I get it. Not many women get the opportunity to see someone like me up close." He contracted his abs, making them ripple down his stomach, and flexed his biceps.

Thankful for the humor he inserted into the awkward moment, I offered him a small smile in return. "I've seen better."

Chandler's smile fell as he stuck out his lower lip in a full-on pout. "No such thing."

I rub my hands up and down my arms. "Aren't you cold?"

"Freezing. Pretty sure I'll never see my nuts again."

With a half nervous laugh, half giggle, I shuffled around him into the cabin. The empty cabin. Disappointment stifled my earlier nervous energy, taking a bit of excitement out of the day. Searching the room, I eyed the files stacked on top of the small kitchen table.

"Those the files from the Smokies cases?" I jerked my chin toward the table.

Chandler glanced across the room. "Yep. The special agent's notes are there, but the pictures are on the iPad. Go ahead and dig in while I get some clothes on."

The second his bedroom door clicked closed, I moved back toward the front door. Once, twice, and a third time, I snapped the deadbolt in place. With the cabin secure, I moved to the next order of business—heat.

Kneeling at the fireplace, I tossed a couple more logs on the poorly lit fire and moved the coals around, giving it the attention it needed. After a minute, flames glowed and heat poured into the chilled room.

Shifting to the table, I sat in one of the four wooden chairs and flipped through the various folders until I came to the one labeled with the earliest date. A couple sentences in, a chill raked down my spine. With a huff, I scooped up the files to read by the now-roaring fire.

"You want some coffee?" Chandler asked as he stepped barefoot from his room. Involuntarily my eyes flicked to the other closed bedroom door. "Birdie?"

Shaking off the unwelcome thought that Cas was avoiding me by hiding in his room, I shook my head. "No thank you. I'm not a coffee fan."

"You're kidding me. You sure? Didn't you work all night?"

Ignoring his surprise at my disdain for the black oil most people drank in the morning, I fluffed a pillow to offer a bit of cushion against the hearth. "I'm used to running on little sleep." Leaning back, I raised both knees and laid the file against them like a makeshift desk. "Hope you don't mind me shifting things around to get comfortable down here by the fire."

"Not at all, but"—he grimaced as he gave me a once-over—"you know you don't have to wear your uniform when we're here, right?"

Through my lashes, I glanced up to find him in the kitchen opening and shutting cabinets. He wore a black, short-sleeve T-shirt and gray athletic shorts. Okay, maybe all guys were hot natured. I was in pants, a jacket, and sitting up close and personal to a fire and was still a bit chilled.

"Next time," I said, then looked back to the papers resting against my thighs. "I picked up the first case. Have you read through them all?"

"I have. Take your time. We can discuss when you're done."

I tried to focus, I really did, but the words blurred as my mind drifted. With a sigh, I shoved the heels of my palms into my eyes and rubbed. "Where's your partner?"

At his non-response, I glanced up. Chandler had paused whatever he was doing in the kitchen to face me, smiling. "Reading."

"Reading what?" I snuck another peek at the closed bedroom door.

"Some paperwork I gave him to look over. What, am I not enough?"

Paperwork? What paperwork? Sounded made up. With a long sigh, I shifted my eyes back to the file. "Just wondering," I mumbled under my breath, hoping that would help hide the lie.

"Right, Birdie. Whatever you need to tell yourself."

Two hours and four case files later, my eyes burned, my back ached from sitting on the floor too long, and I had absolutely *nothing* to show for it. Each case had the exact same MO with different names and locations. In each one, the husband and kids had left the wife behind and when they returned, she was gone, vanished into thin air. Not a single person reported seeing anything suspicious, and zero evidence was left behind.

I groaned and lay down on the floor to stretch out my aching back, staring at the ceiling. "There isn't anything useful in these notes," I vented while smacking the file folder against my forehead.

"There has to be something we're missing," Chandler said from the kitchen table. He was on his second pot of coffee, looking just as frustrated as me. His short blond hair was a mess from running his fingers through it with every turn of the page.

With his happy nature, soft features, and warm blue eyes, he'd be good boyfriend material if you liked the lighthearted, center-of-attention type. And based off my body's instant reaction to Cas versus Chandler, I seemed to be attracted to the brooding, threatening, dangerous nature.

Yay me.

I didn't want soft and kind. No, that reminded me too much of *him*. The man who stripped me of my former self and stole my innocence wasn't into rough. No, he was timid, kind, and considerate as he took me against my will during the three days he held me captive. In those three days, my revulsion against touch grew with every gentle kiss, every caress along my incapacitated body.

Cas wouldn't be timid, wouldn't question every touch or move. The red-hot glint in his dark eyes showed a man who knew what he was doing in all aspects of life. That's what turned me on, plus his handsome face and hard body. I wanted to be taken, wanted to be touched—I wanted the dark I *knew* he could offer. With my brokenness, the dark side might be the only place I could ever be free.

Maybe he saw that yesterday and decided I was too much. Our attraction was obvious, but whether it would go anywhere past stolen glances and heated glares was yet to be determined. With him still hiding in his room, it didn't seem that he'd be offering up a piece of his dark soul anytime soon.

Still inspecting the ceiling from my spot on the floor, I mused, "All the cases are the exact same. Women taken with zero evidence, zero witnesses, and zero reasons to up and leave their families. The only difference between those cases and the two here is the stupid location."

"That's my conclusion too, but what does that leave us with, huh? Wait until the next woman is taken and say a fucking prayer to every god out there that this bastard makes his first mistake?"

"You keep saying 'taken,' not 'killed'. You think they're out there somewhere?"

The blunt legs of a chair scraped across the floor. I tilted my head back, viewing Chandler upside down. "I sure as hell hope not."

"Same," I said as I chewed down the cuticle around my thumb. "I was wondering, since I haven't met a lot of FBI agents... how is it? Being in the FBI?" I propped up on my elbows for a better view of the couch where he now sat on the arm, looking down at me.

"The agency does a lot of good. We catch the bad guys, but sometimes the red tape feels more hindering than helping." He massaged the back of his neck as he rolled his head side to side.

"I feel the same way about the park services. We do a lot of good, but sometimes our hands are tied when an opportunity arises to make a bigger impact. Can I ask you something else?"

"I'm intrigued." Releasing his neck, he motioned for me to go ahead.

My vision blurred as I zoned out, staring at the red coals of the dwindling fire. "Were you assigned this case, or did you take it?"

"Why? Does it matter?"

I raised one shoulder in a noncommittal half shrug. "I don't know. Just wondering, I guess. We don't have a lot to go on, no evidence and zero media coverage, so why would someone take it willingly, you know? More than likely the guy will disappear again, leaving all these cases cold, nothing to build one's career on." Out of the corner of my eye, I watched him, waiting for his reaction.

"I took it." He paused. "You're right, it's a tough-as-hell case, but... don't judge me on what I'm about to say."

With my full attention, I situated to face him straight on.

"I'm the only male on our team—surprising, I know—and I didn't want any of my team to get hurt. The special agent who went missing...."

"You didn't want any of your team members to take the case because they'd be a target, not you."

He nodded. "Does that make me a sexist bastard?"

"No, it confirms what I already thought about you."

Chandler's shy smile cracked the solid walls that protected my anonymity. "What about you?"

"Me?"

"Birdie, you don't have to be here. You could've walked the scenes with Mathews and me yesterday and gone back to your normal life."

I huffed a dry laugh. "What's normal again?"

"Why did you choose to work this case with me, knowing you could pin a target on your back?"

"I don't know. I guess—"

The closed bedroom door swung open, severing my train of thought. Like yesterday, the air evaporated from the room and the heat boiled in my veins the second he stepped out, his narrowed eyes immediately locking with mine. Wearing mesh shorts and a gray T-shirt, he fell onto the couch and propped his bare feet up on the coffee table, not bothering with words.

Crap. Even his feet were sexy. Manly. I needed to work on finding a quality about him I *wasn't* attracted to.

"Find anything interesting?" Chandler asked, turning to face Cas.

"Tons," Cas responded, but kept his dark eyes on me instead of turning to his friend.

Awkward seconds ticked by in silence. To avoid the building unease, I focused on studying the file in my hand.

"He has to have resources," I mused as I scanned the words I'd already read twice. "As in a truck or van to get these women out of the park. And...." I turned to stare into the fire. "The women have to be drugged or knocked unconscious somehow, right? The one thing that has stood out is they were all capable of fighting off an attack. But what if they couldn't?" Memories and details of the cases muddled together until they seemed to be one and the same. "It doesn't explain how he got them alone, but it could explain how he got them out of the park, unless he was staying in the park already."

I glanced to Chandler, searching for confirmation. "Have you guys run who stayed in the park then and who's staying here now? Maybe even surrounding cities? Estes Park isn't that big, and several remote areas would be ideal for this guy."

"We did for the Smokies, but not here. Great idea, Birdie."

"Birdie?" Cas questioned.

My eyes shifted from Chandler to Cas, who hadn't dropped his attention from me since he walked out of his room.

"It's what her friends call her," Chandler said, humor lacing his light tone. "Isn't that right, Birdie?"

I nodded and swallowed against a dry throat. Why did he keep staring?

"What else?" Chandler asked me directly.

"Sucks that we don't have the bodies. Then we could determine if he's controlled them with drugs, or maybe a stun gun." I grimaced when my worrying nail snagged on a loose cuticle, ripping it lengthwise along my thumbnail. "But how does he get them to walk into the woods alone?"

"Maybe someone they trusted?" Chandler suggested.

"But that would be a consistency we'd see if it were one person. I mean, all those women having one person in common?"

"What if it's not a certain person but someone in uniform?" Cas offered. His assessing eyes flicked down my chest, over my hips, and along my legs.

An intense heat bloomed between my thighs. Clenching them together to help ease the increasing throb, I watched, mesmerized, as the tip of his tongue darted out, wetting his lower lip.

Wow, it looked like he wanted to eat me.

Oh, how I wish he would.

Where did that come from?

"You mean like a ranger." My heart pounded against my chest, both from him and his subtle accusation.

"Or someone else wearing a uniform: maintenance, park employee, and yeah, a ranger."

"Can you track the online purchases of that kind of stuff?" I asked Chandler.

One hip pressed against the couch, glancing between me and Cas, Chandler rubbed his chin as he considered the new theory.

"You're one smart Birdie." With that as a parting remark, he stalked to his room, phone already pressed to his ear, and closed the door behind him.

8

Cas

UNABLE TO RESIST, I continued to study her as she attempted to distract herself with the file in front of her.

Yesterday after we dropped Alta off, I requested the entire team's files under the ruse of wanting to verify everyone. Of course, Peters saw straight through it, knowing I wanted one report in particular, and why. A part of me wished I'd never asked for it; then I wouldn't be sitting here so fucking pissed off I couldn't see straight. The report gave the basics of what happened to her ten years ago, but no details. Which was both a good and bad thing, considering that, with only knowing the basics I already wanted to dig up the fucker and pound his bones into dust for what he did. There was no telling what I would do if she ever told me the full story.

Same as when I first read the words, my blood boiled beneath my skin, readying to kill. She was innocent, a perfectly happy girl until it was ripped from her unexpectedly. Before the abduction, she was a perfect student, a part of every association on the damn campus, but after, nothing. Alta finished her senior year online instead of returning to college. Then one day a year or so later, she up and left for Tennessee, leaving her family behind in west Texas.

Like a siren's call, her deeply buried darkness sang to my own. But was it a call to protect her from experiencing pain and fear again, or a luring of her dark passion that's been waiting for the right spark to ignite the building want inside?

"What are you looking at?" she asked meekly from her spot on the floor, not glancing up.

"You."

I shouldn't open this door, but I couldn't help it. Somehow, this one woman had a pull over me even when she wasn't around. Past women never invoked this strong protective compulsion—hell, any feelings. Until Alta.

She didn't need me. I'd ruin her. Break her past the point of no return. Her dark desires were fucking rainbows compared to mine.

Stay away.

Run.

For her, I should.

But for me, I wouldn't.

In the cold life I'd been dealt, was it terrible to want one good thing from it?

One good person.

One Alta Lady Johnson.

"Why?" Alta finally peeked up from the paper, allowing her hazel eyes to meet mine.

"You're dangerous, you know that?" I said before thinking better of it.

"Me? Dangerous." She giggled nervously. "Isn't that the pot calling the kettle black? Pretty sure you could break me just with the crazy, intense stare you have."

The corner of my lips twitched upward in as much of a smile as I could manage lately. "You're distracting, mesmerizing, which *is* dangerous."

Hell. Where did all *those* words come from?

"Oh." The fire's coals crackled and the logs popped behind her as she uncomfortably shifted against the floor. "I... I've spent so long being ordinary. You're the only one who's noticed me."

"Why?" I was a bastard. I knew exactly why she wanted to remain anonymous.

"Long story," she said on a sigh. "I was noticed once, and it went sideways." The scraping of her index fingers along the ripped cuticles of her thumbs spoke to her rising anxiety. "Let's just say being around you and Chandler is the first time in years that I feel like I don't have to hide."

The couch complained as I shifted forward, closer to her.

I was a fool.

A weak fool who couldn't resist the enigma in front of him. It wasn't the strawberry-blonde hair or the delicate features of her beautiful, natural face. No, this was deeper.

"You don't. We've got you covered."

"Can I ask you a question?"

"Yes," I said quickly. Whatever she wanted to know, I'd tell her.

"What is this?" Averting her timid gaze, she flicked the file folder between us. "You're super intense, and I'm... I don't really...." A red flush crept up her neck before blooming along her delicate cheekbones, accentuating the small scattering of faint freckles.

Fuck, this is a bad idea.

I'll ruin her.

"Stay away from me, Lady."

Her eyes met mine, daring her to push back. "What? I didn't mean—"

"I'm not the man you think I am. I'm an asshole with more control issues than they can diagnose. I'm not a nice guy."

"But I'm safe," she whispered in a voice so fragile, it chipped at my resolve to stay away for her sake.

Fuck, that weak voice cracked every restraint I had. All she wanted to be was safe, and that was the one thing I *could* offer. "No one—I repeat, no one will touch you while I'm here. That is a fact you shouldn't question."

Her tight shoulders dropped, her lips parted in a relieved sigh. There was trust there, trust I hadn't earned yet, but still she gave it—to me, a nobody.

Fuck it.

Narrowing my eyes, I crouched directly in front of her, inching closer until her back pressed against the brick hearth. Inches from her nose, I inhaled each of her shaky breaths, savoring the heated fear that pulsed off her as her eyes darkened with lust. She needed to be scared of me, to run in the opposite direction.

Still I dared another inch closer, hoping she'd push me off, praying she wouldn't.

I slid a hand around the hot skin of her delicate neck.

"I don't know how to be gentle, Lady," I growled.

Her breath hitched at the minuscule squeeze of my fingers around her throat.

"What if I don't want gentle?" she breathed.

"What do you want?"

Light brown brows pulled together in thought, but her hazel eyes stayed locked with mine. "You."

Instantly I released her neck and retreated to the couch. A trembling hand enclosed around her neck where my finger marks were fading. Breathing still rapid, eyes wide, Alta stared, clearly not understanding my reaction.

That made two of us.

For the first time in a noncombat situation, I was fucking terrified.

This beautiful woman saw me. She saw into my dark soul and wanted more. Wanted me. The emotions she evoked just by seeing me and wanting me were paralyzing.

Frustrated as well as fucking confused, I shoved against the couch, sending it rocking back on its legs with the force, and stalked to the front door. The handle groaned at the jerk I gave it but didn't budge.

"Who the hell locked the damn door?" I grumbled as I flicked the metal lever, allowing the door to swing open at my pull.

A small, fair hand inched into the air by the fireplace.

Of course it was her.

Damn this woman. Damn her innocence, her fucking beauty.

The house vibrated as the door slammed shut behind me. My hands shook as I fumbled with the lighter, the whole time telling myself it was due to the cold, not *her*. The first deep drag of smoke filling my lungs eased the growing jitters. I needed to quit, but what was the point? We all died sometime, and it wasn't like I had a family who would miss me. Hell, I didn't even have a fucking goldfish. I was alone in this hard life, and that was the way it was meant to be. I came into it alone, lived it alone, and knew I was destined to die alone.

Gray smoke curled out between my lips, growing more significant as my hot breath mixed with the icy air. The clear blue sky and bright sun made it appear warmer outside than the actual near freezing temperature. At least it wasn't balls hot out here like in the house. Hell, Peters and I would need to open all the windows after she left to get an hour or two of comfortable sleep.

The next inhale, I held in the smoke until it burned. I needed to get my priorities straight. The case, finding the fucker messing with innocent women, was the goal. Not the edible officer inside who I wanted to devour like the luscious fruit she was.

As the smoke floated away on a light breeze, I adjusted my hardening cock. Inside, gazing into those scared, excited eyes, one thing was clear—If anything happened between us, it would be slow and on her terms.

Not that anything would happen.

Fuck, now I was even lying to myself.

The front door swung open, releasing a wave of warm, dry air from the cabin.

"Fuck, it's hot as hell in there," Peters complained. "But she seems comfortable, so I can't bring myself to be the ass who smothers her stupid fire."

In unison, we glanced through the front window. Alta sat on the hearth, even closer to the fire than before, her knees tucked against her chest as she stared at an iPad.

"Damn, Peters. The FBI has turned you into a soft pussy," I said through an exhale of smoke. "Man the fuck up and tell her to knock it off with the fire if you're hot."

A lone brow arched high on his forehead as he leaned against the post. "You're suggesting I freeze her out."

No. Yes. Hell, I didn't know what I was saying. The woman wasn't even in the same room and I couldn't think straight. But I did know letting Peters think I was into her was still a terrible idea.

To avoid responding, I set the cigarette between my lips and took a long drag.

"We should, you know. Make her run as far from us as possible."

"I'm sure you're going to tell me why, even though I don't give two shits about you or her." Lie. I was a fucking liar. I would tack it onto my growing list of sins I'd be held accountable for one day. The very long list.

"Right, keep telling yourself that, fuckstick. I'm saying she's more innocent than you or I have ever been in our entire lives. More than we can even grasp. When she caught me in my towel—"

I couldn't restrain the low growl that rumbled from my chest as I slid my gaze to him with a pointed glare. His knowing smirk made me curse and shift to look into the dense forest that surrounded our small cabin. Without all the leaves, a few other cabins around us were visible, but still far enough away to have some sense of privacy. I flicked the cigarette butt toward the bucket I set out the night before as a makeshift ashtray.

"She got here early, you jealous fool. Chill the fuck out. It's almost like you care or something. You know"—the way he dragged out the last word told me what was coming next—"if you really don't want her for yourself, then maybe I'll make a pass. It'd be fun to teach her what a real man can do to her."

"Don't fucking touch her," I bit out. "She deserves better than you or me." The truthful words burned in my chest. Most people deserved better than me, but especially her. Innocent, beautiful, a whole life ahead of her to be happy and move on from her past. I was cemented into mine with no hope of ever moving on.

His smirk fell. He pursed his lips as his gaze shifted to the ashtray. "Why do you say that?"

"You said it yourself, she's more innocent than we've ever been. I don't want to see her dragged down by one of us. She deserves someone who could make her happy."

"And you don't think you could." A statement, not a question.

I cut my gaze to him. "You know me. Know what I've done, what we've done. I'm not going to let my demons kill her too."

He cleared his throat and shifted on the post. "You make it sound like we're past the point of saving. Is that what you think?"

In response, I flicked the lighter to light another cigarette.

"We're not the bad guys, Mathews. We're not the ones out there preying on innocent people. We had a job, we were trained to do that job, and we did it. I won't believe what we've done or who we've killed is who we are. We're more than that."

I shook my head. He didn't get it. Peters went into the marines as a good man, only coming out slightly damaged. Whereas I went in damaged and came out an emotionless lost cause. In his optimistic mindset, he thought of us as good guys, the heroes in this world.

Which he might've been. But even as much as I fucking wanted it to be different, I wasn't her hero. And I refused to be her villain.

9

Alta

THE PENCIL ERASER rapped rapidly against the hard surface of the desk as I studied John's closed office door, impatiently waiting for it to swing open. He'd called that morning, telling me to be at the station an hour before the other meetings were scheduled for the day, but didn't give a hint as to why.

Three days had passed since I left Chandler and Cas's cabin, more confused than ever about the case and my strange feelings for the brooding, tatted man. After the hot scene by the fireplace, he shut me out the remainder of the afternoon, avoiding my looks and staying as far away as possible. Then yesterday during a shift, Chandler called unexpectedly, suggesting we schedule meetings with the two missing women's husbands. Knowing Johnny Boy would want to be involved, I called and filled him in on Chandler's request.

As impatient as I was to talk to John, my stomach knotted for another reason. Thoughts of Cas had consumed my every moment for three days, which had felt like an entire week, and now, today, I finally got to see him again.

"What in the hell has gotten into you?" Sarah asked as she snatched the pencil from my hand. "It's John."

"But he didn't say why he wanted to meet me before Chandler, Cas, and the two husbands arrived."

Sarah leaned forward to pet Benny. "I'm sure it's nothing. Want me to distract you with some gossip?"

"No."

With an exaggerated eye roll, she pressed her elbows on the desk. "Too bad. So, my hike with Sadie was quite informative."

As much as I didn't want to get sucked into whatever Sarah was about to say, I still found myself leaning forward, mirroring her pose.

Sarah's eyes flicked around the office, I assumed to make sure no one else was listening in. "Did you know she's here escaping a past?"

I shook my head.

"Didn't think so. Remind you of someone?" she said with a grin. "Anyway, she's running from some crazy ex apparently. It's actually why she doesn't like dogs. Apparently he had a few, and they were mean as hell. Nothing like Benny here."

Okay, now I felt like a terrible human being for not liking her. But on top of the whole 'not liking dogs thing, Sadie was weird. Really, really weird.

Sarah continued as I sat in shamed silence. "Listen, I'm not telling you to like her, but give the girl a chance. Though I doubt you will after what I'm telling you next."

That didn't sound positive. "Maybe you shouldn't tell me, then."

"Fuck that! It's good stuff, girl. You need to embrace this talking stuff. It's what girls do. Just watch, I'll mold you into a woman yet."

"You'll make me a woman? What, you have a strap-on collection or something?"

Sarah tilted her head back with a loud bark of a laugh. "Do you even know what that is?"

"No," I grumbled. But it didn't make the joke any less funny. Damn, I missed being funny and witty. But that drew attention, unwanted attention. No, I held back, kept to myself and stayed as anonymous as possible. That was how I stayed safe.

"John and Sadie, the little freaky wallflower, are going out on a date."

I blinked at my friend as I processed her words. "What?"

"John. Your John asked Sadie out on a date, like a legit 'dinner and coffee and the hope of sex at the end' kind of date."

Unfamiliar jealousy twisted in my gut. I didn't want John that way. His closeness didn't make my body tremble with excitement like Cas's did, but I did love his attention as a friend. His undivided attention.

Here I was, the stupid naïve woman once again.

"Well—" I swallowed back the lump forming in my throat. "—I hope it goes well."

Brows furrowed in concern, she stretched across the desk and grasped my hand between hers. "You okay? Does that bother you?"

"I don't... I don't know." I shook my head. "I don't want to date John, but the idea of him going out with *her* doesn't sit right either. I'm selfish, aren't I?"

"Kind of, yeah." Sarah released my hand to lean back in her chair. "Everyone knowns John had his eye on you since day one, but he fell into the friend corner quick."

With a frustrated eye roll, knowing full well she was right, I leaned back and stared at the popcorn ceiling. "I think I like him," I admitted out of nowhere.

"John?"

"No, the hot guy. The dark and sexy stranger, Cas."

"Do you know him enough to like him?"

"Besides his constant intense staring, no."

"Then what do you like about him?"

"The tattoos?"

Sarah smiled and shook her head. "Then you're attracted to him, babe. Liking means you know him, and attraction means you get all hot and bothered when he's around."

I rolled my eyes once more and glanced to Benny with a silent plea for help. "Fine, I find him attractive."

"How could you not?"

"But he's dark and dangerous, the exact opposite of what I need. Right?"

Sarah's animated features fell, and she pursed her lips. "Listen. You're allowed to be attracted to whoever you want. I'm happy for you. Hell, I'm ecstatic. Run with it, girl. Don't let your past dictate who you are now."

"Can someone be attracted to a guy who's so wrong for them?"

"Have you read a romance novel? Women swoon over the bad guy, but something tells me your dark and dangerous isn't a bad one."

Both our heads jerked toward the sound of John's door swinging open. "Come on in, Birdie," John called from where he stood just inside his office door.

"Okay," I called back. Releasing an anxious breath, I shoved out of the desk chair.

Sarah's hand darted out, gripping my wrist and preventing me from leaving.

"I want to hear more about him. Can we have a girls' night? With ice cream and popcorn and wine and a chick flick while we talk about boys?" The hope in her voice tugged at a part of me I hadn't realized was even there anymore. Those first couple of years in college were the last time I had a real girls' night full of laughter, secrets, and soul-cleansing chatter.

"Sure, but no wine. My place." I glanced to my boots as I mentally mapped out my schedule. "How about tomorrow night?"

Releasing my wrist, Sarah clasped her hands together with a high-pitched squeal.

Benny tucked his paws over his ears to ward off the loud, unexpected noise.

When I was almost halfway to John's office, Sarah squealed from the front room. "Did you hear that, Benny boy? I've won her trust, finally."

With a smile, I strode into John's office and flopped into the uncomfortable standard-issue office chair.

"Shut the door, Birdie."

Huffing my annoyance, hoping to leave it open to catch the draft of hot air from the hall to counteract the cold wind blowing through the open window, I leaned forward and shut the door, locking it three times with the tips of my fingers before turning back. "Shut. What's all this about? If it's about Sadie Lou Who—"

"How did—" He shook his head. "This isn't about her. It's about you."

Interest piqued, I bent forward, resting my elbows on my knees and clasping my hands. "So it's true. You did ask her out?"

"Sure, why wouldn't I?"

Index finger tapping against my temple, I looked to the ceiling, then rolled my eyes to him. "Um, because it's against policy."

"Damn, Birdie, it's one date, not rewriting the Constitution."

"We're dealing with a serial killer right now, you know. Shouldn't your focus be there instead of on her?" Dang it, I sounded jealous. Which I was, but not in the way he wanted.

"I can focus on both just fine. What's your deal? I figured you'd be too busy with the two temporary additions to our team to even give two shits about my love life."

"Is that why you asked her out? Because of them?"

John's face grew red. "No, Alta. I asked her out because she's nice, and attractive, and wants me too. Thought I should start going after women who *want* to date me."

An awkward silence stretched between us as we glared at one another.

"We're friends, and they're here to work on the case. You know I can't date," I whispered. My own words were like a sucker punch to the gut.

What the hell was I thinking with Cas? I couldn't date. I didn't even like to be touched. Even though his touch the other day *wasn't* terrible. It was pretty great, actually.

I shifted my gaze to the floor and shook my head to clear the volleying thoughts.

"Which is why you're here now." Shuffling a few papers around on the desk, he withdrew a file and slid it toward me. "Thought you should know who you're dealing with."

I leaned forward and grabbed the file, flipping to the first page as I sat back in the chair. "How'd you get more information on this guy than the FBI? Is it more than what Chandler has from the previous—"

"Not him. Them."

"Them?"

"Agent Peters and dipshit Mathews."

"Oh." I closed the file, leaving it balancing on my lap while I searched John's blue eyes. "CliffsNotes it for me."

The chair squeaked as he leaned back and interlaced his fingers behind his head. "They were in combat together. Agent Peters has been out for a while and immediately went into the FBI. It's the Mathews guy I wanted to warn you about."

"Warn me," I urged, my gaze on the closed file in front of me. My fingers itched to flip it open and reveal all of their dark secrets. It'd only been a few days, but we'd bonded, and I didn't want their character tarnished in my mind. But I needed the truth now that John had planted the seed of doubt.

"He's dangerous, Birdie." The high-pitched squeak of his chair pierced my ears in the otherwise silent office.

"How did you get this information?" I kept my eyes glued to the folder. Whatever John had to say, I knew it was probably terrible. Just looking at the man, I could tell he was capable of awful things. But I also knew whatever he did wasn't to an innocent victim, wasn't to a woman or a child. I'd only known the man a few days, and yet I knew that for a fact. Whatever John had to tell me wouldn't change my opinion of Cas.

"Sergeant Mathews isn't the only one with friends in high places."

I held back my eye roll. "What did you find out?"

When he didn't respond, I glanced up only to find unwanted sympathy marring his features. My lip curled in a snarl. Sympathy was the one emotion I couldn't stand. It was fake, annoying, and clingy. Sympathy made people think you were too weak to handle what was going on around you. Sympathy made the receiver weak. I would know; enough was tossed my way over the years by strangers who somehow found out about the assault for me to loathe that single emotion.

"Cut the crap, John, and don't look at me that way. I'm fine with whatever you have to say, so say it already."

In a wise move, John schooled his features back to his usual scowl. "He was discharged before his contract was up for medical reasons."

"So?" I huffed, tossing my hands in the air. What the heck was John getting at? And why?

"Mental medical shit, Birdie. The guy is fucked up in the head. He spent over thirty days bunkered down with his men after an ambush. Twelve marines went in. Three came out."

I held my breath as he continued.

"When they did a final count, nine American marines were killed, and over ninety hostiles were dead."

"Okay, I still don't—"

"Birdie, most of the enemy were killed in hand-to-hand combat, not by a gun. That guy you're so fascinated with sliced dozens of men's throats. He snuck up on them and took them out one by one."

I slid deeper in the chair and focused on the plain white wall. "So what you're saying is he saved the lives of two other marines."

"I'm telling you he's a monster."

"Or a savior, if you asked the two who survived."

John shoved out of his chair, sending it flying backward. "You're not listening to me. He's violent. He is fucked up in the head. You shouldn't be alone with him, and he sure as hell shouldn't be on this case. Hell, he should be locked up!"

I stood, echoing his anger. "For what? Serving his country? Protecting his men? Tell me, John, what would you have done in that same situation? Oh wait, you didn't serve in the military, so you wouldn't know."

John's eyes widened, jaw slightly slack. "You're defending him."

Hell yes I was, and I had no idea how John couldn't be as well. We were officers, and he knew anything could happen in the line of duty. It came fast and furious with little time to react, much less think through all the possible scenarios. But unlike me, John wasn't the child of an officer. He didn't have to watch his father justify his actions when it came down to taking a life or having his taken.

No, John didn't understand that sometimes in battle, the lines were blurred and you did what was necessary to survive. Because deep down, you maintained your moral code, and even though it was killing, you were still on the right side.

"I'm defending any man or woman who's been forced to take a life in the line of duty to make sure they came home to their family."

John hung his head. "Maybe it's this case. It's screwing with your perspective on things. The Birdie I know wouldn't be so careless."

My phone vibrated in my pocket. I slid it out, read the message, and reached for the door. After unlocking it, I turned back to the now-ashen man behind the desk. "Christina Brown's husband is here. I'll show him back once Agent Peters arrives." One foot over the threshold, I turned. "And for the record, I agree this case is changing my perspective, but what you can't see through the jealous haze you have over Cas is I'm changing for the better. And next time, show a little more respect for two men who willingly gave years of their lives to protect us. I think they deserve that much from you, don't you?"

Not letting him get another word in, I stormed through the door, down the hall, past a wide-eyed Sarah and Christina Brown's husband, and flung open the front doors.

One step out into the freezing cold, I collided into a hot, hard chest.

10

Alta

THE FAMILIAR MASCULINE scent of cedar and spice infiltrated my senses, sending a flurry of excited butterflies to overtake the growing rage John had conjured. Two large hands wrapped around my biceps, preventing me from yanking away.

"Easy there, Lady," Cas said in a soothing tone.

The soft fabric of his cotton T-shirt brushed along my forehead as I nodded and took a deep breath in, hoping it would halt the building angry tears.

"I'll go ahead and start the interview. Mathews, let me know when the other husband arrives. He should be here any minute," Chandler said at my back, his husky tone radiating restrained anger.

Sealing my eyes shut, I inhaled deeply, savoring his scent, then pulled away from Cas's warm body. I couldn't bring myself to look at him first. Instead, I glanced to Chandler, whose red cheeks and blazing eyes told of the fury boiling just below the surface. The man was all jokes and easy conversation, but his look and posture now were a startling reminder of the marine beneath the suit.

"What, Chandler?" I crossed both arms over my chest in an attempt to ward off the cold wind. *Should have grabbed my jacket off the back of the chair before storming off.*

"I wouldn't go as far as giving him the title of savior," Chandler said with a nod to Cas, who grunted and retreated toward their SUV. "But hero is one word they used when awarding him the Silver Star for valor in battle."

Eyes wide, I slowly turned my eyes to Cas, who was storming toward me with a black coat clenched in his fist. When I turned back, mouth open to ask one of a million questions clogging my thoughts, Chandler was nowhere to be seen.

Heated fingers grazed across the tops of my shoulder, startling me out of the trance I'd slipped into.

"How did he...?" I thought out loud as a heavy coat engulfed my thin frame, smothering me in delicious heat instantly. I peered up at Cas, whose own gaze wasn't on me for once. I turned, following his line of sight to the building. Understanding settled when I locked on John's open office window. "Oh. So you two heard it all?"

"Enough."

The scratch of flint drew my attention back to Cas. Gaze on me, he lit the end of the cigarette, the cherry burning bright with his first deep inhale, then blew out the harmful smoke in the opposite direction of where I stood.

"I don't know how I feel about you two eavesdropping." It was the truth. On the one hand, it was good that they knew I would stand up for them, but I also didn't want them to think I was an ignorant girl for ignoring John's clear warning.

"First." He paused to take a deep inhale of smoke. I watched in fascination as his lips curled around the end. The tip of his tongue flicked against the center of his bottom lip after each drag. "It isn't eavesdropping if two people are yelling so loud that you can't help but hear it. Second, why does it matter if we heard if you meant it?"

"Meant what?"

A muscle twitched along his scruffy jawline. "Don't play dumb, Lady. You're not."

I arched a brow and stepped back to lean against the building's cold brick. "Yes, of course I meant it. Wouldn't have said it otherwise."

"Are you scared of me now that you know the truth?"

"The truth that you're a hero?"

He flinched. Physically cringed, as if my words were poison-laced arrows shot into his skin. At his side, a scarred hand clenched into a tight fist. "I'm no one's hero. I'm the man people call in to wreak havoc, not the hero who saves you from it." He nodded toward the open window. "You defended me. Defended us in there with that dipshit. Why?"

He said it in surprise, as if he'd never had someone stand up for him. Maybe he hadn't.

I focused on the pebble rolling back and forth beneath my boot with each push of my foot. "My dad is a game warden in Texas. A veteran too. As a kid, I remember hearing late-night conversations between my mom and dad, her counseling him through the actions he had to take at work to survive, or even sometimes talking about things he did while serving. It imprinted on me. The bits of a person that get chipped away with each life they took, even though it could've been their own if they hadn't. I'm not defending people who use their power as a way to take lives just because they can. But that's not who you are, or Chandler, or my dad, or most people who put on an officer or military uniform. That's who I defend. The good guys who have to make a tough decision that will haunt them for the rest of their lives."

Mustering a sliver of courage, I peered up into his narrowed, searching eyes.

"What?" I asked.

"There's something else. You're leaving something out. Tell me."

"No I'm not." How in the heck could he tell I left another key person out of my explanation? Was I really that easy to read?

"Lady, I want to know. Tell me. Now."

Inside the long sleeves of Cas's coat, I worked the edges of both thumbs with my index fingers. Other than my family and the officers who'd handled my case, and my friend Beth, no one else knew the truth of how Lance died. It wasn't something I wanted to advertise because of what I did to her. Not me technically, but what she did to save me. She took a life to protect my own, and now she was the one who had to live with it. Not me. I had scars of my own, but Beth, she was never the same either.

I cleared my throat. "It's nothing."

"You're a terrible liar."

An older model navy pickup truck sped into the parking lot before screeching into a spot.

"I've seen firsthand what the weight of taking someone's life can do to someone. Even if it was justifiable."

Before he could press for details, I shoved off the brick and shrugged out of his coat. "The other husband is here. Thanks for this." Without the swaddling warmth of the oversized jacket, a shiver shook down my spine as I walked to meet the husband halfway.

"Hi, Mr. Brandon, I'm sure you remember me—"

"Yep, the woman who couldn't do anything, so they had to call in the FBI. Sure, I remember you."

I stumbled on the flat black asphalt. "Sir, that's not—"

"And you know what, I'm fucking pissed that this didn't happen sooner," he roared in my face, sending a waft of alcohol up my nose. "If you hadn't dicked around when my wife first went missing, maybe she'd be here now instead of still fucking missing." The man stood tall, towering over me with his large build that probably took hours in the gym to maintain.

Instead of backing away, I straightened my spine, prepared to stand my ground against anything else he had to say.

"Step back. Now." Cas's dark, meddlesome voice at my back made my heart rate pick up.

The enraged man's violent gaze lifted from mine and froze. A spike of fear shined in his bloodshot eyes. One step, then another, he backed away until he was well outside my personal space.

"The others are inside. Tell them who you're here to meet with, and they'll show you to the division director," Cas demanded.

I held my breath. Not until the crunch of the dead leaves beneath tennis shoes faded did I turn. Immediately I stumbled backward a step. Shoulders back, pushed-up sleeves exposing the one full sleeve of tattoos, and head slightly bowed, dark eyes peering down, Cas looked as menacing as he sounded.

"Don't you *ever* do that again," he stated, his teeth clenched in his tight jaw.

"Do what? My job?" I protested, even though my voice was no more than a whisper. Somehow the 'I'm a stone-cold killer' look was a turn-on. Every inch of my skin lit on fire with the want for him to reach out and touch me. To have those long, thick fingers wrapped around my throat again, taking from me what I would willingly give.

"He was twice your size, Alta. When dealing with men like him, you need someone else with you, especially when they're emotionally unstable. He just lost his fucking wife—who knows what he'll do. Hell, he could've had a gun, for God's sake."

"So do I."

One small step from him put us nose-to-nose. "Don't. Do it. Again."

Tipping my head back, I stared into his dark eyes. The bright sun illuminated his features, shining flecks of light brown amongst the dark irises. Something he said worried me.

"Size," I whispered, hoping it would help piece everything together faster. "They were both massive men."

Cas stood silent, his eyes searching mine like he could see the wheels of my mind turning.

Maybe....

"Where's Chandler's iPad with the other crime scene and case photos?" I rushed out, a hint of excitement in my trembling voice.

Cas's eyebrows narrowed in confusion. "At the cabin—"

That was all I needed to hear. Turning on the balls of my feet, I took off running across the parking lot toward the exit.

"What are you doing?" Cas yelled after me.

"I think... I might've figured something out. Something we can profile about this guy," I shouted back. At the edge of the road, I turned to see him still standing in the parking lot, hands on his hips.

"I have the car keys."

Looking up the road, I turned back with a broad smile. "Scared you won't be able to keep up? Get Benny, would you?"

Even from where I stood, there was no mistaking the grumbled curses.

Knowing there was no way he could resist the challenge, I turned and took off once again, only to have two dark shadows by my side less than a quarter-mile later.

"Running helps me think," I said through my even, deep breaths.

"We're in hiking boots."

"Already coming up with excuses for why you're going to lose, huh?" I laughed and rammed a shoulder into his ribs.

Retaliating, he shoved me into oncoming traffic with a deep laugh before tugging me back to safety. "Come on, Lady, let's see if you could've cut it in the marines." Without warning, he upped his pace, leaving me to breathe in his dust.

"Well, poop," I exclaimed with a happy smile.

This was fun. I snuck a quick peek down to Benny at my side, who looked up at the same time. I could've sworn he was smiling.

For the first time in forever, we were having fun. And it was glorious.

"What do I get," Cas wheezed, "for winning?"

Shoulder against the side of the cabin, I gripped my ankle and pulled it back, stretching my tight muscles. "It was a tie, and you know it. Don't try to cheat."

His lips twitched upward in an almost smile. "What are we doing here again?"

"iPad."

"Kitchen table is the last place I saw it, I think," Cas said as I squeezed past.

"Thanks." Ignoring the wonderful warmth his body emitted and the sweet smell of manly sweat, I strode to the kitchen table and swiped the iPad open. "Something you said back there, about the husband being twice my size. It made me realize I had the same thought about him and the first husband. Both abnormally large, strong, and fit."

"Could be a coincidence. Aren't most dudes fit?"

An incredulous laugh rattled through my chest. "Um, no. But if you seem to think so, maybe I should go where you hang out, if they all look like you." *Well snap.* "I mean your friends. If you think everyone's fit, I'd love for you to meet your friends. I mean me to meet your friends. You know, because they sound hot like you." *Double snap.* "I'm going to stop talking now and focus on these pictures," I grumbled in complete embarrassment.

Heat crept across my cheeks.

Focus. Focus on the task at hand.

Thankfully Cas didn't mutter a word about my ramblings of finding him attractive; he simply disappeared into his room. At the sound of a shower, I sneaked to the front door, locked it once, twice, and a third time, then went back to my seat, resuming my picture-scrolling with hopes that my random connection wasn't so random after all.

"It can't be a coincidence," I mumbled as I flipped through the pictures again and again. I saved pictures of the husbands in a separate file to make the comparison easier. Like the two husbands here, the others were all fit too—a few looked like they had some illegal steroid help—massive and, by their looming postures in the pictures, also dominant.

I peeked to the couch. Half an hour ago, Cas emerged from his room, freshly showered and dressed in a pair of mesh shorts and a long-sleeve T-shirt. Since then, he lay on the couch in complete silence, just staring at the ceiling. It was unnerving how well he played the silent, hot guy.

I needed to break the silence before I exploded.

"Want to see what I'm seeing?" I asked, swiveling in the chair to watch for a reaction that I didn't get. "Okay fine. I'm going to run back to the station—"

"For fuck's sake, woman, no more running. I had enough of that shit in boot camp. Bring that thing over here. I'm not getting my ass up. My legs are sore."

With the iPad cradled against my chest, I couldn't help my smile as I shuffled across the room to the couch. Tentatively, I kneeled on the floor beside his head and rested the screen on his chest.

"Okay, see this guy? This is the husband of the first woman who went missing." Fingertips on the screen, I spread them wide to zoom in. "He's a head taller than all the people around him, and look at the cuffs of his T-shirt. If he breathed too deep, they'd rip apart." I swiped to the next. "And this guy. I mean, the low-dip tank top is a dead giveaway, plus his anaconda arms."

"Anaconda arms," Cas chuckled. "Is that even a thing?"

"Yes," I responded defensively. "Well, it used to be. Haven't been around a lot of girls recently to be in the know for what's said nowadays."

Before I could swipe to the next example, a hot hand wrapped around my wrist. The iPad slipped from my grasp and fell to his hard stomach. "Tell me one thing about you. One thing so I'll stop feeling so damn stupid obsessing over a woman I don't even know."

Obsessing? That word should've caused fear, but instead, a flood of relief washed through my veins.

This wasn't just a one-way street. He felt it too.

The thumb circling the underside of my wrist created a reverberating shock through my veins with each pass.

"I'm not that interesting," I whispered as I licked my lips.

"One thing. I'm not asking for much here, Lady. And make it something terrible so I'll be able to stay away, like I should."

Lady. My middle name. Keeping my focus on his still-brushing thumb, I smiled as I spoke. "My name. I'm named after my great-great aunt. Most people knew her as Lady Bird Johnson, which is why my nickname has always been Birdie. No one ever uses my middle name. Well, except you. And bonus answer, I kind of like it."

"Me too. Suits you."

Cas's hand inched up my arm until his palm pressed against my cheek.

Turning my face to his, I kept my gaze on his chest. "I don't know what's going on. It's... I haven't—"

"This is me hanging on by a fucking thread. Every second you're in the room, it's torture to stay away. I want you in ways I haven't wanted in a long damn time. In ways I shouldn't want you. Tell me to stay away, Lady. Make me stay away."

He pulled me closer, brushing his nose against the sensitive skin of my lower neck and inhaling deeply. Every thought, every nerve and sensation narrowed on the places he touched. Every breath, every brush of his skin against mine sent a wave of lust and heat to my core, increasing my already rapid breaths.

"Make me pull away," he whispered so softly that it almost got lost in the sounds of my heavy breathing.

Too long ago. Way too long ago was the last time a man made me feel this way—needed and desired and okay with allowing it. And not just allowing it, but *requiring* it.

Make him pull away? Heck no. I wanted this.

Slick lips tentatively pressed against my pulsing vein, urging a trembled moan to pass my lips. His hand tightened around the back of my neck, making it arch and giving him more area to explore.

"Fuck, you taste good." He dragged the tip of his tongue up the length of my neck before wrapping warm lips around my earlobe.

"What are you doing to me?" he whispered into my ear. "I should stay away from you, for your own good, but I can't. I want to taste every inch of you, hear you when you feel safe enough to let go, feel you giving me the control to make it the fucking best you've ever had."

Words stuck in my throat, and all energy went to my pounding heart, on the verge of a heart attack. Yes, to everything he said. Yes, and tack on a please to the end. It'd been so long. Too damn long.

Now, with him, it was time to end the ten-year dry spell.

11

Cas

I couldn't stop.

I needed to pull back. To stop tasting her delicious skin. Stop fantasizing about the way she tasted elsewhere. Stop my roaming hands.

But I couldn't.

Call me selfish. Call me disturbed and an asshole, but I wouldn't stop. She was too much, yet at the same time I couldn't get enough. The sense of belonging enveloped me each time our skin touched, a type of belonging I'd never known, even in the marines.

This was home. She was home.

We were meant to be together. Somehow in this crazy world, we led different paths to be here—two royally fucked-up paths—but we made it to each other.

With each flick of my tongue against her soft, fair skin, each suck of my lips, I dove deeper into her pull.

Mine.

The word pulsed in my brain over and over like a flickering neon light.

This delicate, beautiful, damaged soul would be mine—this innocent woman wrapped in a strawberry-blonde, freckle-faced package.

Strands of her hair tangled between my fingers as I tugged it out of the tight bun that held it back, urging her face closer.

Alta's hot, erratic breaths brushed against my cheek, and mine caught in my chest. She felt it too. Every hot pulse between us wasn't just me. No, she wanted this too.

I grazed my lips down her cheekbone toward her plump, pink lips, and our breaths mingled. Heart hammering against my chest, I shifted along the couch to pull her lips to mine just as a loud engine roared up the gravel drive. Lips hovering over hers, I peeled my eyes open to stare down at the most innocent face I'd ever been that close to.

Innocent.

Perfect.

Deserving.

Everything I wasn't.

"We have company," I whispered against her lips.

"Hmm" was the only acknowledgment I got in return.

Pulling back, I sat against the couch and lifted her from the floor. With Alta still lost in a lusty daze, I retrieved the iPad from where it had slid to the floor, set it on her lap, and flicked the screen alive just as a loud thud boomed through the living room and the front door shook.

I barked a laugh. She did it again. Locked the damn door.

My leg muscles protested as I stood to open the door. An angry Peters stormed through the second I unlocked it, that dipshit John guy hot on his heels.

"Where in the hell did you two run off to?" Peters bit out, even though a fraction of his temper eased the second he saw us both safe. Maybe there was more to this case if Peters was scared that something had happened to us, or perhaps just her. He knew I could handle my own, plus the deranged fucker we were chasing wasn't after someone with my anatomy.

Before I could respond, John stomped to Alta and dropped to a crouch before her as she stared at the iPad.

"You okay there, Birdie?" When he didn't get an immediate answer, his gaze shot to her disheveled hair before turning. "What the fuck did he do to you?"

His accusing tone must've sunk into the deep spell she was under —which I had to admit was fucking amazing, since *I* put her there with only a hint of a kiss. She mentioned it'd been a while for her; surely she didn't mean... no, no way a man hadn't intimately touched her since she left Texas. That was ten years ago.

"I'm fine. Sorry, just lost in thought." Alta looked everywhere other than where I stood as she rose from the couch. "Give me a second, but I want to show you something, Chandler. I think I found something." At that she turned, walked to the small bathroom off the hall and softly clicked the door closed behind her.

Behind the furious John, Peters smiled, probably knowing full well he and John cock-blocked me.

"Calm the fuck down," I grumbled to the man who was still glaring. "She wanted to come back here to look at something on that thing." I hitched my chin to the iPad on the couch. "She fucking took off, ran here."

"You could've left the keys, bastard. I had to bum a damn ride." That mischievous smile of his grew. "Then what happened?" Peters prodded. "Once you two got here, that is."

I shot him a glare and ran a calloused palm down my face. Peters was officially a bastard. "Fuck off," I growled just as the bathroom lock clicked and the door swung open.

Calm and collected once again, Alta snagged the iPad and shifted to show Peters the screen. "When I saw the husbands today, something clicked. They're both huge."

Peters frowned. "Huge is a slight overstatement. I mean, they're big—"

"To me they're huge, just like you and Cas." She gave him a

patronizing pat on his shoulder. "There, does that make you feel better about your size?"

"Yes," he said, seemingly satisfied.

Her hazel eyes rolled to the ceiling, but a small smirk twitched at the corners of her lips. "Whatever. Anyway, it got me thinking about the pictures I flipped through the other day when I was here."

"You were here? Alone? With them?" John cut in, sounding wounded.

Alta didn't flinch. "Yes. Can I talk without being interrupted?"

The two men hung their heads and nodded, completely chastised. I couldn't help the small smile of pride that crept up my lips.

"I remembered having the same thoughts about a few of the husbands from the Smokies cases," she continued. "That's what I wanted to see before I brought it to your attention, Chandler. And after looking at all the pictures again, I think I have something."

"What, that all the husbands are big? That's not much of a profile for the type of women the unsub goes after."

"Maybe it is," she said, straightening. "What if he targets the women *because* of the husbands?"

Peters fell onto the couch beside me as he flipped through the pictures. "But none of the women have the same build, the same hair color, background, nothing. I don't see how—"

"They're all married to the same *type* of guy," Alta continued. "Large, arrogant, dominant, huge egos. And that is a type. What if it's not about the women at all? What if it's about torturing the husbands, because this guy takes the one thing they feel the most possessive about? What if he's taking them not to do whatever cruel things other serial killers do to their victims, but to watch the aftermath, the husband's downfall? Because as big as they are, they couldn't save the one person who mattered most."

Silence took over the room as we all processed her theory. It was crazy, but it made sense, especially if the guy wasn't like the husbands.

"The guy could be weak, comparatively speaking," I mused as I scratched at my days-old scruff. "Maybe he was the small guy his whole life and resents men who're stronger than them." Knowing I was about to set off an explosion, I caught John's attention and asked, "Is that how you felt?"

"Fuck you," he seethed and took a step closer. "Just because I don't 'roid out like you doesn't mean I'm weak."

"So you're just small," I retorted with an arrogant smile. It was too easy, and way too fun.

Arms folded across his puffed chest, he looked to Alta, who ignored us by flipping through her phone. "I'm big in all the right places."

I caught Alta's eyes widening a fraction. So she *was* listening.

"Keep telling yourself that, boss—"

A small but strangely strong hand smacked against my chest, knocking the breath from my lungs.

Hell. The woman could pack a punch. She wasn't exaggerating about the black belt.

"Enough, you two. Focus on the task at hand. You can schedule a time to meet on the playground after the work's done to finish this juvenile fight." Turning to Peters, she asked, "What do you think of the guy targeting the women based on their husbands, not the women themselves?"

Peters leaned back, sinking deeper into the couch after tossing the iPad in my direction. "You could be on to something, but it doesn't give us any details to how he's finding them."

"What's something all of them would have in common?" I asked, looking to Alta as she paced in front of the fireplace, hands resting on her lean hips.

"Haircuts, protein shakes, favorite coffee, places they ran while they were here. It could be anything," Peters said with a groan. "It's a lot of work to go back to all those husbands and track their every move while they were in the parks and outside of it, but it's worth a shot. It's more than we've had to go off of besides the notes."

"Notes?" Alta skidded to a halt, almost tumbling forward over her own two feet. "What notes?"

"I was planning to tell you in the interviews today, but you ran away." Peters leaned forward, clasping his hands between his bent knees. "I couldn't tell you before because it's the one piece of the investigation no one knows about. Not the press, not even the husbands. Each of the wives received a card, a love card of sorts, sometime during their stay. All found on their windshields one morning. Every single one of them brushed it off as a mix-up because of the message inside."

Her chest stopped moving like she couldn't breathe. "What did it say?"

"'See you soon. We'll have so much fun.' Or something along those lines. Since they trashed the cards assuming it wasn't meant for them, we can only go off what the husband remembered, which was very little. Some said it was in print, a few others said cursive like a woman's handwriting, and a few others said it was chicken scratch."

Scared, accusing eyes shot to me. "Did you know about this?"

I nodded, feeling a little guilty, though not sure why.

John stepped toward her. "I just found out or I would've told you. I'm sure this brings up a lot of old memories because of—"

The 'shut the fuck up' glare Alta shot him could be felt by everyone in the room.

John cleared his throat and looked to his watch. "Listen, I need to get back. I've got a ton of shit to wrap up before tonight. Birdie, want me to drive you home?"

She shook her head, resuming her back-and-forth pace. "No thanks. I'll walk Benny home before heading out for my shift."

"I'll take that ride," Peters chimed in. "I need to get the Suburban."

John headed for the door as Peters shoved off the couch, turning to me with an extended hand. "Keys, you asshole. And don't lock the fucking door again."

A small hand rose from the other side of the room. "My bad. Force of habit. Can't say I'll be able to stop, but I'll try."

The back of the soft, worn couch molded around my back as I dug into my shorts' pockets for the keys. One-handed, Peters snatched them before they could soar over his head.

"Be back in a few," he said with a smile. "Don't do anything I wouldn't do."

"I know I'm onto something," Alta muttered after the door had clicked closed behind Peters. "It can't be a coincidence. I've seen the general public in this park, and those guys are not the average man around here."

Instead of turning on her heels to make another fast-paced loop, Alta stayed straight, rounded behind the couch and stopped in front of the door. Her right fingers twitched on her thigh like there was an internal battle urging her to reach up and flip the lock.

"I have to lock it," she whispered, then turned with an apologetic glance. "I know it sounds silly to you, but it's one more defense I put up to not be taken by surprise."

The cushions groaned under the fists I plunged into them to help me stand. Not looking away from her hazel eyes, I paused just out of reach. "I'm here."

"I know, and I do trust you. I do know you'll keep me safe, but it's been a part of me for so long. I've kept myself safe for almost ten years by keeping doors locked, windows secure, a deadly dog by my side. I hide water bottles under the sink so no one can find them and slip something inside. I only drink from things I can break the seal myself or pour myself. There's a gun by my door, Taser under the couch, a knife under my pillow and mace hanging in my shower."

Her back hits against the door with a soft thump and rattling of the hinge. Each breath looked to be a struggle, but her watery gaze never left mine.

"I don't know how to be normal, and I might never figure out how, but this is how I cope. This is how I survive." Using the pad of my thumb, I swiped a single rogue tear trailing down her freckled cheek as she whispered, "I've avoided physical contact for so long." Flush crept up her neck before turning her whole face a bright pink. "It's been years since I've kissed anyone." She broke our stare to look down at the floor.

Emotional shit had never been a strength, so when she paused, still not able to look back up, I wasn't quite sure what to do. Instead of saying the wrong thing or giving in to what my dick wanted to do—shove her against the door and break the dry spell she'd sentenced herself to—I stood silently, waiting for her to continue.

"Right. Okay, nothing else to say, then, huh? I'm quirky and not worth the trouble? I get it, don't worry. I need to get Benny home."

Her soft voice cracked my hard, cold heart. The door creaked open an inch before I slammed my palm against it, shoving it closed.

My chest pressed against her back, forcing her against the door to support my heavy weight. A shudder shook my fingers as I yanked her hips back, sealing us together.

"Normal isn't something I understand or want, Lady. It's fucking overrated." Jerking her collar low with a single hooked finger, I slid my lips up and down the length of her neck. A jolt shook her shoulders, and a happy, mischievous smile curled the corners of my lips. Every cell in my damn body twitched to take her against the door, sink in deep, and show her just how much I didn't fucking care about her quirks.

But I wouldn't, even though her firm, round ass kept shifting against my hard dick, making it near impossible to resist fucking her right then and there. To silence my groan, I bit her soft flesh, savoring the way my teeth sank deep, which would no doubt leave the lasting mark I hoped for.

"More," she begged between rapid pants, eyes sealed shut, her forehead resting against the hard wood of the door. "More. More. More."

"No," I growled at my tipping point.

Releasing her hips, I smacked both palms beside her head to keep them from ripping off her pants. "I'm going to do right by you, Lady. You're not ready for all the things I want from you." A faint whimper escaped her parted lips, making my dick pulse against the soft fabric of my shorts. "And right now, I wouldn't be slow, wouldn't be fucking gentle like you need. Right now," I gritted out into her ear while grinding my hard cock against her ass, "I want to fucking claim you, make you scream my name so that fucker boss of yours can hear it and know you're mine."

12

Alta

"Do it," I begged with what little breath I had left. "Please."

Never in my life had I been so turned on, so hot and wet for a man. Even boyfriends in the past never provoked this kind of need. And we hadn't even done anything yet, except for that erotic bite that sent my head spinning and a steady pulse to pound between my thighs.

Each place he licked, each touch, every breath against my skin, I wanted more. Zero disgust, no withdrawing from his touch. This—*him*—was what I'd been waiting for. This primal, sexual, undeniable pull. And here it was delivered in a hot-as-hell, tattooed killing machine who knew all the right buttons to push.

"No, Lady. Not yet." I whimpered at the sudden disappointment. "We talk first."

"Talk?" Apprehension bloomed in my gut severing the lust-induced daze I'd sunk into. "Talk about what?"

His massive hand tugged my shoulder, flipping me to press my back against the cold wood. Hooded dark brown eyes roamed down my face and lingered on my heaving chest. "You." A deep groan rumbled in his chest as he turned on his bare heels and strode with purpose toward his bedroom. "Lock the damn door. We'll talk after I'm done."

"Done? Done with what? Where are you going?" I called out, a bit panicked. Craning my neck to see inside the room he disappeared into, I startled and jumped back, nailing my backside and head against the door when he appeared shirtless.

Holy hell. My mouth watered at the sight of his defined pecs, hard stomach, and full left arm covered from wrist to shoulder in blue and black ink. Every breath caught in my chest, sweat beading along my forehead and spine.

"To take *another* cold shower." Taut muscles flexed and ripped down his arms as he jammed a finger in the direction of the couch. "Sit. Do not leave. Understood?" With another long perusal down my trembling body, he turned back to the bedroom and disappeared with a low string of curses.

The way he looked at me, wanted my body, was empowering instead of degrading or overwhelming. The want radiating off him and the constant struggle to hold himself back was more strengthening than demeaning. With Lance all those years ago, knowing someone longed over my body was belittling. But not Cas Mathews. Oh no. The control he had over his actions was sexy as hell, and so was the knowledge that he had to fight the persistent urge to pin me against a wall.

The throbbing between my thighs faded the longer Cas was out of the room, allowing worry and self-doubt to fill the void. I'd only slept with two guys before the assault, and neither was earth-shattering. What if I was terrible at sex? Or what if I couldn't even do it? What if I freaked out the second we were naked? How embarrassing would a panic attack be in such an intimate moment?

This was a bad idea.

On the couch, exactly where he told me to wait, I tucked my anxious hands beneath my thighs.

Now that I could think clearly, the idea of doing anything with Cas would be terrible for many reasons, but mostly because I was scared, intimidated, and a lot embarrassed by my lack of experience. He would expect more, and when I couldn't give it, would he walk away or even worse, feel sorry for me?

A quiet creak from the direction of his room signaled he was back, watching.

I had to end this before we went too far.

Mouth open, I turned toward him, ready to call it all off, but not a single word escaped. The sight of him wrapped in just a towel sucked every word, every thought from my head. The man was more than handsome. Water dripped from his hair in streams, cascading down his naturally tan skin as he scrubbed another towel against his hair.

"We... we need...." I willed my body to turn away to think straight, but my eyes remained glued to his naked chest. "Talk. We need to talk."

"Isn't that what I suggested?" At the undercurrent of humor in his tone, I peeled my gaze from his body up to his face, which was just as ruggedly beautiful. "Let's go take care of the dog, and then we can talk." With a smirk, he stepped back into his room, leaving the door open, and dropped the towel from around his trim waist.

Eyes wide, I ogled his naked backside. Each step sent a butt cheek flexing, making my mouth water.

I stumbled from the couch and bolted to the door. "I'll meet you outside," I squeaked out as the door swung open, and Benny and I dashed out into the cold.

By the time the front door opened again and Cas stomped down to the front porch, fully dressed, I had my nerves under control and speech prepared. Gazing out into the naked trees that surrounded our little cabin community, I felt more than saw him approach.

"Left my coat back at the ranger station. This is all I have." A large black sweatshirt was clutched between his fingers. "Wasn't sure how far of a walk your place was."

Taking the soft cotton from his hand, I pressed it tight against my chest. "Thanks, but it's not too far." I was cold and desperately wanted to slip the sweatshirt on to ward off the crisp mountain air. But the second his scent-laced shirt enveloped me, there was no doubt I would lose the nerve to tell him we couldn't happen.

His eyes followed each of my steps as I started down the gravel path.

"What's wrong?" he asked at my side. "Something's off."

"Nothing. Well, not nothing. I'm worried that… I think us doing anything, you know, in private… it's a bad idea. We're working a case and need to focus on that."

"I'm amazing at multitasking." His warm breath brushed against the shell of my ear. The toe of my right hiking boot caught the ground, causing me to stumble forward. Hands around my biceps, Cas caught me mid-fall and pulled me to a halt. "Spit it out. What's going on in that mind of yours, because I'm at a fucking loss. Just a few minutes ago, you were begging me to keep going, and now you sound like you don't want this at all."

"I don't."

"Bullshit," he spit out and dropped his hands. "I'm calling bullshit, Lady."

"It's not," I said defensively. "Well not technically. The case—"

"You changing your mind has nothing to do with the case. It's why I wanted to talk. So before you end this, before we can get to the good stuff—because, Lady, it's fucking great—I need to know a few things."

The gravel crunched under my boots as I shifted my weight from one foot to the other. "What if I don't want to tell you a few things?"

The cold wind brushed where his warm hands had held me tight, leaving me colder than I'd ever been. "Then you get your wish of this not going anywhere. I want you, Lady, but I'm not the guy who will pressure you into doing something before you're ready. It's your choice on what happens next."

My choice.

Yes or no.

Tell him everything he wanted to know or walk away.

The easy way out would be to keep my mouth shut and pretend I didn't want him as desperately as he wanted me.

"What do you want to know?" I asked. My gaze darted to where Benny raced into a cluster of trees after a chattering squirrel.

Cas gestured for us to keep walking. "I pulled your file, so I know the basics of what went down in Texas while you were in school."

I wet my lips and swallowed past the lump building in my throat. "That's good, I guess."

"Tell me what happened and how that fucker ended up dead."

He made it sound easy, but it wasn't. Might never be.

"Start small. What made you want to study wildlife management?"

Benny bolted from the trees with the same angry squirrel hot on his heels. Sweet Benny. He was trained to kill, but that wasn't who he was in his heart. If the other animals would allow Benny the chance, he'd befriend every animal on the mountain.

"Animals. I wanted to be a game warden just like my dad. The ecosystem is a balancing act, and a Texas game warden's job is to make sure the scale never tips. They protect the animals from poachers and illegal fishing operations, render aid or removal when necessary, all to keep the animals safe."

"But you never did," Cas added as he walked at my side with Benny trotting between us.

I hitched my chin to the right, indicating the turn to my cabin. "No, I never did. I couldn't stick around after everything. It became too much. My parents wouldn't let me out of their sight. They booked me an appointment with every therapist in town in an attempt to help me cope. The first few months, they had every right to worry, I was a mess. I couldn't sleep, couldn't move. Fear paralyzed me for a long time." I paused to slip the sweatshirt over my head. As the dark cotton slid down my face, Cas's strong masculine scent filled my nose and lungs, somehow offering a boost of strength to keep going.

"Not sure what all the file said, but it started as a stalking case. I worked at the local H-E-B as a cashier to help pay for the portion of school that wasn't covered by my track scholarships. Who I am now is a shell of who I was before it all happened. Before, I was outgoing, funny, charismatic. I'd talk to anyone and everyone, with the core belief that everyone deserved a kind smile." Out of habit, I brought my right thumb to my lips and chewed on the edge. "That was what caught his attention during the spring semester of my junior year. At first, it wasn't anything big, just him coming in every time I was on shift and hanging back to talk to me, which I didn't mind. Then notes appeared on my car at work, at school, when I was home.

"I told my dad, but he knew there was nothing we could do unless he made a threat, which he hadn't. Everything he wrote was loving, telling me how beautiful I was, how he was glad to have a friend like me, stuff like that."

The old wooden steps to my cabin creaked under our weight as we climbed in unison to the porch. Benny sat by my feet while I dug out the keys and unlocked the first deadbolt, then the next, and the next.

"Safer than Fort Knox," Cas muttered as a joke.

He had no idea how right he was.

"There are deadbolts on the door, jams on the windows, and I had them cover the glass panes with a coating that makes them unbreakable."

"Nice." He nodded as he glanced around my filthy cabin. His lips pursed at the sink overflowing with dirty dishes. "So what changed?"

I tugged off my tactical belt, situated everything like I always did in my routine, and locked all three locks three times each. Unease rolled through my stomach, nausea building. Index fingers scraping at the cuticles of both thumbs, I turned to him.

"I don't have people over," I said as an excuse for the mess. With a cringe at the day-old bowls lying on the coffee table and empty water bottles strewn about, I quickly shuffled through the room, picking up the dishes and hauling them to the already full sink. As I started on the tower of dirty dishes, Cas snagged a clean dishrag from a drawer on the other side, ready to dry.

"Thanks. What was your question again?"

"What changed with the creeper? What made him go from leaving you nice notes to kidnapping you for three days?"

The dish in my hands slipped and dropped into the sink. "I

started dating someone, and Lance, the creeper, wasn't a fan. That's when the notes changed. I stuck around that summer to keep working and take some summer school classes. The notes turned from angry and hurt to demeaning and scary. One had an undeniable threat toward my boyfriend and me. After talking with my dad, I decided it was time to go to the police. I filled out a restraining order and thought it was done."

Beneath the sudsy water, my fingers quivered as I scrubbed at a spoon with dry ramen noodles stuck to it.

"The notes stopped, and he stopped showing up at work, so I took it as a win. The Sunday before Thanksgiving break, my roommate left, but I had to work that Monday and Tuesday, so I stayed behind. We planned for me to meet her in Dallas that Wednesday before I headed home for Thanksgiving."

After the last dish was washed and dried, I hopped on the counter, allowing my legs to dangle. "I never made it to work on Monday. Sunday night, after my nightly run, I came home to the empty apartment, downed a bottle of water that was out on the counter and went to take a shower. My nose went numb first." I scrubbed at the tip, remembering the tingling sensation. "It was so strange. Then my legs and feet grew heavy. Halfway to the bathroom, my legs gave out completely, sending me crashing to the floor. Face pressed against the apartment's old carpet, my arms lost all feeling, but I could still see. Once I was completely immobile, Lance stepped out of the bedroom closet. His proud, sinister smile is the last thing I remember of that day."

Clearing my throat, I made to jump down, but Cas maneuvered his way between my legs, holding me in place. "Stop. I can't hear any more. Not now." I glanced down to where he gripped the counter. Every knuckle was stark white, completely void of color. "Tell me, is there anything I shouldn't do or say or mention? Any triggers I should know about now?"

I shrugged. Chewing on the edge of my thumb, I said, "That's why I said earlier that we can't do this. I don't *know* if I have any triggers. What if... what if everything you do is, or nothing at all? With everyone else, touch is a big one, but with you it isn't. Then there's the whole worry of being out of practice. I don't want to be bad, you know."

A hot hand pulled the thumb from my teeth. "*That's* what you're worried about?"

Again I shrugged and attempted to pull the same thumb back to my lips, but his grip tightened, holding my hand against the counter.

"I mean, yeah. It's been a long time, and what if I have a panic attack while we're... you know." I groaned and slapped a palm over my eyes.

Acting like this wasn't the most bizarre conversation he'd ever had, Cas continued his questioning. "Do you have a lot of panic attacks?"

"I used to, but not as many lately. I manage them better now with the over-the-top rituals and Xanax."

Cupping each cheek, he brushed the pads of his thumbs along my scorching cheekbones. "Don't worry, Lady. We'll go slow. I'll take care of you, but you have to trust me and be honest. If something takes you sideways or I'm pushing you too far, you have to tell me."

"Okay," I whispered, unable to tear my gaze away from his. The dark depths held me, engulfing me in the now-familiar sensation of safety.

I never wanted it to end.

"Slow doesn't mean gentle, Lady. Get that straight now. I told you before, I'm not a gentle man."

"Honestly," I said on a sigh, "that's what I'm hoping for."

13

Alta

I groaned and kind of whimpered to myself for the hundredth time in the two hours I'd been on shift, as I replayed our slightly random, very awkward conversation. I bet I sounded like a freaking lunatic, spewing all my quirks and issues one second, then 'hoping' for him to not be gentle. Who in the heck said stuff like that?

Me, it seemed.

Desperate me.

Ugh, this dark, outspoken, needy side was not the best side of Alta Johnson. I wasn't weak except when he was around, but somehow it was empowering, knowing I could be weak because he was with me. How did any of that even make sense? Either way, all that security evaporated the second he stepped out the door to let me get ready for work. The paranoias and fears bubbled back to the surface, reminding me of the scared, anxious woman I really was.

A familiar female voice screeched over the radio, a faint crackle of static in the background, making me jump and my foot slip off the gas pedal. The dispatcher reported that a hiker called in, stating a man was seen camping along a trail, which was illegal outside of designated camping grounds in the park, and bonus, he seemed to be taking full advantage of Colorado's legal marijuana law. Stretching across the seat, I snagged the radio and responded that I was somewhat close and would check it out.

As I U-turned to take a shortcut across the park, the bright rays of the setting sun momentarily blinded me until I could lower the visor. Pinks and blues highlighted the pre-evening sky, creating a beautiful backdrop to the snow-capped mountains. That was what kept me here the past couple of years. These beautiful mountains, the animals, the scenery—everything was the perfect example of serenity. Something I desired on a daily basis.

Fifteen minutes later, I killed the truck's engine and radioed that I was on scene. The truck door creaked as I shoved it open, putting my shoulder into it against the excessive wind. Rubbing my hands together, I surveyed the empty parking lot. At that altitude, the temperature was significantly colder than the bottom, but at least I would be protected from the wind on the trail. Taking my flashlight, heavy coat, gloves, and beanie from the seat, I slammed the door shut, the bang echoing through the dark silence.

Investigating before the sun set would've been ideal, but it didn't work out that way, and I had a job to do. Who knew what that dumbass was doing camping illegally, but poaching was my number one concern. The animals in the park weren't too scared of humans because of the millions of visitors each year, which made them prime prey for illegal hunting. That was why I had to go out now and not wait until morning; I wouldn't forgive myself if an animal was slaughtered because I was too scared of the dark to do my job.

"Birdie," John called through the radio. "Birdie, answer me. Over."

Only after I pulled on both gloves and situated my hat over my already frozen ears did I pull the radio from my belt. "Yeah, Johnny Boy? Over."

"Do not go out there alone. I'll send someone out to meet you. That's an order. Over."

Again I glanced around the empty, dark parking lot. Nearby branches creaked and groaned as the high wind whipped through the trees, creating an eerie feel. "I'm already here and don't want to wait. I'll be fine. Over."

"Alta, we had another report come in that they saw a man matching our illegal camper's description with a rifle slung over his back. Do not, I repeat, do *not* go in there alone. Over."

My nostrils flared as anger fostered in my veins, warming my chilled blood. "You know what that means, John. You can't expect me to wait while that idiot hunts one of our animals. I'm going up there. Tell whoever's coming up to meet me when they can. Over."

"I'm giving you a direct order. Over."

The unmistakable pop of gunfire rattled through the parking lot. I held a breath, waiting for more. "I heard gunshots. I'm going in."

Poor John. His belligerent voice bellowed through the radio, but instead of listening, or having him give away my position to the idiot who just shot a gun in a national park, I twisted the knob all the way down to silence him and clipped the radio back onto my belt.

The worn dirt trail hushed each of my soft steps. Gun in one hand, flashlight in the other, I concentrated to pick up on anything out of the ordinary in the dense forest. Every snap of a twig or rustle of leaves spiked my nerves higher. Sweat built and dripped down my spine and temples despite the cold temperature. With each step, I fought the urge to sprint back to the safety of the truck. But I couldn't go back, not when a helpless animal out there needed me to muster my courage to protect them.

Another, much louder boom echoed amongst the trees. Self-preservation kicked in and my knees buckled, sending me falling face first to the dirt. After several failed attempts, my trembling fingers finally found the flashlight's switch and flicked it off. Dense blackness engulfed the surrounding area. Lying on the cold ground with the nocturnal animals calling all around, panic set in, stealing my breath and train of thought.

He could be anywhere, maybe even hunting me now.
What if he's watching?

He's watching. I know it.

If he takes me, I won't survive. I can't do that again.

Heart hammering against my chest, I pushed out all the anxious thoughts.

I had to focus. Now was not the time to be paralyzed by a panic attack.

Closing my eyes, I inhaled deeply and held it until the welcomed burn in my lungs provided the calming center I needed. Again I inhaled a deep breath, but the shriek of a wounded animal shattered any sense of calm I'd managed.

Palms against the moist dirt, I pressed up to all fours, readying to move. I held a breath, waiting for another cry for help. My attention whipped to the right at another screech. Something crashing through the trees and underbrush grew louder and closer with each of my shaky breaths.

This was my chance.

Flashlight pressed to my thigh to keep the light as minimal as possible, I crept low and moved off the trail, heading toward the animal that needed me.

The unmistakable pungent scent of gunpowder floated past on a gust of mountain wind. Far away from the trail, deeper and deeper into the thick cluster of trees, I stalked forward as the smell grew, now mixed with the metallic scent of fresh blood.

A rustle of leaves swung me around. Panting in fear, I angled my gun toward a cluster of boulders. Squished between two rocks, I found her.

I fell to my knees several feet away to avoid startling her. Blood bubbled from a gunshot wound in her neck, and another steadily seeped in her long, lean leg. In the darkness of the night, in the now-silent forest, the beautiful doe's dark eyes met mine, allowing all her pain and fear to pass through in the single look.

One inch, then another, I moved closer. Each second I waited, I knew her murderer grew closer, desperate to locate his illegal kill.

Again those dark eyes, so full of pain, met mine. I knew what she was asking.

In the distance, a new sound echoed through—the eerie howl of wolves growing closer.

If I left her mortally wounded to pursue the fucker responsible for her misery, Darla the deer would be left as easy prey for those wolves to eat her alive.

That left only one choice. One humane option. One I'd witnessed several times growing up. It was my duty to take care of this precious animal, to end her pain.

Withdrawing my pistol, I shined the light into her eyes, stunning her and highlighting my target, and pulled the trigger.

I screamed in anger and misery as the gunshot echoed. Tears dripped down my cheeks as I crawled to the deer I was forced to put down. Gripping her neck, I tugged her limp body close, allowing my tears to fall on her coarse coat.

For several long minutes, I sobbed while clutching Darla until the hairs along the back of my neck stood on end, halting my sobs. Making quick work of the flashlight, the area was once again doused in darkness. Restraining a ragged breath, I listened for any signs of someone close by.

I swallowed down a whimper at the snap of a branch. Everything stilled; even the nocturnal animals quieted, waiting to see what would happen next. Palming my gun, readying for anything, I listened as another branch snapped, then a rustle of leaves, followed by the distinct pounding of footsteps moving farther and farther away.

"Bastard," I grunted under my breath as I stood. Of course the coward was running.

Instead of following farther away from the trail, I moved back toward path. The reports mentioned his campsite was along the trail; hopefully I would get lucky and he would return to his campsite instead of leaving it behind.

Three bounding steps through the dark, my foot snagged on something, sending me falling face first into a tree.

Turning the flashlight on would draw attention, but a tree to the face was a brutal reminder that I was no mountain woman. No way could I navigate this rocky terrain with only the light from the half-moon out.

A mile up the trail, the clinking of metal and mumbled curses slowed my steps. He did return to camp. The man paced around his small campsite, talking to himself. From behind a tree, I scouted the well-lit campsite in search of his rifle.

Snapping off my flashlight, I crept closer. White, mid-thirties, long beard—which didn't say much since most men grew beards these days—and a short joint hanging from his moving lips.

Perfect. High and armed. This night went from bad to worse fast.

I stifled a yelp and spun on my heels at a hand on my shoulder, only to relax at the sight of a familiar officer.

"That our guy?" he asked as he checked the clip of his Glock.

I nodded. "Killed a doe about a mile back."

The ranger's head dropped forward with a sigh. "Ready?"

Steeling my spine with what little energy I had left, I nodded. "You have no idea."

14

Cas

THE RATTLE of a truck pulling into the drive pushed me deeper into the darkness the forest provided. Bright beams of light cut through the trees, forcing me behind a thick oak trunk to ensure I wasn't seen. Not that waiting was wrong, but watching from the shadows for her to return from her shift might come off as disturbing instead of why I was really out there.

I was freaked the fuck out.

The more Peters and I studied the bastard abducting those women, the more I knew my Lady was a potential target. Alta coming home three hours late from her shift didn't help my over-the-top protective instincts either. Which was why I was out here at three in the morning, waiting and watching to make sure she made it home safe.

Just as she killed the truck's engine, a new truck roared up the short drive and skidded to a halt beside hers.

Jealousy set my lip in a snarl as her dipshit boss stepped out of the other truck and stormed to her door, which still hadn't opened. On silent feet, I weaved between the trees, moving close enough to hear their conversation.

Okay, maybe now it was creepy, but fuck, I needed to know why he was there so late.

A rogue thought dropped like lead in my stomach. *What if they were together? What if she played me?* My feet paused. My fingers twitched against my thigh, desperately wanting to dig into my pocket and pull out a cigarette.

I shook my head to dislodge the idea. No, Alta wouldn't do that. Something else was going on.

"Birdie," John yelled at the windshield. "Open the fucking door."

The driver door swung open. Shoulders slumped, spine rounded, she looked exhausted as she climbed out. Exhausted and dirty. Unease dropped my gut as Alta stepped into the light from the front porch. That wasn't fucking dirt. I had seen enough in my lifetime to know exactly what covered the front of her uniform. Blood.

"John," she said with a sniff, her voice hoarse and weak. "Go home. You can lecture me tomorrow, but tonight, I need a shower and would like to forget today ever happened. We got the guy, that's what matters."

"You could've been killed," John yelled in her face.

Red-hot rage set one foot in front of the other. By the time I made it to the edge of her lot, Alta was halfway up the front steps with John two steps behind.

"Go home, John," she said just as I stepped around the corner of the house, still hidden by the shadows. "I want to be alone, okay? Go home."

"Birdie—"

"I said go home!" she screamed.

"No," John responded, his voice cold and determined. "I'm not leaving you alone."

The grind of the flint of my lighter snagged their attention. After a deep, soothing inhale of glorious cancerous smoke, I moved into the light. "She won't be," I stated while releasing a cloud of frosty breath and smoke. "Listen to the Lady and leave."

Alta faced the door, almost like she was scared to make eye contact, while the idiot John stepped closer, cutting off my path to her.

"What the fuck are you doing here? You stalking her?" Jealous anger dripped from each of his accusing words.

"Making sure she's safe." My gaze locked on John, I said, "You okay, Lady?"

Keys rattled in her hand as she lifted them to the first lock instead of answering.

"Just go, John," she whispered. Her voice sounded as tired as her body looked. "I'll come in tomorrow."

"Then he goes too."

"Nope," I said, letting smoke filter through my wide smile.

"John, please," Alta begged. At the second lock, her hand slipped, sending the keys falling to the porch. "Go."

Five seconds, maybe less, was all the fucker had to obey her order. Hell, I should've clocked his ass for the fact that she had to repeat herself, twice. But I couldn't trust myself like this. Not with the anger and unease flooding my veins. Who knew what I would do to him. Every instinct commanded me to protect her at all cost.

Protect my Lady.

Mine.

Hadn't even kissed her, and yet every cell in my damn body screamed it. She imprinted on me in a way no woman ever had. Alta Johnson was mine, but I was just as much hers too.

"Now," I said in a voice so calm there was no mistaking the underlying threat.

Smarter than I took him for, John heeded the warning and stepped off the porch, never taking his eyes from mine. In the most drawn-out retreat in history, the bastard's truck finally sped away, kicking gravel and dust in its path.

Her mouth opened.

"Don't waste your breath." Between two fingers, I pinched out the cherry of my cigarette and stuffed the filter into the pocket of my coat. "I'm not leaving."

Alta's hazel, tear-rimmed eyes found mine.

At the sight, my heart, hardened by years of being unwanted and having any sympathy or useless emotion beaten out of me in the marines, splintered.

A sob bubbled from her chest. Without warning, her knees buckled, sending her tumbling to the porch.

Within seconds, her lean frame was tucked in my arms, held tight to my chest. I cursed her fucking three deadbolts as I worked to hold her and open the door at the same time.

Inside, a pitiful whimper brought my attention to where Benny sat on his hind legs, paws reaching for the beautiful creature in my arms.

"Down, boy. She'll be okay." The sole of my foot slammed against the door, securing it shut. "You watch the door, and I'll take care of her."

I swear the dog nodded before swinging his dark eyes to the door.

Having memorized the layout earlier, I carried her into the small bathroom. My knees cracked as I squatted, setting her on the floor with her back resting against the tub. I unlaced her boots and placed them beside the door in a perfectly straight line. Next came her socks, which were tossed into the overflowing hamper.

I stayed quiet as I worked. She would talk about what happened when she was ready, but I did have to make sure the blood on her clothes wasn't hers. Each second that question went unanswered was torture.

"Are you hurt?" I asked in a calm, even tone, completely different than the mess of emotions inside me.

The top of her black beanie wobbled up and down as she nodded with her forehead pressed against her bent knees.

"Show me. I need to stop the bleeding." Fuck. Fuck. Fuck. She had to be okay. But it wouldn't surprise me if my bitch of a life gave me a hint of one good thing, then ripped it away before it could be great. Why did I ever think someone like me could have a sliver of something wonderful like her?

"My heart," she mumbled through a sob, both delicate hands clasped over her heart. "My heart is... my heart is broken."

Um.

What?

"I shot her." Swollen hazel eyes peered up to meet mine. "I killed her," she cried.

What. The. Fuck.

"It's okay, Lady. You'll get through it. I'm sure she deserved it—"

"She was innocent," Alta seethed, narrowing her bloodshot eyes. "That bastard made me kill her."

"John?"

"No," she huffed, like I wasn't smart enough to keep up with the flow of the conversation. "The other guy. But we caught him, poaching jerk."

Okay, maybe I was starting to catch on.

Reaching up, I tugged off her hat and held her tear-streaked cheeks between my calloused hands. So tiny, so frail tucked between the hands of a trained killer.

"Poor Darla," she cried and slammed her eyes shut. "She was so beautiful."

And I was lost again.

"Darla?"

Slick cheeks slid against my palm as Alta nodded.

Yep. Very, very lost.

"How do you live with it? Taking a life?" Once again, those eyes fluttered open to search mine.

Leaning closer, I unzipped her thick coat. "You're asking the wrong person, Lady. I'm perfectly okay with taking a life."

One long blink, then another, and I swore she read through the lie. Through that lie and every lie I'd ever told to keep from allowing anyone in. If no one mattered to you, then no one could disappoint or hurt you. That was the one truth I held on to and believed wholeheartedly since I could remember. But one ferocious, scared, stunning Lady saw straight through it all, she saw me.

Unnerved by the way she cut through my bullshit, I stood from the floor and reached into the shower. After turning the faucet all the way hot, I spun toward the door.

"Cas?" Hand on the doorknob, I peered over my shoulder to where she now stood, nervously fumbling with the zipper of her coat. "Thank you."

My brows furrowed, not understanding. "For what?"

"For being you."

BENNY'S coarse fur tickled my palm as I ran my fingers along his head. The denseness of the early morning air made the quiet night deafening. Through a puff of smoke, I watched out into the trees to the spot where I'd stood waiting an hour or so ago. Something felt off. The way Benny sat on high alert told me he felt it too. Almost like someone was watching.

Benny's head pulled from my hand to whip toward the door before padding over and sitting on the front mat. The door swung open, allowing a freshly bathed Alta to tiptoe out. Cutting my gaze to her, I sucked in a deep breath. Fuck, she was even more beautiful with her hair down. Visions of my fingers tangling in its depth, holding her exactly where I wanted, filled my mind before I could blink.

"I thought you left," she said while rubbing her arms.

In response, I held up the nearly gone cigarette between my fingers.

"Right," she breathed with a sigh of relief. "I'll be inside when you're done. But you're coming back in, right?"

My brows furrowed together, not understanding. Did she think I would leave?

"It's just that—" She buried her face in her hands. "I'm not good at all this, and I don't know if you're leaving because I'm a mess or if you're going to stay."

"Do you want me to stay?" I asked after the last drag of the cigarette.

Her head cocked to the side. "Only if you want to."

Fuck this bullshit talk.

"Lady, it's a yes or no answer."

"Yes," she said quickly. "Of course I do. I feel... I can be me when you're around."

After pinching off the cherry of the cigarette, I hooked an arm around her shoulders and urged her inside. Benny's long claws clicked along the worn wooden floors toward his bed before he fell into it with a loud huff.

Alta settled on the couch, tucking a random pillow under her arms and crossing her legs in front of her like a pretzel.

"Listen," I said from where I leaned against the kitchen counter, running a hand along the rough stubble along my jaw. "We need to figure out next steps for you. Was Darla armed when you shot her?"

"Armed?" she scoffed. "How would she be armed?"

"People sneak guns into state parks all the time—"

"Oh," Alta said with a cringe. "Sorry, Darla is... wasn't a person."

I felt my brows shoot up my forehead. "Then what *was* Darla?"

Nervously she picked at a seam on the pillow. "A deer."

"A deer?"

"Darla."

"Darla was a deer?"

"Yes," she said with a cringe.

"You named a deer Darla."

Alta's shoulders rose and fell. "It fit her. Darla the deer."

The randomness of our conversation and her utter goodness pulled a wide smile up my cheeks. "Got it. Darla was a deer, and you had to shoot her."

Those hazel eyes rolled to the ceiling. "Yes. She was wounded. It was the only humane thing to do. Stop looking at me like that," she grumbled. "I name all the animals, okay?"

Grabbing a stool, I shifted along the top to get comfortable, then waved a hand for her to continue. Her pointed huff in exasperation made my already broad smile grow.

"Okay, so it varies. The first letter of the animal's type has to match the first letter of the made-up name." One look and she knew I wasn't following. "Examples. Molly the moose, Chippy the chipmunk, Hailey the hawk, Oscar the otter. You get the picture. They all have names because they're personal to me. I take their safety seriously, more seriously than the park visitors."

Of course she did. This woman was beyond anyone I'd ever known with her pure, genuine heart. Staring at her tucked on the couch, far out of my reach, realization smacked me across the face. I would ruin her. The darkness inside her I'd felt when we first met was merely a shade of gray compared to my dark abyss of a soul.

At her widemouthed yawn, I stood and gave a pointed glance to my watch. "It's late. I should go. You good?"

Her head bobbed up and down, but sadness still lurked behind her eyes. "Yeah, I'm good. Thanks again for staying with me." She looked down to Benny, who'd trotted over to say goodbye. "It's nice to have someone to talk to who responds."

"Stop by tomorrow morning. Peters and I want to go over a few things about the case."

"Sure." The soft pitter-patter of her bare feet against the wood floor trailed me to the door. "You don't... do you want to stay?"

Turning from the door, I faced her. "An hour ago, you were a sobbing lump on your front porch. You need time to decompress and sleep. If I stay, Lady, you wouldn't get either."

For the first time tonight, the corners of her lips twitched upward in an almost smile. "And you said you couldn't be gentle. You thinking of me first says otherwise."

Before she could blink, my hand tangled in her long damp hair as I shoved her back against the door. Curling my fingers into a fist forced her neck to arch. "Patient, Lady. I'm a patient man. Knowing when to strike, waiting for the perfect moment is control, not gentle." Her body quivered as I bit down on her long, lean neck.

As quickly as I'd pinned her against the door, I released her and moved aside to open the door. With one last perusing look, I smirked at the tiny indentions in her skin. "Lock the door behind me."

Halfway back to the cabin, still smiling, it hit me.

Those few minutes alone with her, listening to her random ramblings... for the first time in my life, I was happy.

15

Alta

A WET, rough tongue tickled my exposed toes, urging me awake. Squinting one eye open, I glanced to the still-dark window. With a groan of misery, I tucked my foot back under the blanket and rolled over on the couch, putting my back to the panting dog. No idea where he got his 'I love mornings' trait, but I'd love to smack the person who trained him to get up every morning at the butt crack of dawn.

Hard nails scraped along my back as Benny attempted a different tactic to get me off the couch—my makeshift bed most nights. Here in the living room, I felt safer with the multiple exits, and a visual to every access point into the house. Sleeping in the bedroom was too confining; out here, I managed a few hours of sleep each night. Maybe I could get more if Benny weren't so persistent every morning.

Arms above my head, I let out a long screech as I stretched, arching my back off the cushions.

"I'm up, I'm up," I yawned to the ceiling, blindly searching around the edge of the couch until my hand connected with Benny's large head and soft ears. "Where are we going today?"

Every leg muscle protested as I pushed off the couch. The couple falls last night did more damage than I realized. Right knee a bit stiff, I hobbled to the bathroom, flicking on the light to locate my toothbrush.

I gasped at my reflection. My knee wasn't the only part that took a beating. Tentatively, I pressed against my swollen left cheek and stroked down the thin scrapes cascading from my forehead to my chin. Great. One more thing for John to ream me out about today, which I was already dreading.

Disobeying a direct order was grounds for suspension, or worse, termination—even though I didn't think John would go that far. But then again, last night he was pissed, and then Cas showed up, only making it worse. Fingers crossed that John wouldn't let his personal feelings toward me or his jealousy toward Cas cloud his judgment.

After splashing a few handfuls of cold water on my face, I stripped off the flannel pajamas to change into running gear. The laces flipped between my fingers as I tied them tight with a double knot. A deep growl from the living room made me pause. Eyes flicking to the bedroom door, I waited.

Another deep growl caused the hairs on the back of my neck stand on end. A flash of nervous of panic jolted through my veins, sending my pulse racing.

Crouching low to stay below the windows, I sneaked into the living room. Benny stood facing the front door, ears alert and tail up, but the hairs along his back standing straight held my attention.

Benny never showed aggression, even when he didn't like someone.

Each short, rapid breath burned my already-dry throat. Reaching up, I unsnapped the holster on the table and slowly withdrew the gun. Each breath was shallower than the last. I gulped for air but couldn't get enough to fill my lungs. The corners of my vision darkened, the first warning sign that my panic attack was winning. Tears built and pooled. If I passed out, I couldn't defend myself; I had to gain control.

The cold barrel of the gun dug into my lower back as I slid it into the leggings waistband to crawl into the kitchen where the meds were hidden. A metal knob pressed into a shoulder blade as I leaned back against the cabinets. Blindly, I reached up and back, ripping a drawer open and sending it crashing to the ground. With trembling fingers, I shifted through the drawer's contents until three fingers wrapped around the prescription bottle that held my Xanax.

I cursed as I failed time after time to open the lid. My short breaths transitioned into hiccups, jolting me with each inhale. Frustrated, scared, desperate, I ripped at the lid with all the strength I could gather. The lid went one way and the bottle the other, scattering thirty tiny white pills across the floor.

I grabbed one, instant relief settling me as the pill dissolved beneath my tongue. Back against the cabinet, I focused on deep breathing and the reassurance that no one could get through the multiple locks and Benny.

I was safe.

A knock at the door drove Benny into a frenzy, lunging against it with his massive body until the whole cabin shook. Palms suctioned over my ears, I tucked both knees against my chest and burrowed my forehead between them.

Another knock rattled through the cabin, but that time a female voice followed.

"Alta? You okay in there?"

I released my tight, trembling muscles. Sarah.

Tears of relief pooled in my eyes. Of course it was a friend, not someone here to attack me.

Restraining Benny by his collar, I disengaged the various locks and pulled the door open.

My fingers tightened around his collar when I saw her. Sarah's normal bouncy blonde hair was nonexistent, tucked under a black beanie, which matched the rest of her all black outfit.

"What are you doing here?" She never stopped by. Scratch that, she'd never been here, ever. "How'd you—"

Sarah smirked and waved off my obvious apprehension. "Good morning to you too, *friend*. John called me, said you had a bad night and asked me to stop by to check on you."

"Oh." Leaning a shoulder against the doorframe, I looked past her toward Cas and Chandler's cabin. Soft rays of morning light filtered through the trees as dawn broke across the sky. "Why so early?" Maybe questioning her intentions was rude, but what did she expect from a paranoid freak like me?

"You okay?" she asked, her earlier humor now gone. "You're white as a ghost." She shouldered her way into the cabin and I stepped back, allowing it, because that's what you did with Sarah. She *always* got her way.

Benny gave a suspicious sniff at her extended hand before looking to me. At my nod, he shifted to monitor the now-closed door.

"Wasn't expecting the company is all." Ever.

"I listen when you talk, you know. You've mentioned how Benny gets you up super early." She shrugged and spun in the middle of the living room, taking in the cabin. "I figured you would be up."

Had I? I guess maybe I did at some point. Maybe one day when I was irritable from lack of sleep. That made sense. "Why are you up so early?"

Sarah shot me a look of annoyance before falling on the couch. "Seriously, what's with the fifty questions? Unless...." Her face lit up in excitement. "Is he here? Did you do it? Did you fuck him?"

I shook my head and propped myself up by an elbow on the counter. "No, he isn't here, and no, I'm not... you know... with him."

"Mind if I take a shot?"

Standing tall, I crossed my arms. "Yeah, I do. He's mine."

"Easy girl," she said with a chuckle. "So territorial for someone with your past. Fine, I'll go for the other one. Is that a gun tucked into your pants?"

Crap, forgot about that. Reaching back, I tugged the 9mm from the waistband and replaced it in the holster by the door.

"Do you always walk around the house armed?"

"No, just when unexpected visitors pop in." I stretched a wide fake smile to take the bite out of my words. "Benny freaked out, which made me freak out. It's okay though," I said through a sigh. "The Xanax is kicking in, so I'm not on the threshold of a full-on panic attack anymore."

"Good, let's go, then."

"Go?"

"Yeah," she said, moving to stand by the door. "I'm not wearing this getup to look good. Thought you could use a run after your long night. I know it relaxes you."

My shoulders slumped. What was I doing, doubting my only girlfriend about… what was I even accusing her of? I needed to calm the heck down, or I'd lose her trust, and that was the last thing I wanted.

"Right, sorry. Where do you want to go?" I asked over my shoulder as I locked up the cabin.

"How about Lilly Lake? It's my favorite."

Do not read into it.

It's a lot of people's favorite.

She's a friend. A good friend. Stop acting like a fucking lunatic.

"Sounds great. I'll drive," I bit out before yanking the truck door open. I started the truck, but Sarah stood in the opened passenger door, not moving to climb in. "You getting in?"

"I don't know. You're acting weird. I mean weirder than normal, weird. What's with you? Do you want me to go?" She hooked her thumb toward the old Civic. "Because honestly, I'm getting an angry vibe."

Leaning forward, I pressed my forehead against the steering wheel. "Sorry, it's just you showing up and liking my favorite running spot and—"

"Alta, don't take this the wrong way, but you're overreacting. This is what friends do. They show up when they've heard you had a bad day. They listen to what you say when you're talking to pick up on little tidbits about you. And yeah, Lilly Lake is my favorite. It's everyone's favorite. It has the best trail now that the renovations are done."

She was right.

I was acting like the paranoid freak I was.

With a grimace, I leaned back and looked at her. "You're right. I'm sorry, it's just that I'm super bad at this friend stuff. Little out of practice, you know."

Finally she slid into the passenger seat and shut the door. "I know. Now on the way to the trail, you have to tell me how your pretty little face got jacked up."

While backing up, something shifted in the rearview mirror. Not wanting to overreact again, I glanced to Sarah to see if she noticed anything strange.

"Hey, did you...?"

"Hmm?" she mumbled while she fiddled with her phone.

"Nothing, never mind."

It was nothing.

All in my head.

No one was watching me.

Repeating the mantra, I shifted the truck into Drive and coasted down the gravel path.

"You're kidding. John, please tell me you're joking." My voice cracked. Beneath my thighs, I worried over both thumbs, shredding the raw cuticles with an index finger. "I'm sorry. I'm so sorry, but—"

John's raised hand cut me off. "One-week suspension. Be glad I'm not firing your ass, Birdie. Honestly, if it were anyone else, I would. I know why you did it, but it doesn't make up for the fact that you disobeyed a direct order."

The heels of my palms ground against my eyes as I attempted to rub away a looming headache.

"During the suspension, you're not to conduct any park business, including aiding in the investigation of the missing women."

My hands fell back to my lap and clenched into tight fists. "Is this about disobeying your order or about me working with Cas and Chandler so closely?"

He pressed his lips into a thin line. "Go home to Texas, Alta. Visit your family, take a vacation. Get out of Estes Park for a week. Hell, take all your stacked-up vacation days and take two weeks off."

Anger and a sliver of embarrassment shoved me out of the chair, eager to retreat from the suffocating office. Hand on the knob, I clenched my teeth as I gritted out, "You know what working on this case means to me, helping these women and their families. Don't take that away because you're jealous. Please, John. I'm begging you."

Only the shuffling of paper responded to my plea. Crestfallen, I stared him down, willing him to not do this.

"You're too close to the case, to them. It's too dangerous for someone like you. Take the time, Birdie. Take care of yourself for once. Maybe talk to someone, get some help."

He glanced up from the desk with sympathy in his soft gaze.

Anger built within me. The bastard earned my trust, got me to tell him my story, my past, and now was using it against me to get what *he* wanted. How did I not see this whole time that he felt sorry for me, maybe even liked the idea of rescuing and repairing the broken girl?

"Fuck you," I ground out before stepping into the hall. The walls shook at the force of me slamming the door closed.

My fingertips tingled, itching to hit something, hit someone. My anger needed an outlet before I exploded. Focused on the floor, I stormed down the hall only to collide with a willowy figure as I turned the corner.

"Alta," Sadie said, her soft gaze and smile vastly different from my scowl. Her dark brown eyes zeroed in. "I was looking for you."

Still boiling, I shoved past her, not wanting *her* to be the one I vented my anger out on. Making nice with the new girl was not in the cards at the moment. "Not now."

A surprisingly strong hand wrapped around my wrist, yanking me to a halt. My gaze focused on her hot palm touching my skin. "Don't be mad at him. He's just looking out for you." It could've been my imagination, but her grip tightened. "Having someone like John wanting to look after you, that must be nice."

"It's not."

Sadie's dark eyes widened a fraction. "Right, I guess now that you have someone else, you don't need him around."

"I've never... wait, someone else?"

"You're beautiful, you know. In a common type way, I guess."

"Um—"

Her free hand jutted out, holding a small square of paper. I examined the side decorated with hearts and bubble letters. "I found this on your truck and pulled it off. Didn't want you to miss it."

All the blood drained from my slack face. "What did you just say?" Hesitantly, I reached between us and pulled the stiff card from her fingers.

"I can see why he likes you." With an awkward smirk, Sadie shouldered past me toward John's office. "Enjoy your time off. Birdie."

16

Alta

I STUDIED the valentine on the coffee table, rereading the inscription on the back for the thousandth time since I'd walked through the door over an hour ago.

> *Can't wait to see you! We'll have so much fun.*
> *Promise, Birdie.*

The gun resting on my thigh trembled in my sweaty palm.

This couldn't be happening, not again. Nothing would process except for the replay of memories over and over in my mind. Notes, stalking, fear it was all happening again. Benny's wet nose nudged my thigh, trying to get my free hand on top of his massive head.

This wasn't *real*, right? Maybe Cas or Chandler thought it would be funny to—no, neither would do that. But they were the only two who knew about the serial abductor's signature of leaving notes.

Well, them and John, but he was inside with me when Sadie found it. If she *did* find it.

But what would that mean? That Sadie was the person we were after? It made no sense considering we were profiling the person to be a weak male who targeted the wives of strong men. And there was no way Sadie's tiny frame could carry a grown woman's limp body; hell, she looked like she could barely carry her own weight.

After setting the gun on the table, I ground the heels of my palms against my eyes.

Thought my friend was stalking me.

Suspended from work.

Cornered by a weirdo.

And had a creepy note left by a suspected serial killer.

Today was *not* my day.

A pounding knock, so hard the entire cabin rattled, pulled Benny away from my side to trot to the front door, tail wagging. With that kind of reaction, there was no doubt who I would find on the other side.

"Alta. Open the door, would ya?"

Halfway to the front door, I bolted back to the coffee table, snagged the creepy note and tucked it into the side pocket of my running jacket. No need for him to know about it when I didn't even know what it meant.

The moment the last lock clicked free, the door swung open, revealing a frowning Cas.

"Where were you?" he asked after shouldering past me to squat in front of an eager Benny.

"Um, where was I supposed to be?" Behind me, my concealed fingers worked double time on shredding the cuticles.

"Our place for us to discuss the case and any updates." Looking up from where he knelt on the floor petting Benny, those dark eyes bored into mine. "Your face doesn't look as bad as I thought it would. What did you run into anyway? I never asked last night."

"A tree," I grumbled, making a smirk curl his lips up. "Shut it. Little tip—don't run through the woods at night without your flashlight on. You can run into a tree, or two." His deep, carefree chuckle set the day's worries on the back burner. Smiling, I turned for the living room. "I had a visitor this morning, then—"

"Was it him?" he seethed against my ear, his hot breath sending a wave of heat through me.

I stumbled against the armrest, putting distance between us. "What is it with you two?"

Hands tucked into the front pockets of his jeans, Cas paused inches from where I sat. "He's jealous that I get to touch you without you pulling away. Jealous that you look at me like you want me to touch you. Jealous because that's the way he looks at you."

Nibbling the side of my thumb, I avoided his searching eyes. "He suspended me. For disobeying a direct order."

"When did you do that?" he prodded. A pair of black hiking boots moved into my line of sight on the floor.

I shrugged and maneuvered to stand, but two hands rested on my shoulders, keeping me in place.

"Last night," I huffed and pressed both palms to my flaming cheeks. "I was responding to a call about illegal camping when he came over the radio, ordering me to stay put and wait for back-up. But then I heard the gunshot and—"

Warm tingles erupted along the skin of my neck as his hot palm wrapped around it. Thumb beneath my chin, he tilted my face to meet his burning gaze. "You did what?"

"I heard the shot and knew what he was doing, so... so I turned off my radio and went up the trail alone."

He bent closer, his hot puffs of breath caressing my cheek while his dark eyes bored into mine. "Never. Again. Do you hear me, Lady?"

I nodded in shock. Anger laced his words, but something else flicked behind his eyes too. Lightning fast, he tangled a hand in my low ponytail and yanked my head backward, shooting my chin to the ceiling. Towering over me, he stepped closer, putting his nose less than an inch from my own.

"Words. Tell me you understand what I'm telling you. You will not run into danger like some fool again." A soft whimper passed my lips at a light tug on my hair. "Say it."

"I... I won't. It's just—"

There was no warning except a rumbled animalistic growl before his full lips crashed against mine. Holding me captive, Cas's talented lips danced over mine. A light nip at my bottom lip before sucking it between his forced me to gasp, giving him full access to do as he pleased. Lost in his touch, our kiss, I barely noticed as an arm snaked around my waist until it hauled me off my perch and against his hard body. Coolness from the wall seeped through the running jacket into my back, offering a welcomed relief from my suddenly overheated body.

All the negative thoughts and worry from the day melted away, leaving only thoughts of him. Both hands dangled at my sides, fingers fidgeting with the cuticles of my thumb. The fluttering in my stomach and building want for him urged me to reach up and haul him closer.

Pulse pounding, breathing erratic, I rested a hand on his hip, tugging him closer. Tentatively, Cas pulled back. Disappointment flooded through my veins and flipped my stomach. I wanted—no, needed his lips back against my own. Somehow, with just a simple touch, he made everything else disappear. Nothing mattered but him and me. He was the escape I was longing for these past ten years. Someone to distract me long enough to forget the fear, forget the pain and permanent damage left behind.

Our foreheads pressed together, his dark eyes searched mine. "I told you I wouldn't let anyone hurt you, but to keep that promise, you can't pull shit like that. Do you understand? Nothing can happen to you."

I bit back a smile as I nodded. "Okay, but for now can we... can we do that again?"

A softness settled over his features, relaxing his permanently furrowed brow. Palm pressed to my cheek, he ghosted his lips over mine. "Soon, but Peters is waiting for us, and I wouldn't put it past him to head over here, hoping to interrupt us. Fucking bastard."

My new reality of being suspended came flooding back in. Side-stepping Cas, needing space to think, I paced the living room. "But here's the thing. I'm suspended, remember? John was very, very specific that there would be no helping you and Chandler with the cases."

An uncharacteristic eye roll caught me off guard, halting my steps. Like that, relaxed and happy, he looked young and somehow even more attractive. While watching him, I dragged two fingertips along my lips. I wanted his on me again, everywhere.

Cas gripped my hand in his and pulled me against him. "Stop looking at me like that. I'm barely holding back as it is." At my growing smile, he sighed. "Don't worry about dipshit John. You're simply coming over to hang out with us while Chandler and I happen to be discussing the case. How's that for a loophole, fucking jealous bastard."

My smile widened, making the muscles burn. "A few days ago, you didn't want me helping at all."

Once outside, with a freshly lit cigarette between his lips, Cas nodded. "That was me attempting to protect you from me, but that ship's sailed, Lady. You're going nowhere."

A new nervous energy set my feet in motion down the drive. "Why is it like this?" I asked with my thumb between my teeth.

"What?" he asked, matching my long, fast strides.

"When everyone else's touch makes my stomach roll, yours doesn't." Sneaking a peek sideways, I added, "I want it."

"Got me."

Comfortable silence settled between us as we hiked toward his cabin. Birds called high in the trees while kids played in a neighboring yard, offering the mindless distraction I needed to sort through the volleying thoughts.

"Maybe," I said out of nowhere, "it's because you're in control, which makes me feel like I am? You're not tender, or uncertain, which was like—" Memories sent a violent shiver to rack my shoulders and I stutter-stepped. "So it's different. You're different."

Cas said nothing, just nodded with a new cigarette dangling from his fingers.

"And I like it," I admitted while gazing off into the trees. "Even before the assault, there was always something missing with boyfriends." My shoulders rose and fell in a noncommittal shrug. "I'm sure you don't understand any of this, but it's like… it's like you saying you're not a gentle guy woke a part of me I didn't even know existed, a part of me that wants it." I swallowed against a dry throat, trying to get the last word out. "Rough."

"I know," he finally responded. I stopped in front of the cabin, making him pause and turn to face me. "You don't hide anything in those gorgeous eyes of yours."

My brows bunched. "I don't?"

He shook his head as he grinned up to the blue sky. "Nope."

Simultaneously, our boots clomped up the porch steps. Hand on the doorknob, Cas snagged an arm around my waist, hauling me back against him.

"There's nothing wrong with that. It just means you know what you want. And thankfully, you met someone who needs the same."

"Why?" My breaths came in short spurts. Overwhelming heat leached from him, fading the chill from the crisp mountain air.

"Why? Why are any of us the way we are? We just are." Releasing his hold, he spun me around to face him. "What are you doing tonight?"

"Nothing," I responded without a second thought, because I *never* had plans. But the second the word was out of my mouth, I remembered promising something. "Wait, I have a somewhat girls' night tonight with Sarah."

"You don't sound too excited about it."

I sighed and rested my forehead against his chest. "I'm not good at the girl stuff, or friend stuff in general. Just really out of practice." I chuckled, remembering the morning's craziness. "I'm so terrible at it that this morning, I thought she was stalking me."

Fingers beneath my chin, he forced my gaze up. "Why?"

"She showed up unannounced to check on me after last night. John sent her. He thinks I'm in over my head here, too emotionally connected to the case, blah blah blah. He told me I should go home for a couple of weeks. Can you believe that?"

Fine lines appeared around the corners of his eyes as he smiled. "He cares about you, and I already know what he thinks about me. As misguided as it is, he's just trying to look out for you."

"Stop it with that logic stuff," I grumbled and turned to the door. "Just let me be pissed, okay?"

Cas's chuckle reverberated beneath the small covered porch. "Whatever you say, Lady."

17

Alta

I<small>NSIDE THE FREEZING CABIN</small>, I beelined to the small stone fireplace and began stacking kindling into a miniature teepee.

"Can we *not* with the suffocating heat today?" Chandler groaned as he strode out of his room in shorts and a T-shirt.

"Don't you two ever get cold? It's freezing in here." I sat back on my heels and glanced between them. "That wasn't a rhetorical question, boys."

"We've had our balls nearly frozen off. This isn't cold, Birdie," Chandler said after plopping on the couch. "You think it's always hot as hell in a fucking desert, but let me tell you from experience, it's not."

Relenting on the fire—this was their place, after all—I rotated on the balls of my feet to sit on the hearth. "Cas said you wanted to talk about the case?"

Both his light brown brows shot up his forehead as a smirk appeared. "Aren't you suspended?"

"Wha... how...?"

"Your boss called while Mathews was out tracking you down."

"Right," I sighed. "I'll be going, then."

"What did you do, anyway?"

Cas leaned against the door and crossed his arms, officially barricading me from leaving. "Disobeyed a direct order to not run into the mountains alone where there was a reported armed poacher on the loose."

Chandler tipped his head back and his laugh rumbled around the room. "Seriously?"

"He shot Darla," I whispered and nibbled on the edge of my thumb.

"Who's Darla?" Chandler questioned.

"A deer. Darla the deer. She names the animals," Cas said with a more sympathetic tone than I would expect from someone like him.

"Of course she does. The depth of your innocence is unreal. But why do women do that?"

"Do what?" I groaned. The whole conversation was slightly funny, but with me as the butt of the joke.

"React on your emotions, like you did last night."

I shrugged and fell into the chair opposite of Chandler. No point in standing when who knew how much longer the conversation would last. "Because we're emotional creatures. And what's so wrong with that?"

"The second you react with emotion, you lose control." I swiveled in the chair to stare at Cas. "Facts and a plan get you in and out safely. Emotions will get you killed."

I eyed Chandler, who nodded in agreement. "Listen, Birdie. I have a feeling your boss suspended you for more reasons than disobeying an order, which is why I'd like you to stay. Officially you're not working this case with us, just listening in and adding insight when you can. Got it?"

A broad smile spread up my cheeks. "Got it. Thank you, Chandler. Now get to what you and Cas found yesterday."

Chandler massaged his temples with both thumbs. "There

weren't any overlaps between people in the Smokies and here. So that was a dead end." With regret in his eyes, he pursed his lips into a thin line. "It was a good idea though."

"People can change their names," I said to myself. "What's something that he wouldn't think to change?" A puff of dust floated up as I pushed off the old chair to pace. "Hair color, eye color—heck, even his build could be altered." Glancing at the door, which Cas had thankfully vacated, I nonchalantly eased in that direction. "What if he had prescriptions?" The lock clicked once, twice, and a third time. Turning back to the two men, I found Chandler glaring. "I lasted a whole three minutes without locking them. It's a slow process, okay?"

"What about prescriptions?" Cas asked, pulling my focus to where he sat in front of the fireplace, lighting a match. A warmth no fire could offer swept through my body at his actions. Despite Chandler's snide remark, Cas was lighting the fire for me.

"Well," I said, trying to focus back on the case, "that's one thing you could track easily, right? If someone was in that area during the time of the abductions and are now getting their prescriptions filled here?" At their lack of response, I spun to do another lap around the room. "What else did y'all figure out without me?"

Chandler stretched his arms overhead and rested his head along the back of the couch. "We think he's getting these women away from everyone by acting hurt or needing their help in some way. It's the only thing we can come up with that would make them take a chance in walking away with a stranger."

"Unless it was a woman," I said under my breath.

"There's no way—" Chandler started to protest.

"Not just a woman. What if it was a killing team? A man *and* a woman. It sounds crazy, but maybe that's how they can lure these women away."

Chandler shook his head. "I like the prescription angle. I'll look into that if HIPAA doesn't stop us, but the thought of a female accomplice is a little farfetched. Men like this hunt alone. They can't function in a normal relationship. The odds are so slim it's not worth the staff hours to bring up that theory to my boss."

I nodded in agreement.

"As I went through the notes yesterday, I started a basic profile." My feet paused as I turned my full focus to Chandler. "Midthirties white male, inferiority complex, manipulative, average-looking, stalking tendencies. Will probably drive a sensible, late-model car or van, but not one that will stand out in a parking lot as being out of place."

The note in my pocket burned through my coat and seared my skin. I had to show them. Who knew, maybe the handwriting could be of use with refining the profile—which would be huge, considering the current profile described half of the millions of visitors who poured through the park on a yearly basis.

"I think—" I started, but was cut off by Chandler's musings.

"You said women were emotional, so they react on emotions. Like with you last night, you went against your better judgment because you were emotionally focused. Never thought about it from the woman's perspective."

Picking up where he was going with the line of thought, I added, "To pull these women away from the safety of other visitors, to get them to follow him somewhere more secluded, they were reacting on emotion. Like someone hurt, or maybe even him saying he needed help." Mentally, I flipped through all the pictures from each case. "They were all mothers, which means they would be more emotionally inclined to help if someone was hurt or lost or—"

"A kid," Cas said, drawing our attention to where he stood looking out the window. "Most mothers have that maternal instinct, and it doesn't stop with just their kid. What if he's saying his kid is hurt, or lost, or needs a woman's help."

We all sat in silence, absorbing what that meant about the guy. I didn't miss the fact that he said most mothers, not all mothers. Guess that meant he wouldn't lump his mother into that category.

"He must watch them for days before he abducts them. Fucking patient bastard is waiting until the exact moment when he can get them alone," Chandler seethed. His large hands balled into tight fists at his side.

I cringed.

"What?" Cas asked, his intense focus back on me.

"So, um, well...." I cleared my throat and stepped toward the warm fire to ward off the chill that had sunk in. "First, you two can't get mad. I've had a bizarre day, and I didn't know how to react."

Their eyes flicked to each other, then back to me.

"Hell fucking no, we aren't promising that," Chandler blurted out. "Out with it, Birdie."

Both men inched closer, boxing me in with their massive frames.

Not meeting their eyes, I unzipped the jacket pocket and withdrew the note. "This was found on my truck today."

Peering up through my lashes, I found both men studying the pink and red hearts decorating the front of the card with narrowed eyes.

"Turn it over," Cas ordered in a tone that sent a shiver down my spine.

Note to self: never get on his bad side.

Between two fingers, I flipped the note and then stepped backward, stretching my arm out as far as it could go. Not sure why. Not like I could get away from it. I was on this guy's radar whether I liked it or not.

Carefully, Chandler extracted the note from my fingers. "Anyone else touch it?"

"Yeah, the new creepy ranger, Sadie. She's the one who found it and gave it to me. I'd just come out of my stupid meeting with John." Cas's glare burned into me. Instead of giving in, I kept my focus on Chandler.

"Give me a minute," Chandler muttered more to himself than us before disappearing into his room.

The taut tension in the room elevated without Chandler as a buffer.

"Alta." My name came out as a command, but a command to do what, I had no idea.

"I was going to tell you," I whispered. "I just knew you would... you initially wanted me off this case due to the potential for me to be a target, I didn't know how you would react when you found out I am one."

"So keeping me in the dark, exposing you the entire fucking walk here without me being on alert—"

"Aren't you always on alert?" I said with a smile. When I gathered the nerve to look at him, my heart cracked at the hurt and fear behind his brown eyes.

"Not when you're around." His agitation with the situation radiated off him. "Do you not trust me?"

"Of course I do. I trusted you more in the first few seconds we met than I have anyone else in the past ten years. But I just... I needed to process it, and then you showed up, and that amazing kiss." I traced along the edge of my lips with my fingertips, remembering the slight burn of his rough scruff. "My not-so-bright idea of waiting to tell you had nothing to do with you."

With a groan, he ran a scarred hand down his face and massaged his bearded jaw. "I don't like it. If the profile is accurate, then why is this guy going after you? You're not married to a fucking meathead, you're not a mother, someone he could manipulate emotionally."

"Well...." I shrugged and scrunched my freckled nose. "All he'd have to say is there's a hurt animal, which he'd probably figure out since he likes to stalk his victims beforehand."

"You're. Not. Helping," Cas growled. "It's a good thing you're suspended. No way could we let you go out on shifts alone with this crazy bastard following you."

"Or...."

"Don't even think about it." Each word was emphasized with a loud stomp. Feet suctioned to the floor, I watched, wide-eyed, as he prowled closer. "No one would go for the idea of using you as bait. If he's been watching you, then he knows we're here and would plan around it."

Toe-to-toe, I tilted my head, eyes lost in the dark depths of his as we stood silent. Emotions—lust, hate, anger, passion—swirled around us, offering a blurred window into Cas's complicated soul.

"How do you do it?" he asked with awe lacing his tone.

"Do what?" I breathed. That close and all I wanted was him closer, touching, his skin against mine.

"Break me and make me whole again with a simple damn look. You see something no one else has ever cared to see."

My heart shuddered at the utter honesty in his statement. "What do I see?"

"Me."

Somehow his raw confession healed a jagged edge of my soul, cleansing the part that had been left unused for so long. Around us, the fire he'd built crackled, and Chandler's muffled voice filtered through the shut bedroom door.

"What... what do you see in me?" I dared. It was a bold question, considering his choice of words had the potential to slay me where I stood or continue strengthening my resolve to let him into my life.

His head cocked to the side an inch, eyes scanning up and down my face. "I see an innocent, kind woman who has scars deeper than someone as young and perfect as she should have."

Scars, also known as issues.

I tilted my head down, angling my eyes to the floor to keep from seeing the sympathy in his gaze, but two gentle fingers beneath my chin drew my eyes back up to his. "Your scars are what drew me in the most. We're not too different, Lady. Both have pasts which have molded us into the people we are now. I'm fucked up in the head, or so they say," he said with a tight smile. "But you, you're perfectly broken in every way, making you the most beautiful woman I've ever met."

Wow. His words were like fresh air filling my lungs, strengthening my soul.

The balls of my feet pushed down onto the floor. Hesitantly, I leaned closer, putting our lips almost touching. "Others have tried to fix me, but you, you want me because of who my past changed me into, not despite it."

"Ditto, Lady."

A faint brush of our lips made my stomach dip, urging me closer. This kiss was different, not him taking from me, but allowing me to take control and keep it slow like the moment deserved.

Five seconds, maybe ten, our soul-speaking kiss lasted before a loud rumbling engine revved up the drive, pulling us apart. My knees shook, lips burned, desperate to be soothed by his. He was everything I ever wanted in a man, yet still more than I ever expected. A simple kiss and my breath was gone, a delirious fog settling over my thoughts.

Cas said he wasn't a gentle man, but I hoped he'd be gentle with my tender, innocent heart.

18

Cas

OUT OF SPITE for the fucker who interrupted us, I lingered by the door, waiting to swing it open until a few annoyed knocks rattled the hinges. Ice crackled between us as John stood across the threshold, each of us staring the other down. His eyes narrowed at my smile. A part of me wanted him to try something, anything to lay his ass out.

"Agent Peters called, said you had a new development and I should come over."

Still I remained in the middle of the doorway, one arm braced against the frame, preventing him from entering. I wasn't as bulky as some of the other guys at the USPP, but still formidable enough to kick anyone's ass even if they were twice my size.

The boys who knew me best said it was my detachment from people that helped me fight better than anyone they'd ever known. I had no pity, no remorse. I always assumed that was the primary trait I received from my birth mother, whoever the fuck she was.

The system molded me. Each foster home, each person who took me in just for another government paycheck, chipped away any emotion or feeling for people I might've been created with. Then what little hope I had left in humanity or the desires of ever being wanted were beaten out of me in the marines. But what they took from my soul, they gave something back in return—purpose. They needed me, and I needed them. It worked out well for both sides. I was their efficient killing machine.

That's what you become when you don't care if you lived or died.

After making the bastard sweat a few more seconds under my hard stare, I shoved off the doorframe and stepped aside. I braced myself for the yelling and accusations to begin between Alta and John, but they didn't. Not a single word was uttered. Confused, I turned and scanned the room.

My lips curved up as I shook my head.

Of course she hid.

That woman was becoming the one woman I never wanted to be without. Which was fucking stupid, considering I hadn't even fucked her yet. Hell, we hadn't even done middle school hand shit. No way could I be thinking long term about someone I'd only known a few days, even if it felt more real than anything I'd ever had before.

The overwhelming necessity to protect her was the most unexplainable thing. Only in the heat of battle, when the lives of my men and the lives of other American soldiers were on the line, did I have this desperate, all-consuming need to protect what was mine. Somehow within the first few seconds of meeting her that first day, she locked herself in the 'must protect what's mine' category. Every inch of my body, especially one long—and still somewhat hard after that strange kiss—body part, told me she was mine.

And no one messed with what was mine.

I had nothing in life to call my own before her.

My Lady.

Mine.

"Damn," Peters said with a low whistle after walking into the living room. "You got here fast."

"You said it had to do with Officer Johnson."

Peters's brows shot up at my loud, scoffing chuckle.

"Speaking of Birdie—" Peters paused at my slight head shake and pointed nod to my bedroom. "Right," he chuckled. "We do have a new development." The note, now encased in an evidence bag to keep it safe, floated to the coffee table.

John stepped forward, picked up the small baggie and flipped it between his fingers. After reading the inscription, his features hardened.

"I told her to stay the fuck away from this case. I told you two to keep her away from it, and now look." He slammed the note down and stalked closer, looking pissed as hell. "She's been through enough in her damn life. She doesn't need this. If he doesn't kill her, being stalked all over again will break what's not already broken in her."

"She's not fucking broken," I growled, taking a step toward him and putting us face-to-face.

He huffed and crossed his arms across his chest. "Really? And you know that how? I've known her for years, and believe me, that woman needs someone to look after her, to help her get over her fears, not put her in situations where she's in the fucking crosshairs again!"

"Cas," Peters said in a calm tone, sticking an arm between us, "let it go. We have to figure out what we're going to do with her."

"You're not going to do anything with me." Alta's tone was calm and steady. "It's my life. My broken life," she added with a glare to John before focusing back on Peters. "I get that I'm in danger, and y'all don't want me in the middle, but I'm already here, and I think... I think I can help if I stick around. I'm not leaving."

The other two and I looked between us.

"It's not safe," John said, moving closer with his palms raised like he was walking toward a cornered animal. "You need to get out of here, Birdie. Do this... do this for me. For us."

"Or how about I do something for, I don't know, me?"

Pride burned in my chest at the way she put him in his place, solidifying what little doubts I had about her being the right woman for me. Someone just as damaged, just as determined to get through this life in one piece.

Mine.

She was so fucking mine.

If the other two weren't in the room, I'd pin her against the wall and prove it to her over and over again. Images of her long strawberry-blonde hair covering her naked shoulders, of her open mouth taking in pants of air as I pounded into her, had my dick at attention. Again.

"What do you want to do?" I asked as I shifted my weight between my feet, trying to ease the pressure of my fully hard dick.

"I'm staying right where I am." John opened his mouth, but she shot him down with a raised hand. "I won't instigate him, and I'll be extra cautious. I'm not saying use me as bait, but I am saying I'm not running. I've been running for far too long."

"I could order you to leave," John said, somewhat out of breath. He was panicking and grasping at fucking straws, anything to get her to leave.

"Actually," Peters chimed in with a smirk, "she's suspended, so you can't. It would be a huge help to our investigation, and I appreciate you offering to stay if that's what you want."

Alta nodded and looked to me. "I'm staying."

"You're not to work on the case," John said. "What the fuck are you doing here anyway?"

"Hanging out with me. It is something people do when they're a couple." I lifted my hand to Alta, who didn't hesitate a second. John's eyes burned fire hot when she tucked herself beneath my arm and wrapped hers around my waist.

"Right. Guess I wasn't—"

"Watch your next words," Peters said tensely. "I stopped him from snapping your neck earlier. I doubt he'd listen to me a second time."

John pressed his lips together so tight that all the color drained from them. "We can take shifts watching Alta," he said. "Rotate days or something."

Alta's arm tightened around my waist. Her pleading hazel eyes met mine.

"Peters and I will figure it out. You've got enough on your plate."

"Fine." Turning on the heels of his boots, John marched to the door and flung it open. Before it shut, he turned and glared at Alta. "Hope you know what you're doing. Your life depends on it."

The moment the door clicked closed, Alta hurried over and locked it, once, twice, and a third time.

"Well that was awkward," she said with a smile as she leaned back against the door. "Thanks for having my back with my decision."

Peters gave a stiff nod. "I do agree with one thing that ignorant dipshit said. You need protection."

"I thought...." She looked to me. "Can't you do it?"

Calluses scraped down my cheeks, and the scruff of my growing beard abraded my palm. "I need a cigarette."

Being outside eased the increasing constriction in my chest. Of course, I would love to stay with her, to protect her. And I would, during the day. But at night, that was the issue. I couldn't trust myself at night. In my sleep, my nightmares were a reality, and any little thing could set me off. I wouldn't endanger her life even more by staying with her.

The door creaked open, the scent of lavender wafting forward.

"It's not you," I said, not turning.

"I've said that a lot over the years," she joked. Shoulder against my arm, she leaned her head onto my bicep and sighed. "Chandler filled me in. You don't have to say anything. But the thing is... I trust you."

"You shouldn't. I have zero control over what I do or how I react while I'm asleep." Holding a deep inhale of smoke in my lungs, I avoided saying more than needed.

"How are you staying with Chandler, then?"

I rolled my eyes and took another hit off the cigarette. "He stays locked in his room, even though he says he's going to try his luck one of these nights just to see what the fuck would happen."

"What would?"

"Probably a snapped neck or a bullet between the eyes."

"Oh," she breathed. "But what if I promised to stay in my room? At night, you could sleep on the couch, and I'd lock myself in my room, with Benny."

My head dropped forward. "Sorry, Lady. Me staying overnight isn't in the cards. I promised to protect you, even if it's from me."

"Okay," she relented. "So you'll stay with me during the day, and Chandler will come over at night. Babysitting shifts."

I wrapped an arm around her shoulders and pulled her tight against my side. "It's best this way, I promise you. But if you want me there during the day, inside your cabin, I have one condition."

"What?" she asked as she tilted her head up, giving me a full view of her beautiful smile.

"We're cleaning your place, and you'll keep it like that. Understood?"

Not sure how, but her smile grew wider. "Deal, Sergeant Mathews."

"Good. I'll go pack a few things, and then we can run into town and buy some cleaning shit."

"I have—" I cut her off with a single look. "Right, looking forward to it. Sir."

Flexing my arm, I pulled her tighter. "Sir. I like that. Remember it tonight."

19

Alta

By the time Sarah pulled up the drive, I had zero energy left for our girls' night. It took over three hours to clean the cabin to Cas's expectations. Three. Hours. Now my lungs burned, my fingertips were raw, and my arm muscles twitched, but every inch of the cabin was spotless. Someone could do surgery in the living room and feel 100 percent sure the patient wouldn't get an infection.

I loved the results and the time we spent together completing the project. Plus I had drawers full of clean clothes, which hadn't happened since Mom did my laundry in high school. We cleaned in silence mostly, which was kind of perfect. It was a comfortable silence that two ordinary people had in a relationship.

Relationship.

Who the hell would've thought I would be so far in my recovery to use the word and mean it? He healed me in ways hours of therapy never had, just by being him. Maybe he was right; we were both broken in some way, but that just meant our broken pieces filled the cracks of the other. That was what he was doing.

"I know you said no wine," Sarah announced with a grin as she walked through the door. Two paper grocery bags crinkled as they swayed on either side of her legs. "But—" She pulled up short when she looked over my shoulder into the living room. "What's he doing here?" she whispered.

"It's a long story," I said as I snagged the bags to take them into the kitchen.

"You do understand a girls' night means just girls, right? Hence the name," Sarah whisper-shouted as she trailed behind me.

When I set them on the counter, the rattling of glass bottles clinked inside the brown bag. With an arched brow, I offered a pointed look at Sarah, then the bags and back again.

"I need it," she said with a whine. "And you could use some relaxing juice too. You just took away the vaginas-only part of girls' night. Don't take away the required liquids too."

All apprehension of the evening turned to guilt. I needed to try; after all, she was, despite my quirks.

"Fine, but I hope you brought a bottle opener because I don't have one."

"Is he going to be here all night?" she whispered as she withdrew a bottle of red from the bag. "I don't mind the eye candy, but it's rude to flaunt what I can't touch."

I chuckled under my breath and glanced to Cas on the couch, busy on his phone. "Yeah, something happened today, and I need him to stick around for a bit."

"It's all around the station about John suspending you. Is that what you're talking about?"

"No," I grumbled. Great, nothing like being the topic of the office gossip.

"Oh, you mean the confrontation between you and Sadie? You know, I heard she said that you said some pretty mean things to her," Sarah furrowed her fair brows in concentration as she twisted the cap to the wine, sending a familiar crackle to my ears as the seal broke.

Huh. Who knew they made screw tops.

I stared at the bottle in wonder until Sarah's words sank in.

"What?" I exclaimed. "She was the one being all creepy. I didn't say anything to her."

"She's creepy for sure." Sarah looked back to Cas and leaned across the countertop, bringing us closer. "I'd stay away from her. She seems a bit... unstable. The other rangers have been talking about it, and someone said she's a little obsessive with John."

My stomach dipped. "Obsessive how?"

One of Sarah's shoulders rose in a half shrug. "Being up there all the time, coming up with stuff to make him think he needs to protect her. Like today, she said you were aggressive toward her when she stopped you. Wacky."

"Wacky," I mused. "She was the one who found the note."

"What note?" The paper bag crinkled as she dug around the bottom with her head practically inside it.

"Nothing."

"Well I got a random note today. Maybe she put something on my car since we're friends. But it wasn't anything mean, more like a love note. Maybe I should tell her I'm not her type?" With a smile, she leaned back with a package of Oreos clutched in her hand.

"A love note?" Cas said from the couch.

"How in the hell did you hear that?" Sarah's eyes twitched toward the ceiling. Turning to face him, she leaned back against the counter on her elbows.

"What did it look like?" I inched around the counter.

"You know, like a love note. It said something about having so much fun. I don't know. I tossed it, thinking it was from the guy I fucked last night." She shuddered. "Way too clingy for having such a small dick."

"We need more details," Cas interjected.

Sarah cringed. "Okay. Well, I swear it was only three inches—"

"Not his dick," Cas grumbled into the hand covering his face. When it slipped down, I couldn't help but giggle. He looked like he'd rather be anywhere other than here hearing about some guy's small penis. "The note. What did it look like?"

Her shoulders visibly relaxed. "Oh good, because I felt bad talking about it, you know. I mean, it's not like he could help being so small."

Cas turned and walked to the living room, his frustration clear.

"Fine, the note, got it. Okay, so it was like an old-school valentine of sorts, like you'd give in grade school. Why does this matter? Is that like the one Sadie put on your car?" Sarah's eyes flicked from me to Cas and back again. Watching me, she tilted her head. "What's wrong, Bridie? You look paler than normal."

Of course I was pale, I couldn't breathe.

What was this guy doing targeting Sarah *and* me? Neither of us were his usual target, so did that mean Sadie was the one who put the notes on our cars? Maybe this had nothing to do with the serial abductor, but how would Sadie know about the type of notes that were left for the victims?

"I'm so confused." I paced between the kitchen and living room. "We need to call Chandler and John. Maybe John mentioned something to Sadie about the note, and she's just playing mind games. We need to ask him."

"What the hell is going on?" Sarah demanded, her tone high-pitched. "You're freaking me out."

Cas held out a hand, silencing us both as he pressed a phone to his ear. "Peters. Mathews. Come down to Alta's. We have some new information. Call that dipshit John too. We need to ask him a few questions."

"Worst girls' night ever," Sarah sighed and looked to the ceiling. "Just saying, we need a redo."

"If we're still around," I murmured.

"What does that mean?"

I glanced to Cas, whose forehead seemed to have a permanent worry line stretched across it.

"It means we both better hope Sadie is as crazy as we think, or those notes could be our death sentence."

"You sure you don't want to come to Denver with me?" Sarah asked as she tugged on her coat by the door. "I'm sure my friend wouldn't mind another person crashing on her couch."

Gripping the doorknob, I shook my head before twisting it and swinging the door open, allowing a blast of cold night air to sweep inside. "I'll be fine. I wish you'd let one of the guys go with you to pack your stuff."

She waved a hand between us, dismissing my worry. "Nah, I'll be fine. Just watch yourself, okay? It'd suck to come back to town and find out you're missing too."

"Thanks?"

"Be safe," she yelled over her shoulder as she hurried to her car. She climbed in, started the engine and drove off into the night.

"She'll be fine," Cas said at my back. "Something tells me she's one of those people who could survive anything."

I nodded in agreement. After the door shut, I locked each deadbolt three times and leaned my head against the warm wood. The last hour was more draining than the earlier cleaning extravaganza. No one knew what to think of Sarah also getting a note. John had stormed out when we accused Sadie writing the notes, not the serial abductor. He swore on his life that he hadn't mentioned it, considering that would be discussing an active investigation, which he'd never do.

I believed him.

Which left us where?

Here. Confused, dead ends all over the place, and a hot, brooding male as my new roommate until we figured it out.

That last part wasn't so bad.

"We'll figure it out," Cas said from several feet behind me.

Turning, I leaned against the door and tried to press the back of my head against it, but my ponytail stopped me. With an annoyed sigh, I pulled the hair tie out, raked my fingers through my long hair to ease the ache in my scalp, and leaned my head back with a thump.

"It's been days since you and Chandler arrived. Two missing women here, plus all those in Tennessee, and we're no closer to catching this guy. I feel anxious, like we're just waiting for him to take someone else. And after tonight, I'm afraid it might be one of my friends." Opening my eyes, I found his gaze focused on the door right above my shoulder. "What?"

His head shook like he was trying to rid himself of a thought. "I'm taking a shower. Keep the doors locked—"

"Duh."

His eyes narrowed. "Stay armed." He turned to face Benny. "Auf Wache," Cas commanded and pointed to the door. Benny trotted to the front door, sat his furry backside on the floor and stared forward.

I gaped at him. "How did—"

"Guy in my unit, remember? We need to figure out dinner. I'm fucking starving."

"I have a near-lifetime supply of ramen noodles in the pantry."

He gave an uncharacteristic nose crinkle in disgust. "Had my fill of that shit in the marines. Anything else?"

My hair swished across my upper back as I shook my head.

"Fine, we're going out. You want to shower first, then?"

"Is that a hint?"

A feral smile climbed up his cheeks, sending my heart racing. "That's an 'I'd prefer you to be clean when I eat you for dessert later.'"

"Oh." Heat filled my cheeks, threatening to leave actual burns. "Um, that sounds... good."

Cas's deep rumbling laugh filled the cabin, making Benny turn to see what was going on. "You're so fucking innocent. I can't wait to ruin that. Go shower before I strip your clothes off right now to see how far down that blush of yours goes."

Keeping my back to the wall, then the counter all the way around the kitchen, I eased across the room, never dropping his hungry gaze. Inside the bathroom, I focused on the lock for a few seconds before turning and flipping the hot water on. The potential for sex was the ultimate motivator, it seemed. Who knew the hope of him walking in on me in the shower to fulfill his promise now instead of later would be what I needed not to lock a door.

Eyes closed, I fantasized that each soapy swipe of my hands up and down my torso, over my breasts, between my legs was his instead of my own. At the heat boiling beneath my skin and the nearly scalding water, sweat beaded along my forehead and beneath my arms. I had to stop thinking about him if I ever expected to get clean.

Propping my foot along the edge of the tub caused delicious friction between my thighs, causing a louder-than-expected whimper to pour out.

"Everything okay in there?" Cas asked on the other side of the door.

More than you know.

"Yeah, almost done. Trying to hurry to not use all the hot water."

"We could always save water and shower together."

Mouth gaping, I stared at the plastic shower curtain, half expecting it to rip aside. Fantasizing about him in here with me was one thing, but it actually happening was another. I mean, I'd just had my first kiss in ten years. Things needed to slow down, or my fear of having a panic attack in front of him would become a reality.

"I'll be done in a minute," I said breathily. Hopefully he couldn't hear that part.

A deep chuckle sounded on the other side of the door. "Okay, Lady."

With a sigh of relief, I went back to scrubbing my leg. My hairy leg.

Fuck.

I hadn't shaved since shorts season, which was last month. Or maybe the month before? In a panic, I hastily searched through the products crammed into the corners of the tub for shaving cream. Relief washed over when I picked up the near-full bottle; seemed I didn't use it that much, even during shorts season. My gaze traveled from the bottle clutched in my hands to the very, very, *very* unkempt patch of hair just below my belly.

Under my terrified stare, the puff of blonde, coarse hair seemed to fluff and grow.

Again I whimpered, but that time for an entirely different reason.

I needed a pair of hedge clippers, or maybe a lawnmower. At least a pair of scissors, which, of course, were hidden under the spare pillow in my bedroom.

"What do I do? What do I do?" I whispered into the warm stream of water.

One problem at a time. That always helped calm the rising panic in the past.

Armpits.

Legs.

Crotch.

I'd tackle one hairy mess at a time. With a quick prayer that the razor blade was sharp enough to undertake this challenge, I squirted a dollop of shaving cream into my hand and lifted my arm to start on step one.

20

Alta

THE WATER COOLED within seconds of wrapping up project de-hair. Stepping out of the tub, I snagged a towel and flipped my hair to wring out the gallon of water trapped in the thick locks. Being hairless everywhere other than my head felt sexy. With renewed confidence, I tucked the towel around my chest and swung the door open, only to be stopped by a muscular chest preventing me from vacating the bathroom.

"That wasn't quick," he stated as his gaze roamed up and down my near-naked body, pausing at my heaving breasts pressing against the tight towel. Time stood still as his teeth sank into his lower lip. "Are you scared?"

Scared?

Yes.

No. Not in the way he was undoubtedly thinking. With wide eyes, I focused on the indentions left along his lower lip. My thighs squeezed together to ease the pounding throb those tiny indentations caused.

"You have a choice, Lady. I'll respect your decision either way, but I need to know. Push me away if you don't want me to rip that towel off you right now and bury my face between your legs. Because the control I normally have around you is wearing thin."

My choice. Of course it was. He might not be a gentle man, but he sure as hell was a gentleman.

The wetness pooling between my legs decided for me. Releasing the death grip on the top of the towel, I dropped my arms to my side and let my eyes flutter closed. Every other sense heightened. His scent wrapped around me like a warm blanket, warmth radiating off him as he took a step closer to my trembling body.

"Open your eyes," he commanded, but in a softer tone than earlier.

My lids lifted, eager to do as I was told.

"All you have to say is stop." The pad of his thumb pressed against my lower lip, dragging it down until it popped back into place. "If it's too much... if I take this too far. Promise me, Alta."

"I promise," I whispered around the index finger roughly dragging along my upper lip. "Please, Cas," I begged just as a shudder of overwhelming need overtook my body, shaking my spine.

His teeth quickly replaced his fingers, nipping at my lower lip and pulling back, tugging it past the point of comfortable, but somehow turning me on even more. I whimpered for more as his lips sealed over mine, sucking all the air from my lungs and the strength from my legs.

With ease, he shifted us around the small bathroom. The cold doorframe dug between my shoulder blades, the back of my head smacking backward at the force of his possessing kiss. Each flick of his tongue against mine was deeper, more sensual than the last. This wasn't just a kiss. No, it was a claiming, a marking—a taking.

And I loved all of it.

Lust made my skin tingle with pleasure and my thoughts foggy.

Perfection. This was pure perfection. Holding back the past ten years felt worthwhile because it meant I'd waited for him.

My lips burned as his scruff scraped to kiss across my cheek. His fingers looped around my neck, tightening slightly, my arousal peaking beyond anything I'd ever known.

"You're. Mine," he snarled against my ear. Thumb pressed into the corner of my jaw, he arched my neck, stretching it beneath his slick lips.

A low, aggressive growl yanked me from the haze. Peeling my eyes open, I found Benny staring at Cas, teeth exposed.

Whoops. Forgot about the attack dog.

"Gehen," I said with a shaky voice. When he didn't obey, Cas eased the restraint around my neck so I could take a full breath. "Gehen," I commanded, that time clear and sure. With a look of doubt—I swear he did—Benny turned and made his way to the dog bed in the corner of the living room. Dark eyes still on Cas, he lay down with a huff.

Unfazed, the tightness around my neck returned, shoving my head back against the wood with a light smack. Teeth sank in deep where my neck and shoulder met, making me cry out in surprise and loving every damn second of it. The pain turned to pleasure as quickly as it had come, fogging my brain once again.

Damn this man.

Slowly he sucked and nipped lower. Lips against the swell of my heaving breast, he locked onto the skin and sucked. Hard.

"Mine," he said with a smirk as he stared at the various marks he was leaving on my fair skin.

Hooking a thumb between my breasts, Cas gave a rough tug, releasing the makeshift knot I'd made. The worn terry cloth slipped down my waist and legs before pooling on the floor at my feet.

His hungry gaze singed each place it touched, but spiraled into an inferno when he zeroed in on my hairless mound.

"Fuck me," he said around a heavy breath.

"That's what took me so long. I used all the hot water too."

"Take the last drop of hot water on this fucking planet if it means you're bare for me every day."

There was no controlling my erratic breaths. Each short gulp of air wasn't enough. Either the lack of oxygen or his lips back on my skin made the room spin. Shutting my eyes, I focused on Cas. Like the inexperienced woman I was, I eased my hands up his shoulders unsure of what to do but needing to touch him. There was no way he couldn't feel the tremble in my fingers as I felt up his neck.

"Yes, Lady," he praised as I weaved my fingers into his short hair.

Daring a peek, I found him staring up at me while his tongue circled closer and closer to my hard nipple. On their own, my fingers flexed, pushing his mouth against my breast. I felt more than saw a smirk.

"Your hands on me, your fingernails digging into my scalp, tell me I'm doing something right. Don't be afraid to touch me, because I'm sure as fuck not scared of touching you."

To emphasize his point, warm lips wrapped around my nipple, sucking hard, almost to the point of pain, before flicking the tip back and forth with his tongue.

Giving up on holding back, I pulled him closer by gripping what little hair I could.

"Fuck," he groaned around me. Swift, light kisses coated my skin as he moved to the other side, repeating the same motions but with more urgency. "I'm going to taste you." He released my neck, skimming his hand down my waist and clamping around my left thigh. In the same movement, my leg was hoisted over his shoulder and a warm breath brushed between my legs.

"You're so fucking perfect. You smell like heaven." His nose buried between my folds as he took a dramatic inhale. When his tongue swiped up and back down again, I reached back, gripping the doorframe for support. "You taste like candy," he muttered against me. After another long swipe, his glazed eyes flicked up and found mine. "Like the best fucking salty-sweet candy I've ever had."

His lids closed like he was savoring the flavor.

"Cas," I begged.

My plea was like a spark against gunpowder to his focus. Cas's dark eyes flew open, and his lips sealed against my body. Arching my back, I shifted back and forth, unable to stand still while he devoured me whole.

My fingers tightened around the wood. The slight tremble in my right leg turned into a full-on shake as his tongue flicked and plunged inside me. The twinge of pain as he slid one thick finger inside quickly shifted to pleasure.

"More," I breathed. How had I gone so long without this? Without the worship of a man? Oh, because this right here had never happened before. The intensity with Cas was soul-engulfing.

He slid in another finger as his free hand pried mine from the doorframe and wrapped it around his head. Taking the hint, I dug my short nails into his scalp, yanking him harder against me.

His deep groan of pleasure vibrated to my core, setting off a cosmic burst. I cried out his name as the most intense orgasm pulsed through every square inch of my body at the continued laps of his tongue. My knee buckled, sinking me deeper to the floor. Arm around my waist, Cas held me up as his fingers continued their fast pace, pushing me higher. With another flick of his tongue and curl of his finger, I fell apart once again, his name a breathless scream pouring from my lips.

The world spun, lights dancing behind my closed lids. Everything was peaceful and right in the world.

A stinging sensation flung my eyes open to see what was going on, only to find Cas smirking at a set of teeth indentions inside my left thigh.

"Mine."

I cringed at the already sore muscles of my thigh as he removed my leg from his shoulder and gently set my bare foot on the ground. Hands around my waist, he eased me down to the floor, putting us eye-to-eye.

The shimmer of his lips reflected the bathroom lights. As I stared at the lingering visual display of my orgasm, his mouth twitched into a mischievous grin.

"Here, see how good you taste." Before I could object, his slick lips pressed over mine and his tongue dove in, tangling with my own. As the delicate taste filled my mouth, all revulsion of the act disappeared. I slid a hand into his hair and tugged him closer.

Kissing Cas solved all the world's problems. Nothing else mattered. I was safe in his arms, cherished by his lips and tongue. That was all I needed to know for the rest of my life.

With a light nip of my lower lip, he pulled back, a wistful smile lighting up his face. Reaching up, he brushed a wet lock of hair from my forehead. "Now, I'm going to take a shower so we can go eat."

Like the dazed fool I was, I merely nodded in agreement, unable to find words. With a soft chuckle, he pressed his lips to my forehead and stood.

Uncaring that I sat recovering in the middle of the doorway, preventing him from shutting the door, Cas stripped off his black T-shirt. I blinked once, twice. Yes, I'd seen his bare chest before, but that close, within touching distance, his muscles were even more defined. I blinked several times to wipe away the mirage, because no way guys looked like that in real life.

Ogling every inch of his exposed skin, my appreciative gaze shifted from his defined pecs, down his taut stomach, to where his long fingers fiddled with his belt. The metal buckle clinked open and he tugged the end, yanking it out of the belt loops with a whipping sound. After staring at the long leather, he tossed it across the bathroom toward me.

"That'll come in handy later."

My wide, unblinking eyes continued to watch as he unbuttoned his dark jeans and slid them down his thighs, revealing more incredible, defined strength. Dark hair covered his muscular thighs and calves.

He paused with his thumbs hooked around the tight band of his boxer briefs. Lip between my teeth, I watched, captivated, to see what came next. Cas shoved the elastic over his hips, allowing the underwear to slide down until they pooled at his feet.

That's when the fantasy stalled.

My breaths turned to short wheezes as I gaped at his long, hard cock. Terrible memories of Lance replayed in random succession, unable to control my breathing as darkness encroached in the corners of my vision. Only the steady pounding of my rapid pulse filled my ears.

My muscles wouldn't respond; nothing worked. I couldn't stop the fuzzy images from filling every crevice of my thoughts, flooding from the dark corners of my mind. Three days, three whole days I suffered under the lunatic who thought I loved him back—he just needed some reassuring. Even high on Special K, enough memories were imprinted in my mind to haunt me. Images of him on top, grunting, taking me as I lay there, unable to respond. Of him forcing my mouth open while he shoved himself down my throat. His hand over mine, squeezing tight as he pumped our hands down him. Every minute, every second was there, waiting to emerge when I least expected it.

Like now.

Bile built in my stomach and pushed up my throat. Angling to the side, I smacked a palm against the hardwood floor before I vomited what little I'd had to eat into the hallway. More pictures. More dry heaving.

My abs ached and burned at the constant clenching. Hot tears streamed down my cheeks, mixing with the strings of saliva dangling from my lips. I felt like shit, and I was sure I looked awful too, but it didn't matter. Getting out of the attack in one piece was.

I flinched at a cold towel swiping across my mouth.

Fingers gripped my chin, turning my face into the bathroom. Dark, searching eyes met mine. Anger, concern, and fierce determination were what I found in their depths, not sympathy or disgust like I'd expected.

"Breathe through it," he coaxed in a commanding tone my body immediately responded to. "Take control. Fight it, Alta. Focus on me."

"Xanax," I somehow got out.

He shook his head. "You got this on your own. You can't change your past, so don't dwell on it. Push those memories out. Focus on me." His grip tightened as he shook my chin, gaining more of my attention. "Own it. Don't let it own you."

It struck me fast and hard—he believed in me. I freaked out on him because I saw him naked, I threw up, and yet there he was, inches from my face, walking me through the panic attack. Something lingered behind his eyes, and I got lost trying to figure out what it was he was holding back.

"Focus on what you can control, nothing else. You can control your breathing. You can control your thoughts. Focus. You can do it, Lady."

Little by little, I clung to his confidence in me and began pulling myself out of the downward spiral. Instead of picturing Lance, I focused on Cas. Instead of remembering the all-consuming fear I lived for those three days, I focused on the touch of Cas's fingers, the fluttering and happiness it brought.

Minutes later, the tremble in my fingers faded, my vision cleared —minus the embarrassed tears—and my breathing calmed.

"Why are you crying?" Cas asked, sincerity filling his voice.

"Why?" I glanced away to avoid making eye contact with him. "Oh, maybe because what I was nervous about just happened. I freaked out because I saw your… you know, your…." Without looking, I waved a hand toward his still-exposed crotch.

"Oh, that?" Humor laced his words. "Don't worry about that, happens a lot. Most women pass out when they first see me. I'm used to it."

I smirked at his valiant attempt to lighten the mood until I remembered the next part. "And then I threw up and—oh my goodness, I threw up." Flush heated my cheeks. I buried my face in my hands and shook my head back and forth. "I'm more fucked up than I realized. Here I thought it was just the paranoia. Nope, bonus, that bastard left me with the inability to be intimate with anyone ever again. You can go if you want to. I understand. I—"

"Alta, look at me."

Dropping my hands, I took a deep, steadying breath in. He was leaving; why wouldn't he? I peered up beneath my lashes, prepared for the worst.

"Did you think this would be easy? You were held captive and...." He glanced away, the muscle of his jaw twitched. "This is the first time in ten years you've let someone touch you without pushing them away. Give yourself a little credit, Lady."

A relieved sigh pushed past my lips. "You're not leaving?"

His brown brows furrowed, causing a deep line to form between them. "Did you really think I would?"

My wet hair brushed across my shoulders as I shook my head. "Did you expect something like this would happen?"

He nodded. Sitting his bare backside on the floor, Cas grabbed the towel beside me and laid it over himself, leaving me naked. I narrowed my eyes at the towel.

"Not a chance. I love this view. And yeah, I figured there would be some triggers, but since you hadn't been with anyone since the assault, we didn't know what. Now we know."

"We know I can't look at a nude man," I grumbled, disgusted with myself.

"That'll come with time, which is fine. You're okay being naked with me, and I'm golden with that, Lady. As long as I get to play with you, I'm happy."

"You make me sound like your new favorite toy."

His smile faltered, and his features turned serious. "For the first time in my life, I have something to call mine. So yeah, I might be possessive, but when you've grown up with nothing, you learn to appreciate the things you do have. And I plan on appreciating the fuck out of you."

21

Cas

THROUGH THE SMOKE, I monitored the black SUV as it turned into the drive and parked. At my side, Benny growled at the newcomer and looked up for instruction.

Damn, best dog ever.

His coarse hair tickled my palm as I patted his head to ease his concern. The second Peters came into view, Benny's tail twitched along the porch in excitement. I took the last hit off the cigarette and tossed the butt in the makeshift ashtray Alta set out. That woman was serious about litter.

I suppressed the smile that wanted to emerge at just the thought of her.

"She asleep?" Chandler asked as he stomped up the steps.

"Yes."

"You tuck her in all nice and tight in there?" With a smirk, he nodded to the cabin. "Or is that my job tonight?"

"She's in her room, yes," I grumbled around the new cigarette between my lips as I lit the end.

"You wore her the fuck out, didn't you? You bastard, I told you to take it slow with her. Bet she won't be able to walk for a fucking week."

I turned my steely eyes to him. "Watch it."

Palms up in mock surrender, he stepped out of my swinging reach. "You getting riled up all over a woman?"

Instead of admitting he was spot-on, I leaned a shoulder against the post, placing my back to him.

"Never thought I'd see the day. Knew something would end up happening between you two. Fucking knew it."

"Enough," I demanded. He acted like it was national fucking news. Yes, this was the first time, maybe ever, that I had even a glimmer of emotions over someone. Even in the marines, the boys always counted on my ability to stay detached, emotionless and focused on the facts.

"Wow," Chandler said with an exaggerated sigh. "Anything happen tonight after I left that I should know about?"

I shook my head and took another deep inhale, enjoying the way the smoke burned my lungs. "We went out for dinner because she had shit to eat here. Don't worry, we stopped by the store on our way back, so there's food in there now."

"And?"

"And what?"

"How was dinner?"

I shrugged, not understanding where he was going with his question. "Fine. We mostly talked about the case. We both agreed that something else seems to be going on with this guy. Why switch up the type of women he targeted from 'married to meatheads' to 'single and working for the park'?"

"So all business, then," Peters sighed and leaned back against a post. "Sounds like some date. You don't get out much, do you? Need some pointers?"

"Fuck off."

"All I'm saying is she seems like a nice kid, and you're a little"—he angled his head one way and then tilted it the other, like he was getting a good look—"rough around the edges. Maybe you should, I don't know, shave. And how about wearing clothes other than a black T-shirt or something with 'marines' stamped across it?"

"I know how to fucking date," I grumbled, even though he had me doubting myself at that point. "Lay off my ass, okay? She's fine, and I'm fine."

"Just trying to help a friend out. You respond to her, which is a fucking miracle. Don't want to see you fuck it up before we head home."

"Keys." After catching them midflight, I flipped him the bird and strode to the SUV. Peters had made it halfway through the door when I called out, making him pause. "Don't fucking touch her, you hear me." I started to climb in but stopped. "And don't go telling all our shit tomorrow morning. No one else needs that stuff in their heads." I cranked the engine and backed out. "I sure as hell don't want it," I muttered to myself.

Yes, I was still an emotionless shell of a person, but since leaving the Marines, I was wound tighter now than ever before. The lack of purpose, something to be responsible for in the civilian life, kept me on edge on a daily basis. Sure, I had a job to do, and I did it well, but what could I do with the other hours in the day? Since the demotion, all I did was sit at home, sulking and drinking until liver failure was imminent. I didn't have friends, didn't date; most of my time was spent alone, trying to forget. But with her, the emotions she evoked, I had purpose. She needed me, and I needed her.

This unknown side of me, the possessiveness and all-consuming desire for only her, was fucking terrifying and freeing at the same time. What I told her earlier was true. I'd never had anything of my own, nothing to form an emotional connection to; then she walked into my life, cracking the emotionless cage that held me hostage for so long wide open.

Utterly exhausted, I unlocked the cabin door, stumbled to the living room and fell face first onto the couch, still fully dressed.

Thumbs shoved against my temples, I massaged in small circles, trying to ease my headache as I toed off my boots, letting them clatter to the floor.

My mind raced with thoughts of Alta and the case. Something was going on behind the scenes, something we hadn't figured out yet. Every lead led to a dead end. Which left Alta vulnerable and me on edge, because the one place I wanted to be right now was with her, protecting her, but I couldn't.

No way would I endanger her life so I could be there tonight. Peters was a good guy and a hell of a marine. He would take care of her.

But what rubbed was he wasn't me.

After several minutes of talking in circles, my lids grew heavy. Not bothering with stumbling to my room, I stretched out on the couch, grabbed a spare pillow and gave in to the pull of sleep.

SOMEWHERE IN THE fog of deep sleep, the sound of glass shattering urged me awake. Still, the nightmare held me hostage until slicing pain pulled me awake. Disoriented, I blinked the early morning fuzziness away and shook my head to aid in bringing me back to reality. Streams of sweat trickled down my temples, between my bare pecs and back.

Damn. I went to bed fully clothed, and now here I stood in the middle of the kitchen in nothing but black boxer briefs.

I lifted my hand to wipe the sweat from my forehead before it dripped into my eyes when a searing throb of pain drew my focus down. Blood dripped from the tips of my fingers in steady drops, pooling on the laminate kitchen floor. Brightness assaulted my unprepared eyes after switching the overhead light on to inspect my hand.

Fine lacerations sliced through the skin of my right hand with several deeper, wider ones scattered in no apparent order. Flexing and tightening my fingers into a fist, I ground my teeth to hold back a cry of pain, but the mobility did mean nothing important was cut or damaged. I hoped.

Reaching into a drawer, I yanked out a clean towel and carefully wrapped the injured hand to stop the blood from making more of a mess. After tying another towel tight around my wrist to staunch the flow of blood, I shifted to the sink to clean up. Something sharp bit into the sole of my bare foot.

Glass littered the floor, along with several knives and the knife drawer, which had been ripped from the cabinet and now lay in splinters amongst the glass. Squatting where I stood, I inspected the various knives until I located one with a bloody handprint along the hilt.

What the hell did I dream about?

Standing with a groan, I turned to the microwave to check the time.

"Well fuck," I gritted out. The microwave hung precariously by bolts that held it in place. The front had splintered, with a massive hole in the middle like someone had beaten it repeatedly with something hard.

Like a fist.

My fist.

Turning toward the living room, I found a trail of clothes leading to the kitchen.

"Fuck, fuck, fuck," I yelled at the top of my lungs in utter frustration.

It wasn't the first time I'd attempted to attack my reflection. Back in DC, mirrors were constantly shattered in my small apartment, windows punched out, and now it seemed I'd been reduced to beating the shit out of even a blurred image of myself in a microwave door.

Wonderful.

So fucking wonderful.

That was why I couldn't be around her. Why I'd needed to be alone. Who'd want someone who might beat them to death in their sleep and have absolutely no recollection of it? The answer was no one.

It didn't happen every night, just during periods of high stress. I stared down at the blood-soaked towel. This was my reality. I was fucked in the head. I had enough control when I was awake to manage it, but, when asleep all bets were off.

The sleeping issues didn't start in the marines. It probably stemmed from my love-lacking childhood. I never knew if I'd be yanked from bed by another foster kid who proceeded to whip my ass. Or sometimes the adults looking after me decided nighttime was the best time to treat you like the disposable human punching bag you were. Or it could also be from always being on edge at school, because yet again, threats lurked everywhere; people loved to gang up on the poor, shittily dressed, and most of the time reeking of body odor kid. Whatever started it, it only escalated in the corps and turned into what it was now after the standoff three years ago.

We fought for our lives every fucking second during those thirty days. The little sleep our bodies forced us to take was filled with gunshots in the background and true, unfiltered terror coursing through our veins. After I made it home and saw the shrinks the military required, it was clear—to them anyway, not me—that I wasn't fit to continue serving my country. Which was another blow. I always imagined being a lifer with the marines; they were the only family I ever knew. Then they were gone, leaving me fucked and alone.

Alone.

I'd always been alone. But after meeting her, the thought of spending the rest of my life that way seemed pitiful. She changed me, changed my outlook, but that didn't mean it would change the outcome.

OUTSIDE OF THE closest pharmacy to the cabin, I dumped the bandages, gauze, and antibiotic ointment I purchased onto the passenger seat. At least the worst part was over. Before I left, I painfully removed every sliver of glass embedded in my skin before running out for supplies. Only a few of the gashes looked deep enough to require stitches—like that was going to happen. Instead of waiting at an emergency clinic all day, I drew the separated sides of skin tight together and stuck several butterfly Band-Aids along the cut. I had more important things to do than wait on some doctor who'd ask too many questions.

Twenty minutes later, I had it tightly bound, but loose enough to have full mobility, and pulled the SUV onto the main highway toward the cabin community we shared.

Damn, I was so fucking ready to see her.

And not to have sex, which was a first. No, I just wanted to see her, talk to her, make sure she was safe. Hell, we didn't even have to speak; just being in the same room with her lifted the weight of loneliness from my chest.

That morning, standing in the middle of the damaged kitchen, nearly naked with a fucked-up hand, you'd think I'd feel embarrassed, but I wasn't. No, I felt achingly alone. More alone than I ever had been. Maybe because I wanted to be with her, but my fucked-up head prevented me from doing so.

And I hated it.

Ten minutes later, I skidded to a halt in front of her cabin. After three calming deep breaths in and out, I shoved the driver door open wide and climbed out. There was nothing to be nervous about, but then again there was. I didn't give two thoughts to her panic attack yesterday, but sometimes women were funky about stuff like that, getting all embarrassed and then shutting down. Hopefully Alta was different.

At the front door, I raised my fist to knock, but loud voices and cackles of laughter stilled my hand. Whatever they were doing inside, it sounded like they were having a good time. At eight in the fucking morning.

The door rattled beneath my fist.

One second, I waited.

Two seconds.

I pounded against the door again.

A click, then another and another before the door swung open. Peters stood in the doorway, the door open only wide enough for his body to block the rest of the cabin from view, with a devilish grin. "Oh hey. Was wondering when you'd finally decide to wake up."

A blip of uncertainty that I hadn't felt since high school had me tucking my injured hand behind my back. What in the hell were they doing in there?

"Move," I grunted as I dug a shoulder into his bare chest. I took everything in at once, but peace settled my raging thoughts the second my eyes landed on her. Sitting on the couch, feet tucked under her and wearing the marines sweatshirt I lent her the day before. I smirked.

"Hey," Alta said with a smile while twirling the end of her ponytail between her fingers. "I was beginning to wonder if you were ever coming back."

"It's eight in the morning, you two, not noon," I grumbled, leaning against the counter so I could keep an eye on her and one on him.

"We've been up since five," Peters said as he walked by. Plopping on the couch beside her, he leaned back and laid his head next to her thighs.

I bit back the swarm of pain that pulsed from my injured hand as my fists clenched in fury. Too close. Way to close to my Lady.

"We've been on a run, had breakfast, fed the dog." Peters rolled his head to look up at Alta. "Okay, new category. Ladies choice."

Eyes to the ceiling like she was deep in thought, Alta gnawed on the side of her thumb. "Animals," she said, smiling.

"Fine. Is it a mammal?"

"Yes."

"Does it run on four legs?"

"No," Alta giggled.

What game were they even playing?

"Does it fly?"

"No."

"Does it hop?"

"Yes," Alta groaned and thumped her head against the back of the couch.

"I'm telling you, Birdie, I'm the best at this game. Doesn't help that you tell the world what you're thinking through those beautiful eyes of yours." Peters shot a look across the room that told me he knew everything that went down yesterday between her and me. "You don't hide your emotions well. You're thinking of a kangaroo."

"Unbelievable. You're ten for ten," Alta grumbled, clearly unhappy that he guessed correctly. "Let's play a new game. One I can win."

"No," I stated and stepped into the middle of the living room. "His shift's up. Time to go, fucker."

Peters nestled into the worn couch. "I'm quite comfortable, actually. Birdie here is quite the host, even though you said otherwise."

"Hey," Alta exclaimed, looking hurt.

"I didn't say—" I rubbed my hand down my face in frustration, but the second the smooth cotton bandages slid down my forehead, I jerked it down.

"What happened to your hand?" she asked, more concern than hurt in her tone now. Unfolding herself from the couch, Alta tiptoed on bare feet to where I stood and tugged my injured hand from behind my back.

"Nothing. It's fine." Jerking it from her delicate grasp, I glared at Peters, who remained on the couch, grinning. "Get the fuck out now. Don't you have a case or something to work on?" I arched a dark brow in challenge.

"Yes, but I'll be back later to talk through some of the information that came through overnight." With a groan, he pushed off the cushions and stretched his arms overhead, causing his muscles to ripple every which direction. At my annoyed grunt, his smile grew wider. At the door, he slipped a shirt from his bag and zipped up the army-green duffel. "I'll text you before I head over in case you're... you know, otherwise indisposed."

The moment the door swung open, I shoved my good hand into

his upper back, propelling him forward and out of the cabin. The wooden door slammed shut before he was off the porch.

"Did he hit on you?" I asked Alta while staring at the door.

"Seriously?" Even though I couldn't see her face, there was a hint of amusement in her tone.

"Did he or didn't he? If he did, then I'm going back out there and kicking his ass until he can't fucking walk." Turning, I strode toward her. Eyes wide, she stood her ground as I stalked closer. Good hand cupping her cheek, I pulled her lower lip down with the pad of my thumb. "Or maybe it's you who needs a reminder of whose you are."

Her jaw popped open with a gasp, allowing me the opportunity to swoop down and claim her beautiful mouth.

22

Alta

W‍HOA.

Just like yesterday, his declaration of possession, of being his, should've scared the heck out of me.

But it didn't. The opposite happened. My knees went weak and my heart raced. The tips of my fingers and nose tingled. My stomach dipped and trembled in a way that made me want more. Every part of my body honed in on the purely masculine man holding me the way I'd only ever dreamed of being held.

Cas radiated control, confidence, and patience when he held me in his strong arms.

And there was nowhere else I wanted to be.

It was different with Cas from the man who stole three days of my life. With Cas, I felt safe, not terrified. I had a choice with Cas; when held captive those three days, I had none, no matter the tears and pleas for him to stop. With Cas, the way he made me feel desired, desperately needed, was empowering.

All in all, Cas breathed life back into my petrified soul. With each touch of his hands against my skin, each embrace and slide of his lips against mine, a fractured piece of me fused. The scars would always be there, and that was okay.

My scars were what he liked the most.

And that made me more whole and sure of myself than I'd ever been.

"Did he?" Cas asked before angling his head to deepen the kiss.

With his lips pressed to mine, I smiled.

"No, he was trying to get a rise out of you." Palm against his hard chest, I pushed back, putting a bit of space between us. "And it seems like it worked." Cas leaned down for another kiss, but I pressed harder. "Now, what happened to your hand?"

Taking the hint that now was time for talking, not making out, he huffed and tugged our lower bodies together. I held back a whimper at the hardness behind his zipper digging into my belly.

"How was your night? Any flashbacks?" he asked, those dark brown eyes searching mine.

"Just my usual nightmares, Nothing better, nothing worse. Stop avoiding my question." Needing friction, I shifted back and forth, rubbing against him. A loud groan of pain and frustration erupted from his chest and echoed around the cabin.

"We need to get out of here," he said, wrapping my hand in his and tugging me toward the door. I smiled as he snagged the keys, commanded Benny to stay, and yanked me out onto the porch. "Where to, Lady?"

"Sure it's safe out there?"

The condescending look he shot over his shoulder as he locked up made me giggle. "Why can't we stay here, where it's warm?"

"You mean hotter than Hades on a summer day? And because I don't trust myself being around you anywhere with a bed, or walls, or any smooth surface your back could be shoved against."

I wrapped my arm around my waist and squeezed while biting back a smile. All thoughts of yesterday making him rethink us or him being turned off vanished. I wanted him too, and we'd figure it out. I was sure of it.

Slow. We'd do this slow, and everything would be fine.

"So the park it is," I said. "No smooth surfaces on the trails."

Inside the truck, he twisted the key and turned. After snatching my thumb from my teeth, he intertwined our fingers, locking them in place between us. "Where to, my Lady?"

"Are you trying to kill me?" Cas grunted as we scaled another boulder. "I'd rather die by a bullet than this shit." His deep intakes of air could be heard through half the park.

"Just a bit farther. It's my favorite view," I said with a smile while I waited for him to catch up. Granted, he had more bulk to haul up, and he could only use his left hand because of the other's mysterious injury. "On my days off, I hike up here and sit for hours just watching, listening. It's peaceful."

"If you don't die before you make it," he grumbled. With a loud grunt, which sounded mostly for dramatics, he stepped up beside me.

"Are you going to tell me what happened to your hand now?" I asked, then started up the trail once again, this time with Cas close behind.

"Are you going to keep asking until I tell you?"

"Well yeah." I chuckled and tossed my hands in the air. "Spill it, Mathews."

"I preferred the 'sir' nickname. Fine, I punched our microwave."

I pulled up short, causing him to stumble against my back. "The microwave? What was its offense? Not heating your food, or dinging too loud?" Chin over my shoulder, I shot him a smirk.

"It looked like me."

My smirk fell. Turning, I placed both hands on my hips. "I have no idea what that means."

"It means exactly what I said. I saw a reflection in my sleep, and I… it's why I said I couldn't stay the night with you. I'm trained to take out any threat, and in my sleep, I can't decipher between a threat, a friend, or a fucking reflection." Shouldering past me, he started walking ahead. "Back home, I've just stopped replacing mirrors. This is the first time I've hit a microwave though." Stopping, he held his wrapped hand up to his face. "Hurt like a bitch too."

For several minutes, we walked in silence.

"Do you want to talk about it?" I finally asked, unable to take it any longer.

"Not really."

"Is that kind of a yes?"

"That's a hell no."

Even with the weight of the conversation, I couldn't help but smile. At least he told me about the hand. He could've just kept avoiding the question. Opening up didn't seem to be his thing, which was fine since it wasn't mine either.

Half a mile later, we reached the end of the trail. We stood at the edge of a steep drop-off, surrounded by the best view of several snow-covered peaks down to the stream-filled valleys.

"You were right." A muscular arm wrapped over my shoulder and hugged me close. "This was worth almost dying."

"You're kind of dramatic, you know that?"

Cas huffed a small laugh and flexed his arm, tugging me tighter against him.

"I can see why you don't go back to Texas. How could anyone ever leave this?"

I nodded but frowned at the same time. "I miss it though. I miss my parents."

"Why'd you leave?"

I wrapped an arm around his lean waist, savoring the contact. How had I gone so long without the touch and feel of comfort, of another human's loving touch?

"I couldn't be there anymore. Everywhere I turned, there were places that used to make me happy. I missed my life, I wanted the old me back so bad, but nothing was working. Therapy, drugs, hypnotism." Cas looked down with an arched brow. "Yeah I know, but we were desperate to fix me. When we realized nothing would work, I left. I couldn't take being there anymore, and my mom was suffocating me, afraid I'd sink too deep into depression and hurt myself."

Stepping out of Cas's warm hold, I sat on a large flat boulder and leaned back against a tree. "Remember me telling you Benny and I had a lot in common because we both lost someone?" Hand over the brim of my hat to shield the bright afternoon sun, I eyed Cas, who nodded. "I mourned me. The person I was. The happy spirit who thought everyone deserved a friend. The girl who not only wasn't afraid to step out into public, but who relished in it. I spent way too much money making my hair silky and shiny, which of course everyone noticed and commented on."

I tugged on the end of my ponytail and flicked the dull, dead ends back and forth in front of my face. "That was the first thing I tucked away. Now whenever I go out, I wear a hat of some kind, and I keep it back in a bun, hidden from view while I work. I guess because it's the one thing I knew made me stand out."

"Which you don't want," Cas said with a groan as he sat down next to me. "Because you're afraid it'll attract the wrong attention again."

I nodded as I kept my eyes on the pebbles I rolled between my fingers.

"I saw you."

"You did," I said with a smile. "Even when I tried to hide."

"It was your eyes. Peters was right earlier. You let people see inside you, see your emotions, everything. And somehow it was like you saw me too, all my darkness, and you didn't flinch away. It's what drew me in." Turning his gaze from the beauty in front of us, he locked eyes with me. "It's what won't let me go."

"Can I ask you something?"

"You're going to no matter what I say, so sure."

A broad smile spread up my cheeks. "Touché. This morning, you got worked up when you saw me with Chandler, and any time John is in the room, you're an ass. What's with that? You know I don't... I don't like them as I like you." My cheeks burned.

His gaze swung back to the scenery and leaned back on his elbows. "I'm not used to having something like this, like you in my life. Something I want only for myself. I've never had something that's just mine."

"Even as a kid? Come on." I nudged his shoulder with my knee, urging him to look back, but he didn't turn.

"My childhood wasn't like yours. I was moved from foster home to foster home until I aged out at eighteen. I was the scrawny kid who everyone picked on. Anything I was given, someone would take away."

"I don't believe you were scrawny." My nose wrinkled trying to imagine it. "You're so formidable now."

"Formidable," he said with a laugh. "Not sure my ego can take any more compliments."

That time I sailed my knee hard into his shoulder.

"Fuck, that hurt. And yeah, I was scrawny. I was picked on at whatever home I was in, and at school. I had zero relief from it. When I turned eighteen, I signed up for the marines. I wanted to become this badass no one would ever pick on again. I was terrible in boot camp." A nostalgic laugh had me watching his profile. He looked lost in memories as he stared at the mountains. "But eventually I started putting on weight—imagine what having three meals a day would do to a growing kid—and I learned to fight. I liked it, the fighting. It helped take the edge off the simmering anger that always sat just below the surface, ready to erupt. The marines taught me how to hone the anger, control it, use it. But still, even then I didn't have anything of my own. Until you fell into my life." He smirked.

"Stupid Benny knocking me over that day," I said as I leaned back and closed my eyes to absorb what all he'd said. "So what you're saying is you've never had a girlfriend?"

"First, no. I've had a lot of fuck buddies—"

Eyes still closed, I flung my arm out, nailing him in the forehead. "I don't need details."

"Touchy," he laughed. "No, I've never had a girlfriend. Never someone who I knew wanted me exclusively, and I wanted the same way. Someone who made me feel." The last word was barely a whisper, almost like he didn't understand. "Does me calling you mine and being slightly possessive—"

"I'd lean more toward overly possessive and protective."

"Fine, overly possessive and protective. Does that mean you're my girlfriend? We haven't even had sex."

The flush came back in full force, heating my cheeks. "I don't think having... you know is a requirement."

With a contemplative look, he closed his eyes and sighed. "I don't know what this is, and I don't know how long we'll be here, but I do know I want you while I am. You're addictive. What you're doing to me is too."

I swallowed and nodded. The reminder that he was only here for a short while made my stomach flip with disappointment. "Maybe you're the one who'll fix me so I can date after you're gone."

Cas groaned and shot a glare over his shoulder from where he now lay flat on the rock. "If I can't talk about past fuck buddies, you sure as hell can't talk about future ones."

True.

A happy, content feeling washed over me, making my eyes heavy. Rotating on the rock, I lay back, resting my head on top of Cas's hard stomach. Up and down, my head rose and lowered with each of his deep breaths, lulling me to sleep.

"I can't believe it," I sighed.

"What?" His wrist rested on my shoulder, allowing three of his fingertips the reach to brush up and down the length of my neck.

"I'm relaxed, comfortable. I'm about to fall asleep." Rotating my head, I tipped my chin to see above the bill of my hat to look at him. "It's because of you. I've wanted to do this exact thing in the past but couldn't. Thank you." Shifting back and forth, I nestled to get comfortable and let out a deep, whimsical sigh. "You're my hero."

"I'm no one's hero."

My heart sank at his words. His tone made it sound like he believed what he said. How could he not see how amazing he was? Thoughtful, caring, protective—all the qualities I hoped to find in someone one day. Never expected it to come wrapped in a sexy-as-hell package too.

My eyes fluttered closed. Just as I slipped into the beautiful space between awake and asleep, a soft, deep voice whispered, "If I could be anyone's hero, Lady, I'd die to be yours."

A SHIVER SNAPPED ME AWAKE. Blinking against the bright sun, I pushed onto my elbows with a groan. Hand at my lower back, I massaged the sore muscles that had pressed into the rock while I napped.

"Come here," Cas said with a tug on my arm as he also sat up.

After scooting back, his injured hand wrapped around my shoulder, holding me in place while the knuckles of his good hand pressed into my tight muscles.

"Oh," I moaned. "That feels so good. Harder, right there."

"Lady," Cas growled and pulled my back against his chest. "Do you want me to strip you naked and have my own personal picnic with you splayed out on this fucking rock for everyone to see?"

Well, when he put it that way....

The tip of my ponytail swished along my back as I shook my head.

"That's what I thought. So kindly stop making noises and saying shit that makes me want to, understood?"

Remembering his words from earlier, I smirked. "Yes, sir."

"Fuck," Cas grumbled, but went back to kneading the muscles along my spine.

A soft chuckle died on my lips as the hair on the back of my neck and arms stood on end. Pressing up to my feet, I turned to scan down the trail.

Beside me, Cas stood too. "What's wrong?" Mouth open to explain, I gaped at the gun dangling from his left hand.

"That was fast," I said in awe.

The corners of his lip twitched upward. "That's the only time I'll be okay with you saying that."

"It just felt like someone was watching us," I whispered, following Cas as he stalked toward the trail. "Maybe you should give me the gun since you have a bum shooting hand."

"I'm trained to use both," he whispered over his shoulder. "I'm keeping my gun."

"Fine," I sighed as I gripped his black T-shirt. Even though I'd been trained since childhood, there was zero doubt that he was a faster and more accurate shot than me.

To our right, a barely audible cascade of sediment and rocks fell, shifting both our focus between the rocks. Cas's back muscles tensed beneath my hand. Nerves drew me closer to him, pressing my front against his back for protection. I wasn't the fragile girl type, but he was the one with the gun, so I snuggled in closer.

"Let's keep moving," Cas directed. "I don't like this."

Next thing I knew, he was hauling me down the trail as I fought to keep up. My grip on his shirt loosened as we weaved between the rocks. Just as his shirt slipped through my fingers, something snagged my foot. Everything stilled as I tilted forward, hands extended in front of me to soften the blow that was to come.

But it didn't.

Unclenching my eyes, I found a pair of amused dark brown ones staring back. "You thought I'd let you fall?" A flash of pain swept across his gaze as he used both hands to haul me upright. Mouth open to say something else, he glanced over my shoulder. His shoulders rose, muscles bunched, ready for action.

"Alta, get behind me. Now."

Not understanding what was happening, I peeked over my shoulder and froze.

A beautiful mountain lion stood not twenty feet from us, stock-still—watching.

"She must've been what I sensed earlier," I breathed. "It's okay. At least it's not the serial killer, right?" I let loose a nervous laugh, which Cas didn't reciprocate. "We need to make some loud noises."

"Like what? Yelling?" Cas shook his head and raised the hand holding the gun.

Anger at the movement, at what he *considered* doing, filled every pore. Reaching up, I smacked his arm as hard as I could—which was pretty hard considering all I'd learned in karate classes over the years. Cas grunted as his arm dropped down and the gun clattered to the rocky ground.

"What the fuck, Alta?" he said, his teeth clenched so tight that I could hardly understand his words.

"You shoot her, and I shoot you." I grimaced, realizing it was an empty threat at the moment. "When I get my gun."

Once, twice, Cas slow-blinked, obviously not understanding.

"You will not shoot that beautiful animal," I whisper-yelled. "She's not doing anything to us."

"That 'beautiful animal,'" Cas countered angrily, his voice rising with every word, "is stalking us like we're her next meal. I've prepared myself to die in a lot of fucked-up ways, but death by cat isn't one I'm okay with."

Nervously, I glanced back again, only to find the large cat several feet closer.

Shit.

"Our phones," I mumbled, thinking out loud. Fumbling in the back pocket of my jeans, I tugged mine out. Hitting the music note icon, I chose whatever song came up first and hit Play. Daya's "Sit Still, Look Pretty" blared from the speakers as I cranked the volume up to full blast.

Catching my idea, Cas did the same. Soon Daya and Metallica blared from each device, competing for attention. Fear and excitement pulsed through me as I watched the large predator in awe. I worked in parks for years now and had never been so close to one. It was more beautiful than expected, with her long, muscular legs, gorgeous tan fur, and enormous paws. I bounced on the balls of my feet.

"Jump and wave your arms now." The scowl he shot me was a

clear 'hell no.' "We need to make her think we're bigger and stronger. Now jump."

Cas grumbled something under his breath before hopping from foot to foot and waving his arms.

"I want to pet it," I said to Cas, not taking my eyes off the animal.

"Don't. You. Dare," he said between jumps.

"Please?"

"Alta, I fucking swear...."

After a minute of the combined music and Cas looking like an idiot, the lion yawned, looking bored, then turned on her massive paws and prowled back up the trail. Still trembling, I turned to Cas with a broad smile and fisted his T-shirt in excitement.

"Did you see that?" I exclaimed. "Wow. I mean, wow." I tossed both hands in the air to accentuate my astonishment. "Beautiful, beautiful animals. I've never seen one—" I stopped short and tilted my head at his pursed lips and furious glare. "What?"

"What? Seriously? You knocked the gun out of my hand, Alta. What if she would've charged?"

"Then I would've sacrificed myself," I said stubbornly.

"You're crazy," Cas grumbled as he picked up his gun and dusted it off.

"And you're an ass right now."

"What? How am I being an ass?"

I pointed back up the trail. "You wanted to shoot her."

"So?"

"So?" I said in disgust. "It's an animal. What did she ever do to you?"

"Besides look at you like her next fucking meal? What is it with you and animals?"

I blanched. He made it sound like it was a fault to be so connected to the animals. Without replying, I shook my head and started down the trail once again.

"Wait up."

Okay, maybe I was a tad over the top when it came to them. Naming them was a little strange, and putting my safety in jeopardy to save them could be seen as foolish. But they'd always been there for me, offering the serenity, the escape I'd needed the past ten years. Animals didn't know evil, didn't seek me out just to hurt me. No, that was only humans. So yeah, maybe I had shifted the connection most people had with other humans to animals, but that wasn't a bad thing. It was survival. Because even though I'd been alone for a while now, I was never really alone. Not with them.

They gave to me what I couldn't accept from anyone else.

"Alta, I said to wait the fuck up," Cas shouted from several feet back. His loud grunts as he scaled the rocks and trotted down the trail penetrated through the quiet.

Shaking my head, something farther up caught my eye. Slowing my steps, I drew closer, narrowing my eyes to try and see better. Another step closer. Then a loud gasp pushed from my lungs. My eyes widened in shock and disgust as the realization hit of what I was looking at. Turning to scream for Cas, my cheek smacked into his chest. Instinctively I wrapped both arms around his waist, burying my face in his shirt.

"What—" Cas cursed under his breath. "It's okay. You're safe, Lady."

His consoling words and soft, rhythmic strokes along my spine did nothing to erase the horrific display behind me.

23

Alta

"Shhh, it's okay, Lady," Cas whispered over and over in my ear while his hand stroked down my back. But my heart continued to race faster as the image of the murder scene behind me continued to flash in my mind.

"It's in my head. It's not real. It's not real," I whispered into his shirt. "Tell me I'm crazy."

Rough calluses scraped down my damp cheek, but he didn't make a move to push me away from the safety of his hold. "You're not crazy. I see it."

"Please tell me it's not what I think it is," I choked out. "Please tell me someone didn't...." I couldn't finish the thought.

Seconds ticked by before he responded. "They did."

The sob I held in broke loose, rattling my shoulders as tears poured out of the corners of my closed eyes. The image of the poor murdered chipmunks flashed before my eyes, causing bile to churn in my stomach.

"It's meant for me, isn't it?" I asked, even though I knew the answer. Someone had killed and staged them in the heart shape, and we were the only ones on the remote trail that afternoon.

"We need to get out of here," Cas said before peeling me from his strong chest, dark eyes searching mine. "We'll have to walk past it. Do you want me to carry you?"

I shook my head even though I desperately wanted to say yes. Long fingers wrapped around mine and squeezed. Keeping my eyes focused on the rocky terrain, I followed each of Cas's footsteps. Where he stepped, I stepped. Taking a wide diversion, we climbed back onto the trail minutes later.

"I... I need to... I need to stop," I breathed and shook my hand loose of his. My knees slammed onto the rock. My breaths turned to short pants, each eager inhale demanding more and more oxygen. At my side, Cas spoke, but the words were muffled like my ears were filled with cotton. I peered up, hoping he could talk me through the panic attack like he did last night, but instead of finding him, my gaze zeroed in on the disturbing display.

A flick of movement caught my eye.

Then another.

I gasped. My hand flew up to my mouth to suppress a gag.

"What?" Cas roared and wheeled around to where I pointed with the hand not clasped against my lips. "What the fuck is it, Alta? Talk to me."

"They're...." I turned and dry heaved. Fist kneading my stomach, I tried to breathe through my nose and out my mouth. "They're not dead," I finally got out. At my words, I pivoted and gagged again.

Some sick, deranged person left injured, suffering, innocent chipmunks. For me.

As a sign of love, hate, or maybe a bit of both, which I learned a long time ago was called obsession.

Cas took one step toward the injured animals, then turned back with his brows furrowed and lips pursed deep in thought. Closing the space between us once again, he shoved his gun into my hands and wrapped my fingers around the grip. "I'm going to take care of it." A loud, painful whimper made his concerned wrinkles deepen. "Hold it together, okay? I need you to hold it together for a few more minutes. If you see anything, shoot, you hear me?"

Shock overtook my body and began the process of shutting it down little by little. My fingers and toes were the first to tingle, then grow numb. All outside noises ceased; only the steady rhythm of my pulse thundering in my ears remained. The grip of the gun felt weightless in my palm while the scene around me blurred.

Something gripped my shoulders and shook me forward and backward. My neck stopped wanting to hold up my head, allowing it to loll from side to side with each jostle. I needed to pull out of it, wanted to be strong, but I was tired. So, so tired.

Darkness encroached from the corners of my eyes, sealing off my vision until everything was dark, even with my eyes open.

Internally, I thrashed against the growing dark cloud, desperate to wake up, to watch for more threats.

But for the first time in a long time, the panic attack won, and I gave in to the blissful pull the darkness offered, knowing I would be safe, with him.

"Why isn't she waking up?" someone said close by, the voice familiar enough to not cause fear even though I still couldn't see.

An animal-type growl rumbled near me, and for some reason it made me want to smile—if I could work my facial muscles. "She walked up on some psychotic asshole's makeshift heart made out of tortured rats." That time my lips responded, ticking upward. "That would be enough to send anyone into shock, but add in her past—" A loud, frustrated groan vibrated in my ears. "We should call a doctor."

"Chipmunks," I somehow got out past my desert-dry throat and mouth. Willing my eyes to open, I blinked several times before the two men's faces cleared. Cas was at my side, hand tangled in my hair within seconds.

"What?" he asked. Concern and worry dripped from his words, making my heart flutter with something I couldn't identify.

"Not rats, chipmunks." Ribbed material pressed into my palm as I pushed to sit up. My mouth fell open. We weren't at the park anymore. Somehow he got me back down the mountain, into the truck and back home all without me waking.

"Jiminy cricket, my head," I said with a tight breath. Leaning forward, I wrapped both hands around my skull and pressed hard to ease the throbbing.

"Here." He moved one of my hands from my head and set two small capsules in the palm. I squinted up to find a glass of water held out as well. "It's Tylenol. It'll help."

I stared at the glass. I knew there was nothing in the water. He wouldn't do that to me. But still, I couldn't take it from his hand. My throat seemed to crack and bleed from dryness the longer I looked at the thirst-quenching goodness, but the battle raged in my mind. One side desperate for the relief the water would provide, the other flinging up horrible memories of being drugged and the days that followed.

The fear won.

With a sad smile, I looked to Benny, whose head rested on the couch with his dark brown eyes staring up. "Water," I said and pointed toward the kitchen. Like he was happy to be useful in the situation, he trotted to the kitchen. The scratching of his nails against wood made both men's heads swivel toward the kitchen just as Benny rounded the lower cabinets, bottle of water clutched between his jaws.

"If that dog can do that with a beer, I might steal him," Chandler laughed. The seat cushions popped up as he fell to the couch beside me and stretched a long arm down the back.

Now for the Tylenol. The water bottle crackled in my hand as I withdrew it from Benny's teeth. Holding it to my ear, I listened to the snapping of the plastic pieces before twisting the cap off and chugging half in one swig.

A loud pop of the bottle releasing from the pressure made me flinch. Inspecting the two white tablets in my hand, I hesitantly placed both on the back of my tongue and took a long gulp of water.

Seconds ticked by with none of us saying anything until I couldn't take it any longer.

"What happened?" I leaned back against the couch and massaged my temples with both thumbs. "I remember the chipmunks—" The now-clear memory shot me back up.

Cas cringed. "I took care of them," he said in a dead tone, and my heart broke all over again for the poor innocent creatures. "Hauled you down the mountain. Thank goodness the trail going down was easier than the way up. When you didn't wake up in the truck, I called this dipshit, brought you here. That was—" Looking over his shoulder toward the kitchen, he sighed. "—ten minutes ago."

If my math was right, which it probably wasn't, that meant I'd been out for over thirty minutes.

Goose bumps sprouted down my arms. I didn't realize I was rubbing my hands up and down them until a thick blanket covered me. Resting my chin on my shoulder, I smiled up at Cas. "Thank you."

"Listen, Birdie," Chandler said and leaned a little closer. "Mathews and I were talking it all over while you were out, and none of this makes sense. The bastard in the Smokies never stalked women this way, so it's odd that he's started with you."

"You think I'm lying?" I couldn't keep the hurt out of my voice. Before the notes started, I'd told my supervisor at the time about some random customer who gave me the creeps, which he blew off as me being a dramatic female. Then again when the notes began to appear. No one took me seriously until Dad stepped in and vouched for my... sanity, I guess.

"No." The coffee table made a pained groan as Cas's weight settled on the edge. Leaning forward, he gripped my hands in his and squeezed. "We need to know a few things though. Could this be in any way related to what happened in Texas ten years ago?"

I tugged the blanket tighter around my cold shoulders and gripped the edges in one hand to gnaw on the thumb of the other. "There's no way." I focused on a chip in the coffee table until it blurred in my vision. "He died."

"Are you sure?" Chandler pressed.

Still focused on the chipped wood, I nodded. "My roommate shot him in front of me. See, we'd made plans to meet up in Dallas before Thanksgiving, but I didn't show or answer any of her messages. Beth came back to school to make sure I was okay." Needing space, I stood on shaky legs and began to pace the room. "She walked in on him—" Embarrassment flooded my veins, heating my cheeks and urging me to tighten the blanket as a makeshift shield. I faced the wall. "He had me tied down on the bed and was too focused on me to notice her come through the front door. Not everything is clear because of how high he kept me those few days, but I remember the gunshots, all five of them."

"Your roommate happened to have a gun?" Chandler asked.

My shoulders rose and fell as I nodded and smiled. "That's a Texas woman for you. We're always packing. He was pronounced dead at the scene. Beth put five 9mm slugs in his chest."

"How'd—"

"Later they told me he spotted her and charged, leaving a clear shot for her." I cleared my throat. "So your answer is there's no way he could be a part of his. He's dead, really dead. And considering no one came forward to claim the body or charge Beth in a civil suit, I assume he didn't have any family."

"Peters will confirm," Cas said, still on the other side of the room.

My stomach sank at the distance between us.

"Anyone else know about what happened in Texas?" Peters asked.

Summoning up a bit of courage, I glanced over my shoulder. Cas stood with a shoulder against the wall, looking out the back window.

"John, I guess. I told him about it, and my friend Sarah, but she's in Denver now. Only those two. I don't open up about it a lot, but I trust them."

"We're done," Cas stated, still focused on something out the window. "You have enough to go off of, and the original file you gave me. Go do your motherfucking job and find out what this is all about."

Shocked at his rude tone and words, I swiveled around with a scowl, expecting to find a pissed-off Chandler, but it was the exact opposite. Smiling, he stood from the couch and tucked his T-shirt deeper into his jeans.

"Yep, I have what I need, and looks like you do too, fucker." Eyes locked with mine, his smile grew. "And you know what? I'm happy for you. Don't fuck it up." On his way to the door, Chandler stopped beside me. "I'll be back later tonight, but don't worry. We'll catch this guy."

"I'm as confused as you two. Why me? He didn't put this much effort into the other women."

"Maybe you're special," Chandler said, his happy smile dipping to a frown.

"I'm so fucking tired of being special," I whined. "I want to be normal. What is it about me that attracts men like this?"

"It's not about you." He gripped my shoulder and squeezed. "It's about them and power, nothing else. There's nothing you could've done differently. My guess is he saw you at a crime scene and has decided to have a little fun with you before attempting to snag you."

I pulled the blanket up to my mouth in hopes to cover my whimper.

"We won't let anything happen to you," Chandler said with a steely look of determination in his eyes. "And that guy"—he tipped his head toward the corner of the room where Cas stood, arms crossed, watching us—"is the best I've ever had the privilege of serving and working with. No one will get past him." A nod to Cas and he was gone.

Seconds after the door shut, I reached for the locks.

Once.

Twice.

At the third click of each deadbolt, I turned to lean my back against the door. Cas's dark eyes caught my immediate attention. Intensity pulsed between us. The air in the cabin shifted, heating my core as we gazed at each other in silence.

He moved first. Shoving off the door, I matched him step for step until we collided in the middle of the room. Arms around his waist, I nuzzled against his chest as he rested his chin on the crown of my head. The still mysterious unlimited warmth soaked into my skin, heating me to the bones.

"It'll be okay. We'll find out who's doing this, and I'll kill them."

My muscles tightened at the coldness in his words, so at odds to the firm, steady beat of the heart pounding in my ear.

"I don't want you to kill whoever's doing this."

His near scoff tightened his chest muscles beneath my cheek.

"I've seen what it does to someone. Each life you take, a piece of you fades, and I don't want that for you. Not for this. Not for me."

I gasped in surprise as he shoved me back and his fingers gripped my chin, holding me in place. Eyes blazing with an intimidating fury, he gritted out, "I'll go to Hell and back to keep you safe. Don't worry about my soul, Lady. It's already gone. But you." His dark eyes softened. "You're the one worth saving."

An ache radiated from my chest into my belly. "How could you even say that?" My eyes searched his, hoping to find some humor there, but I found none. "You're not gone. None of us are. Until we're dead in the ground, none of us are past the point of saving. Even you, Cas Mathews." Sometime during my passion-filled words, I had gripped his black T-shirt and fisted the soft cloth between my fingers.

Sadness engulfed his features, almost resembling pity. "Lady, I love your optimism. I do. But I know the truth. I was nothing when I came into this world, and I'll be nothing when I leave it. You're the only good thing I've had in my life, and even that's temporary."

Tears welled. "You think I'm good?" After everything, I needed to know a piece of me was still pure, still good.

"You're a motherfucking angel, Lady. Don't you ever forget it. You hear me?" His fingers tightened on my chin. "Not for one damn minute do you ever forget that you're the best person I've ever met."

I wasn't the type of woman to kiss a man—that took confidence in one's sexuality, which I lacked—yet I pressed to my tiptoes and pressed my dry lips against his anyway.

24

Cas

Without hesitation, I angled my head to seal my lips over hers, controlling our kiss. A soft moan of pleasure seeped from her lips into mine, sending a bolt of want straight to my cock. She was perfection embodied. I kissed her with the passion I felt for her, hoping she understood what I couldn't put into words. Nothing else mattered, just her and me, together. I could protect her against everything except me, which was the scariest threat of them all.

"Cas," she said against my lips.

"Lady."

"Tell me one thing."

"Anything." I meant it. Whatever she wanted, I'd tell her. I'd tell her government secrets to make her happy.

"Tell me that when this is all done, when the bad guy is caught and gone, that this feeling won't stop."

My lips paused. Eyes open, I waited for Alta's to meet mine. "We will never be done. Whatever this is between us is never-ending, I'll ache for you for eternity. I can't promise we'll be together." Gripping her hands, I wrapped both arms around my neck and pressed my forehead against hers. "But wherever I am, you'll be with me. Time, distance, even death can't stop me from thinking of you, from wanting you." My heart thundered against my chest. "I have no fucking idea what this is, but whatever it is, it's not temporary, that's for damn sure."

Her eyes sealed closed. "I'm... I'm scared."

"Of what?"

"My past, the memories, the sicko chasing me, you, the way I feel about you, what I want...." She swallowed hard as her hazel eyes fluttered open to meet mine. "What I want from you."

All the blood that flowed through my veins shifted straight to my cock. "And what is that, Lady?" My voice was so guttural, it didn't sound natural, or like my own.

Her voice shook. "Something I can't have." Tears welled in her sad eyes. "I'm sorry I'm so damaged that I can't—"

Instead of refuting her with words, I poured my overpowering desire for her, and all the broken slivers she believed were ugly instead of the beauty I found in the damage, from my lips to hers. Sucking, nipping soft and slow, savoring each delectable bit of her plump lips, I ate up the soft moan she released as she pressed closer.

"Do you trust me?" I asked as I sucked down her neck. Fuck, she tasted like innocence—sweet and perfect.

"Yes." The lack of hesitation and her clawing at my arms, begging me to squeeze her tighter, confirmed her quick response.

My hands trembled with tremendous restraint to not strip her out of her damn clothes right there in the living room. Fingertips against her back, I brushed lower and lower down her tight T-shirt. A groan escaped as I gripped each of her perky ass cheeks. Not caring about my injured hand, I squeezed each one and lifted her. Immediately, muscular, lean legs wrapped around my waist, squeezing the breath from my lungs.

One step.

One fucking step was as far as I got before my cell rang through the small cabin.

"Fuck," I grunted. Set to ignore the interruption, I strode across the room while it continued to ring. A sigh of relief brushed across her neck, only for it to turn into a groan when the phone began ringing again. Still ignoring it, I shoved her back against the wall of the short hallway, pressing my rock-hard cock against her and grinding firmly.

"Oh my," Alta breathed with a content sigh. "Yes."

The phone stopped ringing only to pick back up its cock-blocking shrill tone.

Every curse word ever invented sailed through my head. Heat from my forehead sizzled against the chill of hers. "I have to get that." Each inch her perfect tits and warm center slid down my body was torture.

When her feet safely reached the ground, I planted a rough kiss on the top of her head and stormed toward the still-ringing phone. Annoyance played with the fuse to my anger, leaving me fidgety and on edge, which was the worst possible combination with Alta in the room. I was going to explode, and no fucking way did I want her there when it happened.

I accepted her the way she was, but there was no way I could ask that of her in return. She was perfect; I was a motherfucking atomic bomb.

"What," I snapped the second I put the phone to my ear.

"Interrupting something?" Peters said in a steely tone that immediately caught my attention, raising caution flags.

"What happened?"

Alta tiptoed closer with questions in her eyes.

"Who is it?" she whispered once she was by my side.

Ignoring her question, I turned my back to her and focused on Peters.

"Another woman went missing. Be ready in fifteen." The line went dead.

Holding the phone out, I stared at the blank screen. "Another woman went missing," I stated, monotone. "Peters will be here in fifteen minutes."

The sound of something falling onto the couch made me turn. Alta sat on the old worn couch with a hand covering her mouth.

"When? Where?" she asked from behind her hand.

"He didn't give any details." My gaze traveled from her disheveled hair—I wasn't too gentle when I ripped the hat from her head earlier—to her long-sleeve T-shirt and jeans. "Get dressed. You're coming with me."

"What? I'm suspended."

Glaring down, I widened my stance and crossed both arms across my chest. A flick of lust-filled heat flashed in her eyes, stirring my cock back into action. "If you think I give a shit about what that asshat John has to say, you're wrong. I'm not leaving you unprotected. You're coming with us, and that's final, Lady." I pointed toward her bedroom. "Go get changed. It's grown colder since the sun's set, and it looks like a storm's blowing in."

A mischievous smile played on her lips, making her look even more irresistible.

"Yes, sir."

"Go." I jabbed my finger for emphasis.

Against my better judgment, I watched each of her steps, loving the way her ass bounced.

"I need a fucking cigarette," I mumbled to myself. The dog perked up, eyeing me from where he lay on a massive bed in the corner of the room. "Seriously, I get it. It's going to kill me. Stop it with the guilt trip."

Not dropping his stare, I walked back toward the door. The second my hand wrapped around the doorknob, I swear he shook his head in disappointment.

Outside, the wind whipped through the trees as the first glimpses of the moon peeked over the mountains. I snagged the spare pack I left on the windowsill and pulled a cigarette out with my teeth before tossing the rest back to my not-so-secret hiding spot.

Cancerous smoke filled my lungs, easing the tension from the day.

That woman kept me on my toes, that was for sure. From the second I pulled into her driveway that morning till now, it was nonstop. And that incident with the mountain lion.... I huffed a laugh as I slid the butt of the cigarette back and forth over my lower lip. She was a mess, a highly entertaining mess.

Headlights cut through the dark, signaling Peters's arrival. Steeling my frustration at him for the interruption of my next few hours, I leaned against the post and watched as he climbed out of the SUV.

"You look murderous." Not that he seemed to care with his constant knowing smirk. "Don't kill the fucking messenger, okay."

Instead of confirming what he already knew, I sealed my lips around the cigarette and took a deep inhale.

"You ready?"

"Waiting on her." I tilted my head toward the cabin. "She needed to change."

"Her wet—"

"Careful," I said in a tone that cut through his shit.

He sighed. "You're no fun like this." With a wave of his hand, he gestured up and down my face with a cringe. "But you weren't the other way either, so I guess there isn't any change in your normal sour attitude. Either way, I didn't make this shit happen. We have a job to do, and duty calls."

"I get that duty fucking calls," I seethed. "What do we know?"

"Nothing." I shot him a glare. "Fuck, man, all they said was a man reported his wife missing this afternoon. Somehow my office found out about it, called me, and I called the Estes Park police station. The lead investigator isn't giving me shit since I'm not a cop, which is where you come in. I need you to strong-arm this asshole captain into giving us all the details of the case."

Around us, darkness blanked the area along with a thick cloud cover, sealing off the moon's bright rays. Dampness in the air mixed with the cold mountain wind made everything feel heavy and foretelling—though of what, I had no idea. Everything was off about this guy and his fascination with Alta. The fucker had gone off the rails, which was never a good thing.

We had to figure out the connection, if there was one, and get ahead of this bastard before he tried to snag her. So far, the note and creepy mutilated rat heart were all he'd done, but at some point that wouldn't be enough. He'd escalate, and that fucking scared the shit out of me. This wasn't battle; it was fucking guerrilla warfare. We had no way to fight him except to be on guard at all times.

"I'll get the information." The tip of the cigarette singed the ends of my fingertips as I pinched it off before tossing the butt into the ashtray. "Give us a second."

Inside, the dry, hot air seared the inside of my nostrils. "You ready?" I called out impatiently. "Peters is here."

My breath caught when she rounded the short corner from her bedroom into the living room. Long, bright strawberry-blonde hair cascaded over her shoulders, which directed my gaze straight to the sweater's V–neck, showing off a hint of pale-skinned cleavage. The red sweater brought out the unique hues of her hair and gave her hazel eyes more of a green tint than brown.

"I'm used to wearing my uniform or sweatshirts everywhere," she said, making her pale, freckled cheeks flame pink. "Is this okay?"

"You're beautiful." Understatement of the year.

The pink of her cheeks turned a bright red.

Extending a hand, I urged her closer. The moment she was within arm's reach, I pulled her flush against me, allowing her to feel just how 'okay' I thought her choice of outfit was.

"If any of the officers look at you—"

Her hand slammed against my chest with a force that knocked the breath from my lungs. "They all know me. And this late at night, why would anyone be at the station?"

Shit.

"We're not going to the ranger station."

"Then where?"

"The Estes Park police station."

All the color drained from her face. "I'll go get my hat—"

"Don't you fucking dare."

"Cas," she said while nibbling at the edge of her thumb.

The nervous energy radiating off her spoke to her rising fear. This woman who was born to stand out was terrified of allowing her natural beauty to shine, all because of one fuckstick. With a grip on her hand, I tugged her toward the door. "Don't worry. You look extraordinarily ordinary."

The corners of her lips twitched. "You sure? Because the rest of your body doesn't seem to agree."

"Positive, Lady."

Peters's eyes lit up in surprise and appreciation—the fucker—as she stepped out onto the porch behind me. I gave a slight shake of my head, and he cleared his throat and looked toward the SUV.

"Seriously, Birdie," Peters sighed. "Couldn't you've dressed up or something? Dressed like that, maybe we can take you to McDonald's or something after we're done."

I watched as her smirk grew into a full-blown smile. "Sounds perfect."

The ride to the station turned awkward the moment we were all piled into the Suburban. Not a word was said the entire thirty-minute drive, the pelting of ice against the windshield and roof from the forming storm the only sound in the confined space. My thoughts were too consumed by the case and preparing for a battle at the police station for idle conversation.

The brakes squeaked as Peters slowed to back into a tight parking space.

"Let me do the talking," I said, rubbing a hand down my face. "I have no idea what kind of resistance, if any, we'll face inside. Most cops don't like someone like me snooping around on their turf. And Alta?"

She swiveled in the passenger seat. Apprehension glimmered in her bright eyes.

Fuck, she was gorgeous.

"Don't talk to a single person in there. You're still suspended, so technically you shouldn't be here, but stay close. I don't want you out of my sight. Peters, I'll make sure you get the information you need."

At that, I flung the door open and stepped out into the freezing drizzle. Peters and Alta followed suit. I hugged her close to shield her from the blasting wind, and we jogged in sync to the front doors.

25

Alta

I DIDN'T SMOKE. Never even tried it in high school or college.

But right now in the freezing temperatures, with the eerie fog descending on the small parking lot, the idea of a cigarette seemed nice. More than nice, it felt necessary.

Rotating to peer over my shoulder, I sighed. Cas and Chandler were still locked in conversation with the police chief. It ate at my anxious nerves not knowing if this case was connected to the others, but I had to wait. Soon I'd know what they knew.

Headlights beamed through the thick fog as a truck pulled into the back of the parking lot. Only the bright beams were visible as it sat there idling. Lights still on, the driver door swung open. Shielding my eyes from the brightness, I watched as a familiar gait ambled closer.

"Birdie?"

At John's voice, I pressed up from where I slumped against the metal railing to stand straight. "John? What are you doing here?"

Halfway up the stairs, he stopped. "You look... different."

At my nod, he continued up the final few steps, which was when I noticed he looked different too. Dressed in slacks, a pressed button-up and a nice coat, and smelling divine too, this John standing in front of me was a far cry from the division manager I was used to seeing—and sometimes harassing—on a daily basis.

"You have a hot date tonight or something?" I joked, trying to ease the weird tension that settled between us. Only it made it worse. His cheeks, already red from the cold wind, blushed even further. "Oh." Right, stepped into that one.

"She's in the truck," he said with a resigned sigh. "Agent Peters said someone in town went missing, and I wanted to see if it had anything to do with the cases in the park."

"Me too," I mused before glancing back to the idling truck. "I don't know how much longer they'll be. I can tell Chandler to give you a call after, if you want to get back to your date."

"Nah." He leaned against the railing that was barely protected from the storm. "I like her, don't get me wrong. It's just this case is... consuming, you know."

I nodded.

After a few seconds of silence, he looked over his shoulder through the glass doors.

"So you and the USPP guy."

I raised a shoulder and nodded. "He's not what you think."

John let out a sarcastic laugh. "Funny, that's what I was going to tell you."

Annoyance at his words pricked at my patience. "I'm going inside." The cold railing bit into my bare palms as I shoved against it.

"Wait." John tugged on my wrist, pulling me to a halt. "I'm sorry, it's just... for so long... then he showed up and now everything's... different. I want you to look at me the way you look at him." His Adam's apple bobbed as he swallowed.

"John," I breathed. Hand over my heart, I pressed hard to keep it from pounding out of my chest. "I can't explain it. He makes me feel whole again."

"How?" he said through clenched teeth. "You've known him all of a fucking week, Alta. I've known you for two years. What in the hell does he offer that I don't? I love you, not him."

My head drooped, allowing my hair to shield me from his exploring eyes. The answer was simple. Cas didn't want to fix me, didn't see me as damaged or give me sympathy. No, Cas accepted me and wanted me, all of it. All the broken bits.

"He—"

"You love her?"

We both whirled toward the bottom of the stairs, where Sadie stood glaring at us.

John hurried down toward her. "Sadie, sorry, I—"

"I thought you said we were here because of the missing women case, not her," Sadie said, staring past John's shoulder straight to me. Even in the little light from the flickering bulbs on either side of the doors, her hatred was apparent.

My stomach rolled as unease settled with a bit of fear mixed in. Sarah was right, this chick was unhinged. No way did I want to instigate Sadie to show her true crazy.

John's voice turned apologetic as he lowered his tone to talk to her without me overhearing.

My frozen hands and numb nose confirmed it was time to go back inside. Initially, I stepped out to get some air away from the stale coffee and day-old donut smells. It was all too similar to the station back home, where I'd visited several times after everything went down in my apartment. Even though no one pressed charges against Beth, lots of paperwork and interviews were needed to make sure the self-defense case was airtight.

Inside the quilted lined pockets of my coat, I worked on shredding each thumb's cuticle. "I'm going—"

The two doors at my back swung open, a burst of warm air blowing over my shoulders rustling my hair.

"What the hell are you doing out here?" Cas demanded. Even with my fluffy coat, his grip on my bicep felt tighter than necessary.

"Needed air," I said, yanking my arm from his grasp before massaging where his hand had been.

Realization flicked behind his eyes as he watched my movements. "Sorry." Bandaged hand scrubbing at his face, he said, "Don't walk away like that again, please."

"Did he hurt you?" John stormed up the stairs, making a beeline for me.

"Can everyone just calm down for a second?" I said, my words dripping with pure annoyance. "What did you two find out in there?"

"You're not working this case—"

"Fucking hell," I yelled, cutting John off. Everyone quieted. I never cussed. Guess Cas was a bad influence after all, but hey, it got them to shut up. "Stop it, would you? I'm sorry you're not in control anymore, and I'm sorry it's not going the way you wanted, but stop." Face burning, I turned to Cas, who wore a cocky smirk. "And you." His smirk fell. "You could see me the entire time, so don't act like I was breaking any of your rules. And not only that, but I highly doubt the guy doing all this is stupid enough to snatch me in front of a police station!"

The freezing rain trickled in the parking lot as a gust of cold wind barreled through the five of us.

"Wow," Chandler said, allowing a minute of the other two men's quiet sulking to pass. "It's a mix of *Law and Order* and *Jerry Springer* out here tonight. If you two are done upsetting my friend Birdie, I say we take this somewhere warmer. If we stand out here discussing everything we just learned, I might never see my dick again."

THE CONSTANT YELLING around the sports bar rang in my ears as someone scored, sending the crowd into near hysterics. Had to hand it to Chandler—this was the perfect place, neutral ground for Cas and John to discuss the case without anyone overhearing our conversation. Heck, we'd have to yell at each other as it was.

A young server with her boobs pushing out of the top of the deep

V-neck uniform bounced up to our table, eyeing the three men. Immediately Sadie's arm snaked around John, claiming him as hers, in case the death stares weren't enough.

"Hi, I'm Becky, and I'll be helping you all tonight. Want to start with some body shots?" she asked while laying a few cocktail napkins around the table. "I have the perfect place." Eyes twinkling, Becky looked to Cas.

"Whatever IPA you have on draft," Cas responded while looking at his phone. I couldn't stop the smirk that crept up my lips, which of course Chandler caught and returned.

"Same," Chandler said, still smiling like a fool with a secret.

John ordered some light beer while Sadie ordered a white wine. Cold wine in this dreary weather—no thanks. Becky didn't bother looking up from her notepad when it came to my turn.

"Bottled water, please."

"We're out."

"Oh, um, okay. How about sparkling bottled water?"

"Aren't you the life of the party?" Becky grumbled under her breath.

My cheeks burned hot. Under the table, I tucked both hands under my thighs to keep them still.

"You know what, I changed my mind," Cas said, now very interested in the conversation. "I'll have the same as my girlfriend here." He nodded my way before leaning in for a quick peck on the cheek.

"Same goes for me," Chandler said. "That's all."

Embarrassment shifted her earlier snarky attitude to a humble one as she turned on her black sneakers and sulked toward the bar.

"Where do you get your hair done?" Sadie asked out of nowhere.

Eyes a bit wide, I shook my head and said, "I don't."

"It's really pretty."

Dang, where was that water? My throat was on fire. "Thanks."

"Out with it, Agent Peters," John said while eyeing Sadie and me. "Is it the same guy or not?"

Chandler's smile dropped, turning his features grim. "Looks like it. The husband remembered seeing a note earlier in the week, but like all the others, he dismissed it. We didn't get to meet with the guy in person, so I can't say for sure if he fits the physical type. She went missing earlier this morning, never came home from a morning run through the trails."

A shiver of dread snapped my shoulders up to my ears. "Which... which trail?" I asked, even though I knew the answer. There was no way this was all a coincidence.

"One the park just renovated, Lilly something," Chandler said absentmindedly.

John's blue eyes shot to me. "Birdie."

"I know," I breathed, which was becoming more and more difficult. An invisible weight settled on my chest, applying pressure. With a fist against my breastbone, I pressed hard in an attempt to alleviate the building tension.

"What?" Cas and Chandler said in unison.

Short wheezes kept me from gaining a full breath. A heavy hand rested on my thigh and squeezed. Focusing on the heat pouring from him to me, on the simple touch I now craved, the pressure eased, allowing a full breath to fill my lungs.

"It's her favorite running trail," Sadie chimed in. Everyone at the table—excluding Sadie, who looked to be enjoying my discomfort—watched with concern in their eyes.

What the...? How in the heck did she know that?

"Why... why does it keep coming back to me?" I bit out, anger quickly replacing the diminishing fear.

The table fell silent. No one knew, which meant we were nowhere closer to catching this guy than we were yesterday or the day before that.

"It started in Tennessee and now followed you here," Chandler said solemnly. "I'm beginning to think it does have something to do with you. Maybe this guy saw you in Tennessee, or maybe one of your friends?"

"I don't have friends," I gritted out. Once again, the table fell silent as Becky deposited the round of drinks to our table. Holding the cap close to my ear, I listened for the crackle of plastic teeth, ensuring it wasn't tampered with. Satisfied, I lifted the bottle to my lips, allowing the crisp bubbles to soothe my dry throat. "I didn't have any there for sure."

"Question," Sadie said and leaned against the table. The green sweater drew out the brightness of her cunning green eyes. Something was alluring about her, something that pulled you in, much like a black widow spider or colorful venomous snakes. "Why isn't Alta dead yet?"

Cas slammed his glass bottle on the table while Chandler mopped up the dribble that had escaped his gaping mouth with a cocktail napkin.

I slid across the stool, putting more distance between Sadie and me. "What?"

"I mean, based on what's going on here, you should be dead, right? Sounds like someone's playing with you. Kind of like a cat with a mouse." With a sad smile, she added, "I love the way cats stalk their prey. Mesmerizing to watch."

Half my right butt cheek was off the stool as I continued to slide closer to the safety of Cas.

"Right," Chandler said, looking at Sadie like her head might start spinning with green vomit spewing from her lips. "We figure out how this is all tied to Birdie. Once we do, then we'll find our guy. I'll request every file you touched that last year you were in the Smokies. Which reminds me, you've never told us why you left for Colorado."

Unable to stop myself, I raised a thumb to my lips to gnaw on the edges. "I just needed a change. My routine is no routine, so no one can follow you or learn your schedule. In the Smokies, it just started to feel too... safe, I guess. Which told me I needed to change things up. I applied here and a few other parks, but Rocky Mountain National Park called me first."

"What kind of shampoo do you use?" Sadie asked, throwing me off balance.

"What?"

"It smells really good." To my horror, she leaned in close, dragged her fingers through the ends and held it close to her nose. "Don't you like it, John?"

Stunned into silence, John simply nodded.

Crazy eyes met mine. "I want some. Tell me where you got it."

"Walmart, I think," I whispered.

"What about your perfume?"

"I'm not wearing any."

Sadie's dark brows furrowed together. "How convenient for you."

"Thanks?"

The boys struck up a side conversation, probably to avoid the creepy one I was trapped in.

Leaning closer, Sadie propped an elbow on the table and rested her chin on her hand. With a smile, most likely to make it look like a happy conversation, though I knew right away it wouldn't be, she whispered, "I don't care that he loves you. He'll love me more in the end. They always do."

The noises of the bar came roaring back to life as I watched her lean back against John's shoulder with a menacing smirk.

Chandler was quick to discount my thoughts of the person abducting the women being a woman or at least a killing team, but I wasn't.

I had to find a way to tie her back to Tennessee. There had to be one. Sadie had to be a part of it in some way.

Because this was real life, not some stupid horror movie. I mean, what were the odds of two psychopaths being in the same small town?

26

Alta

Streetlights and darkened storefronts whizzed by outside the window on our way back home. After Sadie's comments, the impromptu meeting only lasted long enough for someone to snag the waitress and pay the bill. Even Cas and Chandler couldn't get out of there fast enough.

"I see what you meant by creepy," Chandler said while trying to stifle a yawn with a fist against his lips. Wrist on top of the steering wheel, he weaved in and out of the late-evening traffic. "I still don't think she has anything to do with the case and everything happening with you, but no doubt there's something going on there." Switching hands, he shifted in his seat to lean closer to the center console. "I'll check her out. If not for your sake, John's. He's an idiot getting involved with that level of crazy."

A part of me felt validated that it wasn't only me who saw her crazy, but another part felt sorry for her. If Sarah's story was true about Sadie running from a bad relationship, maybe she was just a bit broken like me and didn't know how to be normal.

The two men joked back and forth about the various crazies they dated in the past, but I tuned them out to stare out the window into the growing darkness as we drove out of town.

Everything had to be linked to me. But why? Who did I piss off so badly in Tennessee that he started abducting women, one of whom was a federal officer, and followed me here? Ever since Chandler brought up going through my files from that final year, I tried to recall anything memorable from those last twelve months, but nothing came to mind.

"Most women go their whole lives without being the object of someone's obsession," I said to no one in particular. My hot breath fogged a small patch of the cold window. With my pinkie finger, I made two dots for eyes and a frown before it vanished. "And here I am having it happen twice in less than a decade."

Silence reigned for the rest of the drive. Sadness at the situation I'd somehow found myself in again settled deep, making my thoughts heavy. A single tear slipped from the inside corner of my eye, leaving a damp trail down my cheek. Not wanting the two to notice me quietly breaking, I swiped it away with the back of my hand, removing the evidence of my weakness.

By the time the loose gravel of the drive up to my cabin rattled under the tires, my eyelids were almost too heavy to keep open until the Suburban slammed to a halt, throwing me against the seat belt with a jolt.

"What the—"

Every nerve shifted from sleepy to high alert at the familiar slide of a gun engaging. Shifting to look around the SUV, my eyes widened at Cas and Chandler situating their clips and handguns like they were about to head into battle.

"Stay in the car, Alta," Cas commanded. "Chandler, on my six."

"What—"

"Lock the doors after us," Chandler said in a tense, no-nonsense tone he hadn't used before.

First my fingers, then my whole hand trembled. It started making its way up my arms as the two stepped out into the elements. The leather seat groaned as I shifted to watch the two stalk toward the front door of my cabin, using pointed hand gestures to communicate.

Only then did I notice the cabin. A sliver of light from the inside shone through a gap between the door and the frame. I studied the bit of light, brows furrowed, trying to make sense of what was happening.

Either Cas forgot to shut the door when we left, or...

Someone had broken in.

The two men prowled up the steps. Dread dropped in my stomach like a lead weight.

What if the person was still in there?

Hand against my thundering chest, I watched in fear as they entered the house.

I waited. No gunfire, no shouting or them running out. But something was off. I could feel it.

I gasped.

Benny.

I held a breath, waiting anxiously for his familiar snout to pop out the door in search for me. But it didn't. Seconds ticked by without a single sign of my furry best friend.

Desperation to see his dark eyes and feel his rough tongue forced me out of the SUV. Shoulder against the door, I shoved it open, damning the consequences Cas would rain down at disobeying his order.

One cautious step, then another, I stalked toward the door, internally begging for Benny to bound out and prove my fears wrong.

A dark shimmer of something wet on the gravel beneath my feet snagged my attention. Not paying the ripping wind any mind, I squatted low and pressed two fingers to the dark spot.

Dread churned my stomach as I held those two fingers toward the light.

Blood.

A faint whimper somehow escaped on a pushed breath. The

gravel crunched beneath my boots as I swiveled on the balls of my feet in search of more. Two feet away, there was another small puddle, then another a few more feet from that, all leading toward the dark cover of the forest.

The wind howled, shoving freezing air into my already-burning lungs. Phone in hand, I switched on the flashlight feature to follow the dark puddles of blood farther and farther from the safety of the cabin and the two men still inside. The earlier sleet and dusting of snow highlighted the tracks, making them easier to follow. At the edge of the trees, I paused and turned, debating my next move.

It was precisely the type of situation the killer we were after would use to pull me away from Cas and Chandler. I knew it. My head knew it. But my heart... my heart was desperate to find my only true friend.

A faint, pained whine dissolved any building hesitation.

Ignoring the part of my brain screaming at me to turn around and run *to* Cas instead of farther away from him, I pushed back the low-hanging branches and stepped into the trees. Naked branches and twigs snagged at my coat and pulled at my loose hair. The light trembled along the leaf-covered terrain due to my nerves and the freezing temperatures.

My lungs burned. Pausing to catch a quick breath, I closed my eyes to heighten my other senses and waited for any hint of Benny. The faint rustling of leaves snapped my head to the right.

Shoving forward, I kept an ear open for Cas and Chandler, hoping they'd figure out I abandoned the SUV and came searching.

"Benny?" I questioned with a sob when the faint light scanned over his bloody, prone body. My knees hit the cold earth, dampness soaking through my jeans and freezing my palms as I crawled closer to him.

A low, pained cry pierced my aching heart as he attempted to lift his head toward the sound of my voice.

My heart shattered as I took in the pool of blood he lay in. The tears I held back up to that point drenched my icy cheeks.

"Shh," I whispered, pulling him close to my chest. Cold. He was way too cold. Falling on my backside, I carefully pulled his limp body onto my legs to get him off the ground. Ripping off my coat, I flung it over his blood-slick body. "Benny?"

No movement. No response

"And here I thought getting you away from those two would be more difficult," a man's voice said from the darkness.

Terror locked all my muscles; even my lungs stopped working. My vocal cords were silenced by fear, preventing me from screaming out for the guys.

This was it. This was how it happened. I knew coming out here was a bad idea, but still, I did it.

A low, short growl sounded from my lap. I tugged Benny's large frame closer, feeling somehow protected even if he could barely move. A branch snapped somewhere behind me, but I couldn't will my body to turn, too afraid of what I would find. Something brushed through my hair, tugging at the long strands like fingers catching on the knotted mess. A cold deeper than Colorado had ever offered chilled my back, freezing my spine.

"So pretty," the voice said with an evil chuckle. "Soon. I'm beginning to like the hunt too."

"Why?" I somehow got out, my voice barely louder than the wind. "Why me?"

"Not bright though." Fabric-covered fingers wrapped around the back of my neck, tilting my head at an odd angle. "We'll have so much fun. They all did." The slide of wet fingers across my face forced my eyes closed and my mouth sealed shut.

I was going to die right there in the woods.

"Alta!" Cas yelled from somewhere in the dark. Footsteps thundered through the underbrush, growing closer.

Without the protection of my coat, my teeth chattered, threatening to shatter, and my body seized tighter around the whimpering dog in my lap. What felt like hours later, the ground shuddered beneath me. Frozen and lost in the certainty of my death, I barely registered Cas's face in mine, hands cupping my cheeks.

"Alta," he gritted out. The hands holding me trembled, or maybe it was me. "What the fuck are you—"

Unable to get words out about the killer, the looming threat, I focused on the bloody mass of fur in my arms. "Benny?" I begged. "Benny, wake up, buddy." Slick wetness coated my hands each time I rubbed down his furry chest.

Still too cold. Tugging him closer, I wrapped both arms around his neck and tucked his limp head beneath my chin. Only the short puffs of air against my neck told me he was holding on.

"Alta." Sympathy dripped in his tone. "He's gone."

"No," I gritted out. "He's breathing!" I carefully shifted his heavy frame to the ground so I could stand. "We need to get him to the vet. Now!" I screamed. "Save him. Somebody save him. Please."

Two hands dipped beneath my arms and hauled me up. I clenched my teeth as more and more anger flowed through my blood. "Get off me," I yelled. Jerking my arms back, my elbow slammed into something hard, and the hands restraining me released enough for me to squirm to freedom. Before I could kneel, strong arms wrapped around mine like a vise, holding them to my sides as I floated in the air.

"Stop," I screamed while flailing my legs and shoulders to get out of the person's hold. Sobbing, my tears mixed with mucus from my nose as I repeated Benny's name over and over. Maybe he didn't hear me. He could be okay, just asleep. Yeah, asleep.

"He has to be okay. He has to be," I repeated.

"Take her back to the cabin," Cas ordered. His voice cracked at the end, giving away the flood of emotions he wouldn't let show. "Fuck, where is he bleeding?" With the light from his phone, he searched through Benny's blood-matted fur. "There." He tossed his phone to the ground, ripped off his shirt and shoved it against the still-seeping wound. "I'll get him to an animal hospital." With that, Cas scooped Benny up with ease and sprinted in the direction of the cabin.

I screamed at nothing in particular, needing an outlet for the fear and sorrow bubbling inside me. "Tell them to save him," I pleaded. "He has to be okay. He's my best friend."

"Okay, Birdie, okay." All the fight drained what little energy I had left from the day, making me turn limp in Chandler's arms. "Birdie?"

His voice grew muffled in my thundering ears. Every muscle tensed as shock took hold, violently jolting me in his arms. Soon we were moving. My bones and teeth rattled with each stomp through the dead leaves and rocky terrain. The soul-snuffing numbness I never wanted to feel again settled like a thick, impenetrable fog, shutting down each muscle one by one.

By the time Chandler stomped up the cabin steps with me still in his arms, nothing had obeyed my command. Only the involuntary reflex of breathing kept me alive.

And at that point, I prayed my lungs would follow suit, allowing me to slip into the peace only death could grant.

27

Cas

Dried blood, patches of fur, and streaks of mud coated the expanse of my chest and up both arms. The heaviness of Benny's dead weight triggered long-buried memories. Each step with him in my arms was almost too painful to endure. All I could do in the grueling five-minute sprint back to the cabin as I ducked and weaved through the trees and rocks was relate his weight to that of a dead soldier, a dead friend.

Those were the painful, ugly wounds I kept locked away, hidden from those who would see it as a weakness. Alone, I was stronger. Alone, I was free. And the sadness draining my heart due to the gravely injured dog in my arms was a rude reminder of what happened when I got too close.

After racing through town I screeched the Suburban into the parking lot of a twenty-four-hour vet hospital, barreled through the double doors with Benny in my arms. I didn't say a single word. I couldn't. The woman behind the desk did a wide-eyed double take before springing into action, yelling at doctors and me to hurry back. Loss engulfed me as his limp body slid from my arms onto the operating table. Staring down, I gave myself five seconds to mourn the dog who didn't deserve the pain he was in. Four seconds—I allowed tears to well as my heart clenched for the woman who could potentially lose her best friend. Three seconds—I let one tear slip through. Two seconds—bending forward, I brushed the thick fur of Benny's neck, silently vowing to protect her with my life until he could once again. One second—one last pat on the head, one final goodbye before someone tugged me away. Nurses and doctors huddled around him, not paying me any attention now that they had him.

I left my number, credit card information, and specific instructions on evidence I wanted collected from Benny with the wide-eyed receptionist. Following her gaze, I winced at my still-bare chest. With a final reminder to call me with any updates, I pushed through the heavy metal doors and climbed back into the SUV, desperate to get back to my Lady.

At the cabin, I paused at the first porch step to roll both shoulders, hoping to ease the painful tension in my aching muscles. Eyes closed, I mentally prepared myself for what needed to happen next. Seeing her in shambles earlier shredded a piece of my heart I didn't even know existed, and it hurt like I never imagined emotional pain could cause. But I had to go in there. I had to take care of my Lady, even if I would rather die than see her in agony again.

A pang of dread reverberated through my core with each step toward the door.

I was a fucking marine, yet I was terrified to walk into a cabin with zero hostiles, all because seeing the woman I loved in pain had the potential to kill me faster than ten automatic rifles pointed at my chest.

The door creaked faintly as I pushed it open wide with two fingers.

Stealing whatever bit of courage I could muster, I stepped into the cabin.

Chandler's laser-focused eyes were sad and red-rimmed. Slowly, he lowered the 9mm, allowing it to rest beside him on the couch. Still in his arms, tucked against his chest, Alta blinked at the ceiling without a single response as I moved closer.

"She can't stay here tonight," I said, grimacing at her blood-streaked face.

Chandler nodded.

"I'll get her cleaned up. You pack her a bag," I nodded back in the direction of her room. "We need to get someone from the crime lab to the animal hospital. "Just hearing it made a low sob bubble from Alta's throat. Clearing my own, I looked over Chandler's shoulder to focus out the back windows. "Even if that dog were on his last breath, he would've fought back. I bet my life and yours that there's evidence on him. Saving him comes first, then evidence."

Again Chandler stayed quiet, nodding as I spoke, telling me he heard it all.

Shaking out the numbness in both hands, I reached out and tucked them under Alta's shoulders and legs. Mixed feelings of relief and trepidation swept through me as I curled her body to my chest.

Shit, she was cold.

My lips pursed at the sight of her blue-rimmed lips and glassy eyes. *Shit, shit, shit.* Storming to the bathroom, I gently sat her on top of the counter. I steadied Alta with one hand so she didn't fall while I fumbled blindly behind the shower curtain with the other, turning the faucet all the way hot.

Within seconds, steam billowed through the room.

"I have to get these clothes off you," I whispered, running a hand down her tangled hair. Blood coated her pretty red sweater and the small patch of exposed pale skin that had tempted me all night. "We need to get you warm." And clean, but preventing hypothermia was the most important.

Taking her nonresponse as permission, I tugged the sweater off while somehow managing to keep her upright on the counter. The jeans proved challenging, but I managed to get those, her socks and boots off without incident. With a flick of my fingers, her bra fell to the ground, adding to the pile of clothes.

"Alta." I held her chin and tilted so her glassy gaze met mine. "I'm going to put you in the shower, okay? It might sting at first since you're so cold, but we have to get you warm."

The hot water pricked my numb fingers, sending jolts of pain through them as I lowered her into the tub. Angling the shower head for the water to rinse the dried blood and dirt off her arms and chest, I rinsed my hands too. She was still unresponsive, so I shifted through the stupid amount of half-empty bottles along the tub in search for shampoo.

With a muttered curse, I gave up reading the tiny labels and snagged a bottle of something that looked like shampoo, squirting a massive amount into my palm. Gentler than I ever thought I could be, I massaged the soap into her scalp and pulled it down to the tips of her hair. Twigs and leaves floated along the bottom of the tub as I rinsed out the thick suds.

I made quick work of cleaning her face, neck, and chest before tackling her blood-caked hands.

"You gotta be fucking kidding me," I muttered under my breath as I scrubbed and rewashed beneath her fingernails to remove the last bits of Benny's blood.

The color in her cheeks returned, as did the pretty pink tint of her lips as I rinsed her one more time to make sure all evidence of the night was washed down the drain.

The shower handle squeaked as I shut it off.

"I need you to stand up so I can dry you off," I whispered against her wet ears. "I can't do this without your help."

Her faint nod was all the acknowledgment she gave before leaning forward and using the sides of the tub as leverage to help her stand. Easing her out, I wrapped a large multicolored towel around her shoulders. With another, I kneeled at her feet to wipe up the streams of water still pouring off her onto the wet floor.

Steam billowed from the bathroom as we stepped out into the small hallway. Chandler wisely kept his eyes on his cell phone as we shuffled toward her room.

"Everything all set?"

"Just waiting for you two," he said with a sigh. "Working on the evidence piece now."

Less than five minutes later, I had her dressed in some old sweat pants I found in a bottom drawer and my marine's sweatshirt that was discarded on the floor.

Alta in my arms, I marched out of the cabin with Chandler at my side, gun at the ready. Neither of us relaxed until we were situated in the Suburban with the doors locked. It was a false sense of security, but it was better than being in the cabin, where the asshat had already proved he could break in and do whatever the hell he wanted.

I needed to tell her about the note we had found inside, but not now. Hell, she wouldn't even remember it right now. Still not a single word. And who could blame her? Fuck, *I* was traumatized, and I'd known the dog only a little over a week.

Curled against my chest, Alta shifted to taking deep and even breaths halfway to our cabin.

"She fell asleep," I murmured to Chandler as we pulled to a stop.

"That's good. It's been a hell of a day for her," he said, sounding just as exhausted. "I feel like a complete fuckup that I haven't caught this guy yet, for her sake."

"It's not your fault," I sighed, tugging her closer. "This guy is so fucking evasive, but we'll get him. I'm willing to bet my left nut that Benny scored us some blood evidence of some kind."

"I've never seen you like this, so connected." Back against the driver door, he watched me watch her. "Not many women can put up with our level of issues." His eyes shifted to look out the windshield. "I think it'd be nice to find someone who knew how fucked up you were but wanted you just the same. And after getting to know that one in your arms, I don't think it has anything to do with her past. It's just her. She's so naïve, so innocent that she only sees the good in us."

"Yeah." Careful not to wake her, I brushed a lock of strawberry-blonde hair from her forehead. "Nothing can happen to her."

"Nothing will happen to her."

"I still don't trust myself sleeping with her, but I don't want her to wake up alone." Defeated, I hung my head. "Will you— "

"No sweat, man."

"With your clothes on," I added through gritted teeth. Fucking hell, this was torture.

"With my damn clothes on and hers," Chandler chuckled. "Like I would risk getting on your bad side."

Both brows rose high on my forehead. "You would, and we both know it."

"Where's the fun in being predictable."

"I'll kill you if you touch her."

"Is that a bet?" he said with a face-splitting grin.

Narrowing my eyes, I shook my head. "No, motherfucker. It's a promise."

28

Alta

INSUFFERABLE HEAT WOKE ME. My eyelashes were sealed together, making it challenging to peel them open on the first try. I blinked several times, clearing the dryness and allowing my eyes to focus in the dim light. An unfamiliar room came into view, with a few faint streams of buttery sunlight pouring through a set of blinds on a far window.

My annoyance at the sweltering heat grew as sweat beaded along my brow and between my thighs where they were pressed together, my knees curled against my chest. I made to fling off the heavy blankets but couldn't. Something heavy rested across my shoulders, pinning me to the bed, adding to the heat.

Panic spiked through me. My heart raced and thoughts swirled.

What happened last night?
Where am I?
Who's with me?

"Easy there, Birdie," a familiar voice said from my back, right near my ear. "It's just me, Chandler. You're safe."

Breathing still labored, I willed my body to relax under his hold. "I don't understand what's going on. Where am I?"

At that, the weight lifted. Immediately I shoved off the blankets. I swallowed gulps of the cool air before rolling to my back.

"Mathews didn't want you to wake up alone." Chandler clasped both hands behind his head and focused on the ceiling.

"Is he here?" I glanced back to the windows, the brightness making it seem a little later than I normally woke up because....

Grief engulfed me as the memories of last night hit. "Benny?" I asked, my voice breaking.

"I'm sorry, Birdie, but we don't have an update. He made it through surgery, but he lost a lot of blood. That's where Mathews is now. He got a couple hours of sleep, then went back out to check on him."

"But he made it to the hospital and through surgery, so that's something, right?"

Reaching over, he patted the top of my hand before pulling it back to his side. "Sure is, Birdie. And Mathews thinks that dog of yours could be the key to solving this case. He should be back—" The sound of a door slamming shut in the front room made him smile. "Ah, always on time, that one. Looks like my shift is up. Glad I could be here when you woke up."

"Thank you." I grabbed his hand and pulled it close. "For everything."

"Peters." Cas stood in the doorway with a murderous look on his hard features. "Get out."

"How's that for gratitude for you," Chandler joked with an over-the-top wink. Shoving out of bed, he stretched his arms overhead with a loud groan. "Now it's my turn to get some work done."

Cas glared at Chandler as he crossed the room until the bedroom door shut behind him, leaving us alone in what I now realized was his room.

"You okay out here alone for a few minutes?" Cas asked as he tucked his hands into the back pockets of his jeans. "I need a quick shower. Peters is right outside."

At my hesitant nod, he stripped off his black T-shirt and tossed it into a laundry hamper in the corner of the room.

Sounds of the faucet turning, water streaming from the shower, and him stripping from the rest of his clothes were evident through the bathroom door he left slightly ajar. As the water shifted, indicating he'd stepped in, I inched closer to the edge of the bed to have a direct line of sight into the bathroom.

A bit creepy, yes, but he was the one who left the door open.

Only his large shadowed form showed through the opaque shower curtain, but it was enough. Maybe it was my brain's attempt to forget the trauma from last night, or the ever-present danger I was in, but I needed him. I squeezed my thighs together at the memory of his tongue and fingers teasing me inside and out.

This was crazy. I was a dead woman walking. My best friend almost died last night. Heck, I didn't even know how I got in this room, but there I lay in his bed, panting with want. Only for him.

The shower shutting off sent me scrambling back under the covers. Towel around his hips, another rubbing against his shaggy light brown hair, Cas stepped into the bedroom, eyes on me.

"Hi," I said with a little wave. A blush heated my cheeks as I took in his defined chest and abs. Chest hair covered his pecs and trailed down below the towel. He wasn't hairy by any means, but it also didn't look like manscaping was something he ever considered as an option. It looked masculine—like him. Everything about him pulsed all man. From his tattoos to the now-full beard and thick, muscular legs, every inch was as strong and intense as the rest of him.

"How are you feeling this morning?" he asked over his shoulder as he dug through a black duffel bag on the floor. I stared at his perky, firm ass shoving against the white towel, distracting me from his question. "Alta?"

"Huh?" I responded, still staring. When he didn't respond, I tore my gaze from his backside only to find his dark eyes alight with humor.

"You seem okay," he chuckled.

"Yeah," I said, clearing my throat. "Chandler told me Benny made it through surgery, so I'm hopeful. Thank you for taking him last night. When can I see him?"

His broad shoulders rose and fell. "Going out isn't the best idea for you right now. This guy is upping his game, and I don't want you out there. Here we can protect you, take shifts, but there?" He shook his head. "Anything could happen, and I'm not willing to risk that. Soon though. I promise I'll take you to him soon."

Even though I understood where he was coming from, I still longed to see Benny for myself. Last night was terrible. The whole day was terrible, but with all the sorrow and hell going on around me, here in this room, everything settled. I settled.

"My head is killing me," I grumbled. A slow throb had started the second I shifted to get a better view into the bathroom.

He hitched his chin toward the nightstand. "Bottle of water and two Tylenol already there for you."

While I took the medicine and chugged the water, Cas tugged on a pair of boxer briefs and mesh shorts, only giving me a peek of his bare ass as he did.

Thirst quenched, I snuggled back down into the covers and rolled to my side, facing his side of the bed. Taking the hint, Cas crawled in, staying outside the covers, and lay on his back.

"I'm sorry about Benny." He rolled his head along the pillow until those dark brown eyes met mine. "I really am. He's a cool-ass dog, and I know you love him and relied on him to keep you safe. He's a tough one though," he said with a reassuring smile. "I have no doubt that dog will pull through."

The pillowcase shifted beneath my cheek as I nodded. "Do we know... do they know what happened to him?"

He rubbed a hand along his ever-growing scruff as he thought over my question.

"Not positive, but looks like whoever broke in got through the front door, and then all hell broke loose. The blood in the cabin"—he winced—"suggested he was shot or stabbed there, then carried out into the woods, which I assume was to draw you out."

"It worked."

"No shit," he grumbled. "I get why you wanted to run out there, but why? Why did you do it? You knew this guy's play and still you did it. Thank fuck he wasn't out there waiting for you."

My eyes widened a fraction. Slowly I slipped my hand from under the sheets and held it close to my face like I was raising my hand in a classroom.

"What," he deadpanned. "I don't like that look."

"Well, you see...." I ducked under the covers, tugging them tight around my head.

"Lady, get out here."

I didn't.

"Alta."

Still nope. He was going to be pissed.

"I don't want to tell you," I muttered from under the covers. Beads of sweat formed along my forehead and my palms beneath the sweltering covers. I needed fresh cold air, but no way was I ready to give up the mock safety of my blanket fort.

I yelped when cold air brushed down my face and arms as the blankets ripped from my tight fists. A shiver shook my shoulders and legs at the sudden contrast in temperatures.

"Talk. Now."

I shook my head. This was fun. "And what if I don't?"

"This isn't a game, Lady."

"Could it be?" Wow, okay, who said that? No way those words came out of my mouth.

One eyebrow rose along his forehead, and a mischievous smirk tugged at his lips. It was beautiful. Like that, he looked young, unlike the other 90 percent of the time when he looked pissed or stressed.

"How old are you?" I asked, cocking my head to the side, inspecting every inch of his handsome face.

"Old enough."

"That's vague."

"Would it change your mind about me?"

"No," I said with a laugh. "Why would it?"

"Then it doesn't matter. I'm legal age, if that's what you want to know."

A giggle pushed past my lips, tickling my chest at the vibrations. A sense of awe settled over his face as he stared at my broad smile.

"You amaze me, Lady. All the world has dealt you and hear you are, smiling. How do you do it?" The sense of wonder in his tone made my heart swell.

My shoulders slid the sheets up and down with my shrug. "I don't know if I would be if you weren't here. You make it better."

His scoffing laugh wiped the smile from my face. "Normally I'm the one making things worse."

"Not with me," I said. Reaching over, I tugged on his shoulder, making him roll on his side, facing me. "I've had more fun with you these past few days, even with all this going on, than I have in years. Years, Cas. And that's because of you and who you are. You're inclined to only see the worst in yourself, but I wish you'd be just as inclined to see the good, like me."

His nostrils flared at my words. The bed shuddered as his breathing turned fast and heavy. "Say yes, Lady."

I didn't even think. "Yes."

Lightning fast, his hand jutted across the small space between us to tangle in my hair. With a sharp tug, he slid me across the bed to him. Hand under my shoulder, he rolled my chest onto his.

Once, twice I blinked, staring down at his parted lips. Beneath me, his heart hammered against his chest, matching the racing of my own.

"All you have to say is stop," he murmured as he angled my head to lengthen my neck. Warm, wet lips slid along my pulsing veins before teeth sank deep in the skin just below the collar of my sweatshirt. "I'm trusting you to tell me if this gets to be too much."

"I trust you," I groaned. On its own, my leg swept over his, hauling the rest of me over his long, lean body.

I gasped as the grip on my hair tightened, bringing my face to meet his. Fire burned behind his eyes. "Right now, I don't. I've wanted this since you fell on your ass in the parking lot. I won't stop unless you tell me to, do you understand?"

I tried to nod, but the grip on my hair was too tight to move. "Yes, Cas, yes. Now, please."

The corners of his lips tugged upward in a cocky smirk. "Please what, Lady?"

"Kiss me," I begged. Shifting my hips back and forth, I ground against him. "Take it away. Take away yesterday, the last ten years, all of it." Focusing on keeping my breath steady, I dragged my quivering lips against his. "Give me a good memory to dwell on when everything else is falling apart around me. Give me you."

"You already have me, Lady."

His lips sealed over mine, pressing hard. Desperate to rid my rapid thoughts of yesterday, I gripped his short locks between my fingers and tugged. My need for him must've sparked something inside him, as one second I was on top, controlling the kiss, and the next my back pressed into the soft mattress, his hard body half covering mine.

"Fucking hell, I love kissing you," Cas muttered reverently against my lips. "You make me feel... wanted." He pulled back, his dark eyes boring into my hazel ones. "Mine," he gritted out.

"Show me," I said between labored breaths. "Make me yours."

Whoever this woman was saying these things, precisely what she was feeling, was a badass—I liked her a lot.

He ripped the sweatshirt over my head fast and rough, snapping my head forward and then back against the pillow. Naked from the waist up, Cas stared at my exposed breasts, licking his lips that were pulled into a feral smile. Every inch of my exposed skin sizzled under his perusing eyes. With his focus locked on my hardened nipples, his calloused palm skimmed up from my belly and between my breasts to wrap around my neck.

My breath hitched as his hold tightened, which only made his smile grow wilder.

Deviously slow, he moved closer, so close that his hot, panting breaths brushed over the swell of both breasts. I knew what was coming, based off the last time he had me in a similar hold, but I still gasped, my eyes rolling into the back of my head, when his teeth sank deep into the soft tissue, marking me. A slow, soothing lick quickly followed, almost as an apology, only for him to kiss his way over to the other side and complete the same territorial claiming.

Pulling back, he smiled at his handiwork. Shifting his gaze, he watched me as his free hand dangled over a peaked nipple. I squirmed beneath him, but couldn't go far with his weight on me and his hand still around my throat.

"Patience, Lady," he chuckled. "You wanted to forget, and I'm making sure this is the only thing you ever remember."

The heat from his fingers teased as he lowered them, barely brushing over the stiff peak. My sigh of pleasure at his touch turned into a groan as he squeezed the tight bud between his thumb and finger. Shocks of pleasure and pain swirled, making the slow pulse between my thighs turn unbearable.

Cas watched from his high perch as I squirmed and whimpered with each twist and tug. With a slow grind of his hips, pressing his hardness exactly where I needed it, I shifted back and forth, matching his rhythm and adding to my misery.

Taking my lower lip between his, he sucked hard while continuing his other forms of torture below. My breaths came faster and his pace quickened, thrusting his erection over my sweat pants and creating delicious friction between us.

With his teeth nipping at one nipple and fingers tugging on the other, I crumbled beneath him, gasping for air as stars burst behind my closed lids. His deep, proud chuckle made a slow smile spread up my lips.

Tugging the sweat pants down my thighs, he tossed them and my underwear to the floor. My mind flipped to last night when he helped me get dressed, and now here he was ripping it all off.

"Last night," I whispered. "Last night you took care of me."

The soft lips working their way up my thigh paused. Looking down, I found confusion in his eyes.

"You're mine to take care of, Lady. Never doubt that." When he resumed his sucking up my inner thigh, I felt more than saw his lips spread in a smile. "This is my favorite way of taking care of you, just so you know."

Closer and closer, his mouth moved toward my center. The ache that was tamed earlier had returned, causing a deep, wild throb with my rapid pulse. Everything faded to black when his lips wrapped around me, sucking my nub between his lips and lightly scraping his teeth down. I released the sheets that were balled in my hand to weave them through his hair, pushing and tugging him for more.

A quick pang of soreness hit as his finger slid in deep. His hand and mouth stilled.

"I'm fine," I said, my voice shaking.

"Lady, if you're sore from that"—concern laced his features as he stared where his finger had dove inside my body—"I'll break you. I don't want to hurt you."

"Please, Cas," I begged. Tugging on his hair, I pulled him up my body, putting his face inches from mine. "I need this. I need you."

For a brief moment, I thought he'd say no. Panic set in at the idea of his rejection.

With a deep sigh of resignation, he turned to kiss the inside of my palm.

In awe, I studied every move of his muscled arms and abs as he pushed from the bed. After grabbing a condom from his duffel bag, he placed the wrapper between his teeth and tugged his shorts down. My eyes widened at the bulge restrained in his tight black boxer briefs.

Chewing on the edge of my thumb, I glanced up, only to find him already looking back with his face pinched like he was in pain.

"I'll be fine," I encouraged.

With a nod, his briefs hit the floor and he was standing stark naked before me. I held a breath, ready to fight back the inevitable panic attack. But it didn't come. Instead, scanning every inch of the most masculine man I'd ever seen, Cas's nakedness did the opposite. I needed him. Now.

The tear of the condom wrapper inched up the pulsing anticipation. Every part of me was ready for him, wanted him. Yesterday didn't matter right now. The case, Benny, Sadie, John—nothing mattered except what was going on in this room. Us. Together.

Cas climbed up the bed, hovering over me with a lingering look of apprehension in his eyes.

For encouragement, I spread my legs beneath him, hooking my heels around his thick thighs. A tight hiss passed through his lips as he settled between my legs, sliding up and down my wet folds.

"I'm trying," he gritted out. "I don't want to hurt you, but fuck, I want you so bad. I want to feel you all around me. I want to make you scream my name, make you never forget where I've been. Stop me if I—"

Not allowing him to finish, I yanked him down. His lips collided with my own, our teeth clashing in a fierce kiss.

With a slow roll of his hips, he positioned himself just outside my opening before sliding in an inch. Internal muscles burned as they stretched to the max. Tears sprang up as he pushed deeper. I grimaced as I arched off the bed at the contradicting feelings of wanting more and needing less. The delicious pain was one that I wanted more of. Everything hurt, but in the best way possible.

"Lady, talk to me," Cas said, his voice deep and strained.

"More." It was what I wanted, but I also knew it was what he needed too.

He withdrew gently, only to push back in harder than the first time, his control slipping with each second my muscles squeezed him. His pace increased, pushing me past the pain and shoving me into a deep pleasure I'd never experienced before. Desperately he sucked and nipped down my neck, which I arched out long just for him. The bed shook, thumping against the wall as his thrusts turned demanding. I dug my fingers into the defined muscles of his back, holding on while the fog of lust and pleasure thickened.

One hard thrust, him sinking deeper than ever, my fingers curled and I tossed my head side to side as a shoulder-shaking orgasm barreled through. My lazy eyelids opened halfway to find him wearing a proud smile.

"Wow," I breathed.

He chuckled and shifted. The new angle drew out a loud moan from my core. Still grinning like a fool, he dipped a hand between our bodies. Fingers on my clit, he pressed down while drawing lazy circles. "Oh, Lady, we're just getting started."

I shivered at the promise in his voice.

Eyes closed, I concentrated on every place our bodies touched, focused on the swirl of his fingers and penetrating force. For the first time in a long, long time, no bad memories threatened, no worries clouded my thoughts.

I never wanted it to end.

29

Alta

ARMS ABOVE MY HEAD, I stretched out long underneath the sheet and blanket, slightly exposing parts of my naked body to the cold air. Shivering against the cold, I tucked back under the blanket and rolled to face the other side of the empty bed.

I frowned as I felt along the cold sheets, indicating he hadn't been there for a while. I couldn't remember when I gave in to the pull of sleep, but I did remember him holding me, his chest pressed against my back, as I did. Now he was nowhere to be found.

Keeping the blanket against my chest, I sat up in the bed and searched the dark room.

Mumbled voices floated in from the other side of the door.

Blindly searching the floor, I snatched up my discarded clothes before tiptoeing across the room toward the door, where a sliver of light peeked through the gap. Nose against the door, I pulled it open an inch, allowing a little visibility into the living room and kitchen.

Cas and Chandler stood on opposite sides of the long counter, faces grim, voices low.

Whatever they were discussing so seriously could wait; my bladder could not. After pulling on the sweat pants and sweatshirt, I tiptoed down the short hall and slipped into the bathroom. With a relieved exhale, I flipped on the light, only to barely contain my shriek as I took in my reflection.

What the hell happened to my hair?

With a few sad whimpers, I touched around my scalp where the hair was matted. I leaned closer to get a better look at the hard, crusty coating. Pulling a clump of ends to my nose, I inhaled deep.

It smelled like... blackberries. But that wasn't my shampoo scent. No, my shampoo smelled like lavender. My body wash smelled like... oh. I smirked at my poor hair, fully understanding what happened. Sweet, sweet Cas probably got frustrated trying to find my shampoo yesterday and just used what he could find.

On top of my hair looking like I'd been homeless for months, I smelled like sex and sleep. *One way to fix that.* Turning the shower on, I held my hand under the water until it warmed and then removed last night's clothes. Under the hot spray, I sighed and began massaging the body wash from my hair while my thoughts fixed on Cas.

What we did earlier was beyond words. I wasn't sure how many times he took me over the edge, having lost count after the first few. It was like his body spoke to mine. He gave me exactly what I needed, living up to his threats of not being gentle. Remembering his rough thrusts had my thighs squeezing tight in memory. Everything was sore, from my lady parts to my breasts, which took the brunt of his twisted fingers and teeth. I loved it. Every part of it.

It was shocking that all this had happened in a little over a week, which meant what I was feeling for him wasn't love. No, it had to be purely physical, even though the way I wanted his smile and laugh around me every day, wanted to make him smile and laugh every day, had nothing to do with physical attraction. I wanted to make him happy. He deserved it.

I deserved it.

We'd both been through so much in our lives; it was our time to take what we wanted and move on.

Right?

"Lady?" Cas's deep voice echoed in the small bathroom.

Eyes closed, I smiled into the steady streams of hot water. I was in deep trouble if just his voice could make me wet like it just had.

A cold draft flicked across my backside, directing my attention to where he'd pulled the curtain back to stick his head inside. A flick of approval, of want, pulsed in his dark eyes as he scanned up and down my wet, naked body.

"Can I help you?" I said with a laugh, flicking drops of water at him. He ducked back around the curtain.

"I brought you your clothes. Peters also packed some of your stuff from the shower and your toothbrush."

My interest piqued. "Did he pack my shampoo?"

"I don't know," he grumbled. I smiled at the closed shower curtain. *Men.* "He brought several bottles of stuff."

"Can you hand them to me?" I asked innocently, even though it wasn't. It hadn't been ten minutes since I woke in his room alone, and yet I already needed him inside me again. In his arms, I was safe, and everything else dulled in the background. Plus it felt fucking fantastic. Yeah, I cussed, because that was how great it felt—it needed the extra oomph.

The sound of him digging through the bag, grumbling about what the stuff was and why I needed it all, made me chuckle. Soon both hands shot around the curtain, gripping five different bottles. Not wasting the opportunity, I jerked back the curtain for him to get a good view inside.

Carefully I inspected the bottles, my smirk growing with each one I picked through.

"Alta," he said through clenched teeth like he was in pain. "Pick one."

Pulling the shampoo from the group, I held it out to him. "Want to help?"

The other bottles clattered to the floor, rolling under the cabinet and scattering to the corners. Cas tugged his shirt over his head, his hand immediately going to the button of his jeans as the shirt sank to the floor. Not ten seconds after I offered him to join, he was gorgeously naked and climbing into the shower behind me.

"We need to talk," he said while sealing my back against his chest, engulfing me in his strong arms. "But it can wait. Fuck," he hissed into my ear. "I can't get close enough to you."

The length of his hard cock nestled between my cheeks as his hands explored up and down my body. I flung my hair to one shoulder, offering him access to my neck. The warm water washed away each of his soft kisses from my ear down to my shoulder.

Goose bumps sprouted along my skin as the tips of his fingers skimmed down each arm before intertwining with my own. With his massive weight, he pushed me forward, bending me at the waist until both my palms suctioned against the tile. Dropping his hands, he gripped my hips, yanking them farther back. The nudge of his foot against the inside of mine spread my legs the width of the large tub.

Fingers digging deep into my soft flesh, he whispered, "Is this what you wanted, Lady?"

Bottom lip between my teeth, I nodded.

His smirk broadened against the shell of my ear. "I told you I'd take care of you. Hold on, and don't move your hands, you hear me?"

In one move, his teeth sank into my neck as he slammed inside without warning. Water pooled in my gaping mouth at my gasp. Slowly he withdrew only to smash back in harder, deeper. My heart rate picked up, anticipating the delicious pain that would come with each pound of his hips.

Again and again, he thrust deep. My nails scraped along the tile in an attempt to gain traction to keep my hands from slipping. One of his hands slipped forward from my hip to dip between my legs. His rough touch and quick flicks shoved me over the edge fast, catching me by surprise. My knees buckled, hands slipping from the tile as the orgasm drained the energy from my muscles. Such a delicious feeling of utopia.

An arm snaked around my waist and tightened to hold me up, preventing me from falling face first into the wall. Water cascaded over my head and down my face, muffling my labored breaths.

Hell. This man.

On shaky legs, I stood, shoved the hair from my eyes and turned to smile over my shoulder. Cas's hooded eyes were still heavy with want, and if that didn't give it away, his fully hard cock told me he didn't get the same happy ending.

Noticing my confused stare, he said, "Didn't have a condom. Don't worry. I haven't been with anyone since my last checkup, and I'm clean."

But that wasn't where my mind went. A thought flashed through my dirty mind. Licking my lips, I swiveled around and dropped my knees to the porcelain tub floor. The dark hair of his legs pulled between my spread fingers as I slid both hands up them, savoring the strength beneath my palms. His muscles tensed under my touch, driving my want to take care of him. My touch, my body, and soon my mouth—all of it was his. And I wanted to make him mine.

Yes, there was a deranged man out to kidnap me and do who knew what, and yes that same man had mutilated several chipmunks and tried to kill my dog in one day, but with Cas, it didn't matter.

And right now all I wanted was him. All of him.

I dragged my tongue from base to tip. My eyes fluttered closed as I relished in the shiver it evoked from him. Nails digging into his ass, I rhythmically sucked on the tip before gliding my lips down his thick shaft. Once, twice I guided all of him in my mouth before his fingers tangled into my hair, holding my head in place. Taking over, his thrusts quickened, pushing faster and faster in and out of my mouth, going deeper with each stroke. Tears tickled down my cheeks, mixing with the hot water as I fought to suppress my gag reflex.

With a frustrated growl, he withdrew, popping out of my suctioning cheeks. Tight fist around his base, he pumped his hand in short, fast strokes. My gaze stayed glued to his focused face, eyes sealed shut and mouth gaping while water poured over his hair, causing a waterfall to cascade down his features. He drew his lower lip between his teeth, clamping down, the skin turning white around the edges at the pressure. Hot, thick cum spurted out, painting my chest and my neck. Before the water could wash it away, Cas hauled me upright. I arched against the cold tile, only to be pressed back by his chest against mine.

Our labored breaths mirrored each other's. Eyes locked with mine, Cas grinned as he ran the tips of his fingers through the sticky mess before pressing a coated finger against my lips. Through my smile, my tongue darted out, licking off the remnants of him. Approval sparked behind his dark eyes. A lightness settled over his features, relaxing his brow and softening his usual harshness.

"You could've ... you know. I wouldn't have minded." Even with everything we'd done, embarrassment at saying it out loud brought heat to my cheeks.

Chuckling, he pressed his lips to mine before diving his tongue in to dance with my own. "We're pushing our luck with what we've done and you not having a panic attack. Didn't want that to be the thing that tipped you over the edge. Now tomorrow," he muttered against my lips, "different story. I won't hold back."

"That was you holding back?" I said, my eyes wide. Hell, he fucked my mouth. How was that holding back?

His deep, wicked laugh stirred another bout of lust inside me. I squeezed my thighs in response.

"Plus I kind of like seeing this," he said with a hint of awe in his tone. "Me covering you. Marking you." Eyes blazing with determination, he flicked his gaze back up. "Mine."

"I think the teeth marks you left did that already," I said on a pushed breath. Heat built, making wetness pool in my core. "Let's do it again."

Teeth gripping his lower lip, he shook his head, sending cool droplets of water to rain down. "You need to walk tomorrow." His expression darkened. "And we have stuff to discuss. Peters is waiting."

Without another word, he twirled me around, putting my hair directly under the warm water and ending the conversation.

30

Cas

Eyes on the bedroom door, I half listened to whatever Peters rambled on about. Both my heads were focused solely on the beautiful creature currently changing behind that door. Which meant she was naked. Clean and naked. Ready for me to slip in and get her dirty all over again.

Fuck.

Shifting, I gripped my hard dick to alleviate the uncomfortable throb, which was fucking lunacy. I'd gotten off more today than I ever had in one day, and there I was ready, desperate for her again. It wasn't just her tight pussy that called to me. No, it was all of her. Those all-seeing eyes, the hushed breaths, whimpers she didn't even know she gave, those smiles I didn't deserve but she gave anyway.

Everything. She was everything.

A hard, no-holding-back punch to the shoulder dragged my attention to Peters.

"Fucking hell." He smacked my face hard enough to sting. "Get your head in the game. The right fucking head, you dipshit. I told you," he said, jabbing a finger in my chest. I glared at the offensive finger, debating about ripping it off. "I told you not to let this interfere with the case, and here you are not listening to a fucking thing I'm saying. It's her life on the line, you know that, right?"

Her life. Right.

Shaking my head, I scrubbed my sliced-up hand down my face, allowing the pain to bring me back to the present. "Right. Fuck, what's wrong with me?"

"Good pussy."

I took a step toward him; he took two back. "Watch it."

A small tilt of his chin was all he gave. "Fine. Listen, this guy is stepping up his game. I still have no idea why he's doing this to her—"

"I do." We both turned at her voice. Just outside the doorway, she stood with her small hand raised like she had the answer to Peters's question.

I watched every step she took into the living room. Her eyes cut to the fireplace that was roaring with the fire I'd built for her the second we made it out of the shower. My gaze flicked to her hands, where both index fingers picked at the cuticles of her thumb.

"Oh?" Peters asked, moving closer to her.

My muscles bunched, the protective instincts taking control. It was only sheer willpower that kept my feet planted instead of stalking across the room and putting myself between them, even though they stood more than five feet away from each other and had a couch between them.

"Last night." Her nervous gaze flicked around the room. "I was so focused on...." Clearing her throat, she squatted to the hearth to get closer to the heat of the fire. "I couldn't tell you guys...."

"Tell us what, Birdie?" Had to hand it to Peters, he knew how to turn his anger and frustration on and off. He was seconds from punching me one minute ago, and now here he was showing the extra patience Alta needed.

"He found me."

I felt all the blood drain from my face. Peters glanced to me and held up a hand, letting me know he'd handle it. Clearly, by the look on my face, I wasn't capable.

"What do you mean?" he asked.

Turning, she tucked her knees to her chest and stared into the fire. "Before you two showed up, he was there waiting for me. I had Benny in my arms, and then he was just there."

"In your head? You hallucinated?" As crazy as it would make her, I hoped to every god that it was all in her imagination.

Rotating away from the fire, she shook her head. "He said it was easy to get me away from you two, and that he was beginning...." Her eyes widened as she gawked at her sock-covered toes.

First, the shake in her hands drew my attention to her stunned silence. Next it was the loud, desperate gasps for air. Peters and I both rushed over. Gathering her in my arms, I pulled her away from the fire and laid her flat on the couch, gripping her ice-cold hand in my own.

"Lady, breathe. You're safe. You got out. It's okay. Focus on me." Nothing. With a feral growl, I climbed onto the couch to straddle her lean hips. Her chin between my fingers, I tightened my grip until those hazel eyes focused on me. "Breathe," I commanded. Tears leaked from her eyes, but her chest rose in a deep inhale. "Good girl," I praised. "Again."

Over and over I repeated the same words, commanding one thing and then praising her response.

"He said... he said he was beginning to enjoy the hunt too. *Too.* That means...." Her eyes turned to Peters, imploring him to disagree with what she was thinking.

But he couldn't.

I couldn't.

The fucker had a partner.

31

Alta

THE HOSTILE SILENCE that settled around me after admitting what happened last night churned my anxious stomach. Were they mad? Concerned? Didn't give a rat's heinie? Well, that last one wasn't true; the pure hate and anger boiling out of Cas's dark eyes told everyone he did care—maybe *too* much.

Which, with my past, should've scared me. I'd had too much attention, had someone care too much, but with Cas, he cared too much with my well-being in mind, not his. That was what I saw that first day and what I saw now—he was a protector, didn't take advantage. Every cell in Cas's body was geared to take care of someone else, and it seemed he'd finally found the person he wanted to take care of. The person who would allow it.

Me.

Heck yeah, I'd allow it. I savored it. I relished every second his alert eyes watched me. If I were honest with myself, I would admit that I wanted those watchful eyes on me every second of every day for the rest of my life. Wanted his body on mine, inside mine, until death did we part.

"It would make sense," Chandler said reluctantly. "The way he's able to do all this without a shred of evidence left behind. Someone must be cleaning up after him. And if he said 'starting to enjoy the hunt,' that means his partner is the one who does the watching."

"Has that ever happened?" I asked, my eyes flicking between the two guys. "A killing duo?"

Chandler nodded, eyes unfocused on the wall. "Several. Couples." Looking at the ceiling, he sighed. "Fuck, why didn't I see this before? It's probably why we haven't found the bodies." With a cringe, he looked to me. "They probably both use the women until they're bored, and since there are two, they can bury the bodies where no one would find them. A dead body is easier to carry with a little help."

Pushing up from his seat on the coffee table, Chandler took his phone from the front pocket of his jeans. "I need to make a few more calls before—" His eyes narrowed at the screen. "Your boy John is calling."

"Not my boy."

"Not her boy," Cas and I said in unison.

With a smirk, Chandler rolled his eyes and slid his thumb across the screen. "Peters," he said in a clipped tone. His eyes roamed around the room as he listened. "Interesting. Why don't you two come by? Put the evidence in a plastic baggie of some kind." Another beat of silence. "Great. See you in ten."

After sliding the phone into his pocket, he smiled. "Seems our girl Sadie just eliminated herself from becoming suspect number one in our search for the bastard's partner."

"What?" Cas and I said, again in unison.

"Seems she 'found' a note from the serial abductor on her car this morning. He didn't say much outside of that. Guess we'll learn the details in a few."

In a few. My eyes flew to Cas, who still sat on top of me, smirking.

"I'm good," I said, squirming beneath him. "You can get off now." I shoved against his legs, not getting anywhere.

"I'm quite comfortable."

"Cas," I pleaded as I shoved against his thick thighs again.

His eyebrows rose with a silent question.

"I just don't want to make this worse," I said. "He already hates you because of me... us, and I don't want him finding you like this."

He crossed his arms over his chest but didn't make a move to climb off me. "Like what?"

Exasperated, I pressed my head into the couch cushion and rubbed my closed eyelids. "Cas Mathews. You know exactly like what. You're straddling me. Now get off."

Even though it was my request—demand, more like it—I immediately missed his heavy weight as he climbed off the couch. Standing across the room, he leaned against the window.

"There was a note in the cabin," Cas said, his shoulders tense. "We didn't figure out what it meant until we realized Benny was missing."

A pulse of tension inched up the suspense as Cas took a deep breath.

"It said 'one down, two to go.'"

One down, two to go.

One down, two to go...

Oh.

Oh.

"You think he's coming after you now?" My voice was so high-pitched that even I didn't recognize it.

The two exchanged a long look.

"We're not sure," Chandler said. "But we do know you're in his sights, and he's willing to take out anyone who stands in his way. I'm still waiting on all the files from your last year in the Smokies, but there has to be something there. Something that pushed this guy, this team, to want you specifically."

"When I asked him why last night, he only said I wasn't bright," I murmured, thinking out loud. "So it has to be something obvious.

Even though I can't remember anything, it has to be something big to have gotten his attention."

"Or not," Cas cut in. "It could've been big to him. To you, it could've been you stopping him from littering, or warning him about getting too close to the animals."

"That happens every day," I groaned. Sitting up, I tucked my knees to my chest. "How will I ever distinguish between the ones who were pissed because a woman called them out, those who were pissed because they got caught, or those who were crazy enough to think it had something to do with them?"

A warm hand settled on my knee. Looking up, I found concern and sympathy in Chandler's eyes. "When we first met, I said you were perceptive, and of all the things you've brought to light in this case, you continue to back that up, so I have no doubt you'll know the difference. It's just about triggering your memory. You got this, Birdie."

I nodded, hoping his confidence in me wasn't entirely off base like I felt it was.

"You need to eat," Cas said, his attention back on me. As if my stomach understood English, it growled in response, confirming his assumption. "We have food here, or I can run out and—"

"Something here." No way did I want him going out alone with a possible target on his back. Plus the thought of him leaving my side, me being vulnerable, made my pulse race. "Eggs?" I suggested, edging the word with a hint of hope.

"Eggs it is." When he walked by, he paused behind the couch to press his lips to the top of my head. "Just so we're on the same page," he whispered. I glanced to Chandler, who was too busy doing something on his phone to pay us any attention. "If he gets within five feet of you, or says anything I take as offensive toward you, I won't hold back as I've done in the past."

I blinked. "Before was you holding back?"

"He's not in the hospital, is he?"

I shook my head.

"Then yeah, that's me holding back."

For some messed-up reason, his words lit my blood on fire, making every inch of my body burn for his touch.

Behind me, pans and other things clanged around the kitchen.

Sensing my stare, Chandler looked up from his phone.

"Can you call Benny?"

His brows shot up. "You want me to call a dog?"

I rolled my eyes. "Call the hospital. I need to know if there are any updates. Is he okay? Does he miss me? Maybe I should take him his favorite bed or blanket?"

Chandler barked a laugh. "Only you, woman. Yes, I'll call to see how he's doing, but I'm not taking him his favorite squeaky toy."

"Your phone is ringing, Alta," Cas said as Chandler held his against his ear. "It's been going off like crazy for a while."

Pushing off the couch, I snagged the vibrating phone from the counter and swiped it open.

Dad's voice boomed through the line. I pulled the phone back a few inches to keep from having my eardrum disintegrated.

"Where in the heck are you? I've been calling you all night," he shouted. Zero anger laced his tone, only desperation and worry.

"Sorry," I said. Pulling a stool over, I sat and not so lightly tapped my forehead against the counter in utter frustration—with Dad or me, I wasn't sure. "Things are a little crazy around here."

"Why does your GPS chip show you a few miles from your house? And you didn't go running like normal today. You haven't moved, at all. Alta Lady Johnson, what the hell is going on up there? I'll jump in the truck right now, just say the emergency word."

I cringed as Chandler and Cas stared me down. No doubt they heard every word. "No emergency word needed, Dad. I'm staying at a friend's house for a few days, just right up the road. Don't worry, okay? I'll send you a new schedule soon." Outside, a truck rumbled up the drive. "Listen, Dad, I gotta run. I'll call you later and explain everything, okay?"

Not waiting for a reply, I hung up and tossed the phone on the counter.

"Emergency word? GPS chip?" Cas asked, sliding a plate of buttered toast and scrambled eggs in front of me.

Taking the fork from his hand, I dug in. "Yeah," I sighed before taking a bite from the warm toast. "I have GPS chips in all my shoes. The signal and data are transmitted back to my parents in Texas, you know, to make sure nothing's wrong. I don't tell anyone because it makes me sound...." I wiggled the fork in the air as I searched for the right word. "Like the paranoid freak I am. Same with my emergency word in case they call and I'm in danger. Fireflies, by the way. That's the SOS word."

"You're not a freak," he said through gritted teeth, making me smile. He was even defending me against me. So cute. "What schedule do you send them?" Cas leaned across the counter, shortening the distance between us while sliding a bottle of water to me.

After twisting the cap off, I gulped down the room temperature water, savoring the way it seemed to clear the remaining haze from the earlier long nap. "At the beginning of every month, I send them my work schedule and running schedule. Since I don't keep a normal routine, I like for someone to have all the information of when and where I'll be somewhere. That way if anything goes wrong...." I shrugged and went back to devouring the delicious eggs. "Thank you for the food. I was starving."

The pounding against the front door halted our conversation, even though I could tell Cas had more questions regarding everything he'd just learned. Chandler yanked the door open wide, allowing John to stalk through. His blue eyes searched the room until they landed on me. A strange expression creased his forehead and pinched his lips. I didn't understand what had him so concerned until she walked in two steps behind him.

What. The. Hell.

No one said a word—heck, we maybe didn't even breathe. Only her heeled boots stomping against the hard floor and the crackle of the fire sounded in the small room.

Turning from the smiling Sadie, I stared at my empty plate. My mind was playing tricks on me. There was no way Sadie was that crazy.

A glance over my shoulder confirmed it. I wasn't crazy. Sadie had taken her near-black hair to a color somewhat matching mine. A bit more orange than my strawberry blonde, but there was no question the color she'd attempted.

"You like it, Birdie?" Sadie asked as she crossed the room.

My fingers tightened around the fork. It wasn't much of weapon, but if I could make it to her neck...

Strong fingers wrapped around mine, easing my death grip on the thin metal. Glancing up, I shot Cas a glare, but he merely smiled and shook his head while withdrawing the fork.

"It's different," Cas said carefully.

"Let's get to the note," John snapped from where he paced in the middle of the room. If I were him, I'd be nervous too, though more about Sadie than the man hunting us. "Sadie found it on her car this morning."

"Outside my apartment building," she added, her eyes sparkling with amusement. "As soon as I saw it, I ran back upstairs to show John."

My hands tucked into tight fists beneath the counter. It seemed she was more interested in letting me know John had stayed the night at her place than being worried about the note.

"Where is it?" Chandler asked, his face still locked in shock. "The note you found."

John pulled a clear baggie from his jacket pocket and slapped it onto Chandler's extended palm.

"Why haven't you found this bastard yet?" John's tone was full of accusation. He turned to focus on Cas. "If you were doing your job, maybe Sadie and Birdie wouldn't be in danger."

"I'm an excellent multitasker," Cas responded with a slight lift of his shoulder. "And we are getting closer to finding this fucker, not that we'd tell you."

"And until he's caught," Chandler cut in, "we're keeping Birdie here, and I would suggest you get some protection detail for your girl here."

Sadie's eyes lit up at Chandler calling her John's girl. "I think he has that handled," she said, tucking herself under John's arm and forcing him to wrap it around her shoulders. "Unlike other people, I'm grateful for his concern."

I ground my teeth together to keep from lashing out.

"If Birdie is staying here, where's Benny?" John asked, glancing around the cabin.

Tears welled, but somehow I kept them hidden and maintained my composure.

"Ugh," Sadie scoffed. "Be glad he's not here. That dog is mean and judgy. I don't want him anywhere near me."

That was enough.

I shoved away from the counter, the stool clattering to the floor as I ran to Cas's bedroom. Only once the door was closed, my back pressed against the hard wood, did I take a full breath. It was too much. Sadie's crazy, Benny hurt, Dad threatening to drive up, a killer after me and everyone I knew—all of it.

After hitting the light switch, dousing the room in complete darkness, I carefully shuffled to the bed and fell onto it face first. Sealing my eyes shut, I curled my knees and tucked an arm around my shins.

Their loud voices carried through the door. Grasping a pillow, I shoved it over my ear, blocking out their words.

It didn't matter. None of this mattered.

I was a dead woman walking.

It was only a matter of time before this guy grew tired of the cat-and-mouse game he was playing and ended it.

With me.

32

Alta

THE OPPOSITE SIDE of the bed shifted and creaked. Shortly after, the coolness of the cabin brushed against my hot cheek and ear when the pillow was pulled away. Confident, careful fingers swept through my hair, then skimmed over my forehead and cheek, calming me with each stroke.

"I know you're awake," Cas muttered against my shoulder, his hot breath seeping through the thin cotton of my long-sleeve T-shirt. "But you do need to sleep. Want me to run down to the store and get something to help calm you down?"

I shook my head. Pushing up, I pressed both elbows into the mattress to shift around the bed. Tucking an arm around his waist and hooking a leg around his thighs, I snuggled my cheek against his chest.

"I don't think I can do this anymore," I whispered into the dark. "It's too much, Cas. I can feel my mind slowly shutting down from it all, just like it did ten years ago. I don't want to go through that again, especially when I almost didn't get out alive. If I fall into the dark chasm of my mind, I won't make it out again."

"Ah," Cas said into my hair. "See, that's where you're wrong, Lady. You're stronger than you think you are. Now is the time you need to remind yourself of who you are, what you're capable of. You've held yourself back, telling yourself you're safer in the shadows for so long that you've forgotten."

"Forgotten what?" I almost begged.

"You've forgotten who you are underneath all the paranoia, all the locks and ticks. Those things have defined you for way too long. The Alta I see is stronger than any of those things—hell, stronger than most men I know. But you have to believe it. I can't do that for you."

I tapped my middle finger against his breastbone. "You think I'm strong?"

"I do."

"You think I can survive this?"

"I know you will."

"Because you're here."

"No, Alta." At the earnestness in his voice, I shifted back to look up into his face. "Because you can." Mulling over his words, I tucked my head back against his chest. A light rumble from his chuckle tickled my cheek. "I'm hoping you're the one who catches this guy. With what he did to those animals, I have a feeling you'd put a world of hurt on him before he ever saw the inside of a jail cell."

My cheek slid against his shirt as my smile grew. "I do know a thing or two."

"And you can pack a punch, don't forget that. You've caught me off guard twice with the power in those tiny arms."

"Do you think it'll come to that?" I asked as I gnawed on the edge of my thumb. "You think I'll be the one confronting him?"

His chest rose high, taking my head with it before lowering slowly on a controlled exhale. "I don't know, but it's best to be prepared. One thing is for certain—I'm not going anywhere until the bastard is behind bars or six feet under. I finally found someone to… someone I want to... I'm not letting you go without a fight is what I'm trying to say."

With the steady beat of his pounding heart in my ear and the heat radiating off him, the pull of sleep came fast, dragging my eyelids down. He shifted, scooting to the other side of the bed slowly and slipping my head off him.

"Stay with me," I asked in my sleepy state. "Don't go. I don't want Chandler. I want you here when I wake up."

"Alta—"

Fighting with my lids to stay open, I pressed up on an elbow. "Cas, I trust you. It'll be fine. You won't hurt me."

"You don't know me," he said in a sad tone that hurt my heart.

"I do, and I might know you better than you know yourself. Why do you think you're a villain in this life? Because I don't see it."

"I'm a killer, Lady. I don't mind it either. Where you have this light of hope and forgiveness deep in you, I have this dark, hollow hole. Nothing good comes from knowing me." He sighed and leaned his head against the headboard. "I came into this world alone, and I'm prepared to leave it the same way. Well, I was."

"I don't want you to be alone. You don't deserve this self-imposed exile."

In the dark, I watched his lips pull up in a sad smile. "Funny, that's exactly what I feel about you. You don't deserve the solitary life you've given yourself. You deserve to live."

"Ditto, Cas Mathews. Hey, I have an idea."

"This doesn't sound good." He barked a laugh when I smacked his thigh. "Watch it. Any higher and you'll bruise the part of me you've come to love today."

My face heated. It was true, I was quite fond of that part of his anatomy.

"What's this idea of yours, Lady?"

"I think I need to be alone to be safe, right?"

"Yeah."

"And you feel like *you* need to be alone to keep others safe."

"Exactly."

"We should be alone together!"

The bed vibrated with his silent laugh. "I don't think it works that way."

"Says who? We make our own rules, right? We can strike a deal. You keep me safe, and I'll keep you from slipping into the supervillain you believe you are. It's a win-win."

"Sounds dangerous for you."

"There will be lots of sex," I said seductively while skimming my fingers up his inner thigh.

"Sold."

I yelped as he shoved me back against the bed and climbed on top, settling his weight over my hips.

"So you'll stay with me. Tonight," I asked, to make sure he understood the rules. Not that I did—heck, I'd just made the whole thing up to get him to stay. Where it all became a bit fuzzy was if I was talking about him staying tonight or forever. The forever part sounded better and better every minute we spent together.

"Lady," he gritted out before tugging my shirt over my head. My pants and underwear were next. "It's a terrible idea, but okay. Though don't say I didn't warn you."

I nodded in the dark and stuck out my hand between us. A full, mischievous smile glimmered on his face from the small bits of moonlight pouring through the windows.

Slowly he shook his head. "I have a better way to seal this deal," he said, lowering his lips to mine. My back arched off the bed as he bit down along the edge of my lower lip and slid in deep between my thighs.

Yep. His way was much better.

Low, scared curses from somewhere in the dark woke me what seemed like days after I'd fallen asleep. Blinking back the fog, I glanced around the room, trying to pinpoint what was going on. The bed trembled beneath me, and the sheets had been yanked to the opposite side of the bed. Again a scared cry pierced through the night.

Eyes wide, I swallowed back the fear of what the next few minutes would hold and shifted to my other shoulder to face Cas. In the dark, he twisted on the bed, muttering things under his breath that I couldn't understand.

This was what he didn't want me to see. But instead of being scared, my heart broke for him. What Cas didn't realize was in his nightmares, he wasn't the villain—he was the victim.

At another bout of mumbled words, I stretched across the sheets. My fingers slid over his cold, clammy shoulder until they rested right above his heart. My hand leapt off his skin with every thunderous beat.

"No," he mumbled as his fist beat against the bed. "No. I'll kill you." His arms swung into the air over and over punching something that wasn't there. The scent of sweat and fear leached from his skin. The sheets were ripped from the bed as his legs thrashed back and forth like he was trying to leap up from the mattress.

Unable to resist the urge, I scooted across the sheets, pressing my naked body against his.

"Not her," he gritted between clenched teeth like he was in pain. "She's mine." A desperate roar tore from his lungs, startling me back. "Love her."

My eyes widened. Curling a leg over his thigh, I tugged him closer, sealing my skin against his. For the first time since we'd known each other, I used my body heat to warm his chilled skin. Soon his breathing calmed and his muscles relaxed beneath my hold.

Did he mean... surely he meant... could he have meant...

Me?

Quirks and all.

He loved me?

Did I want him to? I did like him, a lot. More than a lot. These past several days with him, I felt more alive and happy than I had in years. I just assumed I fell fast for Cas because it'd been ages since I found someone with this kind of connection. What's crazy was I knew even before we slept together—heck, maybe I knew from the first day we met. It was never simple attraction. From the moment his hand touched mine, we connected.

In a bold move, I slid the rest of the way over his hips, straddling his naked body. The moment my hot center touched him, his cock stirred to life, hardening within seconds. Leaning forward, I pressed my bare chest against his and wrapped both arms around his shoulders, clutching him tightly. His muscles tensed, then melted within seconds of realizing I was no threat.

Head buried into his neck, I smiled as his strong arms linked around my back, holding me even tighter to him.

"Lady?" he gasped. His arms wrapped around me like a vise, pressing the air from my lungs. "You're here."

My cheek slid against his slick skin as I nodded. "I wanted to be close to you," I whispered.

The silence stretched between us. The stillness in the air pressed in, making the quiet unbearable.

"Close… to me?" The bewilderment in his tone made my arms squeeze tighter.

"Yeah, you."

"Careful, I might never let go," he replied. Within seconds, his breathing evened with deep inhales and exhales.

The scruff along his cheek tickled my lips as I whispered back, "That's what I'm hoping for."

Hot.

Way too hot.

Shoving against the weight on my chest, I gasped for air only to have it cut short by something pressing against my open mouth. I flung my eyelids open to find a pair of sparkling dark eyes gazing into mine.

"I slept. All night." His lips teased mine, tickling with each word. "I've never slept like that. That deep. Normally my nightmares take me all around the house, but last night... I still had them, but it was different. I was more scared than angry and volatile. And this... I've never woken up like this."

"Wanting sex?" I joked, wiggling beneath him to maneuver his hard erection between my folds.

"No." He teased back by rolling his hips back and forth. His hiss of pleasure snapped all my senses wide awake. "In someone's arms. It's comforting, relaxing. Nice."

"Nice? Cas," I begged. Lifting off the pillow, I sealed my lips against his. "Kiss me."

Fine lines burst from the corners of his eyes as his smile grew. "How sore are you?" His hand snaked between us, leaving a trail of fire in its wake. I tried to hold back a wince as his fingers slid in and out. "Looks like sex is out for today."

I let out a pouting whimper. His responding chuckle tickled my neck.

The tip of his tongue left a slick trail as it slid from my collarbone to between my breasts. The first bite of my soft flesh wasn't a surprise, but the second, harder one drew a gasp as his teeth clamped down deeper than ever before. As he sucked the throbbing flesh between his lips, soothing the ache he'd caused, Cas resumed the slow slide with his fingers. The soreness quickly faded, creating a desperate, unrelenting throb between my legs.

Every muscle tensed and relaxed against the bed as his thumb flicked my tiny bundle of nerves. Unable to stop, I circled my hips, mirroring the movement. Each flick of his tongue against my pebbled nipple, every scrape and tug between his teeth, along with his slow, torturous fingers strung me tighter. I let out a loud whimper as he dipped lower, planting kisses and not-so-soft bites down my belly before settling his shoulders between my thighs.

"Breakfast is the most important meal of the day," he said, staring blatantly at where his thumbs spread me wide for him. "And I plan on eating you first thing every morning for as long as you'll let me."

Before I could respond, his tongue slid between my folds. Each plunge of his fingers, every swipe of his tongue left me desperate for more. Sweat beaded along my brow as my fingers dug into his scalp, pushing him harder against me. I groaned his name as my body tensed and my back arched off the bed with my release.

My labored pants filled the hot room until slick lips sealed over mine. The tip of his tongue spread my lips, thrusting inside and forcing me to taste myself.

"Fuck, I want you so bad," he mumbled against my lips before taking the lower one between his teeth with a tug.

"Do it. I want you, Cas. All of you."

Without hesitation, his hips shifted over mine and rolled back, aligning himself outside my entrance. His desperation was clear, but still he restrained from plunging in deep with the first thrust. My internal muscles burned as they stretched to accommodate him. Dark eyes locked with mine, his breaths turned short and quick. Slamming his eyes shut, he let out a roar of frustration. Twisting, he moved us to the edge of the bed, allowing him to stand with my legs wrapped around his waist. The vibrations from each of his footsteps pushed him deeper at the new angle.

One hand on the wall to stabilize us, he bent forward to rummage through his bag with the other. Locating what he needed, he stood straight and removed his hand, causing my back to slam against the wall. A thin metal packet snagged between my teeth. Clamping down, I held the wrapper while he ripped the condom open. Holding me still, his fingers dug into my butt cheeks as he pulled out far enough to roll the thin latex over himself.

My bare back sealed against the wall as his weight pushed against me, thrusting hard and fast. I watched as a random painting near my head knocked against the drywall, threatening to fall to the ground. Cas's roar of possession and satisfaction as he came tilted me over the edge I'd been dangling on. Legs clenching his waist, I held on for dear life, wringing out every pulse of pleasure I could as he continued to ease in and out.

"You'll be the death of me," he muttered, his voice hoarse.

"Death by too many orgasms." I smiled against his sweaty chest, the coarse hairs tickling my cheek. "What a way to go."

His head popped up from my shoulder, a smile tugging on a single corner of his lips.

"What?" I asked, pressing my back fully against the wall to take in his entire face. "Why are you looking at me like that?"

He planted a light kiss on my lips. "When we first met—hell, even just a few days ago—you wouldn't even say the word sex, and now here you are spouting off about death by orgasms."

My cheeks heated. "So?"

"So it means you're getting comfortable with me. Getting comfortable with yourself. It's good, really good."

"Oh." Behind his back, my index fingers worried along the cuticles of my thumbs. "Guess I never thought of it that way."

A sense of loss overtook me as Cas withdrew and set my bare feet on the cold wood floor. "You've been alone for a long time," he said, clearly not embarrassed by his nudity as he slid the condom off and tossed it in the trash. "But even you standing here right now, naked, or earlier when you told me what you wanted, that's progress, Lady. Don't knock these small victories." Rummaging through his bag, he withdrew a pair of mesh shorts. After tugging them on, sans underwear, he came back to where I still stood to lean against the wall. "I'm going to make you breakfast. Then you, Peters and I are going to figure out a plan to catch this son of a bitch before anyone else gets hurt."

The second the door shut, I slid down the wall until my bare backside hit the floor.

He was right; I was changing. On top of me being more comfortable with myself and my own body, the sensations of being watched came less frequently with him around. The fears and paranoias had almost completely gone away, even under the current circumstances. Which meant with Cas in my life, I was happy, but vulnerable.

Only time would tell if my evolving was a good thing or one that would get me killed.

33

Cas

"I'm moving out," Peters grumbled from under the throw pillow on the couch. "I can't hear you two anymore. It's making me horny as fuck, and I'm too damn busy analyzing this bastard we're after to go out and find someone to relieve my issue. Fuck."

I chuckled as I moved to the kitchen. "Suck it up, fucker. Did you figure anything out with the note that crazy chick left?"

The pillow tumbled to the floor as Peters swung his feet over the cushions and sat up. "Nothing new, but my gut tells me there's something different about this one."

"Different how?" I cracked six eggs into a bowl for myself and added two more for Alta.

"I'll take six too."

"You get the last four. We need to go to the store. We're running out of food, and I don't want her out in public. Too many unpredictable scenarios."

"Agreed. I'll go later so you two can have some more alone time." His eyes rolled to the ceiling. "You seriously like this girl? I mean, she's cool as shit and all, but...."

"But what?" I gritted out as I whipped the eggs with more ferocity than needed.

"She's not the type of girl who'll let you go easily. Are you prepared for that?"

"Prepared for what?"

"The end, when we leave and don't come back. This will end, you know. We'll catch this bastard, and we'll go home to DC. The longer you do this with her, the harder it'll be for her."

"What the fuck are you saying?"

"Put more distance between you two so you don't crush the poor girl. Have fun, but remember it'll end."

Mulling over his words, I tossed the last few slices of bread into the toaster and flicked the lever down. "What if I don't want it to end?" I said to the pan full of raw eggs instead of Peters. "What if I don't want to let her go?"

His resigned sigh tightened my grip on the spatula.

"Then you'll figure it out. It won't be easy, but you're a stubborn jackass who's used to getting his way, so I don't doubt that if you don't want it to end, it won't."

"Thanks?" I said with a laugh. "And I've got this covered here, if you do need to go out tonight to take care of the problem your eavesdropping caused."

"Fuck you. It's not eavesdropping when the walls are fucking rattling."

I smiled at the pan as I flipped the eggs over.

Both our heads turned at the slight creak of the door. Fully clothed, hair in a high ponytail, Alta tiptoed out of the room on her sock-covered toes toward the bathroom. The moment the door shut behind her, I turned to Peters, my features set in hard stone.

"Don't you tease her about this shit, got it? I will end you, slowly."

He raised both palms in silent surrender. "Got it." His words said he did, but the mischievous fucking twinkle in his eyes told me he wasn't taking the threat seriously.

"Good morning, Chandler," Alta said as she emerged from the bathroom and slid onto the stool beside him. My focus zeroed in on the too-small gap between them. "Sarah texted me." She held up her phone for emphasis. "She said she needs to come back to Estes, that her friend is kicking her out." She chewed on the edge of her thumb, her gaze focused on the phone in her hands. "I don't want her staying alone. I kind of feel responsible for the mess she's in now that we know I'm the one this guy is after."

"Sleep well?" Peters asked, closing the small space between them by wrapping an arm around her shoulders. I waited for her to tense, pull away or show any sign of discomfort in his touch, but none came. As much as Peters touching her pissed me the hell off, I relished in the fact that this was yet another growing point for her. Whatever we were together was curing us both.

"Can she stay here?" she asked, avoiding his question. I smirked and nodded before returning my attention to the eggs. "Just until we figure all this out, or...."

"Or what?" I divided out the eggs and slid them onto three separate plates.

"Maybe I *should* consider going home to Texas, and maybe take Sarah with me. Then I'd be—"

I chucked the dirty pan in the sink, the clang vibrating in my ears as I gripped the counter. "Then you'd be away from us, completely exposed, and moving this guy to a different hunting ground. No."

Alta stood from the stool to come around the counter. Standing toe-to-toe with me, her determined hazel eyes tipped up to meet mine. "I don't think you—"

"You're the one not thinking." The muscles in her small arms flexed under my tight grip around her biceps. "Here, you have Peters and me to watch out for you. Here, we have the upper hand because we know his end game—you. If you leave, who knows when this bastard will show up again. Months from now? Years? You're. Not. Leaving."

Her eyes blazed into mine before flicking to Peters, who was watching with rapt attention. "We'll discuss this later." After snagging the plate with the least amount of eggs, she rummaged through the drawers for a fork and stomped toward the living room.

With a groan of annoyance, I ran my injured hand down my face and rubbed the long scruff growing along my jaw.

"The note," I said, staring at the plateful of eggs waiting to be eaten. "You said it was different. How exactly?"

After shoving half the plate into his mouth, Peters said, "This one didn't feel right. Everything about it was right, but... I don't know. It could be her. I think she's just crazy enough to put a note on her car to get that dumbass's attention."

"But we have to consider it a real threat," I mumbled. The slightest sway of her ponytail from her perch on the couch's arm gave away the fact that she was listening. "I agree though. Wouldn't put it past her. So what does that leave us with?"

"A deranged duo who enjoys the hunt as much as the kill and, bonus, have their eyes set on me for something I can't even remember doing," Alta chimed in. "The initial profile doesn't matter anymore. We're not looking for their next victim or why he targets the women he does. Now it's time to figure out why me and work backward from there." Turning, she faced us. "I'll call my old boss and see if he remembers anything big from that last year in the Smokies. You two focus on the files and the recent cases."

We nodded in unison.

"I'm going to look into the guy from ten years ago too," Peters said as he stuffed the rest of the eggs into his mouth. Shoving the plate across the counter, he stood from the stool. "I know you said he didn't have any connections, but that was what the local police could gather, I have more resources. I'll do some digging, and if all this is any way connected to that, I'll find it. And—" His attention fell to the phone ringing in his hand. "Hold on, it's my boss. Gotta take this."

Marching from the room, he shut his bedroom door with a quiet click, leaving Alta and me alone.

"Listen—"

She cut me off before I could get another word out.

"I get it. I do. It—"

Rounding the counter, I make it to her in two strides, hauling her off the couch to make her look at me. "You don't. Last night, for the first time in years, my nightmares weren't contorted memories." My grip on her shoulder tightened as the onslaught of last night's visions floated back to the surface. "It was all about you and being taken from me, and it hurt, Alta. It physically fucking hurt." Gripping her hand, I held it over my racing heart. "Nothing can happen to you, do you hear me? I wouldn't survive it. I wouldn't want to survive it."

"Okay, okay," she said in a calming tone. Her fingers loosened from mine to splay across my heart. "I won't do anything stupid. I won't go anywhere."

Clasping the back of her head, I tugged her close, holding her cheek against my chest. Pushing my fingers into the depths of her hair, I raked them down, easing the tangles as I went.

The door to Peters's room flung open, nailing the wall. Both my head and Alta's turned at the sound. He stood just over the doorframe, staring blankly at the phone in his hand.

"That was my boss."

"What's wrong? What happened?" Alta's voice quivered. We both felt the unease rolling off him, even from across the room.

His eyes flicked up, looking from her to me and back to Alta. "A tip came in." The pregnant pause irritated my anxious nerves. "Someone said they knew where all the bodies were buried in Tennessee. They're sending a team out to the site to investigate, but my boss seems to think we need to take it seriously."

"Why?" I asked.

"The caller had his voice disguised, and at the end of the call said, 'We had so much fun.'"

"Deranged bastard," I spit out. "What's he playing at? Why tell you now?"

Dread settled in the pit of my stomach, making me nauseous at the look on Peters's slack face. "My theory isn't a good one," he said.

"What?" I demanded, tugging Alta even tighter.

"Two down, one to go." Alta convulsed in my hold, a shiver of dread shaking her entire frame at Peters's words. "He knows I'll have to leave to be a part of the investigation. If this is true, if those bodies are where he indicated, it could give us the missing pieces we've been looking for. I have to go."

"When?"

Peters looked to the phone in his hand and cringed. "Two hours. I have to leave in two hours to catch the jet. Listen, Mathews; I'm not questioning your ability—"

"Yes," I said before he could finish. "Yes, I want additional help. Anyone the local FBI can spare. Especially if Sarah will be staying here. I can't keep watch twenty-four seven."

Peters nodded, his thumbs flying across his screen as he typed out text. "I'll let you know who I can get. In the meantime, I know you don't want to hear this, but we could use John's help. He can fill in for me until we get you some backup."

I grumbled into Alta's shiny, soft hair. Her head tipped back, allowing me to see the smirk pulling at her lips. "Fine. But not until you leave."

Peters smiled as he shoved the phone into his shorts pocket. Striding past us, he tugged on his coat and grabbed the keys from the side table. "Running to the store. I'll get enough food for an army so you don't have to run out again. I agree with what you said earlier, too many unpredictable scenarios out there. This guy is upping his game, which makes me think he's planning to move fast. His end game is in sight."

Her.

Lady.

My Lady.

The moment the door shut behind Peters, I strode forward, Alta's hand never leaving mine, and flicked the deadbolt. Every step through the house, I tugged her behind me, not daring to let her out of my sight—hell, out of my grasp. The nightmares from last night were quickly becoming a terrifying reality.

"Is that necessary?" she asked around the thumb between her teeth. Her eyes flicked between the loaded assault rifle and shotgun. "You're already armed."

"Yes." There weren't enough guns in this house to make me relax. "I'm not taking any chances. Peters was right—he's circling, focused on his end game. The past year has built to this, and I'll be ready the second he makes his move."

"Does this mean showering together is out?" Two of her fingers pressed beneath my chin, lifting my attention from the guns to her.

I pursed my lips. Vulnerability swirled behind her hazel eyes. Rejecting her would hurt her and me, but keeping her safe was always priority number one. "I'll be out here." Her gaze fell to the floor. That time it was me who drew her attention back up. "It has nothing to do with not wanting to." Reaching forward, I gripped her hand and pressed it against the hard-on I was sporting beneath my mesh shorts. "I'd fuck you until you begged me to stop, but when I'm inside you, when you're with me, I'm only focused on us. Nothing else matters, and that can't happen right now." My eyes slammed shut as her fingers wrapped around me over the shorts. "Lady, get in the damn shower. Now."

I missed the heat of her palm, the closeness of her body the moment she stepped away, smirking. "Fine, have it your way. But so you know...." She paused at the door and turned to wait until I looked up, giving her my undivided attention. "I'll be thinking of you."

"Go," I said through gritted teeth, the word barely recognizable with my restraint stealing the strength from voice.

The hiss of the shower turning on tensed every muscle. Not being in there with her was the hardest thing I'd ever had to do, but I wouldn't cave. No, I'd stay strong for her to remain clearheaded and alert.

Beneath my shorts, my dick throbbed.

"Fuck," I groaned against the hand over my face. The scrape of facial hair against my palm centered me.

I would be strong.

I'd resist the beautiful, naked woman in the next room.

I'd resist in order to keep her safe, even if it physically hurt to hold back.

I'd resist because her life depended on it, which in turn meant mine did too.

34

Alta

Two days.

Two long, dull days sitting around the house under Cas's protective, fatigued stares. Sarah arrived the same day Chandler left, providing a bit of a distraction from everything, but being stuck inside was suffocating. Sarah had the privilege of going out into the real world for her shifts at the local coffee shop in town. John escorted her to work and home, with Sadie at his side each time.

Sadie's curious side-eye glances and outright stares grew creepier each day—or maybe it was my imagination running away with me since I had nothing better to do.

And I meant nothing. Cas hadn't laid an intimate hand, tongue, lips, nothing on me since Chandler left. He said I was the one distraction he couldn't afford, whatever the heck that meant. So not only was I bored but also horny. I kept telling him it was cruel to give me a glimpse of the good life only to retract his gorgeous body from my touch—and bonus, I still had to look at it every day. I didn't even get a chance to seduce him at night. Sarah took up shop in Cas's bed with me each night. John and Cas rotated shifts, and when Cas's time for sleep came up, he made it a point to fall onto Chandler's bed, fully clothed.

He said one positive was that even his mind was too exhausted to drum up the normal nightmares.

So there we were, day three of lockdown. Sarah left around five for an early morning shift, meaning I woke up at five due to the loud racket she caused while getting ready. No wonder her friend in Denver kicked her out.

Unable to go back to sleep, I tossed on Cas's marine's sweatshirt, sweat pants, wool socks, and my running shoes, then tiptoed to the bedroom door. I cringed at the creak it gave as I pulled it open an inch to scout the living room.

Empty.

A deep breath pushed from my lungs. On silent feet, I crept past the couch and tiptoed toward the door. The cold metal knob shot a jolt of excitement through my palm. I wasn't running; that would be stupid, and I wasn't an idiot. No, I just wanted one minute outside in the cold mountain air, alone.

The first gust of wind caught my breath, but a broad smile spread across my cheeks anyway. Everything was quiet; not a single bird sang, no coyote howled. Rubbing my hands up and down my arms, I leaned back against the closed door, taking in the stillness, letting it creep over me, calming my high-strung nerves and overanxious thoughts.

In the darkness of the morning, without anyone watching, my thoughts wandered. So much had happened over the past couple weeks that it was hard to filter through all the emotions that swirled through me. There was a shift, a change brought on by Cas—which was a good thing. It was like he woke me up, breathed fresh air into my lungs, pulling me from a long sleep. Parts of my body and heart thrummed and sizzled only for him, only with him. Even if he didn't protect me from my potential fate, he'd already saved me.

Ten years of my life I'd wasted being scared, hidden, and

ashamed of my past. Like it was my fault. None of it was, and Cas helped me realize it wasn't about me. I wasn't to blame.

Confident, self-assured, and strong were words I'd use to describe myself after just a few days with him.

This version of Alta Lady Johnson was who I was meant to be.

"Just what in the *fucking hell* do you think you're doing?"

The back of my head slammed against the door, and a startled scream tore from my throat. The crunch of crispy cold grass and gravel grew closer. A bright red dot glowed in the dark, marking where Cas stood in the driveway.

"Answer me," he demanded before taking another deep drag. I stared mesmerized as the cherry of his cigarette burned bright. "Lady."

"What are you doing out here?" I asked instead of responding.

"Smoking and patrolling the area, looking for any signs of someone waiting, watching. Your turn."

I sighed and tucked both hands under my armpits. "I just wanted five minutes of fresh air, of quiet, of being alone."

"You want to be alone?"

"Yes and no," I said honestly. "I want to be alone, but then again I want you here with me while I'm alone." I let out a fake laugh. "Just another one of my quirks, I guess."

Cas stepped closer, shifting into the streams of light pouring out from the house's illuminated windows. With his head slightly tilted, the light and shadows accentuated the firm lines of his face. His dark eyes glittered as they stared deep into me. My breath caught as my heart jackhammered in my chest. The intensity, honesty, and desire behind his eyes were too much.

I wanted him. All of him. All of him all over me.

After tossing the cigarette butt into the can reserved for his litter, he strode past me and swung open the door. Mouth gaping, my eyes followed his movements in shock. It had to be a joke. No way would he leave me out here, alone.

The thousands of questions in my mind came to a halt when Cas reappeared with pillows and a quilted blanket tucked under his arm.

Lips parted in shock, I watched as he tossed down the pillows before arranging them like two makeshift chairs. After two fluffs of the blanket, spreading it out evenly over the cushions, he turned, eyebrows raised.

"Well come on. You wanted to be out here, and I know you're fucking freezing."

I was.

Pulling the collar of his sweatshirt over my mouth, I smiled behind the cotton while taking in a deep sniff of his lingering scent.

He got situated first, lounging on the porch with his back against the wall, legs crossed at the ankles in front of him. He lightly patted the cushion at his side, and I sank to my knees and crawled under the blanket, laying on my side and tucking my head against his chest. For the first time in days, I inhaled deep, filling my lungs with freezing fresh air.

His fingers raked through my long hair, carefully tugging each tangle free with more gentleness than I ever gave it. Slowly, pinks and gray burst over the trees. Thick white clouds of morning fog rose from the ground, suspended in the air just feet from us. No sooner had the sun shone its first rays than the birds woke, chirping happily through the trees and singing of another beautiful day.

"Beautiful," I said in awe. It's why I loved the mountains. A west Texas sunset was hard to beat, but mountain dawn gave it a run for its money.

"Yeah, perfection." Smiling, I turned to look up only to find his eyes on me. "I know someone like me—no family, no career, no money—doesn't deserve you, but... I want you to know that whatever happens after all this, I don't want to lose you. I don't know what that means logistically, but if you want to figure it out with me, we will."

I sucked in a breath. Was I ready for this conversation?

"You don't have to say anything. I just wanted to toss that out there." A shy, self-conscious smile tugged at his dry lips.

"We deserve to be happy, Cas Mathews. We deserve to be happy and free." Leaning up, I pressed my lips against the pulsing vein of his neck. "And we made a deal, remember? We'll be alone, together."

Calluses scraped my cheeks as he cupped either side of my face, pulling me up. Both thumbs hooked into my lower lip, tugging down until it popped back into place. Again he dipped both thumbs past my lips, but that time he thrust them past my teeth, filling my mouth. My eyes fluttered closed as heat blazed through my veins, settling deep in my core. A low groan rumbled in his chest when I wrapped my lips around his thumbs and sucked deep, lapping at the pads with tiny flicks of my tongue.

"Damn you, Lady," he hissed.

"You started it," I mumbled around the intrusion in my mouth, which was slowly moving in and out.

A deep rumble of an engine revving broke the spell. As quickly as his thumbs had thrust in my mouth, they disappeared. Jumping up, he tugged his gun free from the holster on his hip and engaged the slide.

John's old Dodge rounded the curved drive, making Cas's shoulders drop from their semipermanent place by his ears.

"Oh good, another day with that dipshit," he sighed as he put the gun back into the holster.

"When are those FBI guys coming to help?" I asked. Chandler called yesterday with the report of them finding all ten bodies, which were being identified with dental records and DNA samples, and told us he was still working on finding Cas some help in protecting me.

"Tonight," he said, crossing his arms over his chest and widening his stance as John approached the porch.

I shook my head.

Men.

"Well that should help. Maybe then you can get more than a few hours' sleep." I knocked his calf with the tip of my toe to get his attention. "With me," I whispered.

"Fucking finally," he grunted in response. "I've never had blue balls so bad."

"What are you two talking about?" John asked as he climbed the steps, his hesitant gaze flicking between Cas and me.

"Nothing," I said at the same time Cas said, "Blue balls."

"Whatever," John grumbled, then pushed the front door open to stomp inside.

Our smiles mirrored one another's when our eyes met. Cas simply shook his head and went back to watching the sunrise.

"Peters called this morning with an update. It seems all the women had traces of a sedative-type drug in their blood. Since we still don't know how long he held on to the women before disposing of them, we don't know if he drugged them only during their capture or if he kept them for a few days, keeping them drugged. But we'll know more after autopsies."

I couldn't blink. Couldn't breathe. A tremble started in my hands and worked its way up my arms, over my shoulders and out, making my entire body shake in fear. I knew what those women went through, but unfortunately for me, I survived it.

"Cas," I barely managed.

Not sensing my struggle, he simply craned his neck to look over his shoulder. "Fuck," he cursed and dropped to his knees. "Fuck, fuck, fuck, I didn't think—" Tugging me against his chest, he pulled me across his lap, allowing me to curl into a ball on top of him.

My eyes slammed shut, not wanting to see the sympathy in his eyes. It was the one thing he hadn't shown me during our time together, and I sure as heck didn't want to see it now.

Should he have known his words would be a trigger? Maybe. But did I blame him? No.

"Breathe through it," he murmured over and over into my hair. "I got you. You're safe." His heartbeat thundered in my ear pressed against him. I listened to the steady beat, mimicked his deep breaths, allowing both to seduce me into a calm trance. "I'm so sorry. You're safe, Lady. Stay with me."

The desperation in his shaking voice kept me from slipping further into my panic attack. Still, my heart raced so hard, so fast, that I just knew I was having a heart attack.

"I love you," he barely whispered with his nose in my hair. "So fucking much."

The memories Cas's earlier words brought to light dissolved back into their hiding spot in the dark corners of my mind.

Loved me.

Me.

Those three little words yanked me from my downward spiral. Steady, calm breaths replaced the earlier frantic ones. My pulse still raced, but for an entirely different reason. Our skin clung together as I pulled away from his neck.

"You do?" I asked with a growing smile.

"Yeah." He closed his eyes and inhaled deeply. "I do. You make me feel...."

"Happy?"

"Wanted. And now that I've found you, I realize that's all I've been searching for my whole life. You."

I brushed the tips of my fingers down his scruffy cheeks. "You make me feel happy, and safe, and normal." I shrugged at his raised brows. "Everyone's tried to fix me. You're the only one who noticed me for who I was—scars and all."

"Ditto, Lady. Ditto."

Something vibrated against my bottom, making me look down between us.

"Don't get too happy. I don't have a vibrating dick. It's my cell," he grumbled. Helping me off his lap, he jammed his hand into the front pocket of his jeans and pulled out the phone. He stared at the number before answering and holding it to his ear. "Hello. Yes.... Really?" A few seconds of him silently nodding drew my ear closer to his phone, hoping to catch a word or two. "Great. Yeah, I can be there in a few. Thanks, see you then."

After running a hand down his face and scratching at his beard, he stood and extended a hand to me. "I've gotta run to the station. Seems they were able to get some evidence off Benny and want to talk to me about it." His large fingers wrapped around mine and hauled me up. "You okay with numb nuts in there?"

I dropped my head back and groaned in frustration. "Yes, I'll be fine."

"I don't like him."

"Really? Hadn't guessed that," I said with a sarcastic bite in my tone. The animosity between those two was becoming unbearable, way past the point of annoyance.

"He wants what's mine, and he can't have it."

My hand froze over the doorknob. Slowly, to give myself time to rein in my frustration, I turned to face him once again. "One, I am not a toy in the sandbox, so stop treating me like one. Two, he might want it, but he can't have it because you have me. And three... three...."

"Three, I'm a possessive jackass who won't stop being a possessive jackass because that's the way I'm made."

I flashed him a narrow-eyed glare. "I don't like point three."

"Point three causes point one and two, so point three is the keystone to all this."

"Whatever." I pushed through the door. As soon as I was inside, the claustrophobic feeling came back in full force.

Cas strode past to his room while John watched from his seat at the kitchen table, where he ate a bowl of cereal.

"What's eating him?" he asked.

"He has to run out to the police station."

"Ah," John said between bites. "Overprotective ass."

With an eye roll, I fell onto the couch and stared at the ceiling. A dark shadow encroached from the other side of the sofa. Flicking my eyes over, I found Cas's concerned dark ones.

"I'm going. We good?"

"Good."

"You sure?"

"I'm sure."

"Because if we're not—"

"Freaking A, Cas, just go. I'll be fine. We're fine. Everyone is fine." Okay, that was a little snippy. What was going on with me?

"Don't take offense, man," John said. I couldn't see him from my prone position on the couch, but the sound of the chair scraping back and loud footsteps told me he was moving closer. "She's about to start."

"Ah," Cas said in relief. "Need me to get you anything?"

I gawked at the two men. *What the heck.*

A look of pure shock or confusion must've been written across my face, because John explained, "We've worked side by side for a while, Birdie. It's one of those things guys just kind of pick up on."

Grabbing a throw pillow, I slammed it over my face and screamed into the dusty fabric. "Go away," I yelled into the pillow, making my words muffled, but unfortunately not my hearing.

"Just go, man. She's fine," John urged.

"I don't want to leave her like this."

"Like what?"

Cas sighed. "Frustrated."

"Man, she's a woman. She's going to be frustrated with you more often than not. Better get used to it."

"Should I get her anything while I'm out?"

The long pause in their conversation had me holding my breath, very interested to hear John's response.

"Dove chocolate. She loves dark Dove chocolate."

Beneath the pillow, my eyes filled with tears. John was a good man. Not the one for me, but his heart was big and intentions pure.

"Thanks, man. I owe you one."

"No problem."

Even after the door shut and the resounding click of the locks slid into place, I stayed where I was, the pillow protecting me from the outside world.

35

Alta

A BURST of cold air wafting through the cabin and then the slamming of the door jarred me awake. For a split second, I panicked at the thing pressing against my face, blocking my air. I swatted at it with both hands, and the felonious pillow dropped to the ground, freeing me from its suffocating hold. Hands wrapped around my pounding head, I swung both legs over the couch's edge and leaned back.

"Good morning." Sadie's cheerful voice grated on my already frayed nerves. "Wakey, wakey, sleepyhead."

"How long was I out?" I asked without looking up. John had to be in the room somewhere.

"Ten minutes, maybe. Good morning, Sadie."

The sound of sucking lips made my stomach roll. What in the heck did he see in her?

Peeking through my lashes, I found them in each other's arms smiling like fools in love. Her hair was still kind of blonde, kind of orange, which did nothing for her fair skin.

Ugh, I was mean. Maybe John was right and I was about to start. Not that I'd seen a calendar lately. Ever since the jackwagon in there suspended me, I couldn't keep the days straight.

"I brought everyone some coffee. Where's Cas?"

"Out," I grumbled and pushed off the couch. I eyed the three cups of coffee sitting on the table as I walked to the kitchen.

"And I've been watching you." Creepy. "And know you don't like coffee." Because it's terrible. "So I brought you an orange juice."

My narrowed eyes flicked from the open fridge to find her staring expectantly. The sweet, doe-eyed look made me hate myself a little more than I already did.

"Thanks, Sadie," I said and slammed the fridge door shut. "That was nice of you."

"I know," she said in response before turning her full attention back to John. Picking up a to-go coffee cup, she thrust it into his hands. "I made it just the way you like it too. I love watching people, seeing what makes them tick. Two sugars and three teaspoons of creamer. Am I right?"

John's eyes widened as he nodded.

Surely now he saw her crazy.

Not interrupting the conversation, I swiped the small plastic orange juice bottle off the table and carried it back into the living room. Shoulder against the glass pane, I zoned out as I stared into the tight gathering of trees.

A bright, happy giggle from Sadie broke my trance. Turning, I found her on his lap, their gazes locked.

I tossed the small plastic bottle into the air once, twice, as I studied it. Everything looked intact.

"Just drink the stupid thing, Birdie," Sadie said like my slow pace annoyed her. "Here." Shoving off John's lap, she practically skipped to me. Taking the bottle from my hands, she twisted the cap off too fast for me to hear the telltale sound of teeth snapping. I opened my mouth to protest, but instead, she held up a hand and took a swig. "See. Fine. I got it directly from the coffee shop. You're safe."

Maybe I was acting like a freak. It was ten years ago, after all. And this guy didn't have anything to do with what happened in Texas. Separate instances. That happened to be similar.

My stomach rolled with nausea. *John's right, I am about to start.*

Sadie flicked her annoyed eyes from the plastic bottle now in my hand to my face and back again. When I lifted it to my lips, her smile grew. The first swallow was small, but still, I forced it down. Then I waited.

Nothing.

Another sip.

Nothing again.

Again and again, I sipped from the plastic bottle and waited until it was all gone. Staring at the empty bottle, relief washed over me, lifting the worry growing in my belly. Nothing happened. Everything was normal. Not everyone was out to get me.

"Thanks, Sadie, I didn't realize how bad I needed that." It was true. The sudden rush of sugar made my head swirl.

"You're welcome. Are we best friends now?"

Avoiding her question, I held up the empty bottle between my fingers and nodded toward the trash. On my way, I eyed John, who sat smirking with his coffee cup at his lips.

"She just wants to be friends."

"I can't be friends with someone who looks like she wants to make a skin suit out of me."

John barked a loud laugh. "Stop it," he chuckled and took a swig from the cup. "So good. Coffee is a must in the mornings. No idea how you live without it."

I shrugged.

Well, *tried* to shrug. I narrowed my eyes at my shoulder.

Odd.

Flexing my fingers, I pulled them close to my face and studied them, wondering why they felt so stiff, so unusual.

Stillness worked its way through my veins, relaxing every muscle as it went.

Fuck.

My eyes went wide as I stared at John, who was too busy talking to

Sadie to notice I was slowly slipping into a drug-induced coma. My feet were lead, tennis shoes stuck to the floor—not that I'd be able to use my legs if I couldn't feel my feet. Euphoria swept in, making me smile.

The room moved in a rush as my legs gave out completely and I collapsed to the floor. My head smacked against the ground, bouncing up after the initial hit, but the pain didn't register.

John's face appeared above me, his pupils large and lips moving, but his words fell on deaf ears. Little by little, my vision darkened. John's eyes fluttered closed and a heavy thump landed against my chest, knocking the wind from my lungs.

Unable to move, I watched the ceiling. My mind raced, trying to keep up with what was happening.

A banging vibrated along the floor, tickling my back. An ear-piercing scream broke through the silence just as the room faded to black.

36

Cas

THREE FUCKING convenience stores to find the Dove dark chocolate John instructed me to get. Three. That clearly demonstrated what I felt for Alta was true love. Never in my life had I gone through that kind of hassle for a woman, and I never would've even considered it after a long damn day like today.

Four hours with the detectives and crime scene geeks was enough to push me over the edge of my limited patience. Tack on this scavenger hunt, and I was done. Done and very ready to see Alta.

My Lady.

Mine.

Even if she didn't say she loved me back earlier, she was mine.

Surely she did though. She wouldn't have said all those things if she didn't, unless she said them as a distraction to not say it back.

"Damnit," I grumbled. The phone in the cup holder vibrated, Peters's name appearing on the screen. "What," I said after flicking the SUV's Bluetooth on.

"How'd it go?" The sound of his heeled dress shoes against a hard floor clicked in the background as he paced.

"Good. They found some human blood between Benny's teeth. They sent it out for analysis yesterday on a rush order. Expect the results later today. It was a gunshot wound to the chest that took him down. I talked to the vet too. Benny's doing better, and they expect him to make a full recovery." I cleared my throat. "I'm telling Alta as soon as I get back to the cabin."

"Anything else?"

"Nothing on the missing women. Still missing, of course. No evidence."

"Fucker. Nothing new here either. The least-decomposed bodies were autopsied, and you'll never believe what they found."

"I'm scared to ask."

"Nothing."

"What?" I chewed on my lip.

"They didn't appear to be sexually assaulted, no abuse, just malnourished and deep wounds around the wrists and ankles like they were restrained. We're dealing with some sick fucker."

"How do you mean?"

"I'm guessing his partner likes watching them free, and the main guy likes watching them as a captive. If he doesn't hurt them, then seeing their fear, them trying to escape, gets him off." He paused long enough that I checked the screen to make sure the call didn't drop. "That gives me an idea. What if he didn't assault them by penetration but got off on the fear, leaving behind evidence on their skin? The sicko could've wacked off and spilled his jizz on them."

"Why not rape them?" I mused. "Seems like after the recon work they do, the work they put in to take these women, why not take it that next step? That doesn't make sense, right?"

"Just a theory."

"They identify all the women yet?"

Another long pause. Fuck, this sucked. This part of the case was awful—no idea how Peters dealt with it day in and day out. I would much rather be out protecting the public with a gun at my side than listening to someone go on and on about decomposing bodies.

"All of them. The DNA results came back an hour ago. The husbands have closure now."

"When you heading back?"

"Soon, tomorrow maybe. I've done enough here, so I need to get back to the active crime scenes. We have to get this guy soon. He's not showing any sign of slowing down."

I tapped my thumb against the steering wheel at a red light. "You still think this has something to do with Alta?"

"Yup. And I did more digging on what happened in Texas ten years ago. She was right that he didn't have any living relatives, at least none who would claim him. He grew up in the system. But I did find something odd." My eyes flicked to the speaker. "Starting around ten, at every foster home he went to, something happened. Like a fire, or reports of him hurting other kids or even the foster parents. There's abundant documentation that he was mentally unstable."

"Not surprising."

"No, but I still feel like I'm not getting the full story. The reports seem... vague. I can't figure it out, but it's like they were protecting someone else. Keeping another name out of it all. I'm still digging."

My hands tightened on the wheel as I switched on the blinker to turn into the cabin community.

"Okay, call me with any updates."

"Same, Mathews. Later."

The second I passed through the entrance, unease grew in my gut. Ignoring the speed limit, I pushed my foot down on the gas pedal, sending me hauling ass down the street. Gravel kicked up behind the SUV as I took the sharp right into our cabin's driveway.

Both feet slammed onto the brake, I skidded forward, the front bumper inches from crashing into the porch.

For a second, all I could do was stare at what was left of the front door. My heart ratchetted against my chest as fear like I'd never known coursed through my veins, turning my entire body cold and my thoughts sluggish. Shoving the driver door open, I drew my pistol from its holster and angled the barrel toward the doorway. Silently as possible, I crept up the porch steps, cursing at a faint creak of the wood.

Standing just over the threshold, I swept the room, angling my 9mm every direction my gaze went. Stepping through the splintered remnants of the door, I moved toward the two bodies lying prone along the ground on the other side of the room. Aware of my surroundings, I squatted by the unmoving Sadie and pressed two fingers against her neck. Internally I sighed in relief at the steady pulse thrumming beneath her skin.

I flexed my hands around the grip of the gun, gaining some blood flow to my locked fingers. Carefully stepping over Sadie, I again lowered to the floor in front of John. Unlike Sadie, John looked like he'd merely fallen asleep on the floor, whereas Sadie's arms and legs were sprawled out as if she'd collapsed.

With the first press of my fingers against his jugular, I couldn't find a pulse.

"Fuck," I cursed under my breath. Moving to a different angle, I shoved my fingers deep into his neck, desperate to find a sign of life. A light, unsteady beat appeared, but it did nothing to calm my rising tension. He was fading. Fast.

Knowing he had limited time, I flew through the rest of the house, clearing every room, every closet faster than any one man ever had. After clearing the last dark corner, I yanked the phone from my back pocket and dialed Peters.

"Miss me already?" he joked.

"She's gone." It was all I could say, the only words that were on repeat in my head. "Gone."

"What?"

"Alta, Lady, she's gone. Sadie, John, drugged. Send an ambulance." The phone clattered to the ground, my knees right behind it, almost cracking the bone with the hard hit. Gone. I scanned the room, looking for something I missed, but came up empty.

"Fuck!" I roared and shoved up with a punch to the floor. Neither Sadie nor John stirred. Not knowing what or how much they were given, I rolled both to their side so they wouldn't choke if they threw up.

Sitting back on my haunches, I pulled at my hair, allowing the sharp bite of pain to ground me.

Think.

I had to think.

But I couldn't. Every nerve, every thought centered around the growing grief and desperation to find Alta. I let her down. I told her she was safe with me and now....

My gaze flicked to John and zeroed in on his blue-lined lips.

Immediately I dropped to my knees beside his head, rolled him to his back and pressed palm over palm on top of his heart.

Where in the hell is that ambulance?

37

Alta

A LOW BUZZING filled my ears, ringing in my head as I eased awake. My fingers and toes tingled, as did the tip of my nose and lips. I ran a dry tongue over my cracked lips as I took in my surroundings. I tugged on my wrists and ankles, but got nowhere except a slice of pain up my arms. Fear pressed against my lungs, shortening my breaths. The room was small, whatever it was—almost like a shed. The walls were made of thin ridged metal, half rusted but the other half shiny, as if they were brand new.

How I got in this tiny shed was a black hole in my memory. As was the way I'd ended up tied to the metal chair.

What felt like thin, tight wire cut into the cold flesh of my wrists. Thankfully my ankles were protected by the wool socks I'd pulled on that morning.

Even with the building fear and panic, two things ran on a loop, keeping me grounded to the present.

First, my shoes. Which meant they could track me. Cas had just learned about the GPS chips in all my shoes; surely he'd think of that quick. All he had to do was call my parents, get my general location and find me. Yes, it was a bit of a long shot, considering the signal had a two-and-a-half-mile accuracy, but it was better than nothing. No doubt this guy had a secluded place tucked away where he was sure I'd never be found again.

And the second reason I wasn't stupid scared was Cas. He would find me. He would save me. If he was still out there, then I had a chance at surviving this. I just had to hold on until he could.

The person who abducted me from the house was a hazy memory at best. It was a male though, that much was sure. Blips of him talking to me in the car, detailing what he was going to do, were unfortunately clearer than everything else.

Again I swiped my tongue across my lips, hoping to find relief.

Saving my energy for when I'd need it, probably to fight the guy off, was important, but I couldn't stop from trying to free my feet and hands. A sob bubbled in my throat, but I pushed it back down. Tears wouldn't get me anywhere except more dehydrated and tired. I had to survive this.

Taking in the dark room for the hundredth time, my gaze landed on the small stream of light coming from what looked to be an adjoining room. The light pouring through the edges of the wood said the place wasn't well constructed, or was maybe just really old. Now and then voices seemed close, but the steady, highly annoying hum of some engine made it hard to tell if they were real or in my head.

I hoped in my head, as crazy as it sounded. The voices in my head wouldn't hurt me.

I gasped at the door swinging open, nailing the back of the other wall. Bright light flooded into the small room, and I slammed my eyes shut, shielding my face at the visual assault. Slow blinking, I allowed my eyes time to adjust before peeking back toward the door.

My heart slammed to a halt.

A man stood in the doorway, but the bright light beaming behind him doused his face in shadows. What I could see was an average man, maybe slightly overweight if the bulges over his hips were any indication. Shorter than average for a guy too. It had to be him. The man we were looking for. Of course someone like that would want to overcompensate and take the wives of stronger, alpha men.

He didn't mutter a single word as he came in and shut the door behind him. With each resounding step against the dirt floor, he drew closer, and I shrank against the metal chair in an attempt to disappear.

The joints of his knees popped as he squatted in front of me. At that angle, the light illuminated his profile, which was about as unassuming as one could get. He was your basic middle-aged white guy. Not handsome, not ugly. Just blah. Of course, I wasn't about to tell him that.

The toe of his boot pressed against my toes, holding them to the ground. My eyes stayed focused on his as he gripped my knees and forced my legs apart as wide as they could go with my feet tied. With every muscle I'd built with my years of running, I pressed my knees back in, resisting.

A low chuckle sounded around the room.

"I like you," he said. A sudden waft of stale breath floated into my nose. Bile rose, burning my throat, but I pushed it down. He wouldn't see a reaction from me. That was what he wanted. "We have to be fast."

His small hands shoved up my thighs, slamming into the apex. Crudely he rubbed the heel of his palm up and down.

That time I couldn't stop, and a small desperate whimper slipped past my lips. His smile grew to show a row of crooked teeth.

"You can be as loud as you want, baby. No one will hear you."

I believed him.

"Watching you, playing with you was fun. Did you like my gift on the trail?" He chuckled at my narrow-eyed glare. "Thought you'd like that. You're special, the one we've been looking for. And finally, here you are."

A soft hand slid farther north, dipping under my sweatshirt and caressing the skin of my stomach.

"Fucking marines," he muttered to himself. "How does that jackass feel now, dumb fuck. I took you from his own damn house. I'm sure he fed you with lies of you being safe, how he'd protect you. Look at how wrong he was."

"He wasn't wrong," I said before I could think twice about my words. "You're the dumb fuck for taking me from him. He won't stop until he finds me, which he will. And when he does, he will kill you." My breaths came in long, deep pants, my anger building with every word I said. "Let. Me. Go."

His knuckles against my cheekbone whipped my head to the side. I only registered the shock of his hit when another blow came from the other side with more force, cracking against my eye socket.

I should be strong. Shouldn't cry, shouldn't feel so desperate. Cas was out there. But I did.

I didn't want to be there.

I wanted to go home.

38

Cas

THE SECOND THE ambulance doors were shut, I pounded my fist against the back, then turned and vomited up what little I'd had to eat, splattering it over the gravel. I stared at the evidence of my inner turmoil. A vision of Alta scared, being hurt—alone—rolled my stomach, shooting more of its contents up my throat and onto the driveway. Hands gripping my knees, I let everything out, all while the dozen or so local police officers and crime scene techs pretended not to notice.

"Here." A bottle of water appeared in my periphery. "Need a minute?"

"No," I grunted as I shoved off my legs to stand at full height. I snagged the bottle of water from the detective's outstretched hand and twisted the cap off with more force than necessary.

"Weak stomach?"

I scoffed, then swished the first couple of sips around before spitting it across the drive. "For the last fifteen fucking minutes, I gave mouth-to-mouth to a mostly dead guy, whom I cannot fucking stand because he's in love with my girl. Oh, and my girl is in the hands of some fucking psychopath," I bellowed. "So no, not a weak fucking stomach. I'm a fucking wreck."

The other men loitering around stopped their work and turned.

The detective just shook his head. "Right. Sorry. Let's get inside."

Several sets of cautious eyes followed my path up the porch steps and into the living room; no doubt they all knew I was at my breaking point.

Inside, I polished off what was left in the bottle and scanned the room. My attention fell to the pillow on the floor by the couch. The same pillow Alta used that morning to avoid me. My stomach churned as fear and anger fought their internal battle with in me. I shook my head to stop the dark path my thoughts were leading me down and looked to the kitchen. That wasn't much better. All I could see was the spot where I'd knelt minutes ago, keeping John alive.

"You bring coffee home?"

"Huh?" I responded but didn't look over.

"Coffee." I followed the path of his pointed finger to the three to-go coffee cups on the table. "Someone brought it from the shop in town. Was that you?"

"No," I mused and stepped closer. His hand swatted mine when I tried to grab one. "Maybe Sadie did, the girl who was drugged."

"So she brought a coffee for you, your girlfriend, and the other guy?"

"Alta doesn't drink coffee. The other cup would've been for her."

"But that still leaves one more. That means she expected you to be here, but you weren't."

Brows furrowed, I tried to follow his theory but failed. "Why does that matter?"

The detective rolled his eyes to the ceiling like I was the stupidest motherfucker he'd ever spoken to. If I weren't so desperate to hear his theory, I would've punched him.

"It matters because that guy they took away didn't look like he put up a fight, which doesn't make sense if someone marched in here and abducted Alta Johnson. That means he was already drugged when the person broke in, and I'm guessing"—he pointed a chewed-on pen at the cups—"that's how they got the drug in their system."

"But Alta wouldn't drink the coffee," I mused.

The detective nodded like he was deep in thought, trying to work through the roadblock I'd erected, halting his theory. With an inspecting eye, he walked around the table, looking for who knew what. In the kitchen, the detective swung open the cabinet under the sink and squatted. Intrigued, I peeked over the counter to find him rummaging through the trash can.

When he stood, his features were grave as he held an empty orange juice bottle in his hand. "Your girl like orange juice?"

39

Alta

"Please don't do this," I pleaded through my tears as his hand scraped up my bare stomach.

His smile grew feral. Instead of halting, he palmed a breast and gave it a painfully tight squeeze.

The pain triggered the despair to shut off and fury to fill its place. Hot, bright-red anger blazed through my core, fueling the strength I needed to fight back. Not giving a second thought to the pain that would surely follow, or how stupid my actions were, I lunged forward with a banshee scream. My forehead slammed against his nose with a sickening crackling of bone. He yelled in pain and tumbled back, taking me with him, still tied to the chair. My face smacked against the dirt, pain searing through my head at the impact against my injured cheek.

Stars sparkled in my vision. Blink after blink, I tried to clear my head.

Roaring curses and rage-filled snarls bounced off the walls of the rickety shed.

"You fucking cunt!" he screeched. Blood pouring down his face, eyes wild with hate, he stumbled to his feet. "Fucking bitch," he yelled again as his foot drew back. Not wanting to watch, I sealed my eyes shut. All the air whooshed from my lungs, preventing me from screaming in pain as his foot crashed into my unprotected stomach. Again and again his foot connected, sending me skidding across the floor. I gasped for air as tears slipped out from my shut lids, streaming to the ground.

Fingers dug into my bicep, hauling me off the ground to set the chair upright. With my back to the door, the light from the other room illuminated the evil in his rage-distorted face.

Hand in my hair, he fisted a clump and yanked my head back, ripping the strands from my scalp. I screamed at the top of my lungs as pain radiated from everywhere. I thrashed against his hold, but it did no good. Ice-cold terror chilled my anger at the distinct sound of a zipper.

"If you promise not to bite, I'll wait until day two to fuck that sweet ass of yours."

Shoulders shaking, tears streaming, breaths heaving, my spirit broke at his disturbing words.

"Now open—"

I jumped and screamed at the gunshot. Ears ringing, I watched as my attacker's eyes went wide. The impact of his heavy body hitting the dirt pushed a small cloud of dust around the room.

Cas. He made it. He saved me.

Frantically I looked over each shoulder, trying to get a view of the door, of him.

"Cas," I sobbed in relief. "Cas, you came."

No response. No hug or warm embrace.

Nothing.

A chill sent goose bumps down both arms and neck. "Cas?" I said tentatively. Something was very wrong.

"Sorry, Birdie. No Cas."

What the hell is going on? I whipped my head left and right, desperate to get a view of the door and the person now in the room. "Wh-what are you doing here? Where's Cas?"

I ducked and shifted away from the soft stroking down the back of my head.

"What do you want?"

"You, of course."

Stepping around the bleeding man, my new captor moved into the light. Her smiling blue eyes met mine, an evil gleam shining bright within them, twinkling in the artificial light.

This couldn't be happening.

Finally finding my words, I choked out the only thing I could think to say.

"Sarah?"

40

Cas

"How quick can we get results on the coffee and empty bottle?" I asked as I followed the detective out of the cabin. "We need to find her. Now."

The detective grimaced and paused, looking everywhere other than me. "Not soon enough to be useful."

I gripped his shoulder and spun him around to face me. "We find her. Now."

He shrugged out of my hold. "Unless you implanted some tracking device in her, we have nothing to go on at this point. I'll check the coffee shop where—"

"Fuck me!" I smacked a sweaty palm against my forehead. Struggling to stay calm, I dropped the phone to the ground twice before I could dial Peters's number. "Peters. Mathews. Get me Alta's parents' information. Now. All their numbers."

I hung up without waiting for a reply. No time for words. No time for anything. The clock was ticking on finding my Lady in one piece.

The phone vibrated in my hand, the screen showing an unknown number.

"Mathews," I practically yelled into the mouthpiece.

"Sir. We got the results back on the blood sample from the dog's mouth. She was in the system, so we have—"

My mouth fell open in shock. "Wait. Did you say *she*?"

"Yes, sir. Rose Bense. She has a record, plus a sealed juvie record. Lots of stalking, some minor violence stuff. Recently she did a long-term stint in a mental facility for disfiguring a man's wife."

"Name doesn't sound familiar. Send me a picture."

After I ended the call, I stared at the blank screen.

Fuck, all this time, Alta was right. It was a team, a man and a woman. Fucking hell.

Rose Bense.

Now we had a name, but what did all this have to do with Alta?

41

Alta

"Surprised?" Sarah quipped as she nonchalantly stepped toward the man groaning on the ground. "Jerry, Jerry, Jerry," she said like she was disappointed. "You had to go and fuck all this up, didn't you? Fucking horny bastard."

This was a dream. It had to be.

Sarah squatted beside the man and turned back to look at me, her eyes narrowing. A flash of anger passed through her eyes as she pursed her lips and turned back to him. "Did you break his nose?"

I kept quiet, not because I knew it was best, but because shock still had a grip on my vocal cords. Even if I wanted to say something, there was no way I could.

"Good for you. Stand up for yourself. I like that in a woman. We don't need men like him thinking we're property, am I right?"

She turned, obviously expecting an answer I still wasn't able to give.

"Jerry, no touching, remember?" Sarah's cold, detached laugh was more terrifying than her calm voice. "See what you don't know is I know about the last one. One fucking rule." She pressed the barrel of the gun into his temple. His eyes went wide. "It was fun while it lasted. Bye, bye, Jerry."

"I didn't touch them. I fucking swear. We had a deal. I didn't—"

I shrieked as Jerry's skull exploded, scattering blood and bits across the room. In the now deafening silence, she turned, her face splattered with blood, and smiled.

She was crazy. Sarah was mad.

Slowly she stood and wiped the gore from her hands down the dark denim jeans she wore. Turning, she gave me a sympathetic smile. "I'm sorry he hit you, but nothing else, right?" Her gaze shifted down to my disheveled sweatshirt. A frown marred her lips. "Right. Well, enough of that. He's gone. And you know what? Good riddance. He served his purpose, and when I learned that he touched the last girl, I knew his time was short. See, you have to keep men like him in line or he'd just be raping every woman we brought in here."

"What's going on? Sarah?"

"Damn, for someone so observant, you're pretty stupid, you know that?"

"I don't understand." I shook my head. "Tell me what's going on." The metal wire sliced deeper into my wrists as I attempted to wiggle free. Warm trickles of blood dripped steadily down my palms and leaked off my curled knuckles.

"Seriously? You don't understand? This, Birdie." A sneer tugged at her upper lip at my name. "This was all about you. Every woman, the move from the Smokies to here. You were one hard bird to find. I spent so long tracking you to Tennessee, and what did you do right before I got there? Up and left, again."

"Me?" I had to keep her talking. The longer she spoke, the more time Cas had to save me.

"You sound surprised. Yes, you. See, you took someone from me, and now you're going to pay for it."

I racked my brain, trying to figure out where our paths had crossed before she came to volunteer.

"Who? Who did I take?"

"My brother." Keeping the pistol in her hand, Sarah paced the small room, not paying any attention to the pieces of skull and brain matter she trampled on. "The one person who ever loved me, who stood up for me, and you took him from me." I gasped at the gun barrel pointed between my eyes. "Do you know what it was like to get out of that crazy house, expecting to be greeted by the only person who ever loved you, and have them never show? Two days I waited for him. Nothing. It took me five months to track him to Texas, only to find out he was dead. Dead!" she shrieked.

Sarah gripped her head as her eyes slammed shut. "You killed him. And now I kill you. You fuck with me, I fuck with you back. I'm a damn lady like that."

"He didn't have a sister," I said softly. Maybe she had it all wrong.

"When you grow up together, you're brother and sister." Her smile turned sinister. "Even if some of the stuff we did was a little more than sibling affection. Damn, that guy could fuck. Maybe because I trained him early on."

"How early?" Keep her talking. Keep her talking. It was a stalling tactic, but at the same time, I was curious as to how all this came about.

Sarah used the gun barrel to scratch her temple, looking to the ceiling. "Let's see here... I was seven and he was ten." In a flash, her demeanor shifted. Teeth over her lips, she nibbled as her eyes flicked around the room. "I knew we'd make a great team the first time he saved me. He made it stop. Every time."

"Someone hurt you."

A cold, harsh demeanor slammed over her face. "They all did. And big brother Lance was there to save the day, every single time. Now *how* to save me always needed some... encouragement from me. The man was dull when it came to being creative with our punishments. That's where I came in. See, we were a good team. Everyone ran from us. Hell, the system even protected us. No one wanted to announce the sexual abuse I was subjected to, which in turn led Lance to do the things he did. Me the mastermind and Lance the executor of my plans. It was perfect. We were perfect. Then you screwed everything up. What happened? What did you do to him?"

"Me?" I screeched. "He stalked me. He kidnapped me. He raped me." Again I struggled against my binds, only making the pain worse. "He got what he deserved. Look at me. I'm a paranoid freak because of him."

The wall groaned as Sarah leaned against it, crossing one ankle over the other. "Yeah, but here you are." Her arms fanned out. "All that paranoia and still here you are, with me, like I planned it from the minute I found out who you were. Two years I tracked you. Two long years to plan this out."

All of this was because of me. All those innocent women died because of me.

I shook my head, trying to rearrange my thoughts. No, not because of me. Because of her and the pervert with his head blown off. I was innocent. I'd always been innocent. Lance, Sarah—nothing was my fault. Even though I was yet again a captive of some twisted loon, a burden I'd carried these last ten years lifted.

It wasn't my fault.

I pushed the pain out and focused on the information Sarah spewed. Some parts made sense, but others, not at all. "The orange juice. Sadie? Is Sadie in on all this too?" Things were falling into place, but the million unanswered questions burned in my mind. Being curious about the cause of all this kept my mind from focusing on the slicing pain in my wrists and deep throb of my cheekbones.

Sarah laughed with a broad smile. "That girl is crazy. You need to watch out for her. I mean, I'm legit crazy—have a certification and everything—but that girl is stupid crazy. Do you know how easy it was to talk her into doing my dirty work? Not once did she think a thing about it. Every bad thing I fed her about you, every tidbit I dropped to make her jealous of you, absorbed into that small brain of hers without another thought. This morning, she didn't even think twice about me urging her to take those coffees and orange juice for you. I outright told her she had to make you drink it because you were too stressed lately to eat." She shook her head in disbelief. "I used to enjoy the game with people like her, but then I grew bored, and well, boredom doesn't sit well with me."

"Ten years. Why now?"

Shoving off the wall, Sarah shrugged and went back to walking the room. "Well see, there was this one... let's call it a misunderstanding."

"How so?"

"It's the watching I love. Seeing others live their lives, not knowing I'm observing their every move. Watching their intimate moments, the lies and deception families keep from each other. There was this one man, he was so cute—tall, dark, handsome, and filthy rich. I loved watching him. He had this power walk that made his ass bounce as he went to work in the morning." She let out a deep, longing sigh. "And the way he fucked his wife with such vigor, that was my favorite to watch. Especially when they forgot to close the blinds all the way or thought no one could see through the glass back door." Sarah's eyes glazed over, lost in thought.

"So you kidnapped him too?"

"No, I took out the competition. Well, tried at least. I thought if she were ugly, he'd see me, want me."

"I thought you loved Lance?"

She laughed. "I did love that bastard, but only when he was needed. We often went our separate ways to have our fun, but we always made it back to each other after."

"I wasn't the first for him, was I?" I gritted my teeth at the sharp wave of pain as my stomach rolled and cramped violently. Something was very, very wrong.

"Nope, but you were the first he touched. See, that had always been our rule. The only one he could touch was me. It was always my one fucking rule," she yelled. "What did you do to him to push him over the edge? He knew, he *knew* what I'd do if I found out he forced you."

"I didn't do anything!"

"Yes you did. You broke him, and then you killed him. Admit it!"

A sob broke from my lips, preventing me from responding. Even if

I could say anything, what could I say to calm down an enraged psychopath?

"I know the truth," she said through her hate-labored pants. "And that's what matters. You broke him, and now I'll break you. Come on, Birdie, get your ass up. It's time."

42

Cas

"We have a two-point-five-mile accuracy on this thing," I said to the team of FBI agents and local police officers looking to me for instruction. "We fan out in groups of two. Everyone has a flare, but only use it after the threat to Alta Johnson is eliminated." My gaze flicked to the setting sun. Four hours had passed since I spoke to her dad and obtained the GPS frequency. Six hours since I first arrived at the cabin and realized something was wrong. Who knew how long Alta had been missing before that.

Each group of men fanned out, guns at the ready. The person we were after was conniving, manipulative, and smart as hell; we had to be on our guard at all times.

How in the hell we missed the glaring signs that Sarah was a psychopath was beyond me. But everything Peters sent over—from her juvie file to her most recent crime, which landed her in a mental ward for four years—confirmed the woman was mentally unstable.

I couldn't make eye contact with the two dogs brought in to help us find Alta. Just seeing them had sadness gripping my heart. Benny was doing better, but who knew when that might change.

While the other officers fanned out, I geared up with the basic firearms I'd tossed in the back of the SUV before leaving the cabin. The grenades might've been a bit much, but I would rather have them and not need them than the alternative. After strapping on the assault rifle and checking the sights of the scope, I slammed the trunk closed.

"What else you got in there?" came a familiar voice at my back.

"Plenty. What's your poison?" I said to Peters with as much of a smile as I could muster in this type of situation.

The trunk light flickered back on as the lid rose in the air. While he rummaged through the arsenal, I checked every clip, making sure all five guns on my body were loaded to the max.

"Is that a grenade?" Peters asked as he slung a rifle over his back.

I shrugged and slammed the magazine back in place. "I like being prepared."

"You look like you're going to war."

Through the headlights of the other trucks and SUVs, I met his gaze. "I am."

His simple nod said everything.

"Ready?" I asked.

"Ready."

Side by side, we stalked deeper into the trees, the crunch of the leaves and twigs beneath our boots the only sound. With each step I slipped deeper and deeper into the marine I used to be. The stalker, the killer. The protector. I would find her. I would save her. That was the fact I had to zero in on, because the alternative would render me paralyzed and utterly useless in the search for her.

Alta would survive, as would I. Together we would live the rest of our lives, broken but not shattered, hurt but not dead. Together we were whole, which was why I had to find her. I'd never be the man she thought I was without her by my side.

She had to survive.

Or I wouldn't.

A sixth sense pulled me short, making Peters pause midstep. I held a tight breath, listening through the dark stillness.

"You hear that?" I said just above a whisper. "There." With the assault rifle in my grasp, I pointed southeast toward the barely audible voices.

"Could be the other officers."

"Could not be. Let's go."

At a quick pace, we raced through the dark, leaping over toppled trees, knocking down young saplings and stomping over the dense underbrush. Nothing could stand in our way of investigating the voices, which grew louder with each step we took.

Sweat beaded beneath my wool cap and dripped down my temples, even with the cold night air brushing past my cheeks and cooling my exposed hands.

A flash of movement dropped us to the forest floor for cover, the cool, damp ground quickly absorbing all the building heat. At my side, Peters pushed up to his elbows scouting the situation.

"Flashlight. Two unknowns." Falling back to the earth, he slid the shoulder strap off and positioned the rifle in front of him. "What do you want to do?"

I held in a tight breath. What I wanted to do and what we should do were two different scenarios. I was a planner, needed all facts before making a move, but in this case, nothing mattered but getting closer to her. This was acting on emotion, which would get me killed, but what was the alternative?

"Let's—"

Sarah's singsong voice several yards away cut me short. "Now, Birdie, this is where I say goodbye and good riddance."

Every muscle tensed to propel me toward the voices. A firm grip on my shoulder forced me back down.

"What the fuck," I said through gritted teeth. "She's going to kill her."

"We need a better visual. You can't just go in there guns blazing, you know that. Stop thinking with your heart and think with your fucking head."

Damn. He was right.

Not a single plan formed, not one idea on how we could save her.

"How much do you love her?" Peters asked, his tone tense.

"I don't want a life without her."

The grip on my shoulder tightened in what I assumed was sympathy. "We need to get Sarah to shine the light around more. I can't get a shot off without knowing where Birdie stands."

Without a hint of hesitation, I shoved to my feet and marched toward a crazy woman and the love of my life, praying with each step that Peters knew to save her before me.

43

Alta

MY FINGERS WERE GONE.

Well, I assumed they were gone, since I couldn't feel them. I only knew my toes were still attached from staring at them the last thirty minutes as we traipsed through the forest. I didn't say a word, didn't even try to escape. I was accepting my fate, owning it instead of being afraid. Fear would get me nowhere, but neither would this downward spiral of despair.

Cas hadn't come, and now he'd be too late.

Even Sarah's sick goodbye didn't register any emotion.

"No words of goodbye?" she asked. In a cruel move, Sarah whipped the flashlight up, directing the powerful light into my eyes. With a hiss I turned my head and slammed eyelids closed. "Come on, just look at what Jerry dug for you. I told him to make it deeper than the others. We wouldn't want any of those pesky animals of yours digging up your body months from now, now would we?"

"Wouldn't that be terrible," I deadpanned. "Just get it over with, would you? I'm cold."

Her fake, over-the-top gasp grated on my nerves, sparking a flash of anger. "Well how rude of me. I should've packed you a jacket. One should be warm for their own funeral."

"She can have mine."

My lungs stopped working. It couldn't be. I shook my head. No, it was in my head.

"He isn't here," I mumbled to myself. "He isn't here."

The light whipped over my shoulder, allowing a reprieve from its bright beam. Blinking past the bright bursts in my vision, I followed the beam of light to the other side of the freshly dug grave. *My* grave. There was no point trying to hold back the pitiful whimper. Happy, scared, angry, terrified—too many emotions swirled at the sight of Cas decked out in all black with guns strapped across every part of his body.

In my ear, the click of a hammer cocking froze every inch of my mind and body. The cold end of Sarah's gun pressed to my temple.

"Don't come any closer or your pretty little Lady gets her pretty little head blown off."

Eyes wide, I watched Cas pause his advancing. His fierce gaze never faltering from mine, he raised both hands in the air.

"Rose, this is the end of the line. We know who you are, what you've done."

I grimaced at Sarah's scoff, the movement making the gun barrel dig deeper against my temple. One flick of her finger and all this would be over. The realization of how close I was to death made me want to live. Really live. To have a family, to raise kids, and be free from all the paranoia and fear. I wanted a life.

With him.

A snap of a twig in the dark shifted Sarah's focus, making the gun slip a fraction. Without thinking twice, I tilted forward and leapt into the grave I was destined for. My hands yanked against the binds as I free-fell through the air, hoping for a chance to catch myself before I landed face first, but the wire held.

Gunfire boomed above me. Just as I smacked the ground, a sharp slice of pain ripped through my shoulder. My scream echoed around the deep dirt cavern as its dense walls muffled the commotion going on above.

Dirt floated into my nose and dry mouth with every short breath. Everything from the tips of my toes to the top of my head ached and groaned at the impact. A small bit of relief calmed my racing heart when both feet responded to the demand for them to move. If I survived this, at least I hadn't broken my back in the fall, leaving me paralyzed.

The ground shuddered, dirt and bits of rock dusting my arms and back.

"Alta? Lady?" Cas called out with pure desperation in his tone. "Please be okay. Please. Oh God please."

I opened my mouth to respond, but nothing came out except a pained cry.

"I got you." Tucking one arm beneath my shoulders, he carefully rolled me over, placing my back against the dirt. Even through my closed lids, a bright light shining above us singed my sensitive eyes. "Get a fucking ambulance. And we need a backboard."

"Then don't fucking move her, you damn moron." Inside I smiled at the sound of Chandler's voice.

Cas grumbled something under his breath that sounded like nothing but a string of creative curses.

Chandler came too. They both came like they said they would.

They saved me. In so many ways, Cas and Chandler rescued me.

EYELIDS HEAVY, I strained to pull them open to find out where the stupid beeping was and why in the heck I was so dang hot. After several blinks to clear the haze clouding my vision, I quickly scanned the small hospital room, only for my gaze to stop on the man asleep in the chair beside my bed.

My muscles protested as I moved to run my fingers through his hair but stopped midair. My lips pressed into a thin line as I rotated both wrists in front of me, taking in the thick bandages encasing them. I didn't want to know the damage beneath the bright white gauze, or think about the scars that would surely be left behind.

The steady throb of my shoulder drew my attention to the thick bandage covering my collarbone down to mid-bicep.

"You're lucky it wasn't your head she shot."

Still staring at the bandage, I couldn't help it as the corners of my lips pulled upward.

"Ah yes, what a lucky day it was."

"You know what I mean." A hot hand engulfed both of mine in a tight grasp. "Watching you fall into that grave while hearing her shot and Peters's go off simultaneously...." I turned to face the man I loved, my heart hurting at the dark circles beneath his eyes, the hollowness in his gaze. "I can't lose you." His voice broke. Pulling a hand to the edge of the bed, he gripped it tight as he pressed his forehead against the top. "I love you, Lady, and I'd rather be dead than live another minute of this life without you in it."

The tears that welled from his sweet, honest words spilled over to trickle down my cheeks.

"I love you too, Cas." Slowly his head rose, his red-rimmed eyes meeting mine. "I do. I love that you love me for me, and I love that you make me feel safe, but more than anything I love the way you make me feel about *myself*. You've shown me who I am again. The girl who was lost ten years ago, you brought her back to life. I never want to hide again, and with you, I never will."

The sheets rustled beneath his hand as it slid up the bed to tuck beneath my head. Careful to only tip my head forward, Cas leaned close to press his lips against mine.

A light rap on the door pulled him away sooner than I wanted, which I let him know with the small pout I shot his way just before Chandler peeked his head through the door.

"You're awake," he said with a relieved sigh. "He was a bear to handle while you were in surgery."

"Surgery?" My attention zeroed in on my shoulder. "What

happened? The last thing I remember was Cas hauling me out of... well, you know."

The two men glanced to one another. Chandler cleared his throat as he stepped deeper in the room. At my bedside, he again looked to Cas, who nodded.

"The bullet was a through and through, but they had to patch up your shoulder and clean it out. There was a ton of dirt and debris in the wound, and the docs didn't want to risk infection setting in. The gel ice packs they put on your face calmed the swelling or you wouldn't be able to see through either eye."

"Damn Jerry." My fingers curled around the blanket into a tight fist. "Did you find his body?"

"You mean what was left?" Chandler scoffed. "Yeah. Was he the one who did that to your face?"

I nodded. Looking to the crisp white blanket, I fiddled with a loose string. "Sarah stopped him from assaulting me. She said that was her one rule, no touching. What does that even mean?" I whispered.

Cas's hand wrapped around mine, stilling the movement. "It means everyone has a limit to what they deem over the line. Rape, touching someone who didn't want to be, was hers. We read her file, and it seems she'd been sexually abused since birth, which probably influenced her habits as an adult. As crazy as Sarah was, she knew that was a line she wouldn't cross or allow her partners to."

"Lance was her foster brother. She said she loved him, and they were a team."

Chandler's nodding drew my attention away from Cas. "It seemed they used Lance as a scapegoat. No one would ever admit he acted out, burned down houses, or hurt foster parents because they were abusing Rose."

"Rose," I said, mystified. "Such a pretty name for someone so manipulative. She manipulated Sadie this entire time. All the creepy things Sadie did were directed by Sarah, or Rose, whoever she was."

Both men nodded.

"When Sadie came to, another FBI agent walked through her day and how she got ahold of the coffee. We put two and two together at that point. Poor girl, she was terrified. But I will say, as much as Rose manipulated Sadie, she still is a bit on the looney side. That note she found?" Chandler rolled his eyes. "She created it, all based on the information she pulled from John. Seems all she wanted was his attention."

"Wow," I said on a pushed breath. "Sarah, Sadie, Lance, Jerry—am I so naïve to think that's a lot of unstable people associated with my life?" A small smile pulled at the corner of my lips. "Maybe I attract the crazies."

Cas shook his head. "Lance was a victim of Rose's. She manipulated him and molded him into the perfect little minion she needed. Even though what he did to you was terrible, at that point he was without the person who controlled his every thought, and he spiraled. And Sadie, like we said, she's a little off anyway and was too easily manipulated by Rose's mind games. That poor girl didn't have a chance once Rose saw how susceptible she was. And Jerry"—he bit out the name in disgust—"had a long rap sheet of misdemeanors, ranging from voyeurism to spying. One charge had him spying in a women's bathroom. Once Rose met him, she knew she'd found the perfect replacement for Lance."

"How did they even meet? 'onlybadguys.com' dating site?"

The two chuckled. "She was a watcher. She probably watched him watch other women for a while and approached him. One thing was clear—on all Rose's testing, she was off-the-charts brilliant. No one stood a chance against her once she locked in on them."

"Is she...?" I didn't want to know, but then again I needed to. Not because I was scared of her coming after me again, but because of all the additional lives she could manipulate and harm in the future if she were still alive.

"Dead." Chandler smiled. "You can thank me later."

"How about now?" I pushed off the bed with a smile, set to hug him, but I sucked in a tight breath at the agony radiating from my stomach. Relaxing back, I sealed my eyes shut and focused on slowing my breathing. "What the heck?"

"Your whole stomach and lower back were beat to hell. There was some damage to your kidneys, but nothing requiring surgery. The doctors want to see how they heal on their own. Their main concerns when you came in were the hypothermia and gunshot wound."

"I broke his nose." When the pain subsided, I peeled my lids back open. Both men stared down with pride in their eyes. "Then he kicked the crap out of me for it. That was when Sarah came in and shot him. I thought it was you. I thought you'd found me."

Out of the corner of my eye, I watched Cas's forehead bunch and lips purse.

"I'm sorry it wasn't me."

Grabbing his hand, I tugged it to my heart. "You did when it mattered most. You and Chandler both. Thank you, thank you, thank you. If you two hadn't come to Colorado to investigate...." I shook my head, trying not to think of my body in that grave they'd dug for me. "The other women, were they buried close?"

"Within a hundred yards. We found them all. The only difference was the woman who was taken from town looked to have sustained vaginal and anal tearing. The other two were like the others in the Smokies: malnourished, abrasions around the wrists, but no rape."

My gaze swept to the dark window. That made sense, based on what Sarah said in the little shack right before she shot Jerry. For some reason, the knowledge of Sarah's childhood, the line in the sand she had on assault, made my heart sad for her. Maybe even feel guilty for her death.

"Hey." Chandler's stern voice snapped me from my thoughts. "Stop whatever you're thinking. You're the victim. Not her, not him. You."

I chewed on my thumb as his words processed. Ever so softly, Cas's finger wrapped around my chin, dragging my gaze to meet his. The love and pride shining in his dark eyes brought on a new wave of happy tears.

"No, Peters, you're wrong." A slow smile spread across his cheeks. "She's not a victim. She's a fucking survivor."

EPILOGUE

I held back a wince, knowing the other rangers were watching as I rotated my left shoulder. Everything healed perfectly, but it still turned stiff if I didn't move it often. Like now, sitting here filling out an incident report for the past hour on the stupid campers who decided to lure and trap six chipmunks to take home.

Idiots.

For the tenth time since I sat down over an hour ago, I glanced to the phone screen, hoping to see a new text. For the past four months, Cas and I had been trying out the long-distance relationship thing. We texted each other every hour, more than that most days. But today I hadn't heard from him. Worry built in my gut, telling me something was wrong.

Reaching down, I rubbed Benny's soft head, hoping he had the magical power to calm my racing nerves. A wet tongue popped out and licked up the back of my hand, making me smile. He was fully recovered—as much as he could be, at least. The physical therapist wanted him to be more active, but I couldn't pull him out of the little doggie depression he'd sunk into.

With another scratch behind his ears, I sighed and pressed the Home button again to make sure I didn't miss a message.

I didn't.

"Birdie." John's loud voice carried past his closed door. "Get in here."

Everyone quieted and watched as I pushed back from the desk and straightened my uniform. Since I came back to work, he had given me a wide berth, not talking directly to me, always giving orders in a group setting. It was awkward to say the least. This was the first time he'd initiated a one-on-one conversation in three months.

Pushing the door open wide enough to pop my head through, I found him pacing behind his desk.

Great.

"Yeah, John?" I said, still keeping half my body outside his office.

"Come in. We need to talk." Not once did his eyes shoot up to acknowledge my entry.

"Okay." Deep breath in, I pushed the door open wider and stepped inside, pressing my back to the wall. "What's up?"

"For fuck's sake, Birdie, I'm not going to hurt you. What's your deal?" he bit out, finally looking up.

"You. Me." I waved a hand between us. "It's awkward, right?"

"Yeah, but we're going to change that. I miss you." I blanched at his words, and his eyes widened a fraction. "No, not like that. I mean I miss my friend. I want us to be back on good terms, as friends."

"Friends," I mulled over the word. He and Cas were on good terms after Cas saved his life, so there really wasn't any reason why I couldn't rebuild my friendship with John. "I'd like that. A lot. But no Sadie."

"No Sadie," he laughed with a grimace. "But I called you in here to discuss something else. Walk with me." After he rounded the desk, he brushed past me and strode down the hall without another look back.

"Okay," I muttered to myself as I turned to follow. This was weird. "John, what's going on?"

"We have a new division chief. He's set to arrive any minute, and I thought we would meet him out in the parking lot."

"Why? It's freezing out there." I pulled to a stop. "Plus, won't we look like brownnosers?"

His cheeks bunched as a broad smile pulled across his face. "Maybe, but I don't think you'll mind."

I held a breath. "Would Cas...?"

John didn't respond, just kept walking. Outside, a black SUV was pulling into the parking spot reserved for the chief.

My heart thundered against my chest.

Please be him.

Please be him.

The last four months apart were torture, and I wasn't looking forward to any more. So much so that I'd recently checked out available jobs in the DC area just to get us in the same city, even though Cas and I both knew I would hate leaving the mountains and my animals.

The driver door swung open. I held a breath as a black hiking boot, then another planted on the blacktop. On their own, my feet moved toward the SUV in search of a better angle to see who the mysterious person was.

His smile was the first thing I zeroed in on. Broad, happy, eager. I smiled back before breaking into a sprint toward Cas, not caring who was watching. With a happy squeal, I leapt into his outstretched arms, our bodies colliding together. Lips pressed against his neck, I nuzzled deep, savoring his heat in the freezing temperatures.

"Well hello to you too," he said into my hair. "I missed you."

"I missed you too, more than you can imagine."

"Birdie," John said at my back, "I'd like you to meet our new division chief, Cas Mathews."

Pulling back, I smiled up at his handsome face. The beard was gone—something we'd rectify immediately—but the love and pride shining back in those dark eyes were the exact same as four months ago.

"I can't believe... why didn't... why not tell me?" I searched his face, taking in every detail I'd only been able to dream about recently.

"I wanted it to be a surprise." He nodded to the SUV. "Everything I own is in the back. Know somewhere I can stay until I find a place of my own?"

My teeth sank into my lower lip as I nodded. "I bet we could find somewhere."

His brows furrowed as his features turned serious. "I did bring a new ranger trainee with me. He'll have to stay with us too, until he goes out for more formal training."

Crap. What kind of impression was I giving the cadet, who was undoubtedly watching?

I slid down his hard body, Cas's arms only releasing their hold when my feet were solid on the ground.

"Ready to meet him?" he said with a smirk.

After straightening my shirt and belt, I gave him a nod. Cas shook his head, swung open the back door and reached inside. "Officer Johnson, I'd like you to meet your new trainee, Mac Mathews."

The soft German shepherd puppy's muzzle buried deeper into his arms as Cas moved from the cover of the SUV into the whipping wind.

I shrieked.

Shrieked.

"What?" Hands extended, I charged toward him and carefully pulled Mac from his arms. "A puppy?"

Cas shrugged, his face-splitting grin somehow growing wider. "You said Benny needs more exercise. What better way to encourage him to get off his doggie bed than to train this little guy?" Cas's large hand wrapped around Mac's head and rubbed back and forth. "You like him?"

"Like him?" I exclaimed as I inhaled Mac's sweet puppy breath. "I love him."

"But not as much as me," Cas said while trying to take Mac from my arms.

I held the nibbling puppy closer to my chest. I smiled as he bit my hand—of course he was a biter, just like his owner. I yanked Cas close, smooshing Mac between us. "There will never be a human, chipmunk, moose, or dog that I'll love more than you. That's impossible. There's no such thing as love bigger than that."

"There is." Cas pulled me up for a chaste kiss. "My love for you, Lady."

ALSO BY KENNEDY L. MITCHELL

Series:

More Than a Threat

More Than a Risk

More Than a Hope (Coming Soon)

Standalone:

Falling for the Chance

A Covert Affair

Finding Fate

Memories of Us

Mine to Protect

ABOUT THE AUTHOR

Printed in Great Britain
by Amazon